THE DARKEST NIGHT

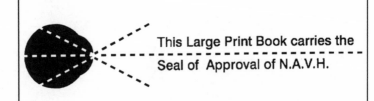

THE DARKEST NIGHT

GENA SHOWALTER

THORNDIKE PRESS
A part of Gale, Cengage Learning

GALE
CENGAGE Learning

Detroit • New York • San Francisco • New Haven, Conn • Waterville, Maine • London

LIBRARY OF CONGRESS CATALOGING-IN-PUBLICATION DATA

Showalter, Gena.
    The darkest night / by Gena Showalter.
      p. cm. — (Lords of the Underworld series ; #1) (Thorndike Press large print romance)
    ISBN-13: 978-1-4104-0915-7 (alk. paper)
    ISBN-10: 1-4104-0915-5 (alk. paper)
    1. Large type books. I. Title.
PS3619.H77D37 2008
813'.6—dc22
                                        2008017967

Published in 2008 by arrangement with Harlequin Books S.A.

Dear Reader,

I'm thrilled to present my brand-new paranormal trilogy, LORDS OF THE UNDERWORLD, which begins with *The Darkest Night*. In a remote fortress in Budapest, six immortal warriors — each more dangerously seductive than the last — are bound by an ancient curse none has been able to break. When a powerful enemy returns, they will travel the world in search of a sacred relic of the gods — one that threatens to destroy them all.

Join me on a journey through this darkly sensual world, where the line between good and evil blurs and true love is put to the ultimate test.

Wishing you all the best,
Gena Showalter

To Kresley Cole and Nalini Singh.
Not only because your
books are beyond amazing and
I get twitchy if I
don't get a KC and NS fix, but also
because you are
such wonderful people.

To Shelly Mykel.
Because you're awesome and
I'm determined to get it
right (at least once).

To Debbie Splawn-Bunch.
Because I'm a terrible
friend, you love me anyway
and I know you wouldn't
have let me title this book
Take This Sword and Shove It.

To Jill Monroe.
Because you're always in my
corner — even if you do have my
adored Lobby.
And speaking of Lobby . . .

To Lobby. Because I miss you.

Max Showalter, you are
my one and only.

CHAPTER ONE

Every night death came, slowly, painfully, and every morning Maddox awoke in bed, knowing he'd have to die again later. That was his greatest curse and his eternal punishment.

He ran his tongue over his teeth, wishing it were a blade over his enemy's throat instead. Most of the day had already passed. He'd heard the time seep away, a poisonous tick-tock in his mind, every beat of the clock a mocking reminder of mortality and pain.

In little more than an hour, the first sting would pierce his stomach and nothing he did, nothing he said, would change that. Death *would* come for him.

"Damned gods," he muttered, increasing the speed of his bench presses.

"Bastards, every one of them," a familiar male voice said from behind him.

Maddox's motions didn't slow at Torin's unwelcome intrusion. Up. Down. Up.

Down. For two hours he had worked out his frustration and anger on the punching bag, the treadmill and now the weights. Sweat ran from his bare chest and arms, riding the ropes of his muscles in clear rivulets. He should be as exhausted mentally as he was physically, but his emotions were only growing darker, more powerful.

"You should not be here," he said.

Torin sighed. "Look. I didn't mean to interrupt, but something's happened."

"So take care of it."

"I can't."

"Whatever it is, try. I'm in no shape to help." These last few weeks very little was needed to send him into a killing haze where no one around him was safe. Even his friends. *Especially* his friends. He didn't want to, never meant to, but was sometimes helpless against urges to strike and to maim.

"Maddox —"

"I'm at the edge, Torin," he croaked. "I would do more harm than good."

Maddox knew his limitations, had known them for thousands of years. Ever since that doomed day the gods had chosen a woman to perform a task that should have been his.

Pandora had been strong, yes, the strongest female soldier of their time. But he had been stronger. More capable. Yet he had been deemed too weak to guard *dimOuniak,* a sacred box housing demons so vile, so destructive, they could not even be trusted in Hell.

As if Maddox would have allowed it to be destroyed. Frustration had bloomed inside him at the affront. Inside all of them, every warrior now living here. They had fought diligently for the king of the gods, killed expertly and protected thoroughly; they should have been chosen as guards. That they hadn't was an embarrassment not to be tolerated.

They'd only thought to teach the gods a lesson the night they'd stolen *dimOuniak* from Pandora and released that horde of demons upon the unsuspecting world. How foolish they had been. Their plan to prove their power had failed, for the box had gone missing in the fray, leaving the warriors unable to recapture a single evil spirit.

Destruction and havoc had soon reigned, plunging the world into darkness until the king of the gods finally intervened, cursing each warrior to house a demon inside *himself.*

A fitting punishment. The warriors had unleashed the evil to avenge their stinging pride; now they would contain it.

11

And so the Lords of the Underworld were born.

Maddox had been given Violence, the demon who was now as much a part of him as his lungs or his heart. Now, man could no longer live without demon and demon could no longer function without man. They were woven together, two halves of a whole.

From the very first, the creature inside him had beckoned him to do malicious things, hated things, and he'd been compelled to obey. Even when led to slay a woman — to slay Pandora. His fingers clenched the bar so tightly his knuckles nearly snapped out of place. Over the years he had learned to control some of the demon's more vile compulsions, but it was a constant struggle and he knew he could shatter at any moment.

What he would have given for a single day of calm. No overpowering desire to hurt others. No battles within himself. No worries. No death. Just . . . peace.

"It's not safe for you here," he told his friend, who still stood in the doorway. "You need to leave." He set the silver bar atop its perch and sat up. "Only Lucien and Reyes are allowed to be close to me during my demise." And only because they played a part in it, unwilling though they were. They

12

were as helpless against their demons as Maddox was his.

"About an hour until that happens, so . . ." Torin threw a rag at him. "I'll take my chances."

Maddox reached behind his back, caught the white cloth and turned. He wiped his face. "Water."

An ice-cold bottle was soaring through the air before the second syllable left his mouth. He caught it deftly, moisture splashing his chest. He drained the icy contents and studied his friend.

As usual, Torin wore all black and gloves covered his hands. Pale hair fell in waves to his shoulders, framing a face mortal females considered a sensual feast. They didn't know the man was actually a devil in angel's skin. They should have, though. He practically glowed with irreverence, and there was an unholy gleam in his green eyes that proclaimed he would laugh in your face while cutting out your heart. Or laugh in your face while you cut out *his* heart.

To survive, he had to find humor where he could. They all did.

Like every resident of this Budapest fortress, Torin was damned. He might not die every night like Maddox, but he could never touch a living thing, skin to skin, without infecting it with sickness.

Torin was possessed by the spirit of Disease.

He hadn't known a woman's touch in over four hundred years. He'd learned his lesson well when he'd given in to lust and caressed a would-be lover's face, bringing about a plague that decimated village after village. Human after human.

"Five minutes of your time," Torin said, his determination clear. "That's all I'm asking."

"Think we'll be punished for insulting the gods today?" Maddox replied, ignoring the request. If he didn't allow himself to be asked for a favor, he didn't have to feel guilty for turning it down.

His friend uttered another of those sighs. "Our every breath is supposed to be a punishment."

True. Maddox's lips curled into a slow, razored smile as he peered ceilingward. *Bastards. Punish me further, I dare you.* Maybe then, finally, he would fade to nothingness.

He doubted the gods would concern themselves, though. After bestowing the death-curse upon him, they had ignored him, pretending not to hear his pleas for forgiveness and absolution. Pretending not

14

to hear his promises and desperate bargaining.

What more could they do to him, anyway?

Nothing could be worse than dying over and over again. Or being stripped of anything good and right . . . or hosting the spirit of Violence inside his mind and body.

Jackknifing to his feet, Maddox tossed the now-wet rag and empty water bottle into the nearest hamper. He strode to the far end of the room and braced his hands above his head, leaning into the semicircular alcove of stained-glass windows and staring into the night through the only clear partition.

He saw Paradise.

He saw hell.

He saw freedom, prison, everything and nothing.

He saw . . . home.

Situated atop a towering hill as the fortress was, he had a direct view of the city. Lights glowed brightly, pinks, blues and purples illuminating the murky velvet sky, glinting off the Danube River and framing the snow-capped trees that dominated the area. Wind blustered, snowflakes dancing and twirling through the air.

Here, he and the others had a modicum of privacy from the rest of the world. Here, they were allowed to come and go without having to face a barrage of questions. *Why don't you age? Why do screams echo through the forest every night? Why do you sometimes look like a monster?*

Here, the locals maintained their distance, awed, respectful. "Angels," he'd even heard whispered during a rare encounter with a mortal.

If they only knew.

Maddox's nails elongated slightly, digging into the stone. Budapest was a place of majestic beauty, old-world charm and modern pleasures, but he'd always felt removed from it. From the castle district that lined one street to the nightclubs that lined the next. From the fruits and vegetables hawked in one alley to the living flesh hawked in the other.

Maybe that sense of disconnection would vanish if he ever explored the city, but unlike the others who roamed at will, he was trapped inside the fortress and surrounding land as surely as Violence had been trapped inside Pandora's box thousands of years ago.

His nails lengthened farther, almost claws now. Thinking of the box always blackened his mood. *Punch a wall,* Violence beckoned. *Destroy something. Hurt, kill.* He would have liked to obliterate the gods. One by one.

16

Decapitate them, perhaps. Rip out their blackened, decayed hearts, definitely.

The demon purred in approval.

Of course it's purring now, Maddox thought with disgust. Anything bloodthirsty, no matter the victims, met with the creature's support. Scowling, he leveled another heated glance at the heavens. He and the demon had been paired long ago, but he remembered the day clearly. The screams of the innocent in his ears, humans bleeding all around him, hurting, dying, the spirits having devoured their flesh in a rapturous frenzy.

Only when Violence had been shoved inside his body did he lose touch with reality. There had been no sounds, no sights. Just an all-consuming darkness. He hadn't regained his senses until Pandora's blood splattered his chest, her last breath echoing in his ears.

She had not been his first kill — or his last — but she had been the first and only woman to meet his sword. The horror of seeing that once-vibrant female form broken and knowing he was responsible for it . . . To this day, he had not assuaged the guilt, the regret. The shame and the sorrow.

He'd sworn to do whatever was necessary to control the spirit from then on, but it had been too late. Enraged all the more, Zeus had bestowed a second curse upon him: every night at midnight he would die exactly as Pandora had died — a blade through the stomach, six hellish times. The only difference was, her torment had ended within minutes.

His torment would last for eternity.

He popped his jaw, trying to relax against a new onslaught of aggression. It wasn't as if he were the only one to suffer, he reminded himself. The other warriors had their own demons — literally and figuratively. Torin, of course, was keeper of Disease. Lucien was keeper of Death. Reyes, of Pain. Aeron, of Wrath. Paris, of Promiscuity.

Why couldn't *he* have been given that last one? He would have been able to journey to town anytime he wished, take any woman he desired, savoring every sound, every touch.

As it was, he could never venture far. Nor could he trust himself around females for long periods of time. If the demon overtook him or if he could not return home before midnight and someone found his dead, bloody body and buried him — or worse, burned him . . .

How he wished such a thing would end

18

his miserable existence. He would have left long ago and allowed himself to be roasted in a pit. Or perhaps he would have jumped from the fortress's highest window and smashed his brains from his skull. But no. No matter what he did, he'd merely awaken once again, charred as well as sore. Broken as well as sliced.

"You've been staring at that window for a while," Torin said. "Aren't you even curious as to what's happened?"

Maddox blinked as he was dragged from his thoughts. "You're still here?"

His friend arched a black brow, the color a startling contrast to his silver-white hair. "I believe the answer to my question is no. Are you calm now, at least?"

Was he ever truly calm? "As calm as a creature like me can be."

"Stop whining. There's something I need to show you, and don't try to deny me this time. We can talk about my reason for disturbing you along the way." Without another word, Torin spun on his booted heel and strode from the room.

Maddox remained in place for several seconds, watching his friend disappear around the corner. *Stop whining,* Torin had said. Yes, that's exactly what he had been doing. Curiosity and wry amusement pushed past his lethal mood, and Maddox stepped from the gym into the hallway. A cold draft of air swirled around him, thick with moisture and the crisp scents of winter. He spied Torin a few feet away and stalked forward, quickly closing in.

"What's this about?"

"Finally. Interest," was the only response.

"If this is one of your tricks . . ." Like the time Torin had ordered hundreds of blow-up dolls and placed them throughout the fortress, all because Paris had foolishly complained about the lack of female companionship in town. The plastic "ladies" had stared out from every corner, their wide eyes and let-me-suck-you mouths taunting everyone who passed them.

Things like that happened when Torin was bored.

"I wouldn't waste my time trying to trick you," Torin said without turning to face him. "You, my friend, have no sense of humor."

True.

As Maddox kept pace, stone walls stretched at his sides; sconces glowed, pulsing with light and fire, twining shadow with gold. The House of the Damned, as Torin had dubbed the place, had been built hundreds of years ago. Though they had modernized it as best they could, the age showed in the crumbling rock and the scuffed floors.

"Where is everyone?" Maddox asked, only then realizing he hadn't spotted any of the others.

"You'd think Paris would be shopping for food since our cabinets are nearly bare and that's his only duty, but no. He's out searching for a new woman."

Lucky bastard. Possessed as he was by Promiscuity, Paris could not bed the same woman twice, and so he seduced a new one — or two or three — every day. The only downside? If he couldn't find a woman, he was reduced to doing things Maddox didn't even want to contemplate. Things that left the normally good-tempered man hunched over a toilet, heaving the contents of his stomach. Though Maddox's envy abated at such moments, it always returned when Paris spoke of one of his lovers. The soft brush of a thigh . . . the meeting of hot skin . . . the groans of ecstasy . . .

"Aeron is . . . Prepare yourself," Torin began, "because this is the main reason I hunted you down."

"Did something happen to him?" Maddox demanded as darkness shuttered over his thoughts and anger overtook him. *Destroy, obliterate,* Violence beseeched, clawing at the corners of his mind. "Is he hurt?"

Immortal Aeron might be, but he could still be harmed. Even killed — a feat they had all discovered in the worst possible way.

"Nothing like that," Torin assured him.

Slowly, he relaxed and gradually Violence receded. "What, then? Cleaning a mess and throwing a fit?" Every warrior here had specific responsibilities. It was their way of maintaining some semblance of order amid the chaos of their own souls. Aeron's task was maid service, something he complained about on a daily basis. Maddox took care of home repairs. Torin played with stocks and bonds, whatever those were, keeping them well-moneyed. Lucien did all the paperwork and Reyes supplied them with weapons.

"The gods . . . summoned him."

Maddox stumbled, shock momentarily blinding him. "What?" Surely he had misheard.

"The gods summoned him," Torin repeated patiently.

But the Greeks hadn't spoken to any of them since the day of Pandora's death. "What did they want? And why am I just now hearing about this?"

"One, no one knows. We were watching a movie when suddenly he straightened in his seat, expression dead, as if there were no one home. Then a few seconds later he tells us he's been summoned. None of us even had time to react — one minute Aeron was with us, the next he was gone.

"And two," Torin added with barely a pause, "I tried to tell you. You said you didn't care, remember?"

A muscle ticked below his eye. "You should have told me anyway."

"While you had barbells within your reach? Please. I'm Disease, not Stupid."

This was . . . this was . . . Maddox did not want to contemplate what this was, but could not stop the thoughts from forming. Sometimes Aeron, keeper of Wrath, lost total control of his spirit and embarked on a vengeance rampage, punishing mortals for their perceived sins. Was he now to be given a second curse for his actions, as Maddox had been all those centuries ago?

"If he does not return in the same shape he left, I will find a way to storm the heavens and slaughter every godly being I encounter."

"Your eyes are glowing bright red," Torin said. "Look, we're all confused, but Aeron will return soon and tell us what's going on."

Fair enough. He forced himself to relax.

Again. "Was anyone else summoned?"

"No. Lucien is out collecting souls. Reyes is gods-know-where, probably cutting himself."

He should have known. Even though Maddox suffered unbearably each night, he pitied Reyes, who could not live a single hour without self-inflicted torture.

"What else did you have to tell me?" Maddox brushed his fingertips over the two towering columns that flanked the staircase before beginning to climb.

"I think it will be better if I show you."

Would it be worse than the announcement about Aeron? Maddox wondered, striding past the entertainment room. Their sanctuary. The chamber they'd spared no expense creating was filled with plush furniture and all the comforts a warrior could desire. There was a refrigerator crammed with special wines and beers. A pool table. A basketball hoop. A large plasma screen that was even now flashing images of three naked women in the middle of an orgy.

"I see Paris was here," he said.

Torin did not reply, but he did quicken his steps, never once glancing toward the screen.

"Never mind," Maddox muttered. Directing Torin's attention to anything carnal was unnecessarily cruel. The celibate man had to crave sex — *touch* — with every fiber of his being, but he would never have the option of indulging.

Even Maddox enjoyed a woman upon occasion.

His lovers were usually Paris's leftovers, those females foolish enough to try to follow Paris home, hoping to share his bed again, not knowing just how impossible such a thing was. They were always drunk with sexual arousal, a consequence of welcoming Promiscuity, so they rarely cared who finally slid between their legs. Most times, they were all too happy to accept Maddox as a substitute — even though it was an impersonal joining, as emotionally hollow as it was physically satisfying.

It had to be that way, though. To protect their secrets, the warriors did not allow humans inside the fortress, forcing Maddox to take the women outside in the surrounding forest. He preferred them on their hands and knees, facing away from him, a swift coupling that would not rouse Violence in any way or compel him to do things that would haunt him forever and still another eternity.

Afterward, Maddox would send the females home with a warning: never return or die. It was that simple. To allow a more permanent arrangement would be foolish. He might come to care for them, and he would definitely hurt them, which would only heap even more guilt and shame upon him.

Just once, though, he would have liked to linger over a woman as Paris was able to do. He would have liked to kiss and lick her entire body; he would have liked to *drown* in her, completely losing himself, without fearing his control would snap and cause him to wound her.

Finally reaching Torin's quarters, he blocked those thoughts from his mind. Time spent wishing was time wasted, as he well knew.

He glanced at his surroundings. He'd been in this room before, but he did not remember the wall-to-wall computer system or the numerous monitors, phones and various other equipment lined throughout. Unlike Torin, Maddox eschewed most technology, for he had never quite gotten used to how quickly things seemed to change — and just how much further each new advancement seemed to pull him from the carefree warrior he'd once been. Though he would be lying if he claimed not to enjoy the convenience such gadgets provided.

Survey complete, he faced his friend. "Taking over the world?"

"Nope. Just watching it. It's the best way to protect us, and the best way to make a little coin." Torin plopped into a cushioned swivel chair in front of the largest screen and began typing on the keyboard. One of the blank monitors lit up, the black screen becoming intertwined with grays and whites. "All right. Here's what I wanted you to see."

Careful not to touch his friend, Maddox stepped forward. The indistinct blur gradually became thick, opaque lines. Trees, he realized. "Nice, but not something I was in dire need of viewing."

"Patience."

"Hurry," he countered.

Torin flicked him a wry glance. "Since you asked so nicely . . . I have heat sensors and cameras hidden throughout our land so that I always know when someone trespasses." A few more seconds of tapping and the screen's view shifted to the right. Then there was a swift flash of red, there one moment, gone the next.

"Go back," Maddox said, tensing. He wasn't a surveillance expert. No, his skill lay in the actual killing. But even he knew what that red slash represented. Body heat.

Tap, tap, tap and the red slash once again consumed the screen.

"Human?" he asked. The silhouette was small, almost dainty.

"Definitely."

"Male or female?"

Torin shrugged. "Female, most likely. Too big to be a child, too small to be a grown man."

Hardly anyone ventured up the bleak hill at this time of night. Or even during the day. Whether it was too spooky, too gloomy or a sign of the locals' respect, Maddox didn't know. But he could count on one hand the number of deliverymen, children wanting to explore and women prowling for sex who'd braved the journey in the last year.

"One of Paris's lovers?" he asked.

"Possibly. Or . . ."

"Or?" he prompted when his friend hesitated.

"A Hunter," Torin said grimly. "Bait, more specifically."

Maddox pressed his lips together in a harsh line. "Now I know you're teasing me."

"Think about it. Deliverymen always come with boxes and Paris's girls always race straight toward the front door. This one looks empty-handed and she's gone in

circles, stopping every few minutes and doing something against the trees. Planting
dynamite in an attempt to injure us, maybe.
Cameras to watch us."

"If she's empty-handed —"

"Dynamite and cameras are small enough
to conceal."

He massaged the back of his neck.
"Hunters haven't stalked or tormented us
since Greece."

"Maybe their children and then their
children's children have been searching for
us all this time. Maybe they finally found
us."

Dread suddenly curled in Maddox's stomach. First Aeron's shocking summons and
now the uninvited visitor. Mere coincidence? His mind flashed back to those
dark days in Greece, days of war and savagery, screams and death. Days the warriors
had been more demon than man. Days a
hunger for destruction had dictated their
every action and human bodies had littered
the streets.

Hunters had soon risen from the tortured
masses, a league of mortal men intent upon
destroying those who'd unleashed such evil,
and a blood feud had erupted. The battles
he then found himself fighting, with swords
clanging and fires raging, flesh burning and

peace something of lore and legend . . .

Cunning had been the Hunters' greatest weapon, however. They had trained female Bait to seduce and distract while they swooped in for the kill. That's how they managed to murder Baden, keeper of Distrust. They had not managed to kill the demon itself, however, and it had sprung from the decimated body, crazed, demented, *warped* from the loss of its host.

Where the demon resided now, Maddox didn't know.

"The gods surely hate us," Torin said. "What better way to hurt us than to send Hunters just when we've finally carved out a somewhat peaceful life for ourselves?"

His dread intensified. "They would not wish the demons, crazed as they would surely be without us, loose upon the world. Would they?"

"Who knows why they do any of the things that they do." A statement, with no hint of a question. None of them really understood the gods, even after all these centuries. "We have to do something, Maddox."

His gaze flicked to the wall clock and he tensed. "Call Paris."

"Did. He's not answering his cell phone."

"Call —"

"Do you really think I would have disturbed you this close to midnight if there were anyone else?" Torin twisted in the seat, peering up at him with forbidding determination. "You're it."

Maddox shook his head. "Very soon, I'm going to die. I cannot be outside these walls."

"Neither can I." Something murky and dangerous shimmered in Torin's eyes, something bitter, turning the green to a poisonous emerald. "You, at least, won't obliterate the entire human race by leaving."

"Torin —"

"You're not going to win this argument, Maddox, so stop wasting time."

He tangled a hand through his chin-length hair, frustration mounting. *We should leave it out there to die,* Violence proclaimed. *It —* the human.

"If it *is* a Hunter," Torin said, as if hearing his thoughts, "if it is Bait? We can't allow it to live. It must be destroyed."

"And if it's innocent and my death-curse strikes?" Maddox countered, tamping down the demon as best he could.

Guilt flashed over Torin's expression, as though every life he was responsible for taking clamored inside his conscience, begging him to rescue those he could. "That is a chance we have to take. We are not the monsters the demons would have us be."

Maddox ground his teeth together. He was not a cruel man; he was not a beast. Not heartless. He hated the waves of immorality that constantly threatened to pull him under. Hated what he did, what he was — and what he would become if he ever stopped fighting those black cravings and evil musings.

"Where is the human now?" he asked. He would venture into the night, even if it cost him terribly.

"At the Danube border."

A fifteen-minute run. He had just enough time to weapon up, find the human, usher it to shelter if it was innocent or kill it if circumstances demanded, and return to the fortress. If anything slowed him down, he could die out in the open. Anyone else foolish enough to venture onto the hill would be placed in danger. Because when the first pain hit, he would be reduced to Violence and those black cravings would consume him.

He would have no other purpose but destruction.

"If I don't return by midnight, have one of the others search for my body, as well as Lucien's and Reyes's." Both Death and Pain came to him each night at midnight, no matter where Maddox was. Pain rendered the blows and Death escorted his soul to hell, where it would remain, tortured by fire and demons almost as loathsome as Violence, until morning.

Unfortunately, Maddox could not guarantee his friends' safety out in the open. He might hurt them before they completed their tasks. And if he hurt them, the anguish he would feel would be second only to the agony of the death-curse that visited him every night.

"Promise me," he said.

Eyes bleak, Torin nodded. "Be careful, my friend."

He stalked out of the room, his movements rushed. Before he made it halfway down the hall, however, Torin called, "Maddox. You might want to look at this."

Backtracking, he experienced another slap of dread. What now? Could anything be worse? When he stood in front of the monitors once more, he arched a brow at Torin, a silent command to hurry.

Torin motioned to the screen with a tilt of his chin. "Looks like there are four more of them. All male . . . or Amazons. They weren't there earlier."

"Damn this." Maddox studied the four

new slashes of red, each one bigger than the last. They were closing in on the little one. Yes, things could indeed be worse. "I'll take care of them," he said. "All of them." Once more he leapt into motion, his pace more clipped.

He reached his bedroom and headed straight to the closet, bypassing the bed, the only piece of furniture in the room. He'd destroyed his dresser, mirror and chairs in one fit of violence or another.

At one time, he'd been foolish enough to fill the space with tranquil indoor waterfalls, plants, crosses, anything to promote peace and soothe raw nerves. None of it had worked and all had been smashed beyond repair in a matter of minutes as the demon overtook him. Since then he'd opted for what Paris called a minimalist look.

The only reason he still had a bed was because it was made of metal and Reyes needed *something* to chain him to as midnight drew near. They kept an abundant supply of mattresses, sheets, chains and metal headboards in one of the bedrooms next door. Just in case.

Hurry! Quickly, he jerked a black T-shirt over his head, pulled on a pair of boots and strapped blades to his wrists, waist and ankles. No guns. He and Violence were in agreement about one thing — enemies needed to die up close and personal.

If any of the humans in the forest proved to be Hunters or Bait, nothing could save them now.

CHAPTER TWO

Ashlyn Darrow shivered against the frigid wind. Strands of light brown hair whipped in front of her eyes; she hooked them behind her throbbing ears with a shaky hand. Not that she could see much, anyway. The night was black, thick with fog and snowflakes. Only a few golden slivers of moonlight were strong enough to peek through the towering, snowcapped trees.

How could a landscape so beautiful be so damaging to the human body?

She sighed, mist forming in front of her face. She should have been relaxing on a flight back to the States, but yesterday she'd learned something too wonderful to resist. Hope had filled her, and earlier this evening she'd raced here without thought, without hesitation, seizing her first chance to find out if it were true.

Somewhere in the vastness of this forest were men with strange abilities no one seemed able to explain. Exactly what they could do, she didn't know. She only knew that she needed help. Desperately. And she'd risk anything, everything, to speak with those powerful men.

She couldn't live with the voices anymore.

Ashlyn had only to stand in one location to hear every conversation that had ever taken place there, no matter how much time had passed. Present, past, any and all languages, it didn't matter. She could hear them in her mind, translate them, even. A gift, some assumed. A nightmare, she knew.

Another chill wind beat against her and she leaned against a tree, using it as a shield. Yesterday, when she'd come to Budapest with several colleagues from the World Institute of Parapsychology, she'd stood in the center of town and begun hearing tidbits of dialogue. Nothing new for her . . . until she'd deciphered the meaning of the words.

They can enslave you with a glance.

One of them has wings and flies when the moon is full.

The scarred one can disappear at will.

As if those whispers had opened some sort of doorway in her mind, hundreds of years of chatter had slammed into her, a blend of old and new. She'd doubled over from the intensity of it, trying to sort the mundane from the essential.

They never age.

They must be angels.

Even their home is creepy — straight out of a horror movie. Hidden on a hilltop, shadowy corners, and damn, even the birds won't go near it.

Should we kill them?

They're magical. They eased my torment.

So many people, present and past, evidently believed these men operated beyond human ability, that they possessed extraordinary skills. Was it possible the men could help her? *Eased my torment,* someone had said.

"Maybe they can ease mine," Ashlyn muttered now. Over the years and in all corners of the world she'd listened to rumors of vampires, werewolves, goblins and witches, gods and goddesses, demons and angels, monsters and fairies. She'd even led the Institute's researchers to many of those creatures' doorsteps, proving they did, in fact, exist.

The whole purpose of the Institute, after all, was to locate, observe and study paranormal beings and determine how the world could benefit from their existence. And for once, working as a para-audiologist might prove to be *her* salvation, as well.

38

Oddly enough, she hadn't led the Institute to Budapest, as was usually the case with a new assignment. She hadn't heard a word about Budapest, in fact, in any of the recent conversations she'd tapped into. But they had brought her here anyway, asking her to listen for any discussions about demons.

She knew better than to ask why. The answer, no matter the question, was always the same: *classified.*

When she had done as ordered, she'd learned that a few of the locals considered the men living atop this hill to be demons. Evil, wicked. Most, however, considered them angels. Angels who kept to themselves — all but one, that is, who reputedly liked bedding anything female and had been dubbed the Orgasm Instructor by a giggling trio who had spent a "single, glorious" night with him. Angels who, through their presence alone, kept the crime levels low. Angels who poured money into the community and made sure the homeless were fed.

Ashlyn herself doubted such do-gooders were possessed. Demons were invariably malicious, unconcerned with those around them. But whether the men *were* angels living on earth or simply ordinary people capable of doing extraordinary things, she prayed they could help her as no one else had been able to. She prayed they could teach her how to block the voices or even help strip her of her ability completely.

The thought was intoxicating, and her lips lifted in a slow smile. That smile quickly faded, however, as another blast of wind cut through her jacket and sweater and seeped into her skin. She'd been out here for more than an hour, and she was chilled to the bone. Stopping to rest (again) hadn't been the smartest of plans.

Her gaze climbed the hill. Through a break in the clouds, a sudden ray of amber light poured down and illuminated the massive charcoal-colored castle. Mist curled from the bottom, beckoning her with ghostly fingers. The place looked exactly as the voice had said, she mused, shadowed and spiked along the top, a horror movie come to life.

That didn't deter her. Quite the opposite. *I'm almost there,* she thought happily, once again trudging uphill. Her thighs already burned from dodging limbs and jumping over elevated roots, but she didn't care. She kept moving.

Until, ten minutes later, she found herself stopping for the thousandth time, unable to walk another step as her shaky, tired thighs morphed into blocks of ice. "No," she moaned. Not now. Rubbing her legs to warm them, she studied the distance again. Her eyes widened when she realized that the castle didn't appear any closer. In fact, it might have been farther away.

Ashlyn shook her head in astonished despair. Damn it! What did she have to do to reach the place? Sprout wings and fly?

Even if I fail, I don't regret coming here. The no provisions and no planning part, yeah, she regretted that, but she'd had to try. No matter how foolish, she'd simply had to try. She would have made the journey naked and barefoot if necessary. Anything for a chance at normalcy.

She loved that she helped safeguard the world with her — gag — *gift,* but the torment she endured was too much. Surely there was another way for her to help. With a little silence, she might be able to *think* of how. Deep-breathing exercises and meditation only did so much for her peace of mind.

She rubbed her legs more frantically, the ministrations finally melting some of the internal ice and spurring her back into motion. *Ök itt. Tudom ök,* she heard as she stepped past a hunched, gnarled tree. *They're here,* her mind instantly translated, *I know they are.*

41

Then someone else said, *Aren't you a pretty thing?*

"Yes, I am, thank you," she said, hoping the sound of her own voice would overshadow the others. It didn't. Deep breath in, deep breath out.

As she continued to slog forward, different conversations from different time periods drifted into her awareness, stacking one on top of the other in her mind. Most were spoken in Hungarian, some in English, and that made them all the more jumbled.

Yes. Yes! Touch me. There, yes, there.

Bárhol as én kardom? En nem tudom hol-van.

One more taste of his lips, and I'll forget him. I just need one more taste.

Ashlyn stumbled over twigs and rocks, the words blending together, growing louder. Louder still. Her heart drummed in her chest and she barely refrained from screaming in frustration. Deep breath in, deep breath —

If you knock on the door, you'll be fucked like an animal and I guarantee you'll love every minute of it.

She covered her ears, even though she knew that wouldn't work, either. "Keep going. Find them." More wind. More voices. "Keep going," she repeated, the words chiming in harmony with her footsteps. She'd come all this way; she could make it a little farther. "Find them."

When she'd told Dr. McIntosh, vice president of the Institute as well as her boss and mentor, what she'd learned about the men, he'd given her a brief nod and a brisk "Well done" — his highest form of praise.

Then she'd asked to be taken to the chateau atop this imposing hill.

"Not a chance," he'd said, turning away from her. "They could be the demons some of the locals paint them."

"Or they could very well be the angels *most* of the locals consider them."

"You're not going to risk it, Darrow." That's when he'd ordered her to pack her bags and readied a car for her departure to the airport, just as he always did when her part of the job — providing the ears — was done.

It was "standard agency procedure," he always claimed, yet he never sent the rest of the workers home. Just her. McIntosh cared about her and wanted her safe, she knew that. After all, he'd seen to her care for more than fifteen years, taking her under his wing when she'd been a scared child whose parents hadn't known how to ease their "gifted" daughter's torment. He'd even read her fairy tales to teach her that the world was a place of magic and endless possibilities, a place where nobody — not even someone like her — had to feel odd.

While he did care, she also knew her ability was important to his career, that the Institute would not be half as effective without her and that as a result, she was something of a pawn in his eyes. That's why she didn't feel (too) guilty for sneaking here the moment his back was turned.

Fingers numb, Ashlyn once again smoothed her hair from her face. Maybe she should have taken the time to ask the locals for the best route, but the voices had been too loud, too incapacitating in the heart of the city. More than that, she'd been afraid an Institute employee would see her and take her in.

Might have been worth taking her chances, though, to avoid this debilitating cold.

There's one way to learn the truth. Stab one in the heart and see if he dies, a voice said, snagging her attention.

Oh, that feels good. Please, more!

Distracted, Ashlyn tripped over a fallen limb. Down she tumbled, landing with a pained gasp. Sharp rocks abraded her palms and scratched at her jeans. For a long while, she didn't move. Couldn't. *Too cold,* she thought. *Too loud.*

As she lay there, her strength seemed to drain completely. Her temples throbbed, the voices still bombarding her. Closing her eyes, she pulled the lapels of her jacket tight and managed to crawl to and huddle against the base of a tree.

We shouldn't be here. They see everything.
Are you hurt?
Look what I found! Isn't it pretty?

"Shut up, shut up, shut up!" she shouted. Of course, the voices didn't listen to her. They never did.

Dare you to run through the trees naked.
Éhes vagyok. Kaphatok volamit eni?

A pop and whiz suddenly sounded, and her eyelids sprang open. Next there was a tortured scream. A man's scream, quickly followed by three others.

Present. Not past. After twenty-four years, she knew the difference.

Terror snaked her in an iron grip, squeezing the breath out of her. Even through the chattering of voices, she heard a sickening thud. She tried to stand, to run, but a sudden whoosh of air held her in place. No, not air, she realized a second later, but a blade. Her entire body jerked in surprise as the hilt of a blood-coated knife swayed just

45

above her shoulder, embedded in tree bark.

Before she had time to scramble away, to scream, there was another whoosh. Another jerk. Ashlyn's attention swung to the other side. Sure enough, a second blade was rooted just above her left shoulder.

How — What — The thoughts hadn't yet fully formed when something burst from a nearby thicket. Brittle leaves clashed together in an ominous dance, the snow that had covered them sprinkling to the ground as limbs slapped and shook. Then the *something* raced past a ray of moonlight and she caught a glimpse of black hair and radiant violet eyes. A man. A big, muscled man was charging toward her at top speed. His expression was pure brutality.

"Ohmygod," she gasped out. "Stop. Stop!"

Suddenly he was there, right in her face. Crouching, pinning her in place, sniffing her neck. "They were Hunters," he said in lightly accented English, his voice as harsh and rough as his rugged features. "Are you?" He grabbed her right wrist and peeled back the material of her jacket and sweater. He ran his thumb over the pulse there. "No tattoo, like they had."

They? Hunters? Tattoo? A tremor cartwheeled down her spine. The intruder was huge, hulking, his muscular frame surrounding her with menace. A metallic tang drifted from him, mixed with the fragrance of man and heat and something she couldn't identify.

Up close, she could see the splatter of red on his too-harsh face. Blood? The biting wind seemed to slither past her skin and into the marrow of her bones.

Savage, the look in his violet eyes said. *Predator.*

Maybe I should have listened to McIntosh. Maybe the men really are *demons.*

"Are you one of them?" the man repeated.

Shocked to her core, frightened beyond belief, it took her a moment to realize something was . . . different. The air, the temperature, the —

The voices had stopped.

Her eyes widened in astonishment.

The voices had stopped, as if they were actually cognizant of the man's presence and were as afraid of him as she was. Silence enveloped her.

No. It wasn't utter silence she experienced, she decided a moment later, but rather . . . quiet. Magnificent, blissful quiet. How long since she'd known such a thing, untainted by conversation? Had she ever?

Wind rustled and leaves smacked together. Snow hummed softly as it drifted through the air, a tranquil melody meant to lull and relax. The trees breathed with life and vitality, branches waving gently.

Had anything ever sounded as magnificent as nature's symphony?

In that moment, she forgot her fear. How could this man be possessed by a demon when he came with such lovely quiet? Demons were a source of torment, not peace.

Was he an angel of mercy, then, as the locals assumed?

Closing her eyes in delight, she drank in that peace, reveled in it. Embraced it.

"Woman?" the angel said, confusion radiating from his voice.

"Hush." Contentment skipped through her. Even at home in North Carolina, in a house that had been built by construction workers forbidden to speak more than necessary, she always heard the echo of deep-rooted whispers. "Don't speak. Just enjoy."

For a moment, he didn't reply. "You dare tell me to hush?" he said finally, angry surprise in his tone.

"You're still talking," Ashlyn admonished, then pressed her lips together. Angel or not, he didn't strike her as the kind of person she should scold. Besides, angering him was the last thing she wanted to do. His presence brought silence. And delicious warmth, she realized as the chill rapidly left her body.

Slowly she cracked open her eyelids.

They were nose to nose, his balmy breath trekking over her lips. His skin glowed like smooth copper, almost otherworldly in the moonlight. All hard angles and fierce planes, his face boasted a sharp blade of a nose and black-as-the-devil's-heart eyebrows.

Those predatory purple eyes bored into her, somehow all the more menacing framed as they were by long, feathered lashes. *I'll kill anyone, anywhere,* his expression seemed to say.

Demon. No, not a demon, she reminded herself. The silence was too good, too pure and right. But he was not an angel, after all, she decided. He'd brought the quiet, yes, but he was clearly as dangerous as he was beautiful. Anyone who could throw blades like that . . .

So what was he?

Ashlyn gulped, studied him. Her pulse should not have fluttered just then, and her breasts should not have ached. But it did. They did. He was like the dragons in the fairy tales McIntosh had read her: too lethal to tame, too mesmerizing to walk away from.

And yet, she suddenly wanted to bury her head in the hollow of his neck. Wanted to wrap herself around him. Wanted to hold on to him and never let go. She even found herself leaning toward him with every intention of giving in to those wants.

Stop. Don't.

Most of her life, human touch had been denied her. At five, she'd been sent to the Institute, where most of the employees hadn't concerned themselves with anything other than studying her ability. McIntosh was the closest thing she'd ever had to a friend, but even he had not hugged or touched her often, as if he feared her as much as he cared for her.

Dating, too, was tough. Men sort of freaked when they learned of her ability. And they always learned. There was no way to hide it. But . . .

If this man was who — what — she thought he was, he might not care about her little talent. He might let her touch him. And touching him and his heat might very well prove to be as potent a sensation as the silence, yet so much more —

"Woman?" he repeated, the word husky now, wine-rich as it cut into her thoughts.

She froze. Gulped again. Was that . . . desire flickering in his icy violet irises, completely obliterating that must-kill glaze? Or was the desire she saw born of pain and brutality, her death imminent? A swarm of emotions bombarded her: another clap of fear, morbid awe and yes, feminine curiosity. She had little experience with men, and even less with desire.

What had she been thinking, leaning toward him like that? He might have viewed her touch as an invitation. Might have touched her in return.

Why didn't the mere thought send her into hysterics?

Perhaps because she might be wrong. Perhaps he wasn't a dragon after all, but the prince who *slayed* the dragon to save the princess. "What's your name?" she found herself asking.

A tension-filled second ticked by, then another, and she assumed he wouldn't answer. Lines of strain bracketed his rough features, as though being near her was a chore. Finally he said, "Maddox. I am called Maddox."

Maddox . . . The name slipped and slid through the corridors of her mind, a seductive chant that promised unimaginable satisfaction. She forced herself to smile in greeting. "I'm Ashlyn Darrow."

His attention deviated to her lips. Despite

the snow, beads of sweat broke out over his forehead, glistening. "You should not have come, Ashlyn Darrow," he snarled, losing all hint of the desire she'd both fancied and feared. But he traced his hands up her arms, surprisingly gentle, and stopped at the base of her nape. Gingerly his thumb tripped over her throat, lingering on the wildly thumping pulse.

She sucked in a breath and swallowed it, his fingers moving with the motion. An unintentional yet wholly erotic caress that liquefied her entire body. Until, a moment later, his grip tightened, almost hurting.

She gasped out a raspy "Please," and he released her completely.

Ashlyn blinked in surprise. Without his touch, she felt . . . bereft?

"Dangerous," he said, this time in Hungarian.

She wasn't sure if he meant himself — or her. "Are you one of them?" she asked softly, not switching languages herself. No reason to let him know she spoke them both.

Astonishment darkened his gaze, and a muscle ticked in his jaw. "What do you mean? One of them?" English this time.

"I — I —" The words refused to form. Fury was blanketing his features, more fury than she'd ever seen another person project.

It radiated from every contour of his hard body. She drew her arms around her middle. No, not a prince after all. A dragon, definitely, as she'd first assumed.

Remaining on his knees, he inched away from her. He drew in a measured breath and slowly released it, the air misting around his face. His hand hovered over the opening of his boot, as if he couldn't decide whether to reach inside or not. Finally, he said, "What are you doing in these woods, woman? And do not lie to me. I'll know it, and you will not like my response."

Ashlyn somehow found her voice. "I'm looking for the men who live at the top of this hill."

"Why?" The single word was spat.

How much should she reveal? He *was* one of the men with strange abilities, had to be. He was too vibrant, too powerful to be solely human. But more than that, his mere presence had somehow chased the voices away, something that had never happened to her before. "I need help," she admitted.

"Do you?" There was a conflicting mix of suspicion and indulgence in his expression. "With what?"

She opened her mouth to say . . . what? She didn't know. In the end, it didn't matter. He stopped her with a quick shake of his head. "Never mind. You aren't welcome here, so your explanation is moot. Return to the city. Whatever you came here for, you will not receive."

"But — but . . ." She couldn't allow him to send her away. She *needed* him. Yes, she'd only just met him. Yes, the only things she knew about him were his name and the fact that he threw daggers with expert precision. But she was already horrified at the thought of losing the silence. "I want to stay with you." She knew desperation seeped from her, but she didn't care. "Please. Just for a little while. Until I learn how to control the voices myself."

Instead of softening, he seemed infuriated by her plea. His nostrils flared and a muscle ticked in his jaw. "Your babbling will not distract me. You're Bait. You have to be. Otherwise you would be running from me in fear."

"I'm not bait." Whatever bait was. "Swear to God." She reached out and gripped his forearms, the flesh firm and solid, unbelievably hot and utterly electrifying underneath her hand. Tingles speared her arm. "I don't even know what you're talking about."

Quick as a snap, he slashed out a hand and caught the base of her skull, jerking her forward into a beam of moonlight. The action didn't hurt her. On the contrary, she experienced another electrical jolt. Her stomach quivered.

He didn't speak, just studied her with an intensity that bordered on cruelty. She studied him, too, shocked as something began to flash . . . swirl . . . materialize under his skin. A face, she realized with macabre awe. Another face. Her heart skipped a beat. *Can't be a demon, can't be a demon. He made the voices stop. He and the others have done wonderful things for this city. It's just a trick of the light.*

While she could still see Maddox's features, she could also see that shadow of someone — some*thing* — else. Red, glowing eyes. Skeletal cheekbones. Sharp-as-daggers teeth.

Please be a trick of the light.

But the more that skeletal countenance stared at her, the less she could pretend it was an illusion.

"Do you want to die?" Maddox — or the skeleton? — demanded, the words so guttural they were barely more than an animalistic growl.

"No." He could kill her, but she'd die with a smile. Two minutes of silence were worth more to her than a lifetime of noise. Scared but determined, and still tingling because of his fever-touch, she raised her chin. "I need your help. Tell me how to control my power and I'll leave here and now. Or let me stay with you and learn how it's done."

He released her, then reached for her again, then stopped and fisted his hand. "I do not know why I am hesitating," he said, even as he eyed her mouth with what might have been longing. "Midnight is closing in, and you need to be as far away from me as possible."

The moment the last word left him, he frowned. A second later, he barked, "Too late! Pain is searching for me." He inched away from her, that skeletal mask still flashing behind his skin. "Run. Go back to the city. Now!"

"No," she said with only the slightest tremble. Only a fool ran from heaven — even if that piece of heaven possessed a transparent face straight from hell.

Cursing under his breath, Maddox jerked the two blades from the tree and pushed to his feet. His gaze lifted skyward, past snow and treetops to the half moon. His frown became fierce, angry. One step, two, he backed away.

Ashlyn used the tree as leverage and stood. Her knees knocked together, nearly collapsing under her weight. Suddenly she could feel the icy wind again, could hear the whisper of chatter closing in on her. A cry of despair rose inside her.

Three steps, four.

"Where are you going?" she asked. "Don't leave me here."

"No time to take you to shelter. You'll have to find it on your own." He wheeled around, giving her a view of his wide shoulders and stiff, retreating back, before throwing over his shoulder, "Do not return to this hill, woman. Next time, you will not find me so generous."

"I'm not going back. Wherever you go, I'll follow." A threat, yes, but one she intended to uphold.

Maddox stopped and whipped to face her, baring his teeth in another fearsome scowl. "I could kill you here and now, Bait, as I know I should. How would you follow me then?"

Bait again. Her heart drummed erratically in her chest, but she met his stare dead on, hoping she appeared stubborn and determined rather than simply petrified. "Believe me, I'd rather you do so than leave me alone with the voices."

A curse, a hiss of pain. He doubled over.

Losing her bravado in the face of concern, Ashlyn raced to him. She splayed her fingers over his back and searched for injury. Anything that crumpled this hulking beast had to be excruciating. He shoved her away, however, and she stumbled from the unexpected force.

"No," he said, and she would have sworn he spoke with two separate voices. One a man's. The second . . . something so much more powerful. It boomed like a thunderstorm, echoing in the night. "No touching."

"Are you hurt?" She righted herself, trying not to reveal just how badly his actions cut. "Maybe I can help. I —"

"Leave or die." He spun and leapt forward, disappearing into the night.

Chatter crashed into her mind, as if it had merely been awaiting his departure. Now it seemed louder than ever before, blaring after the precious silence.

Langnak ithon kel moradni.

Stumbling in the same direction Maddox had taken, Ashlyn covered her ears. "Wait." She moaned. *Shut up, shut up, shut up.* "Wait. Please."

Her foot tangled with a broken limb and she toppled again to the ground. A sharp ache tore through her ankle. Whimpering, she dragged herself to her hands and knees and crawled.

Ate ìtéleted let minket veszejbe.

Couldn't stop. Had to reach him. Wind beat against her, as sharp as the daggers Maddox carried.

On and on the voices clamored.

"Please," she cried. "Please."

A fierce roar split the night, shaking the ground, rattling the trees.

Suddenly Maddox was beside her again, drowning out the voices. "Foolish Bait," he spat. More to himself, he added, "Foolish warrior."

Crying out in relief, she threw her arms around him. Holding tight. Never wanting to let go — even if he did still wear that eerie skeletal mask. Tears streamed down her cheeks, crystallizing on her skin. "Thank you. Thank you for coming back. Thank you." She buried her head in the hollow of his neck, exactly as she'd wanted to do earlier. When her cheek brushed his bare skin, she shivered, those warm tingles rushing through her once more.

"You'll come to regret this," he said, sweeping her up and over his shoulder like a sack of potatoes.

She didn't care. She was with him, the voices gone, and that was all that mattered.

Maddox sped into motion, maneuvering around those ghostly trees. Every so often, he grunted as if in pain. Snarled as if in a rage. Ashlyn begged him to set her down so that she could spare him the burden of her weight, but he squeezed the inside of her thigh, a silent command for her to shut the hell up. Finally she relaxed against him and simply enjoyed the ride.

If only that joy could have lasted.

CHAPTER THREE

Get home, get home, get home. Maddox chanted the command in his mind, trying to distract himself from the pain. Trying to dampen the urge to do violence . . . an urge that was building steadily. The woman — Ashlyn — bounced on his shoulder, an unwelcome reminder that he could break at any moment and slaughter everything around him. Her, especially.

You wanted to drown in a woman, the spirit taunted. *Here's your chance. Drown in her blood.*

His hands curled into fists. He needed to think, but couldn't do so over the pain. She had mentioned a power, asked for his help. Hadn't she? Some of what she had said was lost amidst the roar in his head. All he knew for certain was that he should have left her behind as he'd intended.

But he had heard her cry out, a tortured sound — the sort of crazed groan Maddox himself had often wanted to release. Something inside him had reacted deeply, and he'd been filled with a need to help her, a need to touch her soft skin just one more time. A need that had somehow proven stronger than Violence. An amazing, unbelievable feat.

And so he'd returned to her, even though he'd known she was in more danger with him than she was alone in the forest. Even though he'd known she had most likely been sent to distract him and help Hunters gain access to the fortress.

Fool. Now she was draped over him, her feminine scent teasing his nose, her soft curves his to explore.

Or slice, the demon goaded.

Hauntingly beautiful as she was, it was easy to understand why the Hunters had sent her. Who would want to mar such lush femininity? Who would turn such blatant sensuality away? Not him, it seemed.

Fool, he inwardly cursed again. Hunters! They truly were in Budapest, their tattoos a grim reminder of those dark, dark days in Greece. Clearly they were once more out for blood, for each of the four men following Ashlyn had carried a gun and silencer. For mortals, they'd fought with expert skill.

Maddox had emerged the victor in that

bloody tête-à-tête, but he had not emerged unscathed. His lower leg had been sliced, and one of his ribs was surely cracked.

Time, it seemed, had only honed their skills.

He wondered how Ashlyn would react when she found out they were gone. Would she cry? Scream? Rail? Would she attack him in a grief-stricken rage?

Did any others wait in town?

At the moment, he couldn't seem to make himself care. Holding Ashlyn in his arms, he was transported, the hell that was his life momentarily receding, leaving only . . . something he didn't think he could rightly name. Desire, perhaps. No. He discarded the word instantly. It failed to explain the intensity of the rush, the heat.

Instant obsession, maybe.

Whatever it was, he didn't like it. It was more powerful than anything he'd experienced before, threatening to control him. Maddox did not need another force trying to pull his strings.

She was just so . . . lovely. So lovely it almost hurt to gaze upon her. Her skin was smooth and supple, like cinnamon dipped in a honey pot then churned into lickable cream. Her eyes were that same honey shade and so haunted they made his chest hurt. He'd never seen a mortal look so tormented and felt a strange kind of kinship with her.

While strands of long, silky hair, also the color of honey yet veined with copper and quartz, had wisped around her delicate features, he'd ached. He'd wanted. Wanted to touch, to taste. Wanted to devour. Consume. But he hadn't wanted to hurt. The knowledge still amazed him.

Ashlyn . . . Her name whispered through his mind, as delicate as the woman herself. Taking her to the fortress was against the rules, a threat to their most guarded secrets. He should be ashamed of himself for carrying her forward rather than away, and she should be crying in terror.

Apparently *should* did not mean anything to either of them.

Why wasn't she crying? More importantly, why *hadn't* she cried? When he'd first pounced on her, clearly splattered with the blood of her allies, a delicious smile had lit her face, her plump lips showcasing perfect white teeth.

Remembering that smile, Maddox experienced a jolt of blistering arousal. Underneath it, however, confusion still lingered. Though it had been an eternity since he'd last dealt with Bait, he could not recall the

Hunters' decoys ever being so transparent in their satisfaction.

Not even Hadiee, the Bait who had helped bring Baden, keeper of Distrust, to his knees. Hadiee had played the abused, frightened soul to perfection. Seeing her, Baden had decided to act without suspicion for the first time since his demon had been placed inside him. Or maybe not. Maddox had always wondered if the man had *wanted* to die. If so, he'd gotten his wish. He'd been stabbed in the throat moments after opening his *spiti* to Hadiee — who in turn allowed armed Hunters inside.

Most likely, the stabbing alone would not have killed Baden. The Hunters, however, then proceeded to decapitate him. Baden hadn't stood a chance. Not even an immortal could recover from that.

He'd been a good man, a fine warrior, and hadn't deserved such a bloody demise. Maddox, however . . .

My murder would be justified.

The Bait before Hadiee had seduced Paris. Not that such a thing required much effort. During the act, Hunters had crept inside the woman's bedroom and stabbed the warrior in the back, attempting to weaken him before going for his head.

Paris, though, was strengthened by sex.

Even injured, he'd managed to fight his way free and kill everyone around him.

Maddox couldn't imagine the woman in his arms being cowardly enough to strike from behind. She had faced him and hadn't backed down, even when the spirit inside of him clamored for release. Perhaps Ashlyn was innocent. He hadn't found cameras or dynamite on the trees where she'd lingered. Perhaps —

"Perhaps you are more a fool than you realize," he muttered.

"What?"

He ignored her, knowing it was safer that way. Her voice was soft and lilting and prodded at the spirit, mocking in its gentleness. Best to keep her silent.

Finally he spotted the dark, crumbling stone of the fortress. None too soon. An excruciating pain ripped through his stomach, almost knocking him to the ground. Violence poured through his veins and shimmered in his blood. *Kill. Hurt. Maim.*

"No."

Kill, hurt, maim.

"No!"

Killhurtmaim.

"Maddox?"

The spirit roared, desperate, so desperate for release. *Fight it,* he commanded himself.

Remain calm. He drew air into his lungs, held it, slowly released it. *Killhurtmaim, killhurtmaim.* "I will resist. I am not a monster."

We shall see. . . .

His nails elongated, itching with that inexorable urge to strike. If he didn't compose himself, he would soon assault anything and everything within his reach. He would kill, without mercy, without hesitation. He would destroy this home stone by stone, kicking and clawing. Raging. He would destroy everyone inside of it. And he would rather burn in hell for all eternity than do such a thing.

"Maddox?" Ashlyn said again. Her sweet voice drifted to his ears, an entreaty that was part soothing balm, part kindling. "What's —"

"Silence." He skimmed her off his shoulder, still holding her tight, and burst through the front door, nearly ripping the wood from its hinges. Angry voices greeted him. Torin, Lucien and Reyes stood in the foyer, arguing.

"You never should have let him leave," Lucien said. "He becomes an animal, Torin, annihilating —"

"Stop!" Maddox shouted. "Help!"

All three men spun, facing him.

"What's going on?" Reyes demanded. Seeing Ashlyn, he gaped. Shock settled over his features. "Why have you brought a woman into the house?"

Hearing the commotion, Paris and Aeron raced into the foyer, features taut. When they spotted Maddox, they relaxed. "Finally," Paris said, clearly relieved. But he, too, spotted Ashlyn. He grinned. "Sweet! A present? For me?"

Maddox bared his teeth. *Kill them,* Violence beseeched, a seductive whisper now. *Kill them.*

"You shouldn't be here." The words tore from his throat. "Take her and leave. Before it's too late."

"Look at him," Paris said, his relief and amusement gone. "Look at his face."

"The process has already begun," Lucien said.

The words spurred Maddox to action. Though he found he didn't want to release Ashlyn, even in his madness, he tossed her at the group. Lucien caught her effortlessly. The moment her weight settled on her feet, she winced. Must have twisted her ankle on the hill, Maddox realized, concern slipping past bloodlust for a split second.

"Careful of her foot," he commanded.

Lucien released her to look at her ankle, but Ashlyn scrambled away from him and limped her way back into Maddox's arms. His concern intensified as his arms wound around her. She was trembling. But a moment later, he stopped caring. A pestilent haze fell over his mind, brutality obliterating every emotion in its path.

"Release me," he growled, pushing her.

The woman clung to him. "What's wrong?"

Lucien grabbed her, jerking her backward and locking her in an iron grip. Had she touched Maddox a second longer, he might have clawed her to pieces. As it was, he slammed his hands into the nearest wall.

"Maddox," she said on a tremulous breath.

"Do not hurt her." The words were for himself as much as the others. "You," he grated, pointing to Reyes with a crimson-stained finger. "Bedroom. Now." He didn't wait for a response, but pounded up the stairs.

He heard Ashlyn fight for freedom and call, "But I want to stay with you."

He bit the inside of his cheek until he tasted blood. He allowed himself a single glance over his shoulder.

When Lucien further tightened his hold on the struggling Ashlyn, his dark hair brushing her shoulders, Maddox's need for bloodshed strengthened. He almost changed paths, almost sprinted back into the foyer to hack his friend to pieces. *Mine,* his mind shouted. *Mine. I found her. No one but me should be allowed to touch her.*

Maddox wasn't sure whether it was the spirit or himself who thought such a thing, and he didn't care. He just wanted to kill. Yes, kill. Fury, such fury, exploded through him. He *did* stop. Did change direction. He was going to slice Lucien in half and coat the floor with his friend's blood. *Destroy, destroy, destroy. Kill.*

"He's going to attack." Lucien.

"Get her out of here!" Torin.

Lucien dragged Ashlyn from the room. Her panicked cries echoed in Maddox's ears, which only managed to increase his darkest needs. The image of her pale, lovely face flashed in his mind over and over again, becoming the only thing he saw. She was terrified. Trusted him, wanted him. Her arms had reached for him.

His stomach was a stinging mass of pulsing agony, but he didn't slow his steps. Any minute, midnight would arrive and he would die — but he was taking everyone here with him. *Yes, they must be destroyed.*

"Ah, hell," Aeron muttered. "The demon has taken over completely. We'll have to

70

subdue him. Lucien, get back in here. Hurry!"

Aeron, Reyes and Paris advanced. With the speed of a single breath, Maddox unsheathed his daggers and launched them. Expecting the attack, all three men ducked and the silver blades soared over them, embedding in the wall. Two seconds later, the men were on top of him and he was lying flat on his back. Fists jabbed into his face, his stomach, his groin. He fought. Roaring, growling, punching.

Knuckles slammed into his jaw, dislocating the bone. A knee jammed into the sensitive flesh between his legs. Still he fought. And as the battle raged, the warriors managed to drag him up the steps and into his bedroom. Maddox thought he heard Ashlyn sobbing, thought he saw her trying to tear the men away from him. He jabbed his fist forward and hit something — a nose. Heard a howl. Experienced satisfaction. Wanted more blood.

"Damn it! Chain him, Reyes, before he breaks somebody else's fucking nose."

"He's too strong. I'm not sure how much longer I can hold him."

Minutes passed as he fought, maybe an eternity, then cold metal locked around his wrists, his ankles. Maddox bucked and arched, the links cutting into his flesh. "Bastards!" The pain in his stomach was unbearable now, no longer sporadic but constant. "I'll kill you. I'll take every one of you to hell with me."

Reyes stood over him, a dark glaze of determination and regret blanketing his tanned features. Maddox tried to knock him down by raising his knees and kicking, but the chains held. The warrior, too, held steady, withdrawing a long, menacing sword from his side.

"I'm sorry," Reyes rasped as a clock chimed the hour. And then he stabbed Maddox in the stomach.

The metal sliced all the way to his spine before leaving his body. Instantly blood poured from the wound, wetting his chest and stomach. Bile burned his throat, his nose. He cursed; he bucked.

Reyes stabbed him again. And again.

The pain . . . the agony . . . His skin felt scorched. With only those three slices, his bones and organs were already shredded, each tear a point of anguish. Still he fought; still he felt a desperate urge to kill.

A woman screamed. "Stop! You're killing him!"

When her voice pierced Maddox's consciousness, his struggles became all the more wild. Ashlyn. His woman from the forest. *His.* Get to her, had to get to her. Had to kill her — no! Had to save her. Kill . . . save . . . the two needs battled for supremacy. He jerked at his chains. The metal shackles dug deeper into his wrists and ankles, but he reared up and kicked. The bed shook with the force of his movements, and both the headboard and footboard bent forward with a whine.

"Why are you doing this?" Ashlyn shouted. "Stop! Don't hurt him. Ohmygod, stop!"

Reyes stabbed him again.

Black cobwebs wove over his vision as he searched the room. Paris, he saw dimly, was striding toward Ashlyn. Reached her, wrapped his arms around her. She was dwarfed by the larger man, enfolded in his shadow. Tears glistened in those amber eyes and on her too-pale cheeks.

She fought, but Paris held firm and dragged her from the room.

Maddox uttered an animalistic roar. Paris would seduce her. Strip her and taste her. She would not be able to resist; no woman could. "Let her go! Now!" He strained so fervently for freedom, a vessel burst in his forehead. His vision blackened completely.

"Get her out of here and keep her out."

Reyes stabbed Maddox once more, the fifth blow. "She's making him more crazed than usual."

Had to save her. Had to get to her. The sound of rattling chains blended with his panting as he struggled all the more.

"I'm sorry," Reyes whispered again.

Finally, the sixth blow was delivered.

That's when all of Maddox's strength seeped from him. The spirit quieted, retreating to the back of his consciousness.

Done. It was done.

He lay on the bed, drenched in his own blood, unable to move or see. The pain didn't leave him, nor did the burning. No, they intensified, more a part of him than his own skin. Warm liquid gurgled in his throat.

Lucien — he knew it was Lucien for he recognized the deceptively sweet scent of Death — knelt beside him and clasped his hand. That meant his demise was close, so torturously close.

But for Maddox, the true torment had yet to begin.

As part of his death-curse, he and Violence would spend the rest of the night burning in the pits of hell. He opened his mouth to speak, but only a cough emerged. More and more blood was rushing into his throat, choking him.

"In the morning, you'll have a lot of explaining to do, my friend," Lucien said, adding gently, "Die now. I'll take your soul to hell, as required — but this time you might actually want to remain there, eh, rather than deal with the trouble you've brought into our home."

"G-girl," Maddox finally managed to say.

"Don't worry," Lucien said. Whatever questions he had, he kept to himself. "We won't hurt her. She'll be yours to deal with in the morning."

"Untouched." The request was odd, Maddox knew, because none of them had ever been possessive of a woman. Ashlyn, though . . . He wasn't quite sure what he wanted to do with her. He knew what he should do — and what he couldn't. Both mattered little just then. Because, more than anything, he knew that he didn't want to share.

"Untouched," he insisted weakly when Lucien said nothing.

"Untouched," Lucien agreed at last.

The scent of flowers intensified. A heartbeat of time passed, and then Maddox died.

CHAPTER FOUR

"Who are you and how do you know Maddox?"

"Let me go!" Ashlyn wiggled and squirmed, trying to free herself from her captor's iron grip. Her ankle throbbed, but she didn't care. "They're killing him in there." Oh God. They *were* killing him, stabbing him over and over again. There'd been so much blood . . . such terrible screams. She gagged, remembering.

The voices might still be gone, but she felt more tormented than ever.

"Maddox will be fine," the man told her. Maddox had broken his nose — she'd *seen* it — but it had snapped back into place almost immediately. There wasn't even a trace of blood on his face. Now he removed one of his arms from her waist, only to caress her temple and gently brush aside a lock of hair. "You'll see."

"No, I won't see," she all but sobbed. "Let

me go!"

"Much as I hate to deny you, I have to. You were causing him undue torment."

"*I* was causing him undue torment? I wasn't the one stabbing him. Now let me go!" Not knowing what else to do, she stilled and gazed up at him. "Please." He had brilliant blue eyes and skin as pale as milk. His hair was a captivating blend of brown and black. He was handsome beyond anyone she'd ever seen before, too perfect to be real.

And all she wanted to do was escape him.

"Relax." He smiled a slow, seductive smile. Practiced, even to her untrained eye. "You have nothing to fear from me, gorgeous. I'm all about the pleasure."

Fury and fright, sorrow and frustration gave her strength and bravery; she slapped him. He'd just watched a man stab Maddox, and he'd done nothing to stop it. He'd just watched a man stab Maddox, and he dared to flirt with her. She had *everything* to fear from him.

He lost his grin and frowned down at her. "You hit me." There was surprise in his tone.

She slapped him again. "Let. Me. Go!"

His frown deepened. He rubbed his cheek with one hand and held her still with the other. "Women do not hit me. Women love me."

She raised her palm, ready to deliver another blow.

Sighing, he said, "Fine. Go. Maddox's screams have stopped. I doubt you can upset him now, dead as he surely is." His arm fell away from her.

Ashlyn didn't give him time to change his mind. Suddenly free, she leapt into motion, racing down the hall despite the pain in her ankle. When she entered the room and saw the blood-soaked bed and motionless body, she skidded to an abrupt halt.

Dear God.

Maddox's eyes were closed; his chest was utterly still.

A sob burst from her, and she covered her mouth with a shaky hand. Red-hot tears filled her eyes. "They killed you." She raced to the bed and cupped Maddox's jaw in her hands, tilting slowly. His eyelids didn't flicker open. Breath didn't seep from his nose. His skin was already cold and pale from loss of blood.

She was too late.

How could someone so strong and vital have been destroyed so callously?

"Who is she?" someone said.

Startled, she turned. Maddox's murderers

78

stood off to the side, talking amongst themselves. How could she have forgotten them? Every few seconds, they glanced in her direction. None of them spoke directly to her. They continued their conversation as if she didn't matter. As if Maddox didn't matter.

"We should take her to the city, but she's seen too much," a harsh voice said. The coldest, most uncaring voice she'd ever heard. "What was Maddox thinking?"

"All this time, I've lived with him and I never knew what he suffered," an angelic-looking blond with green eyes said quietly. He was dressed entirely in black and wore gloves that stretched to his biceps. "Is it always like this?"

"Not always, no," the one who had wielded the sword said. "He's usually more accepting." His black gaze was hard, his tone tormented. "The woman . . ."

Murderer! Ashlyn inwardly cried, wanting to attack him. All her life, her ability had revealed more bad than good, forcing her to listen to centuries of hateful accusations and even shrieks of terror. And the one man who'd given her any measure of peace, they'd brutally slain.

Do something, Darrow. She scrubbed her burning eyes with the back of her wrist and straightened to shaky legs. What could she do? They outnumbered her. They were stronger than she was.

An extremely tattooed man frowned over at her. He had military-cropped brown hair, two eyebrow rings and soft, full lips. He also had more muscles than a world champion power-lifter. He would have been handsome — in a serial-killer kind of way — if not for those tattoos. Even his cheeks were painted with violent images of war and weapons.

His eyes were the same shade of violet as Maddox's, but they lacked any hint of warmth or emotion. Blood dripped down his nose as he rubbed his chin with two fingers. "We have to do *something* with the girl." That cold, emotionless voice again. "I don't like her being here."

"Even so, Aeron, we aren't to touch her." This speaker had inky hair that was like a dark halo around his head and different-colored eyes — one brown, one blue. His face was a mass of scars. At first glance, he was hideous. At second, there was an almost hypnotic quality to him, enhanced by the scent of roses drifting from him. "Tomorrow morning she'll be in the same condition she is now. Breathing and clothed."

"Just like Maddox, taking away our fun."

The wry voice came from behind her and

she yelped, spinning. The beautiful pale-skinned man stood in the doorway. He watched her, hunger in his eyes, as if he were picturing her naked and liked what he saw.

A tremor started at the top of her head and worked its way down, all the way to her toes. Bastards, every one of them! Her feral gaze scanned the room and narrowed on the bloody sword that had been carelessly tossed onto the floor. The very sword that had sliced through Maddox as if he were nothing more than a thin layer of silk.

"I want to know who she is," the cold, tattooed one — Aeron — said. "And I want to know why Maddox brought her here. He knows the rules."

"She must have been one of the humans on the hill," the angel said, "but that still doesn't explain why he brought her into our midst."

She would have laughed if she hadn't felt on the verge of a total breakdown. *I should have listened to McIntosh.* Demons *did* live here.

"Well?" Aeron prompted. "What do we do with her?"

Each of the men faced her again, and Ashlyn dove for the blade. Her fingers curled around the hilt and she straightened, pointing the tip in their direction. The sword was heavier than she'd thought and her arms instantly began to shake under its weight, but she held firm.

Her companions merely regarded her with curiosity. Their lack of fear didn't faze her. Though she'd only known Maddox a short while, there was something wild inside her that mourned his loss and demanded she avenge his death.

Maddox. His name whispered through her mind. He was gone. Forever. Her stomach clenched painfully. "I should kill you, all of you. He was innocent."

"Innocent?" someone scoffed.

"She wants to kill us. Hunters *have* come for us, then," Aeron said with disgust.

"A Hunter would not call Maddox innocent. Even in jest."

"Bait would not be above it. Remember, every word out of their mouths was a lie, though their faces were always guileless."

"I watched Maddox slay four men on my monitor, which he wouldn't have done if they had been innocent. And I doubt a coincidence brought a guiltless female to the forest at the exact same time."

"Think she has any skill with a sword?"

Snort. "Of course not. Look how she's holding it."

"Brave little thing, though."

Ashlyn gaped at them, hardly able to keep up with the conversation. "Does no one care that a man was murdered here? That *you* were the ones who murdered him?"

The black-clothed angel laughed, actually laughed, but there was anguish in his green eyes. "Believe me. Maddox will thank us in the morning."

"If he doesn't kill us for being here in the first place," someone retorted.

To her astonishment, several of the men chuckled. All shook their heads in hearty agreement. Only the one who had rendered the fatal wounds remained silent. He continued to stare at Maddox's body, his expression wracked with agony and guilt. Good. She wanted him to suffer for what he'd done.

The sensual one, the one who thought no woman could resist him, leveled his gaze on her, and she was treated to another slow, seductive smile. "Put the sword away, sweet, before you hurt yourself."

She held tight, determined. "Come and take it from me, you . . . you . . . animal!" The words flew from her mouth, a challenge she couldn't hold back. "I may not have any skill with swords, but if you come near me I *will* hurt you."

There was a sigh. A laugh. A muttered, "What kind of female can resist Paris?"

"I say we lock her in the dungeon." This from the one named Aeron. "No telling what she'll do otherwise."

"Agreed," the others echoed.

Edging toward the door, Ashlyn shook her head and gripped the sword more tightly. "I'm leaving. Do you hear me? I'm leaving! And mark my words, justice will be served. Every single one of you will be arrested and executed."

"Maddox can decide what to do with her in the morning," the one with the mismatched eyes said calmly, ignoring her.

As if Maddox could decide anything now.

Her chin trembled. And then her eyes widened as each of his killers stalked forward, determination in their every step.

Don't hurt me. Please, don't hurt me.

A pause. A snap.

An anguished cry.

My arm! Huge, gut-wrenching sobs. *You broke my fucking arm!* Ashlyn's own arm throbbed in sympathy. *I didn't . . . do anything . . . wrong.*

The voices had returned in full force.

She huddled on the floor of a dark, dank cell, shivering and scared. "I just wanted to find someone who could help me," she whispered. Instead, she'd fallen straight into a Grimm's folk tale, but with no happy ending in sight.

I will. I will. Just . . . need . . . a . . . moment.

The one-sided conversation had been rolling through her mind for an eternity, it seemed, now a discordant concerto of anger, desperation and pain. Above it, however, a single voice rose: Maddox's. Not a voice of the past, but a memory. A burst of screams.

"You left the Institute for *this.*" She shook her head in grief and disgust, wanting to convince herself this day had been nothing more than a nightmare. That a man had not been slain right in front of her. Stabbed. Repeatedly. But she knew the truth. His shouts . . . God, his shouts. His rage at being chained and beaten, his torment . . . worse than anything she'd ever heard from another human being.

Tears rained down her face. She couldn't get his image out of her head — not his image before he died and not his image after. Harshly handsome face almost savage in its intensity. Facial bones blurred and sunken. Violet eyes bright. Violet eyes closed. Tall, tanned and muscled body. Broken, bloody, lifeless body.

She whimpered.

After shoving her into this cell, Maddox's killers had promised to bring her blankets and food. The vow had been delivered ages ago, but no one had returned. She was glad. She didn't want to see them again. Didn't want to hear them, didn't want to talk to them. She'd rather endure the cold and the hunger.

Shivering, she tugged her jacket tight at the collar. She was thankful she still had it, that the men, those barbaric monsters, hadn't taken it from her during the seemingly endless trek from topside to underground.

Just then, something scampered across her fingertips, squeaking happily, and she jerked. Oh God, Oh God, Oh God. She scooted into the nearest corner. *Mouse.* A hairy little rodent that would eat anything, and where there was one . . .

Stomach churning, she swept her gaze through the cell. Not that it did any good. The room was too dark, and she wouldn't have been able to see a hand — or a monster — if it were right in front of her face.

"Stay still." Deep breath in. "Stay calm." Deep breath out.

I'll tell you anything you want to know, but please don't hurt me again, Broken Arm said, sobbing his way back into her thoughts. *I didn't mean to sneak inside.* There was a long pause. *Okay, yes, yes. I did. I meant to, but I only wanted to see who had taken residence here. I'm not a hunter, I swear I'm not.*

Ashlyn's ears twitched, and she pressed deeper into the rocky wall. Hunter, the man had said. Maddox's killers had called *her* a hunter. What did they mean? Bounty hunter? She frowned and rubbed her swollen, aching ankle. Who could ever think that of five-foot-five, average Ashlyn?

"Doesn't matter. You have to find a way out of here, Darrow." She had to tell the authorities what had happened to Maddox. Would they believe her? Would they even care? Or had the men here somehow bewitched them as they'd done the rest of the townspeople — angels, indeed — allowing them to do anything they wanted, whenever they wanted?

A sob gushed from her lips; a tremor raked her. No one should have to die that slowly, that painfully. Dignity gone. Cries unheeded.

One way or another, Maddox would be avenged.

Maddox screamed.

Flames licked him from head to toe.

Blistering, melting away his flesh, reducing him to nothing but bone. No, not even bone, he mused in the next instant. The flames had reduced him to ash. But he was still aware . . . always aware. He still knew who he was, still knew *what* he was, and that he would have to return to the fire tomorrow.

The agony was nearly more than he could bear. Plumes of smoke thickened the air, scattering soot in every direction. Disgustingly, he knew that soot belonged to him. *Was* him.

Much too soon, it returned to where he had stood, fused together and became a body, a man — a man that once again caught fire. A body that once again melted bit by grueling bit, pouring flesh from muscle, then flickering orange-gold sparks over muscle before disintegrating altogether. There was another blackened breeze, returning everything to its place so the entire process could repeat itself. Again and again and again.

All the while, Violence roared inside his head, desperate to escape, no longer sated as it had been at the moment of his death. Blending with that were the sounds of the other condemned souls, screaming as the flames of hell devoured them. Demons, those disgusting winged creatures with glowing red eyes, skeletal faces and thick yellow horns atop their heads, fluttered from one tormented prisoner to another, laughing, taunting, spitting.

I have one of those monsters inside me. Except mine is worse.

The other demons knew it, too. "Welcome back, brother," they would jeer before licking him with their fiery, forked tongues.

Always before, Maddox had wished to fade into nothing when the fire overcame him, never to return to hell *or* to earth. He'd wished to end his miserable existence and finally stop the pain. Always before — but not tonight. Not this time.

Tonight, pain was eclipsed by desire.

Ashlyn's image rose inside his mind, taunting him far more than the demons. *You'll find nothing but bliss with me,* her eyes seemed to say, lips parting, softening for a kiss.

She was a puzzle he yearned to solve. His first glimpse of heaven with her warm, amber-rich hair and honey-colored eyes. She was exquisite and lush, and so unequivocally feminine she called to his every masculine instinct.

Surprisingly, she had fought to stay with him. Had even fought to save him from the others, he'd realized only a few minutes ago. He didn't fully understand why, but he liked the notion anyway.

He might not have known what he wanted to do with her earlier, but he knew now. He wanted to taste her. All of her. Bait or not. Hunter or not. He simply wanted. After all his suffering, he deserved a sliver of happiness.

Even in his days as an elite warrior to the gods, he had never desired a specific woman above all the rest. After, he had always taken what he could get, when he could get it. But Ashlyn, he wanted specifically. Ashlyn, he wanted now.

Where had Lucien placed her? In the room adjoining his? Did she lounge on the bed, naked body wrapped in silks and velvets? That's how he would take her, Maddox decided then. Not outside as was his custom. Not on a cold, twig-laden ground. But in a bed, face to face, skin to skin, pumping and sliding slowly.

His body burned with the thought — a burn that had nothing to do with the flames.

She means us harm. We'll harm her first and be the better for it, the spirit urged.

Do not dare suggest it, he commanded, trying to eclipse Violence — who, surprisingly, seemed content to discuss Ashlyn calmly now, rather than roar. *I am not a monster.*

We are the same, and that woman spells danger.

Yes, she did. Yet he'd never encountered a woman quite as vulnerable as Ashlyn. Alone in the forest, secrets in her pretty eyes. Killers on her trail. Whether they'd meant to ignore her, kill her or use her to kill him and the other Lords, he would find out.

In the morning, when Lucien returned his soul to his healed body, Maddox would find and question her. No, he would touch her first, he decided. Kiss her. Taste her entire body as he so desperately wanted to do right now.

Despite the pain, he found himself grinning with relish. The woman had looked at him with ecstasy in her eyes; she had tried to follow him, to save him. Yes, she had made her own bed. And now she would lie in it. With him.

Only after the loving was done would he question her. And if he discovered that she truly was Bait — there was a pang in his chest — he would deal with her as he'd dealt with the Hunters.

"The Titans have overthrown the Greeks," Aeron announced. The knowledge had been bubbling inside him since his return to the fortress an hour ago, but with all the commotion he hadn't had a chance to share. Until now. Things had finally quieted — but he knew the peace would last only until his meaning sank in.

Frowning, he plopped onto the plush red couch, Maddox's human no longer a concern. If only his words could be dismissed so easily — and what was suddenly making all that noise?

He looked around, scowled and grabbed the TV remote, flicking off the "movie" Paris had just turned on. Titillating moans ceased. The wet slap of man against woman faded from the flat screen. "You have to stop buying that garbage, Paris."

Paris swiped the remote from him and switched the fleshfest back on. Thankfully, he punched the mute button. "Not pay-per-view, bro," he said without a hint of remorse. "This one's from my own personal collection. *Oil Wrestlers Gone Wild.*"

"You become more human every day," Aeron muttered. "It's embarrassing. You know that, right?"

"Aeron, you cannot make an announcement like that and simply change the subject. You mentioned the . . . Titans?" Lucien said in his ever-calm voice.

Ever-calm. Yes, that described Death

perfectly. The immortal maintained an iron lock on his temper — on all of his emotions, really — for when it was unleashed, he was a force even Wrath feared. More than a beast, Lucien became a true demon. Aeron had only witnessed the transformation once, but he'd never forgotten.

"I thought I heard something along those lines, as well." Reyes shook his head, as if that would help him understand. "What's happening here? First Torin tells us the Hunters have returned, then Maddox comes home with a woman. And now you say the Titans have taken over? Is something like that even possible?"

"Yes, it is." Unfortunately. Aeron scrubbed a hand over his chopped hair, the short spikes abrading his palm. How he wished he could next deliver happy news. "Apparently the Titans spent their centuries of imprisonment honing their powers. In recent weeks they escaped Tartarus, ambushed the Greeks, enslaved them and seized the throne. *They* control us now."

There was a heavy silence as everyone absorbed the shocking news. No love was lost between the warriors and the Greeks, the very gods who had cursed them. But . . .

"You are sure?" Lucien asked him.

"Very." Until tonight, all Aeron had known

about the Titans was that they'd ruled Mount Olympus during the Golden Age, a time of "peace" and "harmony" — two words spouted by the Hunters who'd risen in Greece all those years ago. "They placed me in some sort of tribunal chamber, their thrones circling me. Physically, they are smaller than the Greeks. Their power, however, was unmistakable. I could almost see it, like a living entity. And on their faces, I saw only uncompromising determination and dislike."

Several tense minutes passed.

"Dislike aside, is there a chance the Titans can release us from the demons without killing us?" Reyes voiced the question they undoubtedly all were thinking.

Aeron himself had wondered. Had hoped. "I do not think so," he said, hating to disappoint them. "I asked that very question and they refused to discuss it with me."

Another silence, this one even more strained.

"This is . . . this is . . ." Paris trailed off.

"Unbelievable," Torin finished for him.

Reyes massaged his jaw. "If they will not free us, what do they plan for us, then?"

There would be no reprieve from the bad news. "All I know for sure is that they plan to take an active role in our existence." The one point in the Greeks' favor was that they had ignored the warriors after cursing them, allowing them to have some sort of life — tormented though it was.

Again, Reyes shook his head. "But . . . why?"

"I wish I knew."

"Is that why they summoned you?" Lucien asked. "To inform you of this change?"

"No." He paused, closed his eyes. "They ordered me to . . . do something."

"What?" Paris demanded when he failed to elaborate.

He studied each of his friends, trying to find the right words.

Torin stood in the corner, his profile to everyone. Distanced, always distanced. But then, Torin had to be. Reyes sat across from him. Tanned like the sun god, the warrior didn't look as though he belonged on earth, much less in the room. He was busy slicing grooves into his lower arm as he awaited Aeron's answer. Every few seconds, Reyes winced. That wince became a satisfied smile as blood trickled, forming tiny crimson rivers over his skin. Pain was the only thing that satisfied him, the only thing that made him feel alive.

Aeron had no idea how the man might respond to pleasure.

Paris was sprawled on the couch beside him, hands tucked behind his head as he switched his attention between Aeron and the movie, his demon probably urging him to watch just a little more. A man with his kind of luck should be ugly. At the very least, he should have to struggle to lure a woman into his bed. Instead, he simply looked at a woman with his handsome face and she stripped instantly, willing to be taken anywhere, available bed or not.

Maddox's woman hadn't, though, Aeron recalled. Why?

Lucien leaned against the pool table, his hideously scarred face revealing nothing. His arms were crossed over his massive chest, and those disconcerting eyes of his watched Aeron intently. "Well?" Lucien prompted.

He drew in a breath, released it. "I've been ordered to slay a group of tourists in Buda. Four humans." He paused, closed his eyes again. Tried not to feel a single shred of emotion. Cold. To get through this, he'd have to be cold. "All female."

"Come again." Paris jolted upright, frowning over at him, television forgotten.

Aeron repeated the gods' command.

Paler than usual, Paris shook his head. "I can buy that we're now under new management. I don't like it, I'm confused as hell by it, but hey. I buy it. What I don't get is that the Titans ordered you, the possessor of Wrath, to kill four human *women* in town. Why would they do something like that?" He threw up his arms. "That's craziness."

He might be the most promiscuous man ever to roam the Earth, bedding his partners and forgetting them in the same day, but women of every race, size and age were Paris's lifeblood. His entire reason for existence. He'd never been able to tolerate seeing a single one of them hurt.

"They did not give me a reason," Aeron answered, knowing a reason would not have mattered. He didn't want to harm those women in any way. He knew how it felt to kill. Oh, yes. He'd killed many, many times before, but always through the undeniable urgings of his demon — a demon that chose its victims well. People who beat or molested their children. People who took joy from the destruction of others. Wrath always knew when a person was deserving of death, their shameful actions playing through his mind.

When the women had been brought to his attention, the demon had tried them and found them innocent. And yet, he was supposed to murder them.

If that happened, if he was forced to spill the blood of the undeserving, Aeron would never be the same. He knew it, felt it.

"Did they give you a time frame for when the deed must be done?" Lucien asked, still seemingly unaffected. He was Death, the Grim Reaper — Lucifer, he'd even been called, not that the people who had called him by that name were still alive — so Aeron's task was probably nothing to him.

"No, they didn't. But . . ."

Lucien arched a dark brow. "But?"

"They did tell me that if I failed to act quickly, blood and death would begin to consume my mind. They said I would kill anything and everything until the day I complied. Just like Maddox." They hadn't needed to warn him, though. Wrath had overtaken him numerous times. When the spirit decided it was time to act, Aeron always tried to resist, but the cravings for destruction grew and grew until finally he would snap. Even in the worst thrall of Wrath, however, he had never been compelled to kill an innocent. "But unlike Maddox, my torment will not end with the dawn."

Gravely, Paris asked, "How are you to do it? Did they at least tell you that?"

His stomach twisted, cramped. "I am to

slit their throats," he said. How he would love to refuse to obey these new gods. Only the horror of being ordered to do something even worse had kept him silent.

"Why are they doing this?" Torin demanded, a question they would each ask at least once, it seemed.

He still did not have an answer.

Paris stared over at him. "Are you going to do it?"

Aeron looked away. He remained silent, but he knew, deep in his bones, that nothing could save the females now. They had been placed on the spirit's mental kill-list, no matter that they were innocent, and they would eventually be checked off. One by one.

"What can we do to help?" Lucien asked, his eyes sharp.

Aeron slammed his fist into the couch arm. If he did this terrible deed when he already teetered on the brink of depravity, he would crumble. He would lose himself to the spirit completely. "I don't know. We're dealing with new gods, new consequences and new circumstances. I'm not sure how I'll react once —" *say it, just say it* "— I've killed the women."

"It is possible to change their minds?"

"We are not to even try," he answered,

dejected. "They again used Maddox as an example, saying we would be cursed as he is if we dared object."

Paris exploded to booted feet and paced from one wall of the spacious room to the other. "I fucking hate this," he grumbled.

"Well, the rest of us love it," Torin said dryly.

"Perhaps you will be doing the women a favor," Reyes said, his attention remaining fixed on his blade as he carved an *X* on the center of his palm. Crimson drops trickled onto his thigh.

He was the reason all of the furniture was dark red.

"Perhaps I will be ordered to take your life next," Aeron replied darkly.

"I need to think about this." Lucien worried two fingers over his roughly scarred jaw. "There has to be something we can do."

"Maybe Aeron can just obliterate the entire world," Torin said in that annoyingly wry tone. "That way, all possible future targets will be eliminated and we'll never have to have this discussion again."

Aeron bared his teeth. "Do not make me hurt you, Disease."

Those piercing green eyes glowed with wicked humor and Torin offered a mockingly feral grin. "Have I hurt your feelings?

I'd be happy to kiss you and make you feel better."

Before Aeron could leap across the room — not that he could do anything to Torin — Lucien said, "Stop. We cannot be divided. We don't know the magnitude of what we're facing. Now, more than ever, we must stand together. It's been an eventful night and it's not over yet. Paris, Reyes, head into town and make sure there are no more Hunters lurking about. Torin — I don't know. Watch the hill or make us some money."

"What are you going to do?" Paris asked.

"Consider our options," he replied gravely.

Paris's brows arched. "What of Maddox's woman? I will be better able to fight any Hunters if I spend a little time between her —"

"No." Lucien stared up at the vaulted ceiling. "Not her. Remember, I promised Maddox she'd return to him untouched."

"Yeah, I remember. Remind me again why you'd promise such a dumb-ass thing."

"Just . . . leave her alone. She didn't seem to want you, anyway."

"Which is even more shocking than the news about the Titans," Paris muttered. Then he sighed. "Fine. I'll keep my hands to myself, but someone needs to feed her. We told her we would."

"Perhaps we should starve her," Reyes suggested. "She'll be more likely to talk in the morning if she's weakened from hunger."

Lucien nodded. "I agree. She might be more willing to give Maddox the truth if she thinks it will buy her a meal."

"I don't like it, but I won't protest. And I guess this means I'm going into town without my vitamin D injection," Paris said on another sigh. "Let's do this, Pain."

Reyes was on his feet a moment later and the two strode out of the room, side by side. Torin followed suit, though he gave them a generous head start. Aeron couldn't imagine the pressure of making sure no part of himself ever touched another. Had to be hell.

He snorted. Life for all the warriors here was hell.

Lucien closed the distance between them and eased into the leather chair opposite him. The fragrance of roses drifted from him. Aeron had never understood why the Grim Reaper smelled like a spring bouquet — surely a curse even worse than Maddox's.

"Thoughts?" he asked, studying his friend. For the first time in many, many years, Lucien radiated something other than calm.

His forehead was furrowed and there were stress-creases further marring his scarred face.

Those scars slashed from each of his dark brows all the way to his jawline, thick and puckered. Lucien never talked about how he'd acquired them and Aeron had never asked. While they'd lived in Greece, the warrior had simply returned home one day, pain in his eyes and marks on his cheeks.

"This is bad," Lucien said. "Really bad. Hunters, Maddox's woman — however she fits into this — and the Titans, all in one day. That cannot be an accident."

"I know." Aeron dragged a hand down his face, his fingertip catching and tugging on his eyebrow piercing. "Do the Titans want us dead, do you think? Could they have sent the Hunters here?"

"Perhaps. But what would they do with our demons once our bodies were destroyed and the spirits released? And why order you to act for them, if they only meant to have you slain?"

Good questions. "I have no answers for you. I don't even know how I'm going to do this deed that's been demanded of me. The women are innocents. Two are young, in their twenties, the third is in her late forties and the fourth is a grandmother. She probably bakes cookies for the homeless in her spare time."

Curious about them, he had hunted and found them in a hotel in Buda after he'd left Olympus. Seeing them in the flesh had only intensified his horror.

"We can't wait. We must act as soon as possible," Lucien said. "We can't allow these Titans to dictate our actions in this or they will attempt to do so over and over again. Surely we can come up with a solution."

Aeron thought they would have better luck figuring out a way to patch the charred, tattered remains of his soul when he killed those women. And even that seemed hopeless.

As it was, they sat in silence for a long while, minds churning with options. Or rather, lack of them. Finally Aeron gave a shake of his head and felt as if he had just welcomed a new demon inside him. Doom.

CHAPTER FIVE

Sometime during the endless night, Ashlyn stood and felt her way around the cramped cell. Her ankle throbbed with every step, a reminder of the hours she'd spent climbing the snowcapped mountains outside and the sense of hope she'd lost with six swings of a sword.

Her search for a way out had proved fruitless. There was no window like the one in Rapunzel's tower, no wicked witch's magic mirror to walk through. Nor had she found any bars to squeeze through or tunnels to burrow into like Alice. Somewhere along the way, she'd lost her cell phone. Not that she could get reception in the dungeon of a castle.

As time ticked by, the darkness seemed to close tighter and tighter around her.

The mice had stopped squeaking, at least.

She just wanted to go home, she thought, once again huddling on the floor. She wanted to forget this entire experience. She could live with the voices now. She *would* live with them. Trying to silence them had cost her too much. Her job, perhaps. Her lifelong friendship with McIntosh, maybe. A piece of her sanity, definitely.

She would never be the same.

Maddox's lifeless face would haunt her, waking and asleep, for the rest of her life. Oh God. Tears streamed down her cheeks, chilling with the cold. How many would she shed before the ducts dried completely? Before the ache in her chest faded?

Please, just let me go, a voice babbled. *Please. I swear. I'll never return.*

Me, too, she thought miserably.

"Have you been here all night, woman?"

A moment passed, the question unanswered as Ashlyn oriented herself. That voice . . . she would swear it came from the present, not the past. The rough, booming sound of it echoed in her ears.

"Answer me, Ashlyn."

Another moment passed before she realized it was the voice that had come to haunt her above all others. A voice that was somehow imprinted in her mind, even though she'd only heard it a few times before. She gasped, eyes straining through the darkness, searching . . . searching . . .

but finding nothing.

"Ashlyn. Answer me."

"M-Maddox?" No, surely not. It had to be a trick.

"Answer the question."

Suddenly a door was opened and rays of light flooded the cell. Ashlyn blinked against the orange-gold spots clouding her vision. A man stood in the doorway, a tall, black shadow of menace and muscle.

Sweet silence — silence she'd only encountered once before — enveloped her.

She flattened her palms against the wall behind her and inched to a stand. Shock pounded through her and her knees wobbled. He wasn't . . . He couldn't be . . . This wasn't possible. Wasn't even fathomable. Only in fairy tales did something like this happen.

"Answer me," the man said yet again. There was violence in his tone now, as if he spoke with two voices. Both dark, thick and thunderous.

She opened her mouth to respond, but no sound emerged. That double voice was guttural, turbulent and yet sensual beyond her wildest dreams. *Maddox.* She hadn't been mistaken. Shivering, she wiped at her tearstained cheeks with the back of her hand.

"I don't understand," she breathed. *Am I dreaming?*

Maddox — no, *the man,* for he couldn't possibly be Maddox, no matter how similar the voices — stepped into the cell. His attention jerked to the side, away from her, as if he needed a moment to compose himself.

Golden rays of sunlight danced over him, reverently caressing his beautiful face. Same dark eyebrows, same thickly lashed violet eyes. Same blade of a nose and lush lips.

How could this be? How had her captors produced the exact likeness of the man she'd met last night, down to that same feral edge? A man who stopped the voices of the past with his mere presence?

A twin?

Her eyes widened. A twin. Of course. Finally, something made sense. "They killed your brother," she blurted out. Maybe he already knew. Maybe he was glad. But maybe, just maybe, he'd take her into town and she could report the horrendous crime she'd witnessed. Justice could be served.

"I do not have a brother," he said. "Not by blood."

"But . . . but . . ." *Maddox will be fine,* the gorgeous man had said. She shook her head. Impossible. She'd watched him die. *But an angel could have been resurrected, right?* A

108

hard lump formed in her throat. The men of this household were most definitely not angels, no matter what the townspeople claimed.

His gaze swept back to her, down her body in a possessive appraisal and up again. He scowled. "Did they leave you here all night?" Countenance darker by the second, he scanned the rest of the cell. "Tell me they gave you blankets and water and only removed them this morning."

Shaking still, she smoothed a hand over her face and through her hair, wincing at the tangles she encountered. Dirt probably caked her from head to toe. *Like that matters.* "Who are you? *What* are you?"

For a long while, he didn't speak. Just studied her as though she were a bug under a microscope. She knew that look well. It was a favorite of everyone at the Institute. "You know who I am."

"But you can't be him," she insisted, not wanting to accept the other alternative. He was not like the others, the demons who had slain him. "My Maddox is dead."

"*Your* Maddox?" Something fiery flickered in his eyes. "Yours?"

She lifted her chin, refusing to answer.

Lips inching into what might have been a smile, he held out one arm and beckoned her over. "Come. We will clean you up, warm you and feed you. Then I will . . . explain."

That hesitation made it clear he wouldn't be explaining anything. He had something else in mind and his tone suggested that something would be intense. She remained in place, scared to the core. "Let me see your stomach," she said, stalling for time.

His fingers gave a swift jerk. "Come."

A part of her wanted to go to him, to follow wherever he would lead. Because he did look like Maddox, and whatever else Maddox was, he'd still been the best thing to ever happen to her. But once again she held her ground. "No."

"Come."

She shook her head. "I'm staying here until you show me your stomach."

"I won't hurt you, Ashlyn." The words *not yet* echoed from the walls — unsaid, but there all the same. Even more unnerving, the sound of her name on his tongue was decadent, as if he couldn't help but savor it. And desire another taste. "Ashlyn," he repeated.

Another shiver raked her and she frowned. He shouldn't desire her, and she damn sure shouldn't desire him. "You can't be my Maddox. You just can't."

That intense, fiery *something* flashed over his face again. "That's twice now you've claimed me as yours."

"I-I'm sorry." She didn't know what else to say. Maddox had saved her from the voices, for a little while at least. She had watched him die. They were connected. He *was* hers.

"Don't be sorry." He sounded almost tender just then. "I *am* Maddox," he insisted. "Now come."

"No."

Tired of her refusal, the man closed the rest of the distance between them. He smelled of wanton heat and primitive rituals performed in the moonlight. "I'll carry you over my shoulder if I must, just as I did last night. If I'm forced to do it, however, I cannot guarantee you'll make it out of this cell with your clothes on. Understand?"

Oddly, his words were heady when they should have been frightening. Comforting when they should have been intimidating. Only Maddox knew the way she'd been carted. He'd switched her to his arms before entering the chateau and yelling at his murderers.

"Please," she found herself saying. "Just show me your stomach." The more she demanded to see it, the more she wanted to. Would she find stitched wounds? Smooth skin? Would there be any indication that this man had been stabbed over and over again?

At first he gave no reaction to her request. Then, finally, he sighed. "It appears *I* am the one who will not make it out of here with my clothes on." He reached for the hem of his black tee and slowly . . . slowly . . . raised it.

Despite her insistence, Ashlyn couldn't yet work up the courage to tear her attention from his intense violet gaze. She told herself it was because his eyes were so beautiful, so mesmerizing that she was lost in them, drowning. But she knew that was only half the truth. If he *was* stitched, *was* scabbed . . . if this *was* Maddox . . .

"You wanted to look. So look," the man commanded, both impatient and resigned.

Do it. Look. Inch by inch, her gaze lowered. She saw a corded neck and a wildly ticking pulse. A collarbone mostly covered by black cloth. She saw one of his thick hands fisting that cloth right above his heart. His nipples were tiny, brown and hard. His skin was that otherworldly bronze she'd admired in the forest, and he was stacked with rope after rope of muscle.

And then she saw them. Six scabbed-over

wounds. Not stitched, but red and angry. Painful.

She sucked in a shocked breath. Almost in a trance, she reached out. Her fingertip brushed the scab that slashed through his navel. The healing sore was rough and warm and abraded her palm. Electric tingles rushed up her arm.

"Maddox," she gasped out.

"Finally," he muttered, backing away as if she were a bomb, detonation imminent. He dropped the shirt, blocking the injuries from her view. "Are you satisfied now? I'm here, and I'm very real."

He — no, not "he." Maddox. Not his twin, not a dream. Not a trick. He'd been stabbed; the evidence was there, those six hellish wounds. He'd had no heartbeat, no breath. And now he stood before her.

"How?" she asked, needing to hear him say it. "You're not an angel. Does that mean you're a demon? That's what some people have said about you and your friends."

"The more you speak, the more you hang yourself. Will you follow me now?"

Would she? *Should* she? After that "hang yourself" remark . . . "Maddox, I —" What?

"I showed you my stomach. In return, you said you would come with me."

Did she really have any other choice?

"Fine. I'll follow you."

"Do not try to run. You will not like what happens." Motions fluid, he wheeled around and marched out of the cell.

Ashlyn paused only a moment before limping after him, doing her best to stay close on his heels. Her hands itched to touch him again, to feel the life pulsing beneath his skin. "You never answered my question," she said. The farther they walked from the cell, the more the cold air gave way to warmth. "If you *are* a demon, I can take it. Really. I won't be grossed out or anything." She hoped. "I just have to know so I can prepare myself."

No response.

Those flaxen rays of sunlight streamed through stained-glass windows, casting rainbow flecks on the stone walls. Fatigue and lack of nourishment must have weakened her, because she fell a few steps behind. "Maddox," she said, a low entreaty.

"No conversation," he replied, his gait never slowing as they climbed a flight of stairs. "Perhaps later."

Later. Not what she'd hoped for, but better than never. "I'll hold you to that." She stumbled and winced, sharp pains shooting through her ankle.

Maddox stopped abruptly. Before she realized what he'd done, she'd slammed into his back with a pained cry. Immediately that tingling warmth returned, sparking, catching fire and spreading.

As she struggled to find her balance, he hissed a breath through his teeth and spun around, pinning her with a vicious stare. His eyes were black, the violet gone as if it had never been. "Are you hurt?"

A tremor swam through her. *Yes.* "No."

"Do not lie to me."

"I twisted my ankle last night," she admitted quietly.

His features softened as his gaze slowly perused her, lingering on her breasts, her thighs. Goose bumps broke out over her skin. It was as though he were stripping away her clothing piece by piece, leaving her in nothing but flushed skin. And she liked it. Her heart fluttered wildly in her chest; moisture pooled between her legs.

Suddenly she didn't care about answers, the pain in her ankle or the lethargy in her muscles. Her nipples hardened and strained. Her stomach clenched and unclenched with need. Her skin felt too hot and tight for her bones. She wanted his arms around her, comforting her, holding her close.

A moment later, she realized she was reaching out.

"No touching." He jumped onto the step behind him, widening the distance between them. All hint of softness left him. "Not yet."

Her arms fell to her sides as disappointment crashed through her. *No answers, no touching,* she silently mocked, fighting off the decadent rush of pleasure that came with finally being close to the man who'd consumed her thoughts all night. His warmth, the silence . . . a combination lethal to her common sense.

One stroke, that's all she'd needed — all she'd wanted, surely — but he was determined to deny her. "What about breathing?" she asked dryly. "Can I do that?"

His lips twitched, smoothing the edges of his fierceness. "If you do it quietly."

Her eyelids narrowed to tiny slits. "Well, aren't you a sweetie. Thanks a lot."

That twitch became a full-fledged smile, the blinding force of it knocking the air from her lungs. He was beautiful. Absolutely mesmerizing. Ashlyn found herself caught in his snare yet again — how did he do that to her? — and again reached up without thought. Craving that spark of contact, yes, yes. Needing . . . needing . . .

He gave a sharp shake of his head, humor suddenly gone. She stilled, annoyed with him, herself.

116

"There is something I need to do before the touching can commence," he said, the words so husky and low she felt them as deeply as a caress.

"What is it?" she asked, biting her bottom lip as violet began to reclaim his eyes, trickling from his pupils to overshadow the black. Amazing.

"Doesn't matter." Frowning, he reached out as if he meant to stroke her cheek. He caught himself and dropped his arm to his side, a mirror of her own actions a few moments before. "What does matter is that *you* never answered *me.* Were you in that cell all night?"

His heady, masculine scent wafted to her nose, summoning her closer. She tried to resist, truly she did, but found herself leaning toward him despite his warning. "Yes."

Again, fury darkened his face. "Were you fed?"

"No."

"Given blankets?"

"No." Why did he care?

"Did anyone hurt you?"

"No."

"Did anyone . . . touch you?" A muscle ticked in his jaw, once, twice.

Her face scrunched in confusion. "Yes. Of course."

"Who?" he demanded. His face began that freaky change, gnarled skeleton flashing and churning under his skin as if he wore a see-through mask. Even his eyes changed again. Black covered violet, then red covered black, glowing ominously.

Another of those hard lumps formed in her throat and she struggled to catch her breath. Not even in the forest, not even while chained to a bed, a sword slicing through his organs, had he exuded such ferocity.

Why are you still standing here? Run!

His expression twisted, as though he knew what she planned to do. "Don't," he said, confirming her fear. "You will only incite me further. This will pass in a moment. Now tell me who touched you."

"All of them," she forced out, remaining in place. "I think. But they had to," she hurried to assure him. She couldn't believe she was defending his murderers, but it seemed the fastest way to calm him down. "It was the only way to get me inside the cell."

He relaxed, but only slightly. The skeletal image receded and the red glow faded from his eyes. "They didn't touch you sexually?"

She shook her head, relaxing a bit herself. He'd been angry with the men, then, not with her for resisting.

"I will allow them to live. Barely." Forgetting his own rule, he cupped his palms over her temples and forced her attention on his face.

She experienced those electric tingles again as his warm breath fanned her nose. He was so big he dwarfed her, his shoulders so wide they engulfed her.

"Ashlyn," he said gently.

The swift change in him, from beast to concerned gentleman, was dizzying.

"I didn't want to discuss this yet, but I find I must hear your response now." Heavy pause as he stared at her. "I killed those four men last night. The ones following you."

"Following me?" Had someone from the Institute seen her and come after her? Had they — the rest of his words finally registered. She gasped as a high-voltage shockwave slid down her spine. "You *killed* them?"

"Yes."

"What did they look like?" she choked out. If Dr. McIntosh had been slain because of her . . . She pressed her lips together to cut off a pained moan.

Maddox described the men — tall, strong warriors — and she slowly relaxed. Most of the employees she'd met at the Institute were older, like McIntosh. Many were pale, with thinning hair and glasses, eyes weakened from constantly staring at computer screens. Relief speared her, which in turn made her feel guilty. People had died last night. It shouldn't matter whether she knew them or not.

"Why would you do something like that?"

"They were armed and eager for battle. I had a choice — kill them or let them kill me."

He said it without a single hint of remorse, as though it were a simple point of fact. What a bloody, violent place this fortress had turned out to be. Maddox, too. Her savior spoke like a veteran soldier . . . or a cold and callous killer like his roommates. He didn't, and wouldn't, hesitate to slay.

So why did she still want his arms around her?

Whatever emotion Maddox saw on her face seemed to answer his unspoken question. His brow puckered and his mouth thinned. In displeasure? But why? Before she could study him further, he turned away and climbed two more steps, saying, "Forget I mentioned it."

"Wait." She leapt forward, winced at the renewed pain in her ankle and grabbed hold of his bicep. A puny move, really, but he stopped.

He stiffened, then slowly turned his head and growled down at her fingers.

She jerked away from him. Not because of his reaction but because she'd felt more of those strange tingles. She'd have liked to believe it was static cling. Something, anything, besides more of that oh, so wrong desire.

"Sorry," she muttered. *No touching,* she reminded herself. It was better for both of them that way. She couldn't seem to control her body's reaction when they were close. Actual, prolonged contact might reduce her to a drooling puddle. "Maddox?"

In profile his expression appeared blank, completely devoid of emotion. "Yes?"

"Don't be mad, but it *is* technically later so I'm going to bring us back to Topic One. What are you?" Before he could jump back into motion as if she hadn't spoken, she added, "I answered your questions. Please answer mine."

He didn't. But he did face her again.

Nervous, she ran her tongue over her lips. His gaze followed the movement and his nostrils flared. She didn't mean to, but she started babbling. "Look, there are all kinds of unusual creatures in the world. No one knows that better than me. Did I mention I know firsthand that demons exist? I just want to know what I'm dealing with here." *Shut up. Stop talking.*

If only he would respond. She'd never had to fill a silence before. Never thought silence could be uncomfortable.

He eased down a step, the action measured and precise as it closed the small distance between them; she eased down a step in response, widening it again.

"No more questions. I want you bathed, fed and resting within the hour. You're covered in dirt, wavering on your feet because of hunger and there are dark circles under your eyes. Afterward, we can . . . talk."

Again that hesitation. It disconcerted her, and she gulped. "If I asked you to take me back to the city, what would you say?"

"Unequivocally no."

I thought so. Her shoulders slumped. No matter how much she might want this man — or maybe *because* of how much she wanted this man — she had to start acting like a rational human being and escape.

What if she was next in line for a stabbing? *She* wouldn't rise from the dead, that much Ashlyn knew.

Yesterday she would've sold her soul to come here. *Who are you kidding? You did sell your soul.* She might not have learned to control the voices unless Maddox was with her, but she simply couldn't stay. There were too many uncertainties and too much violence.

But to escape, she'd have to endure the mountain, the cold, the fog and the voices. *You can do it. You* have *to do it.*

Maddox arched a brow. "Do I need to lock you up again, Ashlyn?" he asked, as if reading her thoughts.

The threat scared and infuriated her, but she shook her head. No reason to upset him and risk getting herself killed or thrown back in that icy, damp prison, freedom unattainable. Outside of it, at least, she stood a chance. Small though it was.

Silence isn't as sweet as you hoped, is it?

"Do you want to leave because there is someone you need to speak with?" he asked. He failed to disguise his growing anger with that polite inquiry — she saw the flickers of it just beneath the surface of his skin. "Is someone anxious to know where you are?"

"My boss," she said honestly. Maybe, if she found a phone, she could call him. He could then call the police — no. She nixed that thought immediately, reminding herself they might be entranced by the "angels."

But if she could call McIntosh, the Institute could devise a way to rescue her. She could return to her old life and pretend the last two days had never happened — even though the thought of abandoning Maddox created an inexplicable ache in her chest. *Stupid girl!*

"Who exactly is your boss?"

As if she would tell him and put an innocent man in danger. Instead, she gathered her courage and said, "Let me go, Maddox. Please."

Another pause, heavier than before. He stepped closer, placing them nose to nose as he had in the forest. His eyes were bright violet now. "Last night I told you to return to the city. You refused. You even followed me. You cried out for me. Remember?"

The reminder stung. "A moment of insanity," she whispered, looking down at her hands. Her fingers were intertwined, the knuckles white.

"Well, that moment of insanity sealed your fate, woman. You're staying here."

Maddox escorted the reluctant Ashlyn to his bedroom. He'd already cleaned the floor and thrown out the soiled mattress, replacing it with a new one from the array in the room next door. In anticipation of her seduction, he'd prepared a bath for her, made up a platter of meats and cheeses, opened a bottle of wine and turned down the clean, sun-kissed sheets.

He'd never put so much effort into a coupling, had only heard Paris talk about how quickly women melted when men pampered them like this.

Maddox hadn't realized Ashlyn would spend the entire night in a cell or that she would *need* all of this care thanks to his friends. His fingers curled into a tight fist.

Her comfort doesn't matter. He wasn't sure who the thought came from — the demon or himself. He only knew it was a lie.

"Bathe, change and eat," he forced himself to say. "No one will bother you." He paused. "Is there anything else you might require?"

She walked around him in a wide half circle, turning to face him almost immediately, as if she didn't trust him at her back. "Freedom would be nice."

"Besides that."

Her gaze scanned the room. He didn't like how pale she was, how wobbly and withdrawn. She had not been so drained last night, even in the bitter chill of the forest. "What about wiping out my memory of the past few days?"

"Besides that," he repeated darkly, not liking that she wanted to forget him.

She sighed. "No. There's nothing, then."

He knew he should leave, give her a

chance to relax and follow his commands, but he found himself reluctant to do so. He leaned against the side of the door. She remained in the center of the room, arms crossed over her middle, stretching the pink jacket she wore over her breasts. His mouth watered.

"Have you done this to many women?" she asked in a conversational tone.

His eyes snapped up and locked with hers, his body tightening. "Done what?" Entranced them? Seduced them? His throat was suddenly blocked by a hard mass.

Now she snorted. "Locked them away. What else?"

The mass quickly dissolved. "You are the first," he replied, doing his best to hide his disappointment.

"And what do you have planned for me, special girl that I am?"

"Only time will tell," he answered honestly.

A shadow of concern darkened her expression. "How *much* time?"

"We shall have to discover the answer together."

Now she flashed him a frown. "You're the most cryptic man I've ever met."

He shrugged. "I have been called worse."

"I'm sure you have," she muttered.

Even the insult did not drive him away. *Just a little longer . . .* "I did not know what foods you would like, so I brought you a little of everything we had in the kitchen. I fear there wasn't much to choose from."

"Thank you," she said, then pressed her lips together. A flash of anger descended over her face. "I don't know why I'm being polite to you. Look at what you're doing to me."

"Taking care of you?"

Her cheeks flushed, and she glanced away from him.

"Do you belong to a man, Ashlyn?" he asked, hating the thought.

"I don't understand your question. Am I married? No. Do I have a boyfriend? No. But I do have friends, and people *will* worry about me," she rushed to add, as if suddenly realizing she'd made herself vulnerable.

Who did she hope to convince? Him? Or herself?

"They'll search for me. They will," she insisted when he failed to respond.

"But they will not find you," he said, confident. The four last night hadn't made it up the hill. Her other friends wouldn't, either.

Her hand fluttered to her throat, drawing his attention to the pulse hammering there.

Why did he find himself so entranced by the beat of her heart, compelled to touch the evidence of its movement?

"I didn't mean to scare you," he told her. He wasn't certain which of them was more surprised by his words — Ashlyn or himself.

"I don't understand you," she whispered.

Neither did he understand himself. And the more he stood here talking to her, the less sense he made. He straightened. "Clean yourself up. I will return later." Not giving her a chance to counter, he stepped into the hall, shutting the door without a backward glance.

Better this way. From the moment he had asked her if she belonged to a man, the demon had begun to churn inside of him, eager for a fight. If he stayed, he would touch her. If he touched her, he would take her. But he did not want to risk tangled bodies and heated kisses turning to biting, clawing and a too-rough pounding.

The delicate woman inside his room would not survive.

"Damn this," he growled. Ashlyn was, beyond any doubt, the sweetest-looking human he'd ever encountered. His mouth still watered for her; his besieged body wept for her. Hurting her was not his desire, no matter that she had admitted to knowing about the demon, as only a Hunter or Bait could. No, he wanted only to pleasure her.

Turning, he locked the door from the outside. Switching the tumblers was something else he'd done in anticipation of her seduction. Jumping from the bedroom's terrace would be the only other way out, and he doubted she wanted to fall five stories and land on jagged rocks. Still, he'd glued the window leading to the terrace shut, just in case.

Maddox stalked down the hallway, praying the other warriors had not fled for the day. When he'd awakened in his already-healing body, his first thoughts had been of Ashlyn. He had prepared his room and a meal for her and sought Lucien, finding him in the entertainment room and demanding to know what happened.

"Dungeon," the man had muttered, a strange glint in his eyes.

Furious, Maddox had raced from the room, desperate to assure himself that she was in the same condition he'd left her in: alive and untouched. He'd thought that at least his friends would have given her food, water and blankets. Wrong. She could have frozen to death. She could have starved. And they wouldn't have known.

Had they expected him to passively accept such a thing?

Wrong again.

One glance at Ashlyn's dirty, frightened features and he'd wanted to kill someone. He'd barely leashed the urge, telling himself she'd soon be lying in his bed, naked, open to him. And while that had calmed *him,* it had not calmed the demon — had only managed to incite it further.

Now Violence needed an outlet for its growing rage. For only then would Maddox be able to touch Ashlyn without fear of snapping that fragile little body.

Body . . . Ashlyn . . . two words sure to arouse him when used in the same sentence. Luminous as she was, she was every fantasy he'd ever had come to life, and he planned to sate himself inside her, over and over again, taking her in every position imaginable and even some that weren't.

Soon she would want that, too.

Desire had glistened in her eyes when she'd looked at him, and she had constantly reached for him, clearly hoping for some sort of physical contact. He'd even smelled her arousal, a perfume of passion, innocence and that delectable honey. He frightened her, though, and that fear overrode her desire.

You should be happy that Bait fears you.

130

Should, he inwardly scoffed. How he was coming to hate that word.

Was she Bait, though?

When he'd mentioned the four humans who'd followed her, she had appeared genuinely surprised. Horrified by his actions, true, but most women were horrified by war and carnage.

More perplexing still, she had freely admitted to knowledge of the demons. He hadn't tortured her for the information. Why would Bait willingly do such a thing? Why not pretend she thought he was human to lower his defenses?

And so far, she had not tried to lead him from the fortress, nor had she tried to let anyone inside. But then, she hadn't yet had the freedom to do so, he reminded himself. And she wouldn't.

What confused him most of all, however, was that she had tried to save him from his friends. *That,* he couldn't rationalize away. Saving someone she'd meant to harm was ridiculous. She could have been harmed herself.

She was a walking contradiction to his black-and-white world.

Tomorrow he would deal with her true reasons for being here. Today, well, today was meant for other things.

His boots clicked against the floor, the sound echoing from the walls. The entertainment room loomed ahead and he quickened his step. The spirit purred in anticipation as his bones ached for a fight.

When he stood in the wide expanse of the doorway, he saw popcorn scattered over the floor and ground into the crimson rug. His trained eye spotted several splotches of dried blood. Obviously Reyes had been here. For once, the TV was switched off. Balls littered the surface of the pool table, as if someone had stopped a game midway through.

But no sign of the men, not even Lucien. Where had everyone gone?

Maddox stormed through the fortress, bypassing the luxuries they'd acquired over the years. The hot tub, the sauna, the gym, the makeshift basketball court. None of that would help him.

He reached Paris's room first and burst inside without knocking. The black silk-covered bed was rumpled but empty. The blow-up dolls Torin had purchased were sprawled in every direction, a rapt but useless audience. Whips, chains and a variety of sex toys Maddox couldn't identify lined the walls. They weren't in use, which meant

Paris should be inside the fortress. Somewhere.

Shaking his head, Maddox stalked down the hall.

Fight. Fight. Fight.

He tried to ignore the demon's voice as he entered Reyes's room. No Reyes, and no sexual toys. Instead there were weapons. All kinds of weapons. Guns, knives, throwing stars. There was a blue wrestling mat on the floor with more dried blood splattered over it. There was a punching bag, a few dumbbells. Several holes marred the walls, as if someone had punched the stone until it crumbled into sand.

He would have to patch those up later.

Fight, fight, fight.

Lucien's room was locked, and no one answered when he knocked. Aeron and Torin's rooms were empty. Frustration rode Maddox's shoulders. Black spots were beginning to wink in and out of his line of vision.

Fightfightfight.

He craved Ashlyn, but he could not have her until the urge for violence was tamped — and that could not happen until he found the men. All of which only made him angrier. He strode back into the hall, his biceps flexed, the blood rushing through

133

them blistering hot.

Fightfightfight!

"Where are you?" he shouted. He punched the wall once, twice, leaving a groove identical to the ones he'd seen in Reyes's room. His knuckles throbbed, but it was a good pain, a pain that made the spirit rumble happily.

Maddox stopped and punched the wall again.

He didn't have a lot of time. Midnight would come again. Death would claim him. Before that happened, he *had* to lose himself in Ashlyn. Had to know every inch of her body, for the torment of not knowing was far worse than burning in hell each night.

What if the woman doesn't truly desire you? the demon taunted. *What if she's pretending to want you so you'll give her information? What if she's thinking of another man every time you're near and her arousal is for him?*

Roaring, Maddox once more slammed his fist into the wall. More of the stone cracked and crumbled. She wanted *him.* She did. *Do not react. Do not listen to the spirit.*

Violence shut its mouth, liking his vehemence, his sense of possession.

"What are you doing, messing up the walls rather than fixing them?"

Maddox heard the familiar voice and

spun. Blood dripped from his hands, warm and invigorating.

Aeron stood at the end of the hallway. Light streamed in from the windows, dancing over the man's tough frame. One beam hit directly atop his dark hair, a bright crown that illuminated his decorated skin.

As if it had never been stroked, never been eased, Violence howled to full life. Maddox pointed at his friend and scowled. "You left her down there."

"So?" The black demon tattooed on Aeron's neck seemed to blink its red-rimmed eyes, awakening from a deep slumber. Saliva seemed to drip from its sharp-toothed mouth. "Did she talk?"

"About?"

"Her reasons for being here."

"No."

"Let me ask her, then."

"No!" She was frightened enough. An image of Ashlyn as she'd looked inside that cell flashed through Maddox's mind. Her skin had been paler than the snow outside, the only color streaks of black-brown dirt. She'd been trembling. When that woman trembled, it should be from passion, not fear.

Fight. Fight. Fight! chanted the demon again.

"Where is she now?" Aeron demanded.

"None of your concern. But someone is going to pay for the state I found her in."

His friend's violet eyes — eyes identical to his, as if the gods had been too tired to create something different — widened in surprise. "Why? What's she to you?"

"Mine," was the only answer he had. "She's mine."

Aeron ran his tongue over his teeth. "Don't be foolish. She's Bait."

"Maybe." Probably. He stalked forward. Seething . . . hungry . . . "At the moment, I don't care."

The warrior stepped toward him, equally infuriated. "You should. And you should not have brought her here."

Maddox knew that, but he wasn't going to apologize. He would do it again, if given the choice.

"Take her back to town and figure out a way to wipe her memory," Aeron said. "Otherwise, she'll have to be killed. She's seen and heard too much, and we cannot allow her to report to Hunters."

They were almost upon each other. Maddox hadn't armed himself this morning, a fact that saved Aeron's miserable hide. He would have thrown a dagger in the man's dead, black heart had he been able. "I would rather hurt you."

The demon tattoo stretched its wings, fully awake now, and Aeron grinned slowly. "We do this, and you'll have to patch up the mess."

"And you'll have to clean it."

"Like I care. We going to get started or just talk about it?"

"Oh, yes. We're going to start." Maddox leapt.

Aeron did, too. They collided in midair.

CHAPTER SIX

Punch. Grunt and duck. Punch.

Maddox landed a hard blow to Aeron's cheek and the man staggered to the side with another grunt. But a second later, Aeron retaliated, lashing out with a strong left across his jaw. Maddox's teeth rattled and blood filled his mouth, the taste metallic but sweet, quenching part of the spirit's thirst.

He was grinning as he kneed Aeron in the stomach. The warrior doubled over, wheezing. More. He needed to inflict more damage. Before Maddox could elbow him in the head, Aeron bolted forward with a savage growl, wrapping his arms around Maddox and tackling him to the ground. They rolled in a bid for dominance. Fists flew; knees knocked. Elbows slammed.

Maddox hissed when Aeron caught him in the mouth again. He lost his smile, the inside of his cheek split. Another trickle of blood slid down his throat.

"This what you wanted?" Aeron barked.

He chop-blocked his friend in the throat, causing the other man to gasp and his skin to quickly color blue. "Is that what *you* wanted?" With Aeron struggling to breathe, he threw four more punches, all in the face. *Crunch.* Eye socket. *Crunch.* Nose. *Crunch.* Jaw. *Crunch!* Temple. *No more Violence today,* he chanted futilely with each strike. *No more Violence.*

Are you sure? the spirit beguiled.

Maddox's eyes narrowed as he threw another punch.

Kill him.

"No!" he shouted, only then realizing he hadn't tamed the demon at all. Not even a little. He stilled, panting for air, not knowing what else to do. He couldn't go to Ashlyn like this, hungry for blood and even more on edge than he'd been.

"Oh, yes." Cut and bruised, Aeron snarled low in his throat and slammed his fist into Maddox's right eye. Pain exploded in his head as the man's rings nicked a vein. His vision was momentarily blackened. Something warm and wet gushed down the slope of his face and finally, *finally,* the sadistic voice quieted.

Perhaps he needed the spirit beaten into

submission. Happy to oblige, he splayed his arms wide, welcoming the next blow.

Aeron did not disappoint. The warrior kicked him in the stomach and Maddox sailed backward. The moment he hit the ground, Aeron was on top of him, strangling him, knees pinning his shoulders. Satisfaction blanketed the man's face, but there were demons in his eyes, ugly demons, tormenting demons, so much more menacing than the tattoo on his neck.

"Want more?" Aeron snarled.

"More."

Punch. Maddox's head flew to the left. Punch. His head flew to the right. Punch. The cartilage in his nose cracked.

Hit me. Harder. Harder! With every blow, the spirit slunk deeper and deeper. Wrath against Violence, he mused, and Violence was cowed. The thought of vanquishing Violence was almost a sexual high. He smiled, thinking this must be how Reyes felt. Happy in pain, desperate for more.

His teeth sliced into his tongue as another blow was delivered. His tongue swelled. *Now I won't be able to kiss Ashlyn,* he thought.

You don't need to kiss her to fuck her, the demon lashed out, rearing its ugly head just long enough to send a lance of fury through him.

140

Enough! He wanted to kiss Ashlyn. Wanted her taste in his mouth as she writhed against him. And he would have it. That's all he had thought about while sucking back flames during the endless night.

Another punch.

"Aeron! What are you doing?" Maddox heard Lucien demand from across the hall.

"Giving Maddox what he needs." Punch.

"Stop."

"No." The next blow sank deeper and harder into his temple, rattling his brain.

"Don't stop," Maddox said as Aeron backhanded him. A little more and the spirit might stay hidden for the rest of the day.

"Stop," Lucien repeated. "Now. Or tonight I'll take you into hell with Maddox."

The punches instantly ceased. It was a threat Lucien could easily uphold.

Aeron was panting; Maddox was, too. He almost reached out, grabbed Aeron's wrist and forced the man to start again. He wanted, needed, more. He would take no chances. If he had to be beaten until he was too weak to do anything but crawl, he would let himself be beaten.

He would *not* hurt Ashlyn.

Not yet, at least.

Reluctantly Aeron pushed to his feet and offered Maddox a helping hand. He accepted with the same reluctance and was quickly hefted to a stand. Together, he and Aeron faced Lucien.

There was no emotion in Lucien's eyes as he perused them. Maddox worked a hand over his battered face, finding cuts that would have needed stitching were he human.

"Does someone want to tell me what was going on?"

"We were trying a new sparring technique," Maddox said through swollen lips. For once the spirit remained quiet. He almost felt normal. The realization was so wonderfully stunning, he grinned.

"That's right. New sparring technique." Aeron slung an arm over his shoulder. One of his eyes was sealed shut and his lower lip was shredded.

Within the hour, Maddox knew, both of them would be totally mended. Immortality had its advantages.

Would Violence return when his body healed?

Lucien opened his mouth to respond, but Maddox held up one bruised palm. "I will hear no complaints from you. You left Ashlyn in the dungeon. You should thank the gods I'm not going for your throat."

"We did what was needed to make her

more acquiescent," Lucien said, and there was not an apology in his tone.

Maddox stiffened, anger washing through him. A remarkably ordinary anger, though. One that didn't compel him to do terrible deeds. Miraculous. "I asked you for two things. Only two. You failed on both counts."

"You asked that she remain alive and you asked that she remain untouched. She is both of those things," Lucien pointed out.

True, but she'd been scared and cold, and for some reason that knowledge cut him deeper than Aeron's fists. She was just so small, so delicate. "I could not see to her needs. You should have." He had always hated that he lost all ties to reality when midnight struck. He hated that he didn't know what happened here during those twilight hours, hated that he could not protect himself or those close to him.

For all he knew, the fortress could be attacked by Hunters, burned to the ground, everyone inside slaughtered. Ashlyn could betray him, leading those Hunters inside. But Ashlyn could also be beaten. Ashlyn could be ravaged or killed, and he would not know.

"Listen, right now your woman doesn't matter," Lucien said. "Much has happened since your latest death. The —"

A growl vibrated in his throat, his head, his ears, drowning out the warrior's voice. *Doesn't matter?* "If she becomes sick . . ." The edges of his anger morphed into razor-sharp points, prodding at the spirit. Not subdued completely after all, he realized with an inward curse, even as his body tightened, gearing for war.

A dangerous haze shuttered over his eyes; his own, all his own, but the demon liked it. *Kill him. He means to take what is ours.* Yes, he needed to kill. His blood heated to a boil. His skin stretched over his bones.

"He's not listening," Aeron said to Lucien. A muscle ticked below the man's eye, and he gave Maddox a rough shake before severing contact between them. "Are you listening to *me?*"

"Yes," Maddox gritted out.

"Just how long do you plan to keep the woman here?"

As long as possible, his mind answered of its own accord.

As long as needed, he corrected.

Keeping her in the fortress was dangerous. For her. For him. For the other Lords. He knew that, but he wasn't going to set her free. He had neither the will nor the desire. Nothing was more important than discovering the delights her body promised.

Nothing. Would she be hot and wet for him? Would she purr his name? Beg for more?

Suddenly a fist connected with his nose, whipping his head to the side. Pain exploded in his temple, loosening fury's grip. Arousal, too. Maddox blinked in confusion and frowned over at Aeron. "Why did you do that?"

"Your face was not your own, but Violence's." Lucien shook his head, suddenly in front of him, his expression weary. "You were about to erupt."

"Get yourself under control, man." Aeron expelled an exasperated sigh. "You're like the Sword of Damocles, ready to drop at any moment and slice us all."

"That's funny coming from you," Maddox said dryly. He might charge swiftly into seemingly unprovoked bouts of violence, but Aeron had been known to charge into rampages, too, spreading his vengeance as far and wide as possible.

"Where's the girl now?" Lucien asked.

At first, Maddox did not answer. He didn't want them to know, for they might go to her. "My room," he finally said, his tone so dark they couldn't mistake his unspoken warning: *Visit her and feel the sting of my demon.*

"You left her alone in your room?" Aeron's

exasperation reached a new high, and he threw his arms in the air. "Why don't you give her a knife, tell us to line up and let her stab us one by one?"

"I locked her in. She cannot cause trouble."

"She might have picked the lock." Lucien massaged the back of his neck. "She could be sneaking Hunters inside this very second."

"No. I killed them."

"There could be more."

Lucien was right. Maddox knew Lucien was right. He ground his teeth together, and his battered jaw ached in protest. "I will check and make sure she is where I left her and alone." He spun on his heel.

"I'm coming with you." Determined, Aeron flanked him.

Lucien followed suit.

Maddox kicked into motion. If Ashlyn had escaped, had brought Hunters into their midst, the warriors would demand her head.

He wasn't sure he could give it to them, no matter her crimes. In fact, every cell in his body shouted with the need to protect her. *Me? A protector?* His blood heated with it, burned.

When — if — the time came, would he be able to do what was necessary? Maddox didn't know the answer. He liked to think he would, but . . .

They rounded a corner, and their steps harmonized into a hard battle drum. Thump. Thump, thump, thump. Thump. From the corner of his eye, he saw Aeron shake his arms at his sides. Two small blades fell into his waiting hands.

The man hadn't lost himself to the demon during their fight, after all, Maddox realized. Otherwise, Maddox would be in tatters right now, his skin nothing more than a fond memory.

He experienced a twinge of guilt. Had Aeron fought him only to help him?

"No one touches the girl," he said, his guilt increasing. He should be more loyal to his friends. "No matter what we find, she is mine. Understood? I'll deal with her myself."

There was a pregnant pause as each man weighed his response.

"Fine," Lucien said on a sigh.

Still Aeron remained silent.

"It's my room. I can go in alone and leave you out here to —"

"Fine," Aeron finally snapped. "She's yours. Not that you'll do what you should. Hunters, though, will be executed on sight."

"Agreed." On both counts.

"What has she done to command such loyalty from you?" Lucien asked, genuine curiosity rather than snide disgust in his tone.

Maddox didn't have an answer. Didn't even want to think about it. He deserved disgust, though. That, he couldn't deny.

"I think our friend's forgotten that sex is sex." Aeron twirled one of the blades with menacing flare. "Who's offering it doesn't matter. This woman is nothing special. None of them are."

Suddenly caught in another dark web of anger, all hint of guilt overshadowed, Maddox shot out his leg, tripping Aeron and jumping on top of him before the man even hit the ground. He used the warrior's surprise to his advantage, swiping one of the knives and holding the tip at Aeron's throat.

But, having realized what was happening midway into his fall, Aeron had the other blade poised at Maddox's throat at the same time. Maddox felt the apex sink past skin, nicking a tendon, but he did not back down.

"Do you want to die?"

Undaunted, Aeron arched a pierced black brow. "Do *you?*"

"Let him go, Maddox," Lucien said, the calm eye of the storm.

He pushed the weapon deeper, his gaze never leaving Aeron's. Fire sizzled and crackled between them. "Do not talk about her like that."

"I'll talk however I please."

He scowled. *I like this man. I admire him. He's killed for me, and I for him.* Yet he knew, deep down, that if Ashlyn were mentioned in such a derogatory manner again, he would snap. The speaker didn't matter. Nothing mattered except *her.* He hated that fact. He didn't understand it, but was helpless against it.

"For whatever reason," Lucien said, "the girl is a trigger. Tell him you won't talk about her again, Aeron."

"Why should I?" was the grumbled reply. "Last time I checked, I had a right to voice my opinions."

Deep breath in, deep breath out. That didn't help. Maddox could feel himself gearing for another attack. *Damn it! I have to get myself under control.* This was utterly ridiculous and wholly embarrassing. He'd never had less influence over his own actions.

"Aeron, you have to be tired of cleaning blood off the floors," Lucien said. "Think how much there will be if Hunters are even now trying to invade our home and we do not stop them from getting inside. Tell him."

Aeron hesitated only a moment before removing the knife from Maddox's neck. "Fine," he spat. "No talk of the girl. Happy now?"

Yes. Maddox relaxed instantly and eased to his feet. He even held out his empty hand to help Aeron stand, but Aeron brushed him aside and stood on his own. Paris had once called Maddox "The Mood Swing"; he had been joking at the time, but Maddox was starting to believe the truth of his words.

"I'm not going to say it, but you know what I'm thinking, right?" Aeron asked dryly.

Yes. He knew. He was as bad as Paris — if not worse.

"Children," Lucien muttered, rolling his eyes.

"Mommy," Aeron replied, but there was no heat in his tone.

Maddox closed his eyes for a moment, concentrating, trying to make himself believe. *Ashlyn is just a woman. She means nothing but temporary satisfaction.* The shadows and pain he'd glimpsed in her eyes meant nothing. They would not soften him, much less bewitch him. Not anymore. He had to start thinking of her as he did the others.

Any more of this absurd fighting, and he

would have to dig his dignity out of the garbage.

Hell, maybe the gods had finally decided to chastise him and had sent Ashlyn to drive him crazy, to cause him pain and suffering. To punish him. Maybe he was no longer to yearn for eternal death at night. Maybe he was to yearn for eternal death all day long.

"Good?" Lucien asked.

Not even close. He might be calm now, but he was worse off than ever. Still, he nodded and stalked down the hallway without another word, up the stairs and into his wing of the fortress. Better to get this over with.

When Lucien and Aeron once again flanked him, Aeron said, "My blade."

"It's nice," he replied, purposely misunderstanding. He did not return it.

Aeron snorted. "I didn't realize you were hard up for a weapon."

"If you want to keep yours, take better care."

"The same could be said of your head."

Maddox offered no response. The closer he came to his bedroom, the more he could smell Ashlyn's honey scent. A scent that was all her own. Not from soap or perfume, but from *her*. His body hardened painfully, his cock filling with heat and need. He'd been

151

waiting for a sip of that honey forever, it seemed. *She's just like other women, remember? Nothing special,* he reminded himself.

He flicked a glance at his companions. They appeared oblivious to the sweet fragrance in the air. Good. He wanted Ashlyn, all of her, to himself. *Nothing special, damn you.*

When they reached the threshold, each of them paused. Aeron tensed and readied his remaining blade. A hard mask covered his face, as if he were preparing himself to do whatever was necessary. Lucien, too, produced a weapon — a .45, cocked and ready.

"Look before you attack," Maddox said through clenched teeth.

They nodded, neither sparing him a glance.

"On three. One." His ears twitched as he listened. No sound emerged from inside. Not the splash of bathwater or the gentle rattle of dishes on the tray. Had Ashlyn really escaped? If she had . . .

"Two." His stomach knotted in anger and fear, and the scabs there burned. His fingers tightened around the hilt of the knife. He might just leave the fortress, might search the ends of the earth for her.

Nothing special indeed.

"Three." He twisted the lock and pushed

open the door. Hinges creaked. All three men stormed inside, silent, prepared for anything. Maddox scanned the room, taking in every detail. Floors — no footprints. Window — still closed. Platter of food — untouched. Some of his clothes had been tossed out of the closet and were now strewn around the floor.

Where was she?

Aeron and Lucien fanned out as he inched along the closet wall, alert, watchful. He jumped into the small space, blade raised. Found nothing.

The covers shifted on the bed and a soft, breathy moan drifted through the air.

"Weapons down," Maddox commanded in a fierce whisper, blood sizzling from the sound of that feminine sigh.

Several seconds ticked by before either man obeyed. Only then did Maddox approach the bed, slowly . . . sweating . . . For some reason, he was trembling like a fragile human. He suspected the image he was about to see would undo him.

He was right.

He found a sleeping beauty. Ashlyn. Angel. Destruction.

Her amber hair was splayed over his snow-white pillow. Her lashes, two shades darker than her hair, cast spiky shadows over her dirt-smudged cheeks. She hadn't bathed, hadn't eaten. She must have tumbled to sleep soon after he'd left.

"Pretty," Aeron said, reluctant admiration in his tone.

Exquisite, Maddox silently corrected. *Mine.* Her lips were red and puffy, deliciously swollen. Had she chewed them from worry? He watched the slow rise and fall of her chest, found himself reaching out — don't touch, don't touch — helpless to prevent the action. But he fisted his hands just before contact. His body was once again rock hard, need simmering inside of him. A dark need, frightening in its intensity and still so much more powerful than Violence had ever been.

How did she elicit such a response from him simply by breathing?

Touch her. Who wanted it? Him? The demon? Both? Didn't matter. Just one caress, then he'd leave. He'd shower and return when she was rested — and he'd have himself under firm control by then. Surely he would.

Finally, opening his hand, his fingertips brushed the side of her cheek. A whisper-soft caress. Her skin was silky smooth, electrical. He tingled on contact, his blood instantly heating another degree.

Her eyelids popped open, as if she, too, had felt the jolt.

She jerked upright, hair cascading down her shoulders and back. Her sleep-rimmed eyes searched, locked with his, widened. "Maddox." She scrambled backward until she was smashed against the metal headboard. Chains rattled from the sides of the bed, the chains that bound him every night. "Maddox," she repeated, scared, awed . . . happy?

He, Lucien and Aeron stepped backward in unison. He knew why *he* moved — he'd seen his downfall in her pretty eyes the moment their gazes met — but he didn't know why the others had reacted that way.

"Wh-what are you doing?" she gasped out. "And what happened to your face? You're bleeding." He heard concern and it shook him deeply. Would she always affect him so?

She glanced at the others and gave a choked whimper. "It wasn't enough for you to kill him last night, you had to beat him up today, too? Get out, you . . . you . . . murderers! Get out right now!"

She leapt from the bed and stood in front of Maddox, wobbling slightly as she held out her arms to ward them off. Protecting him? Again? Eyes wide, he met the equally astonished gazes of the others.

Her actions were those of an innocent . . . or someone pretending to be innocent. Even so, Maddox found that he wanted to touch her again. In . . . comfort? He shook his head. Couldn't be. Had to be pleasure. *That* made sense. He was a man; she was a woman. He desired.

But would that desire grow darker, as he feared?

He gripped her arm and pulled her behind him. He shared a confused look with Lucien, then turned to face her. Before he could utter a single word, she rushed out, "Are you going to take me into the city now? Please."

And never see her again? "Eat," he commanded, harsher than he'd intended. "Bathe. I will return soon." To his friends, he barked, "Let's go." He stalked into the hall.

They lingered only a moment before following. After closing and locking the door, Maddox leaned his forehead against the cold stone wall beside it, measuring every molecule of air he drew in and forced out of his lungs as he tried to soothe his riotous heartbeat. *This has to stop.*

"You've brought trouble into our midst," Aeron said, remaining at his side. "And was she actually trying to protect you from us?"

"Surely not." But that was the second time she'd done so, and he was more confused now than before.

He straightened and scrubbed a hand down his face.

"Let me go, Maddox," Ashlyn called through the door. More than it had yesterday, her voice appealed to him. Soft, lilting. Erotic. "I was wrong to come here. I was. If it will help, I'll promise not to tell anybody."

"I know I've brought trouble," he told Aeron.

His friend arched a brow in that insolent expression Maddox was coming to loathe. "No apology?"

That was the worst of it; he still wasn't sorry.

"Forget the woman for now," Lucien said, waving a hand through the air. He squared his shoulders. "You've seen her. She is well. She doesn't appear to have let Hunters in — yet. Now we have a more pressing concern to discuss. What I tried to tell you earlier is that the gods — they are not who you think they are."

"Maddox, we need to talk to you," a harsh voice called, cutting off whatever response he might have made.

Lucien threw up his arms in exasperation and Maddox pivoted. Reyes approached,

Paris and Torin at his sides. Two were scowling, the other grinning like the madman he was.

"Your woman has to go," Reyes growled. "I smelled her all night long, and I can't stand another second of that thunderstorm scent."

Thunderstorm? Ashlyn smelled like honey. Still, his jaw clenched at the thought of another man being so aware of her. "She stays," he said curtly.

"Who is she, why is she still here and when can I see her naked?" Paris asked with an eyebrow wiggle.

"Someone should kill her," Reyes countered.

"No one touches her!"

Aeron closed his eyes and shook his head. "Here we go again."

"Unlike Reyes, I don't mind her presence," Paris said, rubbing his hands together. "I only mind your unwillingness to share. I'd like to —"

Maddox shoved Paris before the man could finish the sentence. "Do not speak another word. I know what you would like to do to her, and I will die first."

Now Paris frowned, pale skin dusting with angry color. "Back off, asshole. I haven't had a woman today, so I'm in no mood for this kind of bullshit."

Torin remained in the corner, watching, grin spreading. "Anyone else find this highly amusing? It's even better than listening to the brokers when stocks plummet."

Maddox struggled to rein in his temper and shove Ashlyn to the back of his mind. Where she belonged. As a female, as a human, as possible Bait, she was the last person who should rouse this sort of protective reaction in him.

Should, should, should. Argh! *End this.* Finally. Soon. Now.

"Enough!" Lucien shouted.

Everyone quieted and stared at Lucien in surprise. He was not usually a shouter.

"Were there Hunters in town?" he asked Paris and Reyes.

Reyes shook his head. "We didn't find any."

"Good. That's good. Perhaps Maddox did indeed kill them all." Lucien nodded in satisfaction. "But Maddox doesn't know about the gods yet. We need to tell him. What's more, Aeron and I . . . did something last night."

Instantly Aeron's body went rigid. "We said we wouldn't tell them."

"I know." Lucien sighed, clearly at the end of his patience. "I changed my mind."

"You cannot simply change your mind!" Aeron roared, leaping in front of Lucien.

"I can and I did," was the reply. Not exactly calm, but close, only edged with steel.

"What's going on?" Maddox stepped between them and pushed them apart. For once, he was not the one throwing accusations and fists. "I'm ready to listen. You mentioned the gods. I know Aeron was summoned. I was too distracted to ask for details before. What did they want from him?"

"Later," Torin said to Maddox, but he didn't take his eyes off Lucien. "What'd you do, Death?"

"Spill," Reyes commanded.

Lucien's attention never wavered from Aeron. "After their reaction to Ashlyn, we need to make sure they don't accidentally stumble upon *our* secret. What do you think will happen if they do?"

For a long while, Aeron did not reply. Tension filled the air, grave, sinister. Finally, Aeron nodded. "Fine. Show them. But get ready to war, my friend, because they aren't going to be happy."

"Someone had better explain," Reyes demanded, looking between them.

"An explanation will not be good enough.

I need to show you." Lucien started down the hall. "This way."

Prophetic words, Maddox thought. He cast a questioning glance at Torin, who had uttered something similar only last night. *Know what's going on?* he mouthed.

No, was the silent reply.

Nothing good, that much he could guess. Lucien had never acted this mysterious. Confused, intrigued, *concerned,* Maddox glanced at Ashlyn's door before following his friends.

Chapter Seven

Ashlyn fell back onto the bed, struggling to control her breathing. Oh God. He'd come back. He hadn't been a dream, hallucination or mirage. Maddox was alive. She'd really been locked inside a dungeon; he'd really risen from the dead. And he'd really stopped the voices.

When he'd left her in this oddly bare bedroom, she'd searched for a phone, found nothing, then searched for a way out. Again, nothing. Fatigue had quickly settled on her shoulders, nearly crushing her. She'd been unable to fight it, the silence inexorably relaxing, like a beloved drug she'd finally been able to indulge in. So she'd lain down, not caring about the consequences. She'd entertained the notion that maybe, just maybe, all of this was a delusion and when she opened her eyes, she'd find herself in her own home, her own bed.

Not so. Oh, not so.

A moment ago, a shock of thrumming power had slammed through her, dragging her kicking and screaming from the most peaceful sleep of her entire life, a sleep wrapped in that blissful silence. And then Maddox had been standing over her, looking down at her with those fathomless purple eyes.

His face had been, *was,* a mass of bruises and cuts. Black and blue and bloodied, his left eye swollen, his lip split from top to bottom. At the memory, nausea churned in her stomach. Had those monsters tried to kill him again?

Again. Ha! She laughed humorlessly. They *had* killed him. And two of his killers had stood at his side. He'd seemed on affable terms with them, conversing with them as if he had no reason to hate them. How could they still be friends?

She lumbered from the bed. Her body creaked and ached with every movement, as if she were a doddering ninety rather than a spry twenty-four. She frowned. Too much stress, with no real end in sight.

The men must have wandered off, because she no longer heard them beyond the threshold. Good. She didn't want to deal with them right now. Or ever. *Take care of business, then find a way out of here.*

She trekked to the bathroom, awed by its surprising beauty, considering the sparseness of the bedroom and the starkness of the dungeon. Here she found white-tiled walls and a matching marble floor, a built-in chrome and black vanity overflowing with towels, a porcelain sink, a gleaming claw-foot tub with a raised nozzle — in case a giant decided to shower? she wondered, wide-eyed — and a nearly transparent curtain.

For some reason, everything was bolted down.

A tiered light hung from the ceiling, its brass arms stretching in different directions. There were no other decorations, though. No pictures or amenities. Had Maddox removed them, afraid she'd try to steal them?

Ashlyn snorted. The Institute paid her very well to listen for and learn about all things paranormal; money was not a problem. Besides, whatever she wanted, McIntosh willingly gave her. And if she didn't want to ask him, she ordered from the Internet and had it delivered to her doorstep.

She blushed, thinking of some of the things she'd recently ordered. Romance novels, which had invariably led to the purchase of a harem girl costume, a black leather bra and panty set, and after reading one particular book about an undercover agent and former female thief, silk scarves and duct tape. Not that she'd ever used any of them.

With a sigh, she dipped a towel into the now-cold bathwater. Leaving her clothes on, she washed herself as best she could. No way would she strip. Any of the men could return at any moment.

Yeah, but you'd like it if Maddox returned.

No, she assured herself, flustered by the thought. She wouldn't. He scared her.

He brings precious silence.

Not anymore. He wasn't here, yet the voices hadn't returned. Her head was clear, her own thoughts all she heard. *I'm cured.*

No, you're not. You heard voices last night, in the dungeon.

"Now I'm talking to myself," she said, throwing her hands in the air. "What's next?"

She studied her reflection in the mirror. Droplets of water dripped from her forehead to her nose, from nose to chin. Her cheeks were bright with rosy color and her dark eyes gleamed. Odd. She'd never been more aware of her own mortality, but she'd also never looked more alive.

When her stomach rumbled, she recalled the tray of food Maddox had left on the floor. Her feet carried her to it without being ordered, kicking past the clothing she'd scattered when she'd searched the closet for a hidden phone. Black T-shirts, black pants, black briefs.

Her nipples hardened with the thought of muscled Maddox in nothing but a pair of those briefs. He'd lie on the bed, hard and straining, erection peeking through the top, wickedness in his eyes as he beckoned her over with a crook of his finger.

And she'd willingly go to him.

Ashlyn nibbled on her bottom lip. Maddox . . . on a bed . . . wanting her . . . Her knees weakened, and her belly quivered. *Stupid girl.* Apparently, when given a little silence, all she could think about was sex.

She gathered the tray of food and tottered to the window, where she balanced the edge on the wall and popped a grape into her mouth. The sweet juice ran down her throat, and she nearly moaned before ordering herself to focus on the matter at hand — escape. She'd told McIntosh, and thereby the Institute, about the men and this fortress. McIntosh had even known she wanted to visit. Most likely he'd have guessed by now where she'd gone.

Would he come for her? Or would he feed her to the wolves for daring to disobey?

While he'd always been kind to her, he had never tolerated mistakes from his other employees, much less willful disobedience.

He'll come, she assured herself. *He needs you.*

But as she stared out the window, only trees and snow greeted her. Still, she didn't let that disappoint her. He could be anywhere. Standing there, allowing anyone outside to see her, she popped another grape in her mouth and tapped on the glass. *I'm here. Do you see me?*

She needed out as soon as possible. With every second that passed, the warriors' madness seemed to take deeper hold of *her.* She had imagined her jailer in his underwear, for God's sake.

Hopefully, McIntosh would see her, blow a hole in the front door and snatch her out. Boom. Done. Over. No, wait. Rewind. She didn't want McIntosh inside the walls. He would be no match for Maddox and the others. She was going to have to distract Maddox, maybe knock him out somehow, and run. Out of the fortress and down the hill. The cold and the voices were better than the threat of death she'd found here.

So . . . just how was she going to distract the man? Mulling it over, she devoured the rest of the grapes. And when those were gone, she concentrated on the meat and cheese, sipping wine between bites. In a matter of minutes, only crumbs and half a bottle remained. Never had anything tasted so delicious. The ham had been glazed with brown sugar, a succulent feast to her taste buds. The cheese had been smooth, not too sharp, the grapes a perfect contrast. The wine, excellent.

Okay, so this place *did* have a few things in its favor.

Food wasn't a good enough reason to stay, though. *What about sex?* Of course not, she thought, her stomach giving another of those strange flutters. That was —

Everything inside her went on sudden alert — the quiet before a debilitating storm. She didn't exactly hurt, but she became aware that something wasn't quite right in her body. One heartbeat passed. Two. She gulped, waiting.

Then the storm arrived.

Her blood chilled to ice, yet beads of sweat that were as sharp as broken glass appeared on her skin. Crawling over every inch of her like spiders. She yelped, whimpered, tried to scratch at them. But they wouldn't go away, and now she could actually see them. They were on her. *On her,* their tiny legs scampering. A scream bubbled in her throat at the exact moment a wave of dizziness slammed into her, so the sound was nothing more than a groan. She had to grip the window to remain standing. The tray fell, clanging.

All too soon, the dizzying fog became an ache and the ache a piercing knife, slicing its way from her belly to her heart. She swayed, gasping and moaning at the same time. Bright lights flashed in front of her eyes, an array of blinding colors.

What was wrong with her? Poison? Oh God, were the spiders still on her?

Another pain shot through her and she doubled over. "Maddox," she called, the word weak.

Nothing. No footsteps.

"Maddox!" she shouted, projecting his name with all her dwindling strength. She tried to walk to the door, but couldn't force herself to move.

Again nothing.

"Maddox!" *Why do you want him?* He *might have done this to you.* "Maddox." She couldn't stop his name from leaving her lips. "Maddox."

Black cobwebs snaked around her vision, constricting it, blanketing the too-bright rainbow. "Maddox." Her voice was a hoarse whisper now, a trembling entreaty.

Her stomach cramped; her throat was swelling, closing off. And then, suddenly, she couldn't breathe. Every cell in her body screamed and screamed and screamed. *Need air. Need to breathe.* She fell to the floor, unable to support her own weight any longer. *Need to get the spiders off.* No strength, no energy.

The bottle of wine toppled as if in sympathy, the remaining red liquid spilling around her. She lost focus completely, the world crumbling, then disappearing altogether, leaving only darkness.

Maddox could not believe what he was seeing. "This is . . . this is . . . not possible." He scrubbed a callused hand over his eyes, but the sight did not change.

"Obviously, it wasn't Ashlyn I smelled." Reyes slammed a fist into the wall. Dust puffed into the air, bits of rough stone tumbling to the floor.

Torin merely laughed.

Paris sucked in a reverent breath. "Come to daddy."

There, in the far corner of Lucien's bedroom, were four women. Holding hands, they huddled together for strength and support. Each trembled in fear, gazing at the men through wide, panicked eyes.

No, Maddox realized. Not all of them trembled. A pretty blonde with freckles regarded them with fury in her green eyes. Her jaw was clenched, as if she were biting her tongue to keep from shouting obscenities.

"What are they doing here?" he demanded.

"Do not take that tone," Aeron snapped. "You started it with your pretty piece of Bait."

Growling low, Maddox closed the distance between them. One of the women whimpered. "I thought we had covered this," he said. "You watch what you say about her or you suffer."

Aeron did not back down. "You've known her, what? A few hours? You've barely spoken to her. She should be begging for mercy right now, and we should know all her secrets and what the Hunters, if there are more out there, are planning."

"She tried to save me when I was stabbed. She tried to save me from you only a few minutes ago."

"An act."

Probably. He'd told himself that very thing, but he couldn't seem to make it matter. Not then, not now. Frustrated with himself rather than Aeron, *he* backed down this time. He faced Lucien. "Why are they here?" he asked, composed but no less disbelieving.

Or rather, as composed as he was capable of being at the moment.

Lucien glanced at Aeron, who motioned to the hall with a tilt of his chin. Understanding, the warriors filed out. Each hummed with expectation. Lucien was the last to exit and was quick to close and lock the door.

Maddox peered at his friends, most projecting the same disbelief he felt. Nothing like this had ever happened before. None of them had ever brought a woman here, even Paris (that he knew of), and now there were almost as many females on the premises as warriors. It was surreal.

"Well?" he prompted.

Aeron explained how the Greeks had been overthrown by the Titans, those leaders from thousands of years ago, and that these new sovereigns wanted — no, commanded — him to execute those four innocent women. Were he to resist, he would be driven mad with bloodlust. Were he to ask to be released from the deed, he would be cursed as Maddox was cursed.

Maddox listened, stunned. Shock and dread washed through him, all but swimming laps in his bloodstream.

"But why would the new king of gods tell Aeron to —" The answer slid into place and he pressed his lips together. *I did this,* he realized. *I'm responsible. I dared the gods yesterday evening, insulted them, even.* This had to be their way of retaliating.

He flicked Torin a dismayed glance. The warrior was staring at him with a hard glint in his green eyes. Then he turned away and flattened his gloved hands on the mirror hanging just above his head. His reflection was bleak. Only yesterday, the two of them had claimed they didn't care if the gods punished them. They'd thought nothing could be worse than their current situation.

They'd been wrong.

"We cannot allow Aeron to do this deed," Lucien said, interrupting Maddox's dark thoughts. "He's at the breaking point already. We all are."

Reyes once again punched the wall, grunting from the force. There were angry red cuts on each of his forearms and they burst open on impact, splattering flecks of blood onto the silver stone. "These Titans had to know what would happen if Aeron obeyed." He bared his teeth in a scowl. "They had to know what a precarious edge of good and evil we're all balanced on. Why would they do this?"

"I know why," Maddox replied grimly.

All eyes flew to him.

Shame weighed heavily on his shoulders as he recounted what he'd done. "I never expected this to happen," he finished lamely. "I didn't know the Titans had escaped, much less that they had taken over."

"I don't even know what to say." Aeron.

"I do. Fuck." Paris.

Maddox's head fell back and he stared up at the ceiling. *I thought I was goading the Greeks,* he wanted to shout. *They* would have done nothing. *They* would have continued to ignore him.

"Do you think Ashlyn is a punishment from the Titans, as well?" Lucien asked.

His jaw clenched. "Yes." Of course she was a punishment. He'd thought so earlier — the timing of her arrival, the way she'd haunted his mind and fanned his desires — but he'd assumed the Greeks had been responsible. "The Titans must have led the Hunters straight to us, knowing they would use Ashlyn and how she would affect me."

"You did not curse the gods until *after* Aeron was summoned. What's more, you hadn't yet cursed them when Ashlyn first appeared on my cameras," Torin pointed out. "They could not have known what we would later do and say."

"Couldn't they? Perhaps they didn't send her, but they *must* be using her somehow." Nothing else explained the intensity of his feelings for her. "I'll take care of her," he added darkly, but every muscle in his body stiffened, begging him to snatch the words back. He didn't. "I'll take care of all of them."

Paris leveled him with a frown. "How?"

Grim, he said, "I'll kill them." He'd done worse. Why not add this to the list? *Because I am not a beast.* If he did it, he would *be* Violence. He would be no better than the spirit inside him, reduced to only one reason for existence: causing pain.

Yet he'd brought this plague upon their house; he needed to fix it. Could he destroy Ashlyn, though? He found he didn't want to know the answer.

"You can't kill the four inside Lucien's room," Aeron said, just as grim. "The Titans commanded *me* to do it. Who knows how they'll react if their orders are not followed exactly."

"I can hear you, you sick bastards," a female voice cried from behind the door. "You kill us, and I swear to God I'll kill every one of *you.*"

There was another temporary halt to

movement and speech.

Reyes's lips curled in a wry grin. "An impossible feat, but I would almost like to see her try."

Feminine fists beat against the frame. "Let us go! Let us go, do you hear me?"

"We hear you, woman," Reyes said. "I'm sure the dead hear you, as well."

That Reyes, the most serious of the bunch, had cracked a joke was disturbing. Only when circumstances were dire did he resort to humor.

This was a nightmare. After centuries of rigid routine, Maddox suddenly had a woman to interrogate, then destroy before she could be further used against him. He had a friend to save from an unthinkable command. And he had gods to appease. Gods he wasn't even sure how to approach.

These Titans were unknown entities. If he asked for mercy and they ordered him to do something vile — something he refused to do — the situation would most assuredly become worse than it was now.

"Why don't I touch them?" Torin suggested, turning back to the group. His eyes were as bright and green as the girl's inside the room. While hers had been filled with anger, his were filled with despair. "If they die of disease, no one will have to worry about his conscience." Except Torin.

"No," Aeron said at the same moment Paris shouted, "Hell, no."

"No disease," Lucien agreed. "Once it starts, it's impossible to control."

"We'll keep the bodies contained," Torin said, his determination clear.

Lucien let out another sigh. "That won't work, and you know it. Disease always spreads."

"Disease!" the girl cried. "You're going to infect us with a disease? Is that why you brought us here? You disgusting, loathsome, rotten pieces of —"

"Hush," another female voice commanded. "Don't incite them, Dani."

"But, Grandma, they —"

Their voices trailed off. The girl was probably being dragged away from the door. Maddox liked her courage. It reminded him of Ashlyn, how she had stood up to him in the cell and demanded he lift his shirt. She had wanted to run — the desire had shone brightly in her eyes — but she hadn't. Just the memory caused his blood to heat and his body to harden. She had even stroked his wound, sparking something to life inside him. Something he hadn't understood.

Tenderness, perhaps?

He shook his head in denial. He would

fight that emotion until his last breath — which should take place in about thirteen hours, he thought wryly. He did not, *would* not, have tenderness for Bait, or a divine punishment, or whatever she was.

Proof — next time he saw her he would take her hard and fast, pounding . . . pounding . . . She would moan and scream his name. Her thighs would tighten around his waist and — No, no. Of its own accord, the image realigned in his head, shifting to please Violence.

She would be on her stomach, braced on her hands and knees. That lovely hair would cascade down her elegant back and he would grab hold of it, tugging. Her neck would arch; her lips would part on a gasp of pleasure-pain. In and out he would pound, her sheath hot and wet. Tight. Yes, she would be tighter than a fist. His testicles would slap at her legs.

When I finally have Ashlyn in my bed, I'm going to be gentle. Remember?

That thought was ignored. She would beg for more, and he would give it to her. He would —

"This is becoming tiresome." Aeron pushed him, hard, slamming him into the wall. "You're panting and sweating and your eyes are starting to glow with red fire. About to erupt, Violence?"

The image of Ashlyn, naked and aroused, vanished — and that infuriated the spirit, who attempted to jump through Maddox's skin and attack. Maddox found himself snarling, too, craving another glimpse of her in his mind.

"Calm down, Maddox." Lucien's serene voice penetrated the haze. "Keep this up and we'll be forced to chain you. Who will protect Ashlyn then, hmm?"

His blood chilled, sobering him. They would do it, he knew they would, and chains he could not allow. Not during the day. At night, yes. He was a menace then and there was no other way. *I'm a menace now.* But if he were bound now, when he was barely hanging on to his sense of self, he might as well admit defeat and stop trying to be anything other than a demon.

All of the men were staring at him, he noticed.

"I'm sorry," he grumbled. Something was very wrong with him. This hair-trigger dance with the spirit was utterly ridiculous. Worse, it was embarrassing. They usually fought each other, but not like this.

Maybe he needed more time in the gym. Or another round with Aeron.

"Good?" Lucien asked him. How many

times would he be forced to ask that today?

Maddox gave a stiff nod.

Lucien braced his arms behind his back and regarded each man. "Since that's settled, let's discuss the reason I brought you here."

"Let's discuss the reason you brought the women here," Paris interjected, "rather than leaving them in the city. Yeah, Aeron has a job to do, but that doesn't explain —"

"The women are here because we didn't want them leaving Buda, perhaps compelling Aeron to follow," Lucien said, cutting him off. "And I wanted you to see them so that you wouldn't kill them if you caught them wandering around the fortress. If they manage to get loose, just bring them back to my room and lock them inside. Don't talk to them, don't hurt them. Until we figure out how to free Aeron from this deed, the women are our unwilling guests. Agreed?"

One by one, the men nodded. What else could they do?

"For now, leave them to me and relax. Rest. Go about your day. You'll be needed soon enough, I'm sure."

"I, for one, plan to drink myself into oblivion." Aeron scoured a hand down his face. "Women in the house," he muttered, adding as he stalked away, "Why don't we invite the whole city over for a party?"

"A party would be fun," Torin said, once again amused. "Might help me forget all this hive-inducing male bonding." And then he, too, was off.

Reyes didn't say a word. Just unsheathed a blade and stomped down the hall, leaving no doubt about what he planned to do. Maddox would have offered to cut him, to whip him or beat him and spare Reyes the agony of self-infliction, but he'd offered before and always the answer was an abrupt no.

He could understand Reyes's need to do it on his own. Being a burden was almost as bad as being possessed. They all had their demons — literally — and Reyes didn't want to make it worse for any of them.

At the moment, though, Maddox might have welcomed the distraction.

"I'll see you losers later," Paris said. "I'm going back to the city." Fine lines of strain bracketed his eyes — eyes that were now a dull blue rather than bright with satisfaction. "I didn't have a woman last night *or* this morning. All this —" he waved a hand toward the door "— has fucked with my schedule. And not in a good way."

"Go," Lucien told him.

The warrior hesitated and glanced toward the door. He licked his lips. "Unless, of course, you'd allow me inside your bedroom . . ."

"Go." Lucien gestured impatiently.

"Their loss." Paris shrugged and disappeared around the corner.

Maddox knew he should offer to guard the women. After all, he was probably the reason they were here. But he needed to see Ashlyn. No, not needed. Wanted. Better. He did not *need* anything. Especially a human with questionable motives who was already marked for death.

But not knowing what these Titans would do next, he realized he did not want to waste another moment. He would go to Ashlyn even though he hadn't completely subdued the demon. Besides, he might never be calm when it came to that woman. And it was better to do what he wanted with her *now,* before he was forced to — he could not even bring himself to think it.

"Lucien," he began.

"Go," his friend said again. "Do whatever you need to do to get yourself under control. Your woman —"

"Ashlyn is not up for discussion," Maddox responded, already knowing what Lucien meant to say. *Your woman needs to be taken care of as soon as possible.* He knew that, too.

"Just get her out of your system, then do what needs doing so that at least part of our lives can return to normal."

Maddox nodded and turned, part of him wondering if his normal life was worth returning to.

CHAPTER EIGHT

Maddox stepped into his bedroom, unsure of what he'd find. A sleeping Ashlyn? A freshly bathed, naked Ashlyn? A ready-to-fight Ashlyn?

A ready-for-pleasure Ashlyn?

To his irritation, his heart drummed erratically inside his chest. His palms were sweating. *Fool,* he chastised himself. He was not a human, a servant to fear, nor was he inexperienced. And yet, he wasn't exactly sure how to handle this woman, this . . . punishment.

What he didn't expect to find was an unconscious Ashlyn, sprawled on the floor, a puddle of crimson — blood? — around her, soaking her hair and clothes.

Darkness shuddered through him. "Ashlyn?" He was at her side in the next instant, crouching down, gently rolling her over and scooping her into his arms. Wine, only wine. Thank the gods. Droplets splashed her too-pale face and dripped onto him. He almost smiled. Just how much had she drunk?

She weighed so little he would have been unaware he held her if not for the low-voltage tingles seeping from her skin into his. "Ashlyn, wake up."

She didn't. In fact, she seemed to slip deeper into unconsciousness, the movement behind her eyelids ceasing.

His throat was tight, and he had to force the next words out. "Wake up for me."

Not a moan, not a sigh.

Worried by her lack of response, he carried her to the bed, ripping off her wet jacket in the process and tossing it aside. Though he didn't want to release her, he lay her on the mattress and cupped her face in his hands. Her skin was ice-cold. "Ashlyn."

Still no response.

Was she . . . No. *No!* Lead balls settled in his stomach as he flattened his palm over her left breast. At first he felt nothing. No gentle beat, no hard slam. He nearly belted out a curse to the heavens. Then, suddenly, there was a weak patter. A long pause. Another feeble patter-patter.

She was alive.

His eyes closed briefly, his shoulders sagging in relief. "Ashlyn." He gently shook her. "Come on, beauty. Wake up." What in the name of Zeus was wrong with her? He didn't have any experience with inebriated mortals, but he did not think this right.

Her head lolled to the side; her eyelids remained closed. Her lips were tinted a pretty but unnatural blue. Sweat trickled down his temples. She was not simply inebriated. Had the night in that cell sickened her? No, there would have been signs before now. Had Torin inadvertently touched her? Surely not. She wasn't coughing or covered in pockmarks. What, then?

"Ashlyn." *I can't lose her.* Not yet. He hadn't gotten enough of her, hadn't touched her as he'd dreamed, hadn't talked to her. He blinked in surprise. He wanted to talk with her, he suddenly realized. Not just sate himself inside her body. Not just interrogate her. But talk. Get to know her and find out what made her the woman she was.

All thoughts of killing her vanished; thoughts of saving her took their place, strong, undeniable.

"Ashlyn. Speak to me." He shook her again, helpless, not knowing what else to do. Cold continued to radiate from her, as if she'd been bathed in frost and dried in an arctic wind. He gripped the covers, pulled them up and tunneled them around her, trying to envelop her in warmth. "Ashlyn. Please."

Even as he watched, bruises formed under her eyes. Was this to be his punishment instead? Watching her die slowly and painfully?

The sensation of helplessness intensified. As strong as he was, he couldn't force her to respond. "Ashlyn." This time her name was a hoarse entreaty. He shook her yet again, hard enough to rattle her soul. "Ashlyn."

Damn this. Still nothing.

"Lucien!" he roared, gaze never leaving her. "Aeron!" As far away as he was from them, he doubted they could hear. "Help me!" Had Ashlyn called for help? Bending down, Maddox meshed his mouth against hers, trying to breathe his strength into her. Warmth . . . tingles . . .

Her blue-tinted lips parted and she moaned. Finally. Another sign of life. He almost howled in relief. "Talk to me, beauty." He smoothed the wet hair from her face, disconcerted to find his hands trembling. "Tell me what's wrong."

"Maddox," she rasped. Still her eyes remained closed.

"I'm here. Tell me how to help you. Tell me what you need."

"Kill them. Kill the spiders." She spoke so quietly, he struggled to hear.

He brushed his fingers over her cheek as he glanced around the room. "There are no spiders, beauty."

"Please." A crystal tear squeezed past her lid. "Won't stop crawling on me."

"Yes, yes, I'll kill them." Though he didn't understand, he continued to trail his hands over her face, then her neck, then down her arms, stomach and legs. "They're dead now. They're dead. I promise."

That seemed to relax her a little. "Food, wine. Poison?"

He paled, felt the color leach from his face until he was likely as white as Ashlyn. He hadn't thought . . . hadn't considered . . . The wine had been made for *them*, the warriors, not for humans. Since human alcohol did little for them, Paris often mixed in droplets of ambrosia he'd stolen from the heavens and hoarded all these years. Was the ambrosia like a poison to humans?

I did this to her, Maddox thought, horrified. *Me. Not the gods.* "Argh!" He slammed his fist into the metal headboard, felt his knuckles crack further and fill with blood. Unappeased, he punched the headboard again. The bed rattled and Ashlyn moaned in pain.

Stop; don't hurt her. He forced himself to still, to breathe slowly, all the while willing himself to calm for the thousandth time that day. But the urge to brutalize was so dark, so bleak. So intense, it was nearly uncontrollable. Except for that brief time following his fight with Aeron, he'd been on edge all day and this only pushed him further. Any moment he might cross the threshold and cause irreparable harm.

"Tell me how to help you," he repeated.

"D-doctor."

A human healer. Yes, yes. He'd have to take her into the city, for none of the Lords had any medical training. There had never been a need for it. What if this doctor wanted to keep her overnight? He shook his head. That, he couldn't allow. She could tell the Hunters what she'd learned here, what she'd seen — how best to defeat the warriors. What bothered him most, however, was the fear that someone could take her, hurt her, and he would not be able to save her.

He would have to bring a doctor here.

Maddox brushed another soft kiss on her cold, cold lips. Again there was a jolt — this one more muted than the last, as weak as Ashlyn herself. His hands curled into fists. "I'll find you a doctor, beauty, and bring him to the fortress."

She moaned, and her long lashes finally fluttered open. Amber pools of pain stared up at him. "Maddox."

"I won't be long, I swear it."

"Don't . . . go." She sounded on the verge of tears. "Hurt. Hurt so bad. Stay."

The need to give in and the need to fetch help warred inside him. In the end, he could not deny her. He strode to the door and shouted, "Paris! Aeron! Reyes!" The sound of his voice echoed off the walls. "Lucien! Torin!"

He didn't wait for them, but stalked back to the bed. He intertwined his fingers with Ashlyn's. Hers were limp. "What can I do to ease your pain?"

"Don't let go." She gasped out a shallow breath. Red striations streamed from the corners of her mouth. Was the poison spreading?

"I won't. I won't." More than anything, he wanted to draw the pain away from her and into himself. What was a little more suffering to him? Nothing. But she was . . . what? He didn't have an answer for that.

Groaning, she clutched her stomach, rolled to her side and curled into a ball. Maddox used his free hand to brush her hair behind her still-damp ear. "Is there anything else I can do?"

"Don't know." She watched him, expression glassy. "Going to . . . die?"

"No!" He hadn't meant to shout, but the denial had escaped on a burst. "No," he repeated more softly. "This is my fault and I won't let you."

"On purpose?"

"Never."

"Why then?" she breathed. Groaned again.

"Accident," he said. "That wine wasn't meant for your kind."

Whether she heard him or not, she gave no indication. "Going to —" she gagged, covered her mouth with her hand "— vomit."

He grabbed the empty fruit bowl and held it out. She pushed herself to the edge of the bed and emptied her stomach. He clasped her hair back, away from the line of fire.

Was purging herself good or bad?

Ashlyn fell back onto the mattress just as Reyes and Paris raced into the room. Both men looked confused. "What?" Reyes demanded.

"What's wrong?" Paris asked. He was sweating, the lines of strain deeper around his eyes.

Reyes's arms were bleeding again, his hand swollen, and he held two blades, clearly ready for battle. His gaze took in the scene and his confusion intensified. "Need help with the death-blow?"

"No! The wine . . . the ambrosia Paris puts in it. I left it for her." The confession spilled from him, dripping with guilt and desolation. "Save her."

Paris wobbled, but managed to remain upright. "I don't know how."

"You must! You've spent countless hours with humans!" Maddox barely leashed a deafening roar. "Tell me how to help her."

"I wish I could." He mopped his moist brow with the back of his hand. "I've never shared our wine with others. It's ours."

"Go and ask the other humans if they know what to do. If they don't, tell Lucien to flash into the city and find a doctor to bring here." Death was the only one of the warriors who could move from one place to another with a single thought.

Reyes nodded and spun on his heel.

Paris said, "I'm sorry, Maddox, but I'm at my limit. I need sex. I heard your call from the front door and came here instead of leaving. Shouldn't have. If I don't get into the city soon I'll . . ."

"I understand."

"Make it up to you later." Paris stumbled out and disappeared around the corner.

192

"Maddox." Ashlyn moaned again. Sweat trickled from her temples. Her skin was still laced with blue, but was now so pallid he could see the tiny azure veins that swam underneath. "Tell me . . . a story. Something . . . mind off . . . pain." She closed her eyes, those lashes casting shadows on her cheeks again.

"Relax, beauty. You should not be talking." He raced to the bathroom, emptied and cleaned the bowl and swiped a towel. He wet it down and returned, setting the bowl beside the bed — just in case. Her eyes were still closed. He thought she might have fallen asleep, but she tensed as he bathed her face. He settled behind her, unsure of what to say.

"Why did . . . friends stab you?"

He didn't discuss his curse, not even with the very men who suffered alongside him. He should not discuss it with Ashlyn. Anyone but her, in fact, but that didn't stop him. Looking at her, seeing her grimace from pain, he would have done anything to distract her. "They stab me because they must. Like me, they are damned."

"That . . . explains nothing."

"That explains everything."

Several minutes ticked by in silence. She began squirming, as if preparing for another round with the bowl. He had made her ill; he owed her anything she desired. He opened his mouth and let the tale of his life spill from him. "Here is a story for you. I am immortal, and I've walked the earth since the beginning of time, it seems."

As he spoke, he felt her muscles loosen their vise-grip on her bones. "Immortal," she echoed as if tasting the word. "Knew you were more than human."

"I was never a human. I was created a warrior, meant to guard the king of gods. For many years, I served him well, helping to keep him in power, protecting him even from his own family. But he did not think me strong enough to guard his most precious possession, a box formed from the bones of the dead goddess of oppression. No, he commanded a woman to do it. She was known as the greatest female warrior, true, but my pride was stung." Thankfully, Ashlyn remained relaxed. "Thinking to prove a mistake had been made, I helped release the demons inside upon the world. And in punishment, I was bonded to one." He wound his arm around her waist and gently rubbed her stomach, hoping the action would soothe her.

She expelled a slight breath. Of relief? He hoped. "Demon. I suspected."

Yes, she had. He still didn't understand why she admitted it so readily.

"But you're *good.* Sometimes," she added. "That's why your face changes?"

"Yes." She thought him good?

Filled with pleasure, he continued his story. "I knew the moment I had been breached, for there was a shock inside me, as if parts of me were dying, making room for something else, something stronger than myself." It had been the first time he had ever understood the concept of death — and little had he known just how intimately he would soon come to understand it.

Another delicate sigh escaped her. If she actually understood what he was saying now, he couldn't tell. At least she wasn't crying, wasn't writhing in pain.

"For a while, I lost touch with my own will and the demon had total control of me, forcing me to do —" All manner of evils, he mentally finished, visions of blood and death, smoke and ash and utter desolation filling his mind. He could barely tolerate the knowledge himself and would not taint Ashlyn with it.

To the very second, he recalled how the spirit's hold on him loosened, like a dream-haze clearing, the black smoke in his mind wafting away in a sweetly scented morning breeze, leaving behind only its hated memory.

The demon had compelled him to kill Pandora, the guardian it hated above all else. Bloodlust at last appeased, it had receded to the back of Maddox's mind, leaving Maddox to deal with the damage.

"Gods, to go back," he said on a sigh. "To walk away from that box."

"Box," Ashlyn said, startling him. "Demons . . . I've heard something about that." She opened her mouth to say more, then jerked. Crying out, she reached blindly for the bowl.

Maddox moved faster than he ever had before, leaping from the bed and swiping the bowl in seconds. The moment he held it out, she leaned over and retched. He cocooned her against his stomach through the worst of it, cooing to her like he'd never done to another. Giving comfort was new to him, and he prayed he did it correctly. He'd never even comforted his friends. They were all as private about their torment as he was.

When Ashlyn finished, he settled her back on the mattress and once more cleaned her face. Then he turned his gaze to the ceiling. "I am sorry for the way I spoke of you," he whispered to the heavens. "But please do not harm her for my sins."

Peering back down at her, he felt as if an eternity had passed since he'd first met her, as if he'd known her forever and she had always been a part of his life. A life that would collapse into nothingness if she were taken from him. How was that possible? Only an hour before, he had convinced himself that he might be able to slay her. Now . . .

"Let her live," he found himself adding, "and I'll do anything you want."

Anything? a quiet voice asked, relish in the undertones. Not the voice of Violence, he realized, or any voice he had heard before.

Maddox blinked, stilled. A moment passed before his shock settled into mere confusion. "Who's there?"

Startled by his outburst, Ashlyn dragged her red-rimmed eyes to him. "I am," she croaked.

"Pay no attention to me, beauty. Sleep," he said softly.

Who do you think I am, warrior? Can you not guess who has the power to speak to you thus?

Another shocked moment passed before the answer took root. Could it be? A . . . Titan? He had sent pleas to the Greeks for years, and never had he been addressed within seconds. He'd never been addressed at all. And hadn't the Titans called Aeron to the heavens like this, with only a voice?

Hope — and dread — unfurled inside him. If these Titans were benevolent, if they would help, Maddox thought perhaps he *would* do anything. If they were malicious, however, and made things worse . . . His hands clenched.

They'd ordered Aeron to kill four innocent women; they could not be good. Damn this! How should he now interact with this being? Humbly? Or would that be seen as weakness?

Anything? the voice insisted. There was a disembodied laugh. *Think carefully before you answer, and know that your woman could very well die.*

Maddox glanced at Ashlyn's trembling body, her pain-contorted features, and remembered the way she'd been. The way she'd looked at him with ecstasy and asked him to savor the silence with her. The way she'd stood in front of him and thanked him for food. The way she'd leapt to guard him from his own friends.

Until then — now — no one had needed him. That she did brought a heady rush and deepened his awareness of her. *I cannot let her suffer like this,* he thought.

He would have to take a chance on the Titans. Whatever they truly wanted from the warriors here, whatever their purpose, and whether or not they were indeed using the Hunters and Ashlyn to punish him for his lack of respect, he would take a chance.

He suppressed a curse, suspecting *he* was going to suffer as he'd never suffered before. But that didn't change his answer. "Anything."

Reyes was panting as he raced toward Lucien's room. He had lost a lot of blood these past few days. More so than usual. But then, the need for pain, that terrible, beautiful pain, had ridden him harder than ever lately.

He did not know why and could not stop it. He could no longer control it, really. The last few days, he had stopped trying. What the spirit of Pain wanted, the spirit of Pain received. Now, with every day that passed, he lost a little more of his desire *to* control it. A part of him wanted to embrace it, to finally lose himself. To experience the numb nothingness every flicker of suffering brought.

That was not the way it had always been. For a time, he had learned to live with the demon, to coexist somewhat peacefully. Now . . .

He rounded a corner, mottled shards of light seeping through the side window and blurring his vision. He didn't slow. He'd never seen Maddox so torn and frightened. So vulnerable. And over a human, a stranger. Bait. Reyes did not like it, but he counted Maddox as a friend and would help in whatever way he could.

He would help even though he desperately wanted things back to normal, where Maddox raged and died at night, then acted as if he hadn't a care the next morning. Because when Maddox pretended that everything was all right, it was easier for Reyes to pretend, too.

Those thoughts skidded to a halt as Lucien came into view.

He was seated on the floor, knees bent and head resting in his upraised hands. His halo of dark hair was in spikes, as if he'd tangled his fingers through it too many times to count. He appeared dejected, pushed past his limits. Reyes swallowed a hard lump.

If the situation could rock the normally stoic Lucien . . .

The closer he came, the more the scent of roses thickened the air. Death always smelled like flowers, poor bastard. "Lucien," he called.

Lucien gave no reaction.

"Lucien."

Again, no response.

Reyes reached him, leaned down and cupped his shoulder, then gave a shake. Nothing. He crouched and waved a hand in front of the warrior's eyes. Nothing. Lucien's gaze was vacant, his mouth immobile. Understanding dawned. Rather than physically leaving the fortress as he usually did, flashing from one location to another in seconds, Lucien had left spiritually.

That was something he rarely did, because it left his body vulnerable to attack. Most likely he'd wanted something, even an unresponsive form, guarding his bedroom door while he was out collecting souls.

I'm on my own, then. Only one thing left to try.

Standing, Reyes gripped the doorknob to his friend's room, unlocked it and burst inside.

All four women were seated on the bed, heads bent together, whispering, but they lapsed into silence the moment they spotted him. Each of them paled. One of them gasped. The youngest, a pretty little blonde, stood to obviously shaky legs and assumed a warrior stance meant to block him from her family. She raised her chin, eyes daring

201

him to approach.

His body hardened. His body hardened *every* time she was near him. Last night, he'd even smelled her. Sweet powder and thunderstorms. He'd spent hours sweating, panting and so aroused he'd considered fighting Maddox for Ashlyn, thinking it was she who had reduced him to such a state.

This woman was pleasure and heaven, a feast to his castigated senses. There were no scars on her, no signs of hard living. Only flawless, sun-kissed skin and bright green eyes. Only a full red mouth made for laughing — and kissing.

If she'd known a single moment of pain, it didn't show. And that drew him. Even though he knew better. His relationships could only ever end badly.

"Don't look at me like that," the little blond angel snapped, hands balling at her sides.

Planning to strike him? A laughable concept, that. She had no way of knowing he would enjoy it. That he would want more and more and more, until he was begging her to strike him again. *I would do the world a favor if I let the Hunters chop off my head.*

Gods, he hated himself. Hated what he was and what he was forced to do. What he now craved.

"If you've come to rape us, you should know that we'll fight you. We won't be taken easily." She raised her chin another notch and squared her shoulders.

Such courage from one so small amazed him, but he could not be sidetracked from his current task. "Do any of you know how to heal a human?"

She blinked at him, losing a little of her bravado. "Human?"

"A female. Like you."

She blinked again. "Why?"

"Do you?" he insisted, not bothering to answer her. "We haven't much time."

"Why?" she repeated.

Reyes stalked toward her, savagery in every step. To her credit, she did not back down. The closer he came, the more her scent filled his nostrils, heady, alluring. Like the girl herself. Unexpectedly, his anger lessened. "Answer me, and I might let you live another day."

"Danika. Answer him. Please." The oldest of the women reached out a trembling, wrinkled hand and latched onto the girl's arm, trying to tug her back to the bed, away from him.

Danika. The name rolled through his mind. Rolled over his tongue, too, he realized, speaking it aloud before he could stop himself. "Danika." His cock jerked in response. "Pretty. I am called Reyes."

The girl resisted the old woman, shaking off her hold. She continued to face Reyes. Her eyebrows and lashes were as pale as the hair on her head. She would be pale between her legs, he suspected.

He couldn't help himself. Despite the need to hurry, he mentally stripped her. Curve after curve greeted him, a banquet to his starved gaze. Large breasts tipped by raspberry nipples. Soft, flat belly. Soft yet strong thighs.

Reyes no longer allowed himself to bed humans, choosing to take care of himself when the need arose. His passions were too dark, too painful for most women to endure. This one, with her softness and her aura of innocence, would be more hurt and disgusted than most. There was no doubt in his mind. Worse, the women he slept with became drunk on his demon, seeking and inflicting pain as intently as he did.

Even if all he wanted from Danika was a kiss, she would not be able to handle it. *He* might not be able to handle it. The thought of bruising her, of making her bleed, of ruining her, left a hollow ache inside his chest.

"I will ask one more time. Are any of you

healers?" he barked, suddenly eager to escape Danika and her taunting innocence.

She blanched at his harshness, but still did not retreat. "If — if I *am* a healer, will you swear to spare my mother, sister and grandmother? They haven't done anything wrong. We came to Budapest to get away, to say goodbye to my grandpa. We —"

He held up a hand and she fell silent. Hearing about her life was dangerous; already he wanted to wrap her in his arms and comfort her for a loss that had obviously shaken her. "Yes, I will spare your lives if you save her," he lied.

If the Titans could be believed, Aeron would soon break, becoming crazed for blood and death. He would exist for no other purpose than killing these women. Giving them a little peace of mind during their final days was merciful, Reyes rationalized. Final days. He didn't like the reminder.

Danika's shoulders relaxed slightly, and she cast a determined glance at her family. Each woman was shaking her head no. Danika nodded.

Reyes frowned, not understanding the byplay between them. Did she, too, lie? Finally, Danika turned back to him. He forgot his confusion as their gazes locked. Or he simply didn't care about the answer.

Her angelic beauty was more enthralling than Pandora's box, promising absolution it couldn't possibly deliver. And yet, a part of him wished that it could. Just for a moment.

She closed her eyes, released a long, heavy breath and said, "Yes. I'm a healer."

"Come with me, then." He didn't take Danika's hand, too afraid of what would happen if he touched her. *Afraid of a mere human? Coward.* No, smart. If he did not know what she felt like, he could not miss the sensation when she was dead.

What if Lucien thought of a way to save her? What if —

"Come." Refusing to waste any more time, Reyes pivoted and strode from the room, forcing Danika to follow. He locked the other women inside, then sprang into motion, trying to maintain a healthy distance between himself and the angel.

Ohmygod, ohmygod, ohmygod, Danika Ford chanted in her mind. Her heart was trying to fight its way out of her chest, banging on her ribs as if they were a door with frozen hinges. *Why did I do this? I'm not a healer.*

She'd taken an anatomy class in college, yeah. She'd taken a CPR class in case Grandpa had a heart attack in front of her, sure. But she wasn't a nurse or a doctor.

She was just a struggling artist who'd thought a vacation would help heal the grief and sorrow brought on by her grandfather's death.

What was she going to do if this hard, steely-eyed soldier — clearly that's what he was, a soldier — wanted her to perform surgery of some sort? She wouldn't do it, of course. She couldn't put someone's life in jeopardy like that. But anything else . . . maybe. Probably. She had to save her family. It was *their* lives in jeopardy now.

Ohmygod. Trying to find a measure of tranquility, she studied her captor's back as he paced in front of her. He had tanned skin and black-as-midnight eyes. He was tall with the widest shoulders she'd ever beheld. She'd seen him once before, and he hadn't smiled then, either. There'd been pain in his eyes, then and now. There'd been fresh cuts on his arms, then and now.

Ohmygod, ohmygod. She didn't even think about running away from him. He'd only catch her, and then he'd be pissed. Maybe attack. And that was scarier than braving a haunted house at Halloween with chain-saws, coffins and all. Alone.

Ohmygod, ohmygod, ohmygod. She wanted to talk to him, to ask him what would be expected of her, but she couldn't find her voice. There was a baseball-sized lump in her throat, preventing speech. She didn't know why she'd been kidnapped, nearly didn't care anymore. She just wanted to leave this drafty, creepy castle with its freaky, overly muscled owners and fly home to the safety of her apartment in New Mexico.

Suddenly stabbed by a sense of desolation and homesickness, she almost sobbed. Would this soldier keep his word if she helped? She doubted it, but hope was a silly thing. She'd do her best, no matter what, and she'd pray for a miracle.

Too bad she couldn't convince herself a miracle would happen. *You'll probably get knifed by the big brute if anything goes wrong.*

Ohmygod, ohmygod, ohmygod. If she failed, there was no question in her mind that she and her family would die — very soon.

CHAPTER NINE

When Reyes strode into Maddox's bedroom with the angelic-looking blonde Aeron was supposed to kill in tow, Maddox almost wept with relief. Ashlyn had vomited over and over again, until there was nothing left in her stomach. And then she had vomited some more.

Afterward she'd fallen back onto the mattress and stopped breathing. Desperate, Maddox had hailed the Titan again, but the god had done nothing whatsoever. Once Maddox had agreed to repay him for any aid rendered, the all-powerful entity had abandoned him.

The Titan had raised his hopes and then dashed them completely. Maddox had wondered at the being's intentions, and now he knew: utter cruelty, sadistic amusement.

Reyes stepped out of the way and the little blonde rushed forward.

"Help her," Maddox commanded.

"Ohmygod, ohmygod, ohmygod," she chanted. She paled as she knelt at the side of the bed. She was trembling, but gave Maddox an accusing glare. "What did you do to her?"

Guilt intensifying, Maddox tightened his hold on the fragile, sick, *dying* Ashlyn. He barely knew the woman, but he wanted her to live more than he wanted to avoid hell's hottest flames. It was too sudden to feel this strongly, yes. It was completely out of character, yes. That, too. He could ponder his foolishness later.

"She's not breathing," he rasped. "Make her breathe."

The blonde's attention returned to Ashlyn. "She needs a hospital. Someone call 911. Now! Wait, crap. Do you have emergency service here? Do you even have phones? If so, we need to call immediately!"

"No time," Maddox snapped. "*You* must do something."

"Just call. She's —"

"Do something or die!" he roared.

"Oh God." Absolute panic filled her eyes. "I need — I need to do CPR. Yes, that's right. CPR. I can do it. I can," she said, more to herself than anyone else. She jackknifed to a stand and leaned down, hovering directly over Ashlyn's lifeless face. "Lay her flat and then get out of my way."

Maddox did not even think of protesting. He rolled Ashlyn to her back and hopped onto the floor, crouching beside the bed. He refused to release her hand, however, retaining a tight clasp. The girl stood there for a moment, unmoving, panic still lighting her eyes.

"Danika," Reyes said, a warning.

The girl — Danika — swallowed and flicked Reyes a nervous glance. The warrior's dark eyebrows winged into his hair as he stared at her and asked, "Are you sure you know what you're doing?"

"Of — of course." Rosy color seeped into her cheeks as she once again returned her attention to Ashlyn. Flattening her palms just below Ashlyn's breasts, she pushed once, twice, and said shakily, "Don't worry. I've practiced. A dummy is the same as a human, a dummy is the same as a human." Then she meshed her parted lips over Ashlyn's.

For the next several minutes, surely an eternity that was worse than the hours Maddox spent burning each night, she alternated between pumping on Ashlyn's chest and blowing air into her mouth. He'd never felt so helpless. Time became an enemy more hated than ever.

Reyes waited by the door, still and silent. His arms were crossed over his chest. He wasn't watching Ashlyn, but Danika, his expression shuttered. Maddox rubbed the back of his neck with his free hand, his own breathing so labored he could hear every exhalation echoing in his mind.

Finally, blessedly, Ashlyn coughed and sputtered. Her entire body spasmed as she opened her mouth and struggled to suck life into her lungs. In — she gasped, choked. Out — she gagged.

Maddox gathered her to his chest in the next instant. She struggled against him. "Hold still, beauty. Hold still."

Gradually her movements ceased. "Maddox," she rasped, and it was the sweetest sound he'd ever heard.

"I'm here." Her skin was still cold, still clammy. "I've got you."

Danika remained at the side of the bed, wringing her hands. White teeth bit down on her bottom lip, drawing a bead of blood. "She *needs* a hospital. Doctors, medicine."

"The journey from fortress to city would be too much for her."

"Wh-what's wrong with her? A virus? Oh God! I put my mouth on hers."

"Wine," Reyes answered. "She is sick from our wine."

Her green eyes widened and she flicked Ashlyn a glance. "All this from a hangover? You should have told me. She needs water and coffee to dilute the alcohol." She paused. "For what it's worth, I hope — *think* she'll live, but you really should take her to a hospital and get her on an IV. She's probably dehydrated." Even as she spoke, shades of color trickled back into Ashlyn's cheeks.

"Hurt," Ashlyn whispered. Her hands clutched at Maddox's back, drawing him closer. Perhaps she felt as he did, that they could not be close enough. He would have burrowed under her skin if possible.

"What else can you do for her?" Maddox demanded of Danika. "She is still in pain."

"I — I —" Danika pursed her mouth and glanced away from him, her gaze locking on Reyes. The warrior looked suspicious. Her eyes widened, and she snapped her fingers again. "Tylenol! Motrin. Something like that. That always helped my hangovers."

Maddox glanced to Reyes. "I've seen a commercial for such things, I think, but don't know where to obtain them. Do you?"

"No. There's never been a reason to pay attention to human medicines." Reyes didn't remove his eyes from the blonde; his voice sounded scratchy for some reason.

Paris would have known, but Paris was

not here. "Where can we get this Tylenol?" Maddox asked the girl, urgency consuming him.

Danika's brows puckered in an imitation of Reyes as she glanced between the two men. There was an odd gleam in her lovely green eyes, as if he and Reyes had been speaking a foreign language and she could not grasp the specifics. "I have some in my purse," she finally said.

When she failed to elaborate, he gritted out, "Go fetch your purse, then."

"Unless you free me, I can't. It's in my hotel room. What — what kind of wine did she drink?" she asked with barely a pause.

"One you have never heard of, *healer,*" Reyes said softly.

He knew, Danika realized, suddenly petrified. What had given her away? Her panicked plea to call 911? Her nervousness? A shudder rocked her. Cold infused her blood. Then he stepped behind her, crowding her with his heat, his vibrant energy chasing away the chill. Her shudder became a shiver. She hastily moved away from him, afraid of her reaction to him.

"You *are* a healer, aren't you?" he asked, his voice a mocking curse.

Oh, yes. He knew. She twisted the material of her pants and swallowed audibly. At

214

least he didn't rat her out — or slay her on the spot.

She gulped. "You can't deny she's breathing now. I did my part. You owe me."

Reyes looked away from her, as if he couldn't stand the sight of her another moment.

"Get Lucien," Maddox said.

"Can't. He is otherwise occupied." Reyes stalked toward the open door. "I'll be back," he called over his shoulder. "Watch the blonde, Maddox. She's wily." With a jerk, he slammed the door shut behind him.

Like an idiot, Danika nearly ran after him. He scared her more than any of the others, but for some reason she'd rather be with him. There was something about him that affected her. Deeply. The pain in his eyes, maybe. The fine lines of stress etched in his face, perhaps. He called to her on a primitive level. A level that claimed he'd keep her safe, no matter what threats he uttered.

"If I have to chase you," the one named Maddox said, "you will regret it. Understand?"

The blunt warning shoved the lingering heat from her skin. This man was completely terrifying. Every time he spoke, she heard a trace of brutality in his voice, as if it were infused in the undercurrents. As if he couldn't wait to inflict maximum pain on anyone who even glanced in his direction. She'd noticed in the past few minutes that his face sometimes mutated, a skeletal mask falling over his features. His violet eyes had flickered to black, then neon red, then black again.

What kind of man — what kind of *human* — could look like that?

A quake traveled from the top of her head to the bottom of her feet. As a child, she'd feared the boogeyman until her mother had told her the creature was a myth, a lie meant to keep children obedient. Danika thought perhaps she was staring at the boogeyman right now.

Only when he gazed at the woman on the bed did he appear normal.

"Understand?" he demanded again.

"Yes." She punctuated the word with a cooperative nod.

"Good." Promptly dismissing the girl from his thoughts, Maddox turned back to Ashlyn. Her trembling had escalated into wracking tremors. Her teeth chattered. Her eyes were open and a lone tear slid down her pale cheek.

"Thank you," she whispered to the healer.

"You're welcome."

"Feel better?" he asked softly.

"Still hurt," she said. "Cold. But yes. Better."

Willing his own heat into her body, he said, "I'm sorry." He rarely uttered those words. In fact, the only apology he'd made in decades was the one he'd offered his friends this morning. "I'm sorry. I'm sorry." He couldn't say it enough. "I'm so sorry."

She shook her head, then moaned and lay still. "Accident."

His mouth fell open in surprise and reverence. So far he'd caused this human nothing but pain, yet here she was, trying to absolve him. Astonishing. "You're going to live. I swear it." Whatever he had to do to keep his vow, he'd do it.

Ashlyn smiled faintly. "At least . . . silence."

Silence. That wasn't the first time she'd used that word. Nor was it the first time she'd said it with such awe. "I do not understand."

Despite her weakened condition, she managed another of those frail, sweet smiles. "Makes two of us."

Fireworks sparked in his bloodstream — that smile, so radiant, so lovely — warming him, arousing him, filling him with so much relief he was almost drunk with it. He opened his mouth to respond, not that he knew what to say, when Reyes sailed into the room, Aeron at his side. The other man's short hair gleamed in the light.

Seeing them, Danika retreated to the wall, realized what she'd done and stepped forward again. She raised her chin again, reminding Maddox of Ashlyn in healthier moments.

He had assumed Reyes had left the fortress and traveled into the city for Danika's purse, but Reyes's hands were empty. Anger slithered through Maddox, provoking Violence as a child would a beast in a cage, running a stick over the bars.

A frown pulled at his lips. He'd hoped to see the last of the wretched demon today — at least until midnight arrived.

"Why are you still here? Go get that purse," he commanded. Words he had never thought he'd say.

"I'll take too long," Reyes said, looking anywhere but at Danika. "Aeron is going to escort the female into town. He says he's fine right now, that he has no desire to hurt her."

"Oh, no. No, no, no. I don't want to leave without my family," Danika rushed out on a panicked breath.

Aeron ignored her and pulled his shirt off over his head. "Let's get this done." He was tanned and muscled, a testament to his warrior's soul. He sported so many tattoos it was hard to distinguish one from the other.

Maddox only recognized two: the black butterfly that flew along the waves of his ribs and the demon that stretched ugly wings over the contours of his neck. Just looking at him, anyone could tell he was a good man to have at your side and a bad one to have at your throat.

"Stop. There's no reason to undress." Danika shook her head violently. "Put your shirt back on. Right now, damn it!"

Grim determination emanated from Aeron as he approached her.

Danika locked her wild gaze on Reyes. "Don't let him rape me. Please. Reyes, please."

"He's not going to touch you that way," Reyes gnashed out. "You have my word."

There was something very odd about him, Maddox noted. His black eyes were edged with scarlet, a color-match to the scarlet butterfly tattooed on Maddox's back. Pain, it seemed, was working himself into a fit of violence. Over Danika?

The girl wasn't pacified by his words, but Aeron continued his approach anyway. Danika scrambled from one side of the room to the other, strange noises emerging from her throat. Small, raspy pants, as desperate and feral as Reyes's suddenly quickened breathing. Maddox felt certain that at any moment, Pain was going to leap at Wrath and attempt to claw it to death.

"Stop," Ashlyn said.

Finally Aeron trapped the frantic woman in a corner.

She screamed as her arms and legs lashed out, trying to keep him at a distance. "Don't touch me. Don't you dare touch me!"

"I'm not going to hurt you," Aeron said calmly.

She kneed the sensitive flesh between his legs. He gasped, hunched a little, but gave no other reaction.

"Fuck you," she snarled, a wildcat that wouldn't be tamed. "I won't let you rape me. I'll die first."

"No rape. But if I must, I *will* knock you out. And you won't like my methods, that I promise you."

Far from subduing her, the threat merely enraged her further. She fought harder, slamming her elbow into Aeron's stomach, kicking him in the groin a second time. Obviously growing weary of her struggles, Aeron raised his fist.

Ashlyn stiffened, moaned. "Stop this. I don't need the pills. I don't."

"Do not hurt her," Reyes growled.

Aeron didn't strike. Yet. He ran his tongue over his teeth. "She made her choice."

If he hit her and Ashlyn witnessed it, Maddox feared she would want to leave again, would once again insist he take her home. "Calm down," he told Danika. "He only needs to accompany you into town."

"Liar!" Snarling, she used her leg to boot Aeron in the stomach.

The warrior didn't budge. Disgust fell over his features, and he tightened the fist he still held in midair. "I warned you."

"Stop," Ashlyn called hoarsely.

Maddox opened his mouth to utter his own command. He needn't have bothered. Reyes beat him to it. One second Reyes was on the far side of the room, the next he was at Aeron's side, gripping the man's wrist. The two glared at each other for a long, silent moment.

"No hitting," Reyes said, and Maddox had never heard a more lethal tone.

A battle raged in Aeron's eyes before he lowered his arm. Had he lied? Was the gods' decree already taking root? Was he fighting the need to hurt Danika? "Calm her down, then, or I *will* knock her out."

Reyes didn't move, just shifted the direction of his gaze. Tears poured from Danika's eyes, making the terror banked there glisten.

"Don't let him do this," she whispered in that same broken tone Ashlyn had used. "I helped you, just like you wanted. Don't let him do this," she repeated.

As quickly as Reyes had leapt to her defense, Maddox half expected him to give in to her plea. He was mistaken.

"Stop fighting him," Reyes commanded, showing no mercy. "We need that medicine, and he is the only one who can take you to get it. You won't even scratch him because you can't afford to anger him. We clear?"

A look of betrayal passed over her face. "Why can't he go into town alone? Why can't he buy the pills at the nearest drugstore?"

"Maddox," Ashlyn said. "I'm better. Swear. I don't —"

He squeezed her shoulder gently, but did not reply. Interrupting the trio would only increase the tension. Besides, he knew Ashlyn was lying. Pain still lingered in her eyes, glowing brightly.

"Aeron is taking you into the city," Reyes continued. "He will not rape you. You have my word." A muscle ticked below his left eye. "He would not know what to buy on his own — you must go."

Silent, shaking, Danika studied his face through the watery shield of her lashes. Searching for truth? Or for comfort? Finally she nodded, a single, nearly imperceptible incline of her head. She straightened and took a wobbly step toward Aeron.

Without a word, Aeron grabbed her wrist and stalked to the room's only window. Its arching glass led onto a wide terrace. Danika did not protest, even as he unlatched the pane with his free hand, the glue Maddox had used earlier nothing to his superior strength. Cold air instantly blustered inside, virginal snowflakes swirling through the room. He released her wrist only to grip her waist and lift her onto the window ledge.

"Stop him," Ashlyn rasped as Danika peeked over the rail and laughed bitterly, a little hysterically.

"What are you going to do?" the blonde demanded. "Throw me? You're all liars, you know that? I hope every single one of you rots in hell."

"We already are," Reyes said flatly.

Aeron gripped Danika's shoulders as he joined her, then spun her so that she faced him. "Hold on to me."

Another bitter laugh. "Why?"

"So you'll live." Large wings suddenly sprang from hidden slits in his back. They were long and black and looked as soft as gossamer, but the ends were pointed, sharp as knives.

Ashlyn gasped in shock. "I'm better. I swear I'm better."

Maddox stroked her cheek, hoping to relax her. "Shh. Everything will be fine."

Danika's eyes widened unnaturally. "Stop!" She tried to wrench herself from Aeron's grip, tried to race back inside the room, but he held tight. She reached for Reyes. "I can't do this. I can't! Don't let him take me, Reyes. Please!"

Expression tormented, Reyes stepped toward her . . . stretched out his arms . . . scowled . . . dropped them to his sides.

"Reyes!"

"Go!" Reyes shouted.

Without another word, Aeron jumped, falling from view and taking Danika with him. She screamed, but that scream soon became a gasp, the gasp a moan. Then the two came into view again, soaring through the air, Aeron's wings flapping gracefully, rhythmically.

"Stop him," Ashlyn breathed. "Please."

"I can't. I wouldn't even if I could. Do not worry for her. The wings of Wrath are strong, well able to hold Danika's slight weight." He searched the room for Reyes, who paced from one corner to another. The man was gripping a dagger by the blade rather than the hilt and blood was dripping from his white-knuckled hand onto the floor.

"We need water and coffee," Maddox told him, remembering Danika's instructions.

Reyes planted his feet and squeezed his eyelids closed, as if he fought for control. As if he teetered on the brink of a total meltdown. "I should have taken her myself, but walking would have taken too long. Did you see how frightened she was?"

"I saw." Maddox didn't know what else to say. Danika's fear was nothing to him when compared to Ashlyn's pain.

Reyes rubbed a hand over his jaw, smearing a trail of crimson on his skin. "Water? Coffee, you said?"

"Yes."

Seemingly grateful for the reprieve, Reyes strode from the room. Obviously Maddox wasn't the only one in the fortress who suddenly had woman troubles.

A short while later, Reyes returned with the desired items and set the tray on the edge of the bed. That done, he left again. Maddox doubted he'd return. Shaking his head in pity — if Reyes felt for Danika half of what Maddox felt for Ashlyn, he was destined for a world of hurt, and not the kind he craved — Maddox reached over Ashlyn and gripped the tepid glass of water. He slid one hand under her neck, tilted her head, and placed the rim of the glass at the seam of her lips with the other.

"Drink," he told her.

Stubborn, she pressed her lips together and gave a slight shake of her head.

"Drink," he insisted.

"No. It will hurt my —"

He dumped the contents into her mouth. She sputtered and coughed, but she did swallow most of it. Several droplets trickled down her chin. He tossed the empty glass onto the floor, heard a *thud.*

Ashlyn glared up at him, accusation in those amber eyes. "I said I feel better, but that doesn't mean I feel great. My stomach is still sensitive."

His mouth edged into a frown. Caring for a human was difficult, that was for sure. He did not apologize for forcing her to drink, however. What she needed, she would get. Whether she wanted it or not.

He gripped the mug of coffee, and his frown deepened when he realized it was cold. Oh, well. It would have to do. "Drink," he ordered. For whatever reason — he still wasn't ready to ponder it — she was important to him. She mattered.

She was not escaping him. Not through death or any other means.

Ashlyn gave no indication that she'd heard him and certainly no hint of her intentions. In the blink of an eye, she shot out her arm and knocked the mug out of his hand. The movement was weak, but the ceramic hit the floor and shattered, leaving a black, caffeinated river.

Twin spots of color dotted her cheeks. "No," she said, drawing out the single syllable with relish.

"That was uncalled for," he chastised, brushing moist strands of hair from her temples, savoring the feel of her silky skin.

"I don't care."

"Fine. No coffee." He stared down at her, this woman who had shaken his entire world. "Do you still wish me to let you go?" The question left his lips before he could stop it. He hadn't meant to put the request before her, since he intended to keep her by whatever means necessary, but there was a need inside him — a foolish need — to give her whatever she desired.

She looked away from him, over his shoulder, past the wall, a peculiar intensity claiming her expression. Several minutes ticked by in silence. Torturous minutes.

He fisted the pillow. "It is a yes or no question, Ashlyn."

"I don't know, okay?" she said softly. "I love the silence, and I'm beginning to like you. I'm grateful to you for taking care of me." She paused. "But . . ."

But she was still scared. "I told you that I'm immortal," he said. "And I told you that I am possessed. The only other thing you need to know is that I will protect you while you're here." Even from himself.

What a change the last hours had wrought in him. Yesterday — this morning, even — he had thought to take her body, question her, then kill her. Yet he had since done everything in his power to keep her alive. And he was no longer certain what questions he wanted to ask.

"Will you protect the other woman?" she asked. "The one who helped me?"

Unless someone figured out a way to defy the Titans, he doubted anyone could protect the healer. Not even Reyes. But he gave Ashlyn a gentle squeeze and said, "Do not give her another thought. Aeron will take care of her." That was not a lie.

Ashlyn nodded gratefully, and he experienced a twinge of guilt.

A few minutes passed in silence. He watched her, happy to note that her color

228

was returning steadily now and the glaze of pain was fading. She watched him, too, her expression unreadable.

"How are demons able to do good deeds?" she eventually asked. "I mean, besides what you've done for me, you've done great things for the town with your donations and philanthropy. The people believe angels live here. They've believed it for hundreds of years."

"How can you know that they've believed such a thing for so long?"

A tremor swept through her and she looked away. "I — I just do."

No, she had a secret, something she didn't want him to know. He cradled her jaw and forced her eyes back to him. "I already suspect you are Bait, Ashlyn. You can tell me the truth."

Her brow puckered, those dark, golden slashes drawing together. "You keep calling me that like it's something foul and disgusting, but I have no idea what bait is."

There was genuine confusion in her voice. Innocent or actress? "I'm not going to kill you, but I expect total honesty from you from this moment forward. Understand? You will not lie to me."

Frowning, she said, "I'm not lying."

Slowly his blood began to heat, the spirit

once again making its presence known. He hurried to change the subject. Hearing more lies might cause him to snap, to hurt. Bait or not, he refused to let it come to that. "Let us talk of something else."

She nodded, appearing eager to comply. "Let's talk about you. Those men stabbed you last night, and you died. I realize you came back to life because you're an immortal demon warrior . . . thing. What I don't know is why they did it."

"You have your secrets, and I have mine." He planned on keeping her here and keeping her alive, and because of that, he wouldn't discuss his death-curse. She already feared him. If she knew the truth, she would despise him, too. Bad enough *he* knew what he had done to deserve such punishment.

More than that, if word spread of what happened to him every night, people might forget his reputation as an angel. Someone could snatch his body, cart him away, set him on fire or cut off his head and there was nothing he could do about it. He might desire this woman more than he'd ever desired another, but he didn't trust her. Some of his brain, at least, was still in his head and not in his cock.

"Did you ask them to kill you so you

could go back to hell to visit your friends down there or something?"

"I have no friends in hell," he said, insulted.

"So —"

"So nothing." She opened her mouth to speak, but he squeezed her side. "It is my turn to ask the questions. You are not Hungarian. Where, then, are you from?"

She settled into his side with a sigh, curling her body around his, back to stomach. That she was comfortable enough to willingly lie with him like this delighted him. "I'm from the States. North Carolina, to be exact, though I spend most of my time traveling with the World Institute of Parapsychology."

He flattened his hand on her belly and gently rubbed as he searched his mind for any reference to such an Institute. "And they are . . ."

"Interested in the supernatural. The unexplainable. Creatures of every kind," she answered on a contented exhale. "They study, observe and try to keep peace between the different races."

He paused. Had she just admitted to working for Hunters? Their hate-filled actions had always been carried out in the name of promoting peace for mankind. His

231

brow furrowed in confusion. An odd thing to do, and certainly a first. "What do you do for them?"

She hesitated. "I listen in order to help find the creatures and any other objects of interest." She wriggled uncomfortably against the mattress, no longer quite so content.

"What happens when you find these things?"

"I told you. They're studied."

When she did not elaborate, he stared up at the ceiling. His confusion intensified. Studied, as in killed? Was this a secret warning, her way of letting him know she did indeed work for Hunters? Did she work for them and *not* know it? Or was this Institute harmless and truly aiming for peace between the species? "Do the people you work with have tattoos on their wrists? A symbol of infinity?"

She shook her head. "No, not that I know of."

Truth? A lie? He didn't know her well enough to gauge. Every fanatical Hunter that had attacked the Lords in Greece — and even those in the forest surrounding the fortress yesterday — had been branded with a tattoo. "You said that you listen. What exactly do you listen to?"

Another hesitant pause. "Conversations," she whispered. "Look, I thought I could talk about this, thought I *wanted* to talk about it, but I'm not ready. Okay?"

Violence sniped at that, and Maddox struggled to contain the demon. What was she hiding? "It doesn't matter if you are ready to talk about it or not. You will tell me what I want to know. Now."

"No, I won't," she said, stubborn again.

"Ashlyn."

"No!"

He was very close to rolling on top of her, pinning her to the bed and forcing the answers from her. Only the knowledge that she was still sick, still weak, held him in place. But he *would* get the answer one way or another. "Beauty, I ask only because I want to know you better. Tell me *something* about your job. Please."

Slowly she relaxed. "People who work for the Institute learn to keep quiet about their jobs. Not many civilians would believe what we do. Most would just consider us crazy."

"I will not think you crazy. How can I?"

She sighed. "All right. I'll tell you about one of my assignments. Which one, which one," she muttered, then clicked her tongue. "I know! You might appreciate this. A few years ago, I — uh, *the Institute* discovered an angel. He'd broken his wings in several places. While we doctored him, he taught us about different dimensions and gateways. That's the best part about my job — with every new discovery we learn that the world is a bigger place than any of us ever realized."

Interesting. "And what does the Institute do with demons?"

"Study them, like I mentioned. Step in and prevent them from hurting humans if needed."

Part of what she described meshed with the goals of the Hunters he had dealt with all those years ago, not to mention those he'd dealt with yesterday. The rest, well, didn't. "Your people do not believe in destroying that which they do not understand?"

She laughed. "No."

Hunters did. Or had. At least, he thought so. So many years had passed since he had fought in that war that he sometimes had trouble remembering certain details. At one time, he knew he had understood why the Hunters wanted him and the others dead: they had done evil things, their abilities giving them the strength and longevity to do so forever if not stopped. But then the Hunters had killed Baden and his understanding had evaporated, for the demise of Distrust had divided the warriors. Half had craved peace, absolution and refuge, quietly relocating to Budapest. The others had sought revenge and remained in Greece to continue the fight.

He'd often wondered if the blood feud still raged and if the Lords who had stayed in Greece had survived these many centuries.

Maddox brushed a strand of hair from Ashlyn's temple. "What else can you tell me of this Institute?"

Frowning, she turned her head and stared up at him. "I can't believe I'm admitting this, but I think they plan to study you next."

Now that did not surprise him. Whatever this Institute was, objective or war-hungry, they would be interested in the demons. But with Torin's sensors and cameras, they would never make it up the hill — and those that dared try would, in fact, be treated as Hunters, whether they were or not.

"They can *try* to study us, but they will not find it easy to do so," he told Ashlyn. With her so near to him, her scent in his nose, he was catapulted deeper and deeper into sexual awareness. With every second that passed, he hardened a little more. She was soft and sweet. She was alive, feeling better with every second that passed. And she was his.

Suddenly he found himself eager to forget the Institute, not learn more about it. "I want you," he admitted. "Very badly."

Her lovely eyes widened. "You do?" she squeaked.

"You are beautiful. All men must want you." He said the words and immediately scowled. If another man tried to touch her, that other man would die. Painfully, slowly.

Violence purred in agreement.

Ashlyn's cheeks colored again, reminding him of the roses he sometimes spied growing beside the fortress. She shook her head. "I'm too weird."

The flat assurance in her tone caused him to frown. "How so?"

She looked away, saying, "Never mind. Forget I said anything."

"I can't." He traced his thumb along her jaw.

A shiver traveled the length of her body, followed quickly by goose bumps. She squirmed against him. Arousal suddenly scented the air, and his nostrils flared as he drank it in. "You want me, too," he said on a low, gravelly rumble of satisfaction, forgetting his question and her refusal to answer.

"I — I —"

"Cannot deny it," he finished for her. "So now I will ask again. Do you still wish me to take you home?"

She gulped. "I thought I did. Only a few hours ago, I thought I was desperate to escape. But . . . I can't even explain it to myself, but I want to stay here. I want to stay with you. For now, at least."

His satisfaction increased, swimming through him, potent, intense. Whether she answered as Bait or simply as woman, at the moment he did not care. *I'll have her yet.*

We'll have her, Violence corrected, frightening Maddox with the fervor of its tone. *We will have her.*

CHAPTER TEN

When Aeron and Danika returned to the fortress, flying through the window and landing on the floor of Maddox's bedroom with a gentle tap, Ashlyn experienced a kick of amazement. So. She hadn't imagined it. The man really did have shiny black wings.

You wanted to meet others like you, Darrow. Well, guess what. You got your wish.

Immortal, Maddox had told her. Possessed. She'd suspected demons, so it didn't really surprise her that that's what they were. But wings? While trekking the hill, she'd heard about a man who could fly. She hadn't given the words much thought; she'd been too busy trying to block out the voices. *Should have known better.* Did that also mean one of the men could sift into the spirit world? One could mesmerize with a look?

She sighed. Maddox *had* mesmerized her with only a look. She'd been ensnared by him since the first, her constant lust as uncharacteristic as her rash decision to stay here.

"Here's the Tylenol," Danika said, her voice shaky. "Well, the generic version." Her skin was tinted green, and she swayed on her feet. She dug into an emerald bag and withdrew a red-and-white bottle.

Beside her, Aeron straightened his shoulders. His wings snapped closed, rolling behind his back, then disappearing altogether. He bent down, grabbed his shirt from the floor and tugged it over his head, covering the menacing tattoos that decorated his torso. He strode to the window and shut it before turning to Danika, arms crossed over his massive chest. He stood there, silent, observing.

"Thank you," Ashlyn said. "I'm just sorry you had to go to such trouble to get them."

Silent, Danika handed her two pills, which she gratefully accepted. Little aches and twinges still bothered her, and her stomach still fought a determined battle with nausea, though nothing like before.

Maddox swiped the pills from her hand before she could toss them into her mouth. He studied them and frowned. "Are they magic?" he asked with genuine curiosity.

"No," she said.

"How, then, will two small pebbles help take away pain?"

Ashlyn and Danika shared a confused look. The men would have had to interact with humans over the years. How could they know nothing of contemporary medicine?

The only explanation Ashlyn could think of was that they'd never paid attention to a sick human before. Besides, only one of the men, Paris, had been seen in the city with any sort of frequency. She remembered that much from the voices.

Did Maddox keep himself locked away in this castle, then? Ashlyn suddenly suspected he did, and that made her wonder . . . did he ever feel forgotten? Untouched, unloved? Except for the kindness she'd known from McIntosh, she constantly felt that way herself at the Institute, where she was only as good as her ability. *What do you hear, Ashlyn? Was nothing else said, Ashlyn? Did they elaborate, Ashlyn?*

Ashlyn realized she wanted to understand Maddox. She wanted to learn about him, comfort him as he'd comforted her. Maddox couldn't know it, and she wouldn't tell him, but every time he rubbed her stomach and uttered those sweet words of reassurance in her ear, she fell a little in love with him. Foolish and wrong, but unstoppable.

She should tell him about her own ability, but she'd decided against it the moment he'd shown such angry interest. She'd wondered: If Maddox was already angry without knowing the extent of her abilities, would he freak if he knew the truth?

Most of the people at the Institute had been uncomfortable around her, knowing she could divine their most private discussions simply by stepping into a room. Since she'd decided to stay here, weird place though it was, she didn't want to deal with that discomfort. For once, she wanted to be thought of as the normal one. Just for a little while.

Around demons, that shouldn't be too difficult.

She'd spill the truth soon enough. In a few days, perhaps. And maybe then she could learn to keep the voices at bay, even when Maddox wasn't around. Meanwhile, she'd have to find a way to call McIntosh. He deserved to know what had happened to her and that she was okay. She didn't want him to worry.

Hopefully, he was studying the fortress as she suspected and would see that she was happy. Hopefully, her happiness came before her job in his eyes.

"Take them," Maddox said, pushing into her thoughts. He placed the pills in her open palm. "If they make her worse," he added, looking sternly at Danika, "I cannot be held responsible for my actions."

"Don't threaten her," Ashlyn said with a shake of her head. "I've taken this type of drug before. I'll be fine."

"She —"

"Hasn't done anything wrong." Ashlyn wasn't sure where she acquired the bravery. She only knew it was there, unwilling to let Maddox bluster and intimidate.

He wouldn't hurt her, she knew that now — a fact she still had trouble grasping. Beyond the miracle of making the voices stop, this harsh man had tenderly seen to her needs. He hadn't bolted when she'd vomited, as most would have done. He'd stayed with her, caring for her, holding her close, as if she were precious.

As wonderfully as he might have treated her, however, Ashlyn didn't know what he was capable of doing to someone else. She knew what he *looked* capable of doing: any dark deed, every evil deed. But there was no way she'd let him hurt Danika, who had also helped her.

"Ashlyn," he said on a sigh.

"Maddox."

His fingers stilled, splayed on her stomach. Thankfully, he didn't move away. She could have rested in his arms forever. Truly, no one, not even McIntosh, had ever made her feel so special.

She only vaguely remembered her parents. They hadn't coddled her like this, either. Actually, they'd been more than happy to get rid of their crying, screaming little girl. A little girl who'd constantly begged for the voices to stop, never allowing the people around her to sleep or work or relax.

She'd known the very day they'd decided to give her away, though she hadn't understood at the time. She'd walked into their bedroom and the entire conversation had unfolded in her mind.

I can't take care of her anymore. She's too much to handle. I can't eat, I can't sleep, I can't think.

We can't just abandon her, but damn it. I can't take any more, either. The crying never stops.

I want a normal life again, you know? Like before she was born. Pause. *I did some research and found a place that could help her. I . . . called them. They want to meet her. Maybe, I don't know, maybe they can give her what we can't.*

They'd sent her to Institute the day after her fifth birthday. There, she'd become known as "subject." Needles, electrodes and monitors became her daily companions, not to mention fear and loneliness and pain. The day she became "Ashlyn" in the eyes of the staff was three years later, when they learned how to use her ability to their advantage.

That was the day McIntosh had stepped into her life.

He'd been an ambitious young parapsychologist, quickly climbing the ranks thanks to his vision, drive and sheer passion for his work. He'd accompanied her to every location the voices led her to, had even stood beside her while she listened, writing down everything she uttered.

Afterward, he would research what she'd heard and tell her of the results — like the time she'd heard about a vampire intent on draining an entire town. The Institute had been able to find and stop him, and eventually study him. Times like that, she *had* felt special, gifted, like the characters he read about every night.

"Ashlyn," Maddox repeated. Their gazes locked and his eyes blazed with violet fire. "Say my name again."

"Maddox."

His eyes closed for a split second, and for that all-too-quick moment he wore an expression of utter rapture. "I like when you say it."

She liked the joy he drew from something so simple. A shiver slipped along the ridges of her spine. But in the next flash — that all-too-quick moment now passed — his countenance returned to normal. That hint of pleasure vanished from his features, as if he didn't trust himself with the emotion.

"Danika will —"

"Get me some water," Ashlyn finished for him. "For the pills."

"Yes. I'll get it." Danika picked up the empty glass from the floor. She stumbled into the bathroom. The sound of running water filled Ashlyn's ears, then Danika was standing beside her again, holding out the glass.

Once again, Maddox confiscated it. He aimed a suspicious look at Danika, then raised Ashlyn's head and held the cup to her lips. She tossed the pills onto her tongue and swallowed a mouthful of cool, refreshing liquid. Everything slid down her welcoming throat with only the slightest hint of soreness.

"Thank you," she told them.

"It's done, then. I'll escort the girl back to

Lucien," Aeron finally said, his voice so harsh it nearly rubbed her eardrums raw.

" 'The girl' has a name," Danika snapped.

"What is it? Lippy?" he muttered, grabbing her arm and tugging her from the room. Obviously, the man had no manners and no idea how to treat a woman.

If Ashlyn really decided to stay here, she'd have to fix that. "Wait!" she called.

They didn't.

"Is she going to be okay?"

There was a slight hesitation. "Yes," Maddox said.

"Good," she said, her voice echoing off the walls. That was the moment she realized she was alone with Maddox. Of course, that was also the moment she became aware of the awful taste in her mouth. God, she must look like roadkill, and smell worse. Mortification heated her cheeks. "I, uh, need to use the bathroom."

"I'll help." He scooped her up as if she were merely a bag of feathers, and stood. She wrapped her arms around his neck, his strength and warmth flooding all the way to her bones.

He carried her past the threshold and stopped in the center of the bathroom. Suspecting he meant to stay, she shook her head and fought a wave of dizziness. "I can do it on my own."

"You might fall."

She might, but there was no way she was going to let him stay with her, watching. "I'm fine."

His expression was doubtful, but he said, "Call if you need me. I'll be waiting right outside the door." He slowly inched her legs down the hard span of his body.

Her feet hit the floor and her knees almost crumpled. *I will not fall, I freaking will not fall.* She reached around Maddox and grabbed the doorknob, using it to hold herself steady. "Back up, please," she said.

He did — but he didn't go happily. When he stood outside, she shut the thick, polished wood in his face.

"Five minutes," he said.

She flipped the lock, muttering, "I'll take as long as I need."

"No, you will not. In five minutes, I'm coming in whether you're done or not. The lock means nothing."

"Stubborn."

"Concerned."

Sweet. With a half smile, she rinsed off as best she could and used one of the toothbrushes she found in the cabinet to clean her teeth. Twice she almost fell. She made use of the facilities, brushed the tangles from her hair, and decided, after studying her pale reflection in the mirror, that there was nothing more she could do for her appearance without spackle.

With one minute to spare, she unlocked the door and called for Maddox. Her voice was weak, but he threw open the wood as if she'd shouted. His expression was tense. She closed her eyes against the intensifying dizziness.

"You pushed yourself too far." He *tsked.* Once again he scooped her up. He carried her to the bed and laid her on the softness of the mattress before easing down beside her.

She peeked at him through her lashes. More than treating her with care, Maddox was the first man ever to lie on a bed with her. The first man to desire her, really.

She'd tried to date upon occasion, but the voices had bombarded her every damn time. To quiet them, she'd attempted the deep breathing and meditation she'd learned. The men had always assumed she was ignoring them, hyperventilating or having a panic attack and had wanted nothing more to do with her.

Once, she'd even gone on a date with a colleague from the Institute, thinking he would at least understand her, if not sympathize. The next day, she'd heard his whispered conversation with another coworker. *Freak,* he'd called her. *Couldn't spread her legs with a crowbar.*

After that, she'd given up dating altogether.

"Feel better?" Maddox asked. He drew her into the curve of his body, exactly where she wanted to be.

That delicious heat enveloped her and she uttered a contented sigh. She'd searched her entire life, but it had taken a possessed immortal to show her this slice of silent, lust-filled heaven on earth.

"Better?" he repeated.

"Much." She yawned. Warm, safe and clean, pain almost completely gone, she felt exhaustion settle over her, beckoning her to sleep. Her eyelids fluttered closed. She forced them open. She wasn't ready to end this reprieve with Maddox.

"We have much more to discuss," he said.

He sounded far away, and she struggled to pull herself out of the drugging lassitude weaving though her from head to toe. "I know."

If he replied, she didn't hear. She was sinking deeper and deeper. Gently, he kissed her cheek. His lips were firm but soft, and fire burned between them on contact. *Open your eyes, Darrow. Maybe he'll kiss you on the mouth.* She tried, really she did. But though the mind was willing, the body was weak.

"We will talk later," Maddox said softly. "Sleep now."

"You'll stay?" *How can I need him like this? I haven't even known him a full day.*

"Yes. Now, sleep for me."

Helpless to do otherwise, she obeyed.

"I saw them," Aeron told the others grimly. "Maddox didn't kill them all, and Paris and Reyes must have missed them when they went scouting. There are more Hunters, and they're gathered in the city even now. I think I heard one of them say the word *tonight,* but I was too high in the air to be sure."

For the second time in two days, Aeron was sitting on the couch in the entertainment room, warriors surrounding him. He rarely came here, preferring instead to seek his own entertainment outside. From the outskirts of the city and the safety of the shadows, he'd secretly watch the mortals interact and wonder why they weren't more concerned about their weaknesses.

Now, he couldn't seem to get away from this chamber.

Paris had returned and was watching

another movie. Reyes was pounding away at the punching bag, Torin was leaning against the corner at the far end of the room and Lucien was shooting pool, having barricaded his bedroom door with timber and nails to liberate himself from guard duty. Only Maddox was absent, but Aeron was glad for that.

The man was too unpredictable today, not to mention too wrapped up in his human. Aeron snorted. Not him. Never him. While he liked to study that foolish species, he had never joined them. Even the pretty blonde had not tempted him. Humans were too weak, and his demon constantly urged him to destroy them in ways that mirrored their own sins.

A rapist would lose his cock. A wife-beater would lose his hands. More and more, Aeron*liked* what he did, liked meting out his own form of vengeance. Which was why he was so close to the edge.

The girl, though . . .

When they had returned from the city, he had deposited her in Lucien's bedroom, her curves imprinted in his mind but his body completely unaffected. She did nothing for him. None of those puny humans did. They were too easily broken, too easily scared. Too easily taken from those who loved them. But he still did not want to hurt her.

"How do you know they are Hunters?" Lucien asked him. His features were strained, his wall of calm showing signs of crumbling as he nailed the eight ball into the corner pocket.

"They had guns and knives strapped to their bodies, and I saw the mark of infinity on one of their wrists." Branding themselves was foolish, if you asked him. Like putting a neon sign around their necks that read *Shoot here.*

"How many?"

"Six."

"Well, this sucks." Paris dropped his head in his hands. He wore a pair of unfastened jeans and nothing else. Aeron had spotted him in the city, pounding into a woman in a shadowy corner of a building, and had told him to finish quickly and hurry home. Promiscuity must have taken the request to heart. "Where there's six, there's six more and where there's six more and so on and so on."

"Damned Hunters," Reyes snarled, hitting the bag with more force.

Pain was in a dark mood. Darker than usual, Aeron qualified. "I do not wish to pack up and leave this time. This is our home. We have done nothing wrong." Yet.

"If they've come to fight, I say we fight them."

"They haven't challenged us." Lucien scrubbed two fingers over his jaw, a habit of his. "Why?"

"They came up the hill. That is challenge enough. And what about Maddox's girl? The Hunters could be waiting for her signal."

"She's more a complication now than ever," Torin muttered. "I still wonder what role the gods are playing in this."

Aeron plucked at the silver loop in his eyebrow. "We'll have to tell Maddox."

Torin shook his head. "It won't matter to him. You've seen the way he is with her."

"Yes." And he was still disgusted by it. What kind of warrior turned on his friends for a woman who would ultimately betray him?

Lucien laid down his cue and tossed a ball into the air. Catch. Toss. Catch. "We'll be watching and we'll let the Hunters up the hill this time. I don't want innocents killed during the battle."

Reyes gave the punching bag a mean right. "I don't want Hunters here. Not in our home. Let's parade Maddox's human around town, using *their* Bait as *our* Bait. They'll follow us, meaning to save her and attack. We'll draw them into a trap, away from the townspeople, and obliterate them."

Everyone regarded him sharply. "If we're seen," Aeron said, "the city will turn on us. It will be Greece all over again."

"They won't see," Reyes insisted. "Torin can monitor the area with his cameras and radio us to let us know the moment someone approaches."

Aeron thought about it, then nodded in approval. The Hunters would be distracted while trying to save Ashlyn, leaving the warriors to pick them off one by one. More important, Aeron wouldn't have to clean their blood from the walls.

He glanced at Lucien, who looked resigned. "Very well. We will use the girl."

Paris rubbed the back of his neck and Aeron thought he meant to protest. Surprisingly, he didn't. "I guess all we have to do now is figure out how to keep Maddox from handing us our asses when he finds out."

Danika peered at her mother, her sister and her grandmother. Their familiar faces regarded her with hope and curiosity, dread and fear. She was the youngest, but she'd somehow become their leader.

"What happened?" Her mother wrung her hands together. "What did they do to you?"

What should she tell them? Danika doubted they'd believe the truth: that she'd performed CPR, helped save a woman from dying and then found herself being flown — flown! — into the city by a winged man, where she gathered her purse, listened to Aeron as he commanded another warrior to go home — a warrior who had had a forty-ish woman pinned against a wall, screwing her brains out — and then come back here. All in about thirty minutes. And to top it all off, there was the voice that had mysteriously popped into her head earlier this morning, but she didn't even want to *think* about that.

She'd lived through all of it, and yet it was unbelievable even to her. Besides, the truth would scare them. And they were scared enough. "I think they'll let us go soon," she lied.

Grandma Mallory started crying, great sobs of relief. Ginger, Danika's older sister, collapsed on the bed with a soft "Thank God." Only her mother remained unmoving.

"Did they hurt you, baby?" Tears filled her eyes. "It's okay, you can tell me. I can take it."

"No, they didn't," she answered honestly.

"You still have to tell us what happened."

Her mom gripped her hands and squeezed. "Okay? All right? I've been going crazy, imagining all kinds of things."

Realizing they would actually worry more if she left them in the dark, she finally told them what had happened. The warriors had terrified her, yes. And the dark-eyed one had even managed to — God, she hated to admit this — awaken something inside her with that intense stare of his, causing her to plead for his help.

A plea he'd ignored, the bastard.

But she had to concede that the men had surprised her as much as they'd frightened her. After all, the black-haired man with the strange purple eyes had treated the sick woman, Ashlyn, like a treasure. He'd held her gently. He hadn't seemed bothered by the vomit in the bowl and the smell in the room. His concern had only been for Ashlyn.

Oh, to have a man treat *her* like that.

She couldn't imagine the hard-looking Reyes softening so much. Or caressing so gently, even while making love. Instantly an image of him, naked and straining, slithered into her mind. With a shiver, she forced a blanket of black over the image. She'd reached for him, begged help from him, and he'd denied her. She would not forget that

Reyes wasn't a man to rely on.

"What if these . . . *things* don't let us go?" her mom asked on a choked sob. "What if they decide to kill us like they've been talking about?"

Stay strong. Don't let them see those same fears reflected in you. "They promised to let us live if I helped cure that woman, and I did."

"Men lie all the time," her sister said, sitting up. Ginger was twenty-nine years old and an aerobics instructor. Usually calm and reserved. None of them had ever been in a situation like this, and none of them really knew how to handle it.

They'd led normal lives until now, getting up every morning and going to work, carefree and unconcerned, deceived into believing that nothing bad would happen to them. Before this, the worst thing Danika had ever dealt with was the death of her grandpa two months ago. He'd been a loving man with a zest for life, and she'd felt his loss to the marrow of her bones. They all had. *Did.*

They'd thought, hoped, vacationing here would help dull the grief and make them feel closer to a man they'd never see again. Granddad had loved it here, had constantly talked about the magical two weeks he'd spent here before marrying Grandma.

He had never mentioned a group of homicidal warriors with wings.

"We've searched the room over and over again," her grandma said. Her weathered face was more lined than usual. "The only way out is the front door or the window, and we can't open either one."

"Why do they want to hurt us?" Ginger cried. Her blue gaze was watery, her pale hair damp from her many bouts of tears. Red splotches stained her skin from forehead to chin.

None of them were pretty criers.

"They didn't say." Danika sighed. God, what a nightmare. Right before they'd been taken, she and her family had toured the castle district. She'd never seen anything so lovely as the multihued lights shining from hundreds of years of majestic architecture. She'd yearned for her paints, her canvas, wanting to capture the sights.

And that's exactly what she'd planned to do at the hotel. Paint.

But the moment she'd stepped inside her room, a man — a large, scarred man with dark hair and oddly colored eyes — had accosted her. He'd smelled of flowers, she remembered, the scent somehow comforting her even in the midst of the greatest panic attack of her life. The winged man had been there, too, only his wings had been hidden underneath a T-shirt.

How easily they'd subdued her. Shame still filled her at the thought. Four women against two men, and still the women had lost, had hardly put up a fight. They'd been knocked out and carted here, awakening in this very room.

"Maybe we should try to seduce a key from one of them," Ginger whispered to her.

The dark-skinned, black-eyed warrior immediately pushed his way into Danika's thoughts. Every time she'd seen him, he'd been bleeding. Clumsy? He hadn't seemed so, but . . . Perhaps she should have offered to "doctor" his wounds. Maybe he would have been nicer to her. Maybe he would have helped her when she'd asked.

Maybe he would have kissed her.

The thought alone excited her, damn it. "No woman should have to barter her body to escape a prison," she said, angry at herself. The image of Reyes swam before her eyes again, and she found herself adding, "But I'll think about it."

CHAPTER ELEVEN

Maddox held Ashlyn for several hours as she napped, hopefully reviving body and soul. Time was his enemy, midnight fast sneaking up on him, but he didn't wake her. Not even when he stripped her of her shoes and sweater, revealing delicate feet and a T-shirt that clung to her round breasts, his blood burning with arousal.

Lunch had long since come and gone. He was hungry, but he wanted Ashlyn more than he wanted food. Holding her . . . hearing her melodious, sleep-rumbling sighs . . . heaven.

Her breasts, smashed against his side, were unbelievably soft. One of her arms was draped over his stomach, cleaving to him in a tight embrace, as if she feared, even in sleep, that he might slip away.

More at peace than he had been in centuries, he was not surprised when his eyelids began to grow heavy and his mind began to drift.

Awaken, warrior. I have returned, a voice said in his mind. An all-too-familiar voice. Now *this* surprised him.

Maddox stiffened, eyelids springing open as fury speared him, completely chasing away the sleep-fog. Gaze sharp, he quickly searched the room. He saw no one lurking about, no suspicious shadow.

He would rather deal with an intruder, a Hunter, than this Titan who had promised to help Ashlyn and then had abandoned her. Would the being now attempt to rip her from his arms?

Where is my thanks, warrior?

He felt a slight hum of power, the air thickening, twisting. Ashlyn released a breathy sigh and he forced himself to relax. He wanted her to wake up, but not until the god was gone. If she were to anger the being, even unintentionally, she could be hurt.

"Who are you?" he whispered.

I shouldn't have to tell you, was the annoyed reply.

Maddox popped his jaw, doing his best to remain at peace. No violence, no raging. How cruel the Titan was to make him guess. "What do you want from me . . . great one?"

You promised me anything. Everything.

"I promised you anything you wanted if you saved the girl. You did not save her," he said, even as his mind screamed, *Do not provoke the god!* "We did."

And yet she is alive.

"But you did nothing." He pressed his lips together. Antagonizing a god was not wise. But he feared what he would be asked to do if he agreed with the being, knowing it would be payment for aid that had not been given.

Are you sure? The voice was silky now, daring him to contradict.

Was he sure? Danika had helped with her strange pounding on Ashlyn's chest, then by breathing life into her lungs. Reyes and Aeron, too, had done their part. Maddox had held her, cleaned her and comforted her.

What could this being have done? *Does it matter?* he thought then. "What do you want me to do?" he asked, resigned.

There was a satisfied purr. *Tell your friends to visit Kerepesi Cemetery at midnight. They are to take no weapons. They are to tell no one what they are doing. They are to come alone, and I will visit them. I will show them exactly who I am.*

"At midnight, we will be otherwise occupied."

Your death-curse. Yes, I know. Lucien and Reyes have my permission to arrive late.

"But —"

No buts. Midnight. Unarmed.

Maddox blinked. That did not make sense. Why demand the men arrive unarmed? A god could crush them no matter how many weapons were strapped to their bodies.

Will you tell them?

His eyes narrowed. Either this was not a god or the being meant to lead them into an ambush. He already thought the Titans cruel, so he would not doubt that they were capable of such an act. But either way, he was damned. If this *was* a god, Maddox would be punished, for he could not bring himself to ask his friends to approach a potentially dangerous situation weaponless. And if this *wasn't* a god, that meant someone else — some*thing* else — had the power to infiltrate his thoughts.

At his side, Ashlyn smacked her lips and rolled to her back. One hand was draped over her brow and the other was curled on her stomach. Close to waking up, he realized, but fighting it.

Will you tell them? the voice demanded again, too eager now, too uncertain.

In that moment, Maddox knew. This wasn't a god. Couldn't be. An all-powerful being could simply whisk the Lords to the cemetery. An all-powerful being wouldn't betray a single shred of doubt. He ground his teeth together.

Do not make me ask again.

"Of course I will tell them," he said, and it wasn't a lie. He would tell them — just not what the being wanted him to tell.

Until tonight, then, the voice said, practically humming with satisfaction.

Until we learn the truth. Of course, Maddox did not voice the thought aloud. When there was no response, no reaction, he grinned slowly. The being could push its words into his mind, but could not hear his thoughts. Good. Very, very good.

The current of power suddenly vanished from the air.

Probabilities spun in Maddox's mind. Perhaps the being could hear dialogue from a distance. Perhaps, like Maddox and the others, the speaker was an immortal with special abilities.

An immortal Hunter?

Careful not to disturb Ashlyn, Maddox crept from the bed and made his way through the stronghold until he found Lucien. The warrior sat on the couch in the entertainment room, alone, silent, a glass of scotch in his hand.

Maddox told his friend what had happened and Lucien paled, even his scars blanching. "Hunters. Titans. Women. Now unnamed beings with unidentified powers? When does it end?"

He ran a hand through his hair. "Every minute that ticks by, it seems something new arises." And to think, only yesterday Maddox had complained about the monotony of life.

"We have several hours, at least, to decide what to do about this. I need to think before we tell the others. Too much is happening at once, too many changes."

Maddox nodded. "You know where to find me when you need me." He returned to his room, glad for the reprieve. He wasn't ready to leave Ashlyn.

She lay exactly as he'd left her, a vision in his barren chamber. He climbed in beside her, accidentally jostling the mattress.

"Maddox," she murmured.

The single word was sleep-rich, a rumbling moan that fired his blood as surely as a caress from her delicate fingers would. With his renewed desire, Violence once again made itself known, its mood dark and hungry. Needing . . . something. Blood?

Pain? Screams? He did not know, couldn't tell. *I will control myself. I will not harm this woman.*

Ashlyn rubbed her cheek against his side and purred like a contented kitten. "Maddox?"

Violence purred in response.

He gripped the sheets, the cool material shredding under his ministrations. What was Violence trying to force him to do? Its desires were hazy. Sweat beaded over Maddox's skin. His jaw clenched so tightly he felt the tendons in his neck strain.

"Maddox?" Ashlyn repeated. This time, she sounded concerned. She eased up, those glorious honey tresses cascading down her shoulders. Rays of sunlight streamed in from the window and bathed her in a bright amber halo. Her eyes swept over him. "What's wrong?"

He couldn't answer, couldn't speak past the knot in his throat.

Concern visibly intensifying, she leaned over and reached under his shirt, running her palms over his bare chest. The touch was exhilarating, consuming. Always there was that energy between them. He'd never felt anything like it.

But the spirit liked it too, he realized. It roared; not with fury but with arousal.

More . . . The hazy needs of before built again, finally making themselves known. Pleasure and passion. Ecstasy and exquisite longing.

"How are you feeling?" Maddox asked, the lump receding. Amazing, to crave something, someone, without feeling a deeper urge to hurt.

"Better."

"I am glad." He remained in place for a long while, letting Ashlyn pet his chest and reveling in the sensations. Soft, sweet, an erotic dream he never wanted to end. He vibrated, or maybe the spirit did. *Dangerous.* He'd strip her and take her in a matter of minutes if he didn't stop her.

"Your face looks better," she said. "Not as battered."

"I heal quickly. Come." He rolled from the bed and held out one hand.

Her tawny gaze traveled from his face to his hand, then back to his face, searching for some sort of answer. "You change moods faster than anyone I've ever met," she grumbled, but she tentatively reached out, as if she couldn't stop herself. Their fingers intertwined.

Another sizzle.

She obviously felt it, as well, gasping at first contact.

Shaking with the need to claim her, he tugged her to her feet. She swayed and tightened her grip on him. "Where are we going?"

To Paradise, if he had his way. "Shower." He didn't wait for her response, but shepherded her toward the bathroom.

Surprisingly, she didn't protest. "I must look terrible." She smoothed a hand down her hair and grimaced. "Ugh. Bedhead."

"You could never look terrible."

Her cheeks flushed to a rosy pink. "Yes, I could. Just . . . I don't know. Avert your eyes until I'm clean or something."

"I've tried to keep my gaze from you. Believe me." But his eyes always sought her of their own accord, pulled by a force far greater than himself.

They reached the bathroom and he released her. An acute sense of loss filled him. *Almost time. Just a little longer.*

His back to her, he twisted the knobs in the tub. Water burst from the nozzle, cold at first, but gradually heating. Soon steam drifted through the bathroom, curling toward the ceiling, condensing, then falling like tiny drops of rain.

Steeling himself, he faced Ashlyn.

"I'm sorry about your room. I'll, uh, clean it later," she said, gazing down at her bare feet. The nails weren't polished, but the toes were charming, square-tipped.

"I'll clean it," he told her gruffly.

Her gaze snapped to his. "No. I'd rather you didn't. I'm embarrassed enough. I mean, I threw up in front of you. Several times. Maybe even on you. Anything that — oh God, this is mortifying. Anything that landed on the floor is my responsibility."

"My fault. My room. I will clean." He didn't like the image of her doing manual labor. He wanted her in bed, resting. And naked. Yes, naked. Perhaps not resting, then, but licking and biting him.

His cock jumped in response.

"Take off your clothes." His voice was huskier than he'd intended.

She blinked up at him, her lashes casting shadows over her cheeks. "Wh-what?"

"Take off your clothes."

"Right now?" she squeaked.

His brow furrowed. "Do you normally shower with them on?"

"No, but I normally shower alone."

"Not today." He felt as if he'd waited forever for this moment. Ashlyn. Naked. His to do with as he pleased, her curves begging to be explored.

"Why not today?" she asked, the words cracked and pleading.

"Because." Stubborn, he crossed his arms over his chest.

"Maddox —"

"Ashlyn. Take off your clothes. They are dirty."

Behind him, the water continued to beat against the white tile. In front of him, Ashlyn continued to stare, as though flummoxed. "No," she said. She backed away toward the exit. One step, two.

He leaned forward, his nose inching toward hers. He didn't kiss her, though. Didn't touch her. He simply reached behind her and flicked the door shut, blocking her escape.

The soft *clink* echoed off the walls, and she gulped. Paled.

He sighed. He didn't want her scared, he wanted her aroused. "Do not be frightened."

"I-I'm not."

He didn't believe her, didn't know what thoughts spun inside her mind. Didn't know why she resisted something she'd seemed to want only minutes ago. So he said, "How do you feel? Were you lying when you told me you were better?"

To lie or not to lie, Ashlyn thought. If she told him she was still sick, she knew he'd leave and allow her to shower alone. If she told him she really was healed, he'd insist on watching her strip. Something she'd never done for any man, much less a stranger. An immortal one, at that.

He's not really a stranger anymore. He's held you and slept beside you, cared for you and cleaned you. All of that was true, but she didn't know the little things about him. His likes and dislikes or his relationship history, which must be pretty extensive, old as he was. She didn't know if he simply wanted today with her, or something more.

So many times, in dozens of languages, she'd heard men tell a woman what she wanted to hear, then abandon her later. She'd heard them cheat, unconcerned about the partner waiting for them at home. She'd heard pretty lies and even blatant force.

How would Maddox, a self-professed demon, treat her body? How would he treat her once the loving was done?

As scary as the prospect of being with him was, however, she had to admit it was also exciting. Thrilling. There was intent desire in Maddox's eyes, a violet fire as fierce as it was hot.

No one had ever looked at her like that.

She was the weird girl, the freak. The crazy girl who couldn't have a normal conversation because she was too busy listening to other people talk. *Take a chance, Darrow.*

Dare to live for once. You know you want to.

She gazed up at Maddox. Steam swirled around him, giving him a dreamlike, ghostly aura. His face was ruthless but sexy, his hair cut in choppy black ribbons that fell to his chin. She'd always wanted to have a man, a relationship. She'd always been curious about the passion she'd heard so much about. But she'd also always wanted a man who would love her, who wouldn't leave her when the passion-fire burned out.

"How do you feel, Ashlyn?" he repeated.

Every nerve ending in her body reached for him, pleading for attention. "Fine," she finally admitted. "I feel fine. I didn't lie."

"Then why are you standing there? Strip."

"Do *not* order me." If she allowed him to walk on her now, he would always walk on her. *Always? How long are you staying?*

He was silent for a moment. "Please."

Are you really going to do this?

Yes. She was. He didn't love her, and she wasn't sure how he'd treat her afterward, but she was going to do it. She wanted him and had from the first.

Her hand trembled as she reached for the zipper of her pink jacket. But she found that she wasn't wearing the jacket anymore. Or her sweater. He must have removed them while she slept. Cheeks heating, she curled her fingers around the hem of her plain T-shirt. She lifted the material over her head and tossed it aside, leaving her in a white tank, bra and jeans.

Maddox nodded his approval. "So many layers. Remove more. Please."

She rested her hands on the bottom of the tank. Paused. "I'm nervous," she confessed.

One of his black eyebrows arched as his head tilted to the side. "Why?"

"What if — what if you don't like what you see?"

"I'll like," he said huskily.

That primitive tone . . . She shivered. It had scared her in the forest. Now it fanned the flames of her desire. "How can you be sure?"

His gaze raked over her in a heated perusal. "I like what I see right now. What's underneath will be even better."

Ashlyn wasn't so sure about that. She didn't work out; she didn't diet. There had never really been a need. When she wasn't traveling with the Institute, she was content to stay home, watching TV, reading magazines and playing on the Internet. Not the things that gave a woman the type of body men talked about wanting.

Her thighs were a little wider than most said they liked, her stomach a little rounder.

What kind of woman was Maddox used to? He was immortal, after all, and had probably been with thousands of beautiful females.

Her hands fisted. Irrational though it was, the thought of him with someone else really pissed her off.

"Ashlyn," Maddox said, snapping her from her musings.

"What?"

"Mind on the task at hand," he said dryly.

Her lips inched into a smile. "Sorry. I got distracted." She'd have to learn to control her own thoughts, now that silence was a part of her life.

"Let me help you. Please."

Every time he uttered the word *please* she melted, wanting to give him all that he desired and more. She nodded.

His hands closed over hers, and there was that thrilling shock that always followed his touch. She'd expected it this time, but was still unprepared for its ripple effect. Pearled nipples, a warm rush between her legs.

He didn't wait for permission but gripped the tank and lifted.

"Wait," she said.

Instantly, he ceased moving.

"I need to prepare you." He was about to see her underwear — another embarrassing topic. They were plain white cotton. *Granny gear,* she'd once heard a man say. She never wore sexy clothing, even underclothing, while on the job. It just wasn't practical. "I do own sexy underwear, I promise, but I'm not wearing it right now."

"That is supposed to disgust me?" Maddox asked, sounding genuinely confused. "That you aren't wearing sexy underwear?"

"I don't know." She chewed on her lower lip. "Maybe. Does it?"

"Ashlyn, whatever you're wearing will not matter to me. You will not be wearing it for long. Ready now?" he asked.

Swallowing, she nodded.

He tugged the tank over her head and tossed it on the floor beside her T-shirt. She shivered. "W-well?"

"Well?"

"Ugly?" she asked.

"Lovely," Maddox replied. He sucked in a — reverent? — breath and her blood caught fire. He reached out with a shaky hand and traced the plain cotton that shielded her nipples. Though already hard, they strained toward him.

Ashlyn moaned at the decadence.

He trailed his fingers down her stomach and gripped the waist of her jeans. A twist of his wrist, and they were unsnapped. She could feel the heat of his skin all the way to her bones.

He slid the jeans over her hips, past her knees and to the floor. "Step out of them."

Legs shaky, she did as commanded. His gaze locked on her white cotton panties. She fought the urge to cover them, wishing again that he could see her in something sexy. "I know men like to role-play," she told him, nervously trying to fill the silence. How many times had she heard them brag about it to their friends? "At home I have a cop outfit, a harem girl costume and a Playboy Bunny teddy." Not that she'd ever gotten to use them. But she loved owning them, just in case.

"That's nice." Maddox sounded unimpressed.

"Maybe I can, I don't know, show you sometime."

"Take the bra and panties off." His expression was disappointingly blank as he straightened.

Maybe he *didn't* care what she wore.

As he waited for her to obey, he reached behind him and jerked his T-shirt over his head. She gasped in surprise, in delight, and forgot about how ugly her panties were — but she still didn't remove them. Or the bra. She was too busy staring.

Maddox was absolutely magnificent. The scabs had already disappeared, leaving only faint red lines. Rope after rope of bronzed muscle offered a feast for her eyes. He had an innie bellybutton and a faint dusting of black hair that led straight into the waist of his pants.

Never taking his eyes from her face, he unfastened his pants and shoved them down the long, solid length of his legs until they, too, pooled on the floor.

He wasn't wearing any underwear.

Her eyes widened and her mouth dried. He was huge. Long and thick and sublimely aroused. She'd seen the male penis in books, on Web sites she shouldn't have visited and movies she shouldn't have watched, but never in person. Never like this. His testicles were drawn up tight and surrounded by coarse dark hair.

"I believe I gave you a specific task," he said, his pointed gaze between her legs making her quake deliciously.

Need flooded her, more intense than ever before. The need to touch and be touched, to taste and be tasted, consumed her. A sharp ache pounded through her. "Are we really going to have sex?" she asked breathlessly, hopefully.

"Oh, yes," he replied, stalking toward her. "Oh, yes, beauty, we really are."

CHAPTER TWELVE

Maddox gripped Ashlyn under her arms and lifted her off the floor. He tore the center of her bra apart with his teeth. The buttery material ripped easily and fell open, revealing the sexiest pair of breasts he'd ever seen.

They were a little fuller than a handful, with rosy-tipped nipples begging to be sampled. He couldn't hold back a moment longer. Everything inside him cracked, needing contact. Beyond desperate.

He sucked one hard bud into his mouth, surrounding it with hot, wet intensity. Ashlyn moaned. She threw back her head and arched toward him, a plea for more. He let his tongue dabble, flicking back and forth, then sampled the other one, giving it the same treatment.

His blood burned for more, but he set her back on her feet and pushed her toward the sink. Soon. Without a word, he handed her the toothbrush he'd acquired for her earlier and claimed his own. He wanted to be perfect for her.

She appeared dazed, wobbly, as she stared at it in confusion. Slowly her cheeks pinkened in embarrassment. Why? They brushed their teeth and used the mouthwash in silence. Afterward, Ashlyn stood in front of the mirror, gripping the sink as if she didn't know what to do next and was afraid to ask.

"Off," he said, pinching the top of her panties. "Please."

She appeared nervous as she slid them over her hips and stepped out of them.

Gods. He nearly crumpled to the floor in a blubbering, thankful heap. A small triangle of honey-colored hair, deliciously rounded thighs. Nostrils flaring at the beauty of her, he once again picked her up. This time, however, he placed her inside the tub and pulled the curtain around them. She gasped when the water hit her, and then she groaned in ecstasy as the heat pounded gently at her skin. He wished he had caused that groan.

Soon, he promised himself again. Soon.

He stepped in behind her. She was already soaked, hair plastered to the elegant slope of her back. Her bottom was perfectly curved, full enough to overflow in his hands. He liked that, liked that she wasn't skin and bones.

"So lovely," he said, but doubt suddenly filled him. Should he turn her around, or hold her like this? Should he lay her down or let her stand? His first shower with a woman, and he wasn't exactly sure of the best way to go about it.

Mine. Do . . . everything.

As instinct and thousands of years of fantasies took over, he closed all hint of distance between them and rubbed his erection in the crevice of her ass. She gave a shuddering gasp. He reached around her and grabbed the pine-scented bar of soap he used every morning to wash away the lingering effects of his midnight trials.

She tried to turn around, to face him, but he locked her in place by resting his chin on top of her head. At first she stiffened. Gradually, though, she relaxed against him. He was already on edge and didn't want to push himself too far. Yet. He barely had a hold on the spirit as it was; it seemed to want to jump out of his body and touch her itself.

"You were made for sex, weren't you?" he purred into her ear. He laved the delicate shell with his tongue.

"I guess we'll find out," she replied on a trembling breath.

She'd been made for him, really. More perfect Bait could not have been chosen. If she'd been sent to distract him, she was succeeding. If she'd been sent to learn about him and his friends, well, she'd succeeded in that, too. He'd told her more than he'd ever told another.

If she'd been sent to punish him, well, she'd done that, too. He'd never been more ashamed of himself. He should be anywhere but here right now, should be doing anything else. Instead, he *was* here. *Was* going to make love with Ashlyn. And he didn't care about the consequences.

Arms still banded around her shoulders, he lathered his hands. He set the soap on its perch and began the slow — really slow — process of cleaning her from head to toe. His soapy fingers snaked around her nipples, along the soft curve of her hips, on the sweet roundness of her belly.

She gave another of those groans, the sound eager and this time just for him. Her head fell onto his shoulder in open invitation, an action that said, *Do with me what you will.*

"Do you like having someone clean you?" he asked.

"Yes."

"Are you still dirty?"

"Yes."

"Where?"

"Everywhere," was the raspy answer.

He almost smiled. Almost. His desire was too dark for humor. Except blended with the darkness was wonder and awe.

His touch was rougher than he'd intended as he soaped her arms. She didn't seem to mind. He could see that she'd closed her eyes and was nibbling on her bottom lip, breathy little sighs emerging every few seconds.

"Have you ever showered with a man before?" Soap in hand, he dropped to his knees.

She stilled. Whispered, "No."

He was glad. They would discover the pleasures of it together. Even before the demon had become part of him, he had not shown much tenderness to females. He had taken them quickly even then. They had been a pleasant convenience, nothing more. Something he'd wanted but had not needed.

After the curse, affection became more unthinkable. He'd always feared the spirit would show itself if he lingered over a female. Only then had he realized how precious time was, how he should have enjoyed his life when he'd had the chance.

He'd never been more afraid of the spirit than he was right now, but he didn't let it stop him from lingering this time, from savoring. Enjoying. He was too hard, too rough for most to handle, but he vowed not to be that way with Ashlyn.

I will control myself, whatever it takes. I will control the spirit. He kissed the curve of Ashlyn's lower back, then licked his way up several of her vertebra.

"Hmm," she gasped. "I — I like that."

He liked it, too.

He liked everything about her.

After soaping her calves and thighs and biting the inside of his cheek to keep from biting *her,* he washed the suds from his hands. Unable to resist a moment more, he inserted two fingers into the very heat of her.

"Oh. Oh!" She jumped away from his erotic touch, but quickly leaned back against him, spreading her legs wider, silently asking for more.

The lather had been slick, and now, so was she. He stroked her, gently pinched her swollen core. A shiver rocked her. "Like it still?" he asked. Tension beat through him.

Take her. Take her now.

"Love it. I love it," she chanted.

He pumped deep, as deep as he could go. She gasped out his name.

"Tight," he said through clenched teeth. He almost thought he felt . . . No, surely not. "Hot."

"Good. Feels good."

Any moment now, he would be consumed by flames — flames hotter than the ones he battled in hell. He was shaking, more than before. He was hard, achingly hard. He was poised and ready for attack.

If he reacted this strongly to filling her with his fingers, what would he do when he filled her with his cock?

Don't stop. Can't stop. Grinding his teeth, he worked another finger inside of her, stretching her . . . and that's when he could no longer deny the barrier that marked her as virgin. His lips pulled down in a tight glower. His head tilted to the side and he found himself staring between her legs in confusion.

Virgin? Surely not. She was a grown woman. But the barrier could not be refuted.

He withdrew from her and stood. He didn't touch her again, just looked her up and down. Like him, she was trembling.

A thousand thoughts tumbled through his fevered mind. How could so beautiful a woman still be a virgin? And why would Hunters send an inexperienced woman to tempt him?

She wouldn't know how.

Why would the gods send a virgin to punish him? Would that not simply punish the virgin?

Obviously confused by his sudden withdrawal, Ashlyn craned her neck until her eyes met his. Pleasure and pain warred for dominance on her lovely features. "Did I do something wrong?"

He shook his head, not yet ready to speak. Possessiveness was shooting through his every cell. No man had ever penetrated her. No man had ever tasted her sweetness.

"Why did you stop, then?" She turned to face him fully and he saw that her nipples were hard, rosy and wet. They reached for him, begging . . . begging . . .

He'd been about to take her virginity and he'd never even kissed her, he realized. Any woman, even Bait, even divine punishment, deserved better than that. And right now, he didn't believe she was either.

But she'd been out in that forest last night and four Hunters had been following her. The two situations were connected, he was certain of it, but now he thought — what? Could *Ashlyn* have been their target?

If so, why? She didn't hold a demon inside her; he would have sensed it. Wouldn't he? He didn't know anymore. Didn't know anything except that he wanted this woman with every fiber of his being. Had since the first moment he'd seen her. Something about her affected him deeply. Affected the spirit, even.

"Maddox?"

He badly wanted to take her virginity, but he wasn't going to. Not today. Not when she'd been sick only hours before. Not when he wasn't sure how he'd react to being inside her — and being her first. She would be a first for him, too. He'd never taken a virgin before. He would have to find the best way to go about it, the best way to keep Violence contained. The spirit would relish causing Ashlyn even momentary pain. Wouldn't it? He might have to chain himself.

As for now . . .

He backed her against the cool tile. Her eyes rounded, those big beautiful brown eyes. Even though his lips had yet to heal fully, he kissed her. Her mouth opened in surprise, then widened in eagerness, welcoming his tongue. He thrust it inside, angling his head to go deeper, to take more, to feed her as much as she needed. Her flavor tantalized him, minty, feminine.

There was another spark between them.

She gasped, and he swallowed the sound. His chest flattened against her breasts, her nipples so hard they stabbed at his skin. He could feel the erratic hammer of her heartbeat.

He bent his knees and pushed up, rubbing his erection against her. She gasped again. She shivered. Her hands tangled in his hair, gripping, pulling him closer. Their teeth banged together; the kiss continued . . . never stopped . . . lasted forever . . . a kiss of sorcery and dreams and fire.

Yes, fire. There was so much fire. White-hot. Blistering. An inferno inside of him. He bit her lower lip, couldn't have stopped himself even if he'd wanted to, which he no longer did. A bead of blood leaked onto his tongue. He savored the metallic taste.

Good, so good.

She moaned and bit him back, returning the darkness of his passion with a fervor that surprised him. *Gentle, calm.* He gripped her cheeks and forced — gently, calmly — her head to the side. Licking and nipping his way down her jaw, her collarbone, was almost his undoing. Her skin was like a drug and one little taste beckoned him to take more, do more. Experience all.

She arched against him, panting. She pulled back, panting still. She arched against him again. His erection probed between her legs, desperate to enter.

No, not yet. *Innocent, remember? She is innocent.*

Her teeth sank into his collarbone, and he almost came. Almost spilled then and there. She was wild, frantic for release. Her fingers moved to his back and squeezed, kneaded. Her nails scored his skin.

He didn't think she was aware of her actions. Her head was thrashing from side to side and her eyes were closed. "I'll make you come," he told her, fighting for his own control.

"Yes. Come." She released him to grip her own breasts, to pinch the nipples between her fingers.

He'd never seen a more erotic sight.

"Just touch me," she commanded roughly. "Don't stop touching me."

"Will. Need . . . a moment." He closed his fingers over his erection, knowing he'd spread her and take her if he didn't. He pumped once, twice. Hissed in a breath.

"Maddox. Hurry!"

"With my hands or mouth?" he asked, the words barely audible. The water was beating against her, slipping and sliding down her abdomen, daring him to follow and drink.

"Wh-what?" She pried open her eyes, looking at him, looking at herself. When she realized what she was doing with her hands, she dropped her arms to her sides and blushed.

"Should I touch you with my hands or my mouth?" He continued pumping his own hand down his swollen length, wishing it were *her* hand. Or her mouth. Her body.

"Hands?"

He didn't know a lot about humans, but he recognized her true desire. She wanted his mouth to finish her. He wanted it, too. The need probably embarrassed her; well, he would conquer that soon enough.

He dropped to his knees a second time.

"What are you doing?" she whispered, scandalized. In the undercurrents of her voice, however, were tendrils of excitement.

Rather than answer, he licked her right where she needed him. It was something he'd wanted to do to a woman for years but hadn't dared risk, too afraid of Violence's reaction. In that moment, he was too enthralled to be afraid, and suddenly he was glad that he had waited. Ashlyn tasted of pure, innocent female. She tasted of honey.

Passion and slick heat. Drugging, addicting. *His.*

"Mouth," she gasped out. "Mouth. Changed my mind."

He licked her again and her belly quivered. She flattened her palms on the tile beside her, holding herself up. Her hips arched forward, seeking more of his tongue. He gave it to her. Spreading her with one hand and pumping his shaft with the other, he sucked on her hot center. She moaned, she undulated, she writhed.

"More?" he asked.

"More. Yes. Please."

She was close, so close. He could feel her rushing toward release, could taste the abundance of sweetness. *Bite.* The urge scared him. He stopped moving. She screamed in frustration, and he clamped his jaw in aroused pain.

Droplets of water fell from his eyelashes onto his chin. He wanted to brush them away, to see her more clearly, but didn't want to move either of his hands. Air burned his throat, his lungs. "Tell me you want me." *While I calm down.*

"I want you," Ashlyn all but shouted. She stared down at him, as if she couldn't believe they were having this conversation here and now.

"Tell me you need me."

"I need you."

"Tell me you'll never betray me."

"I'll never betray you."

At least she hadn't hesitated. Something inside him softened, melted. "Where do you want to be?" he asked, the words almost a plea. *Need me as much as I need you.*

Maybe it was the water. Maybe it was the steam. Her eyes seemed to mist over, a curtain of vulnerability falling over her face. "With you," she replied. "Only with you."

Both man and spirit were staggered by the magic of her words. Humbled. Maddox again buried his face between her legs, tongue burrowing deeper than before. She sighed in ecstasy, one of her legs curling around his back. Her heel dug into his shoulder, but he didn't care. Even liked it.

Her desire flowed down his throat as he nibbled on her. Couldn't stop himself now. Was helpless against his actions. He didn't want to hurt her, and neither did the spirit. For once in accord, both wanted only to pleasure her.

She reached the edge. Fell. The orgasm rocked her entire body. Her inner walls clamped down on his tongue, holding him captive in those gates to heaven. And when she shouted his name, *he* came. Hot seed spurted from him and onto the tub. His body jerked, muscles gripping bone in an iron clasp. Nothing had ever felt so right. Nothing had ever felt so perfect.

Seconds — minutes? hours? — passed. In that timeless eternity he became Pleasure. He wasn't a being ruled by Violence. He was simply a man who craved this woman. A man who lived in a world where light always stamped out darkness and good always conquered evil.

If only . . .

When he opened his eyes, he was once again Maddox. Once again a man ruled by darkness, living in a world where midnight always triumphed and evil laughed in the face of good.

He was still on his knees. Ashlyn was still in front of him. He could hear her panting rasps and realized he was panting himself. He stood, disconcerted to note his legs hadn't stopped shaking.

Neither had Ashlyn's. Her eyelids were closed, lashes in wet spikes. There was a blissful, satisfied aura surrounding her, but he couldn't dislodge the sudden thought that he'd been too rough, that he could have been gentler. Tried harder.

"Please look at me," he said.

Like butterfly wings, her lashes fluttered

open. Those amber orbs gazed up at him, and she nibbled on her bottom lip, expression uncertain. "Yes?"

"Did I hurt you?" Worse, "Do you regret?"

"No and no." She smiled that radiant smile of hers, sunshine in the tenebrous recesses of night.

"How are you still a virgin?" he asked, dazed.

Slowly, her smile faded. Embarrassment clouded her eyes, darkening the brown to a churning black tempest. "I don't want to talk about it."

"Please."

She peered down at her feet, hiding the emotion, the storm. "I never should have told you to ask rather than demand. It's irresistible!"

He would have to remember that.

"Maybe I should have told you earlier, before we . . . But . . ."

His stomach pitched. Should he want to hear her confession, whatever it was? Yes. Did he? No. Not now. He turned the water off and crowded her against the tile. He couldn't predict the spirit's reaction to being told this lushly beautiful creature had conspired against him. "Ashlyn —"

"No," she said with a shake of her head. "Hear me out. Just promise not to hate me, okay, and try to understand that I can't help it." Pause. Shuddering breath. "Here goes. You're not the only one possessed by something you can't control. I hear voices. When I stand in a spot where a conversation has taken place, I can hear every word that was uttered, no matter how much time has passed." Her eyes landed anywhere but on him as she spoke.

Maddox listened, shocked to the core. She hadn't admitted to Hunters or gods or a vendetta against him, but to voices. He knew, deep down, her words were not a lie. They were too complicated and too easily disproved; true Bait would have opted for something less refutable. More than that, what she described made sense, fitting several pieces of last night's puzzle together.

Which meant she *had* tried to protect him earlier. Not for any ulterior motives, but because she had wanted to. Amazement flowed through him. Amazement and relief and joy.

Now he understood why she hadn't been too brokenhearted when he'd admitting to killing those men. Most likely, she hadn't even known them. As he'd suspected, they could very well have hoped to capture her and use her ability to their advantage.

His fingers itched for a knife; he wanted

to kill them all over again. *Calm down.* They still could have worked for her Institute, and she simply hadn't realized it. No, that couldn't be right. They would have made themselves known to her, for they'd been close enough to hear and see her.

"Why did you fear I would hate you?" he asked.

"I hear secrets," she whispered. "It's hard to make friends, you know? The people who know what I can do want nothing to do with me and the people who don't know can't figure out how to deal with me."

The loneliness in her tone affected him deeply. He understood. But even he didn't like the thought of her knowing — hearing — the violent things he'd done over the years. "What secrets of mine have you heard?" He tried to keep his voice light, but didn't quite manage it.

"None. I swear." She gazed up at him with wide eyes. "When I'm around you, the world is silent."

She'd said that before. He recalled the expression on her face when he'd first approached her. Total bliss. She'd been savoring the silence, just as she'd claimed. The knowledge humbled and baffled him, yet underneath both emotions was an unshakable pride. He had helped her. He, who was unable to fight free of his own torment, had somehow released another from hers.

"You said you hear secrets. What have you heard about us?"

"I've already told you. Most townspeople consider you angels. Some consider you demons. But all of them are in awe of you."

"No plans to attack?"

"Not that I heard."

"Good." He splayed his hands around her waist, lifted and set her out of the tub. He climbed out beside her and palmed a towel from the cabinet. After wrapping it around her shoulders so that the material draped and warmed her, he grabbed one for himself.

"*Good?* That's all you have to say to me?" she asked.

"Yes."

Surprise caused her mouth to fall open. "Well, now that I've told you, I'd like to call my boss and let him know I'm okay."

Maddox shook his head. "I'm afraid that is not an option. No one can know you're here. For your safety, and for ours."

"But —"

"It is not up for discussion. The answer is now and always no."

Her mouth worked open again, as if she meant to argue. But she merely said, "Fine."

From her tone, he knew it wasn't. She probably planned to hunt up a phone the moment he turned his back. Women. For the first time, he understood what Paris meant when he uttered the word like a curse. He sighed. "I swear to you, Ashlyn, this is the best course of action for all involved."

Turning away from him, she patted her arms dry. Her actions were a little too slow, a little too measured, as if her mind were far away.

"What is wrong?"

"Lots of things. I need to call my boss, and I'm going to the moment I find a phone. You can't stop me."

"That is —"

Now she cut *him* off. "And even you, an immortal, have to think I'm weird after what I just told you, so I don't know why you're denying it."

He scrubbed the moisture out of his hair and wrapped the cloth around his neck. "You are not weird. I think you are beautiful, smart, courageous and most important, delicious."

She anchored the towel around her torso, blocking his view. "Really?"

Insecurity that strong had to have been beaten into her. He scowled, determined to kill whoever had wielded the verbal fists. "Really." Hands on her shoulders, he spun her around. Their gazes collided. "If you knew half the things that happen here, you —" He pressed his lips together. Damn, but he should not have said that.

"You mean there's more than stabbings and resurrections?" she asked dryly.

Much more.

"So what are we going to do now?" She splayed her arms wide.

Though he wished to spend the rest of the day with her, he knew that he could not. He still had duties, was still a warrior whose home needed to be defended, now more than ever. After ushering her into the bedroom, he dressed, gathered a shirt, boxers and a pair of sweatpants from the floor and tossed them at her. "Put these on."

She missed every single item and had to bend to pick them up. With every movement, the white towel rode up her thighs. His cock hardened. Again. It should have been tired, but no. Not with Ashlyn. She excited him despite, well, everything.

"There are a few things I must do," he said, more to remind himself than in response to her question.

"And you're taking me with you?" she asked, tightening her grip on the bundle.

"Yes and no."

"What does that mean?"

No sense in lying, he supposed. She would find out soon enough. "I'm locking you up with Danika while I do some . . . chores. That way, you will have company and there will be someone to tend you and call for me if you become sick again."

First a look of panic shuttered over her face. Then anger. Her brows arched and the tip of her tongue traced the outside of her lips. "One, there's no need to lock me up. I said I'd stay. And two, you're telling me Danika is locked up? She's a prisoner?" The last word emerged as a screech.

"Yes." Perversely, he hoped the affirmation would anger her further; he wanted to see that tongue again.

"But, Maddox, you told me I was the first woman you had —"

"*I* did not lock her up. Nor did I lie to you. Now, not another word. *Please.*" If she asked him to release Danika, he would want to do it. He would want to go against the others and grant her request. "Get dressed, or I'll drag you from the room naked."

Silently, she studied him. Silently, she begged him to . . . what? He couldn't tell. He said nothing. He couldn't. Time was not his friend.

"What is it going to be? Clothed or naked?"

She scowled at him, her first real show of temper, and offered him a view of her back. Motions stiff and jerky, she allowed the towel to fall to the floor. Elegantly sloped back . . . rounded ass . . . His mouth watered.

"I should fight you on this, but I'm not going to. Know why?" She didn't give him time to answer. "Not because you ordered it but because I'd like the chance to check on Danika."

She quickly dressed, and he should have been happy those luscious curves were covered. No one else would be able to see her; no one else would have the chance to enjoy the view. But that also meant *he* wouldn't see, and *he* wouldn't enjoy.

"They're too big," she said, facing him.

She was right. The clothes bagged on her, but Maddox thought she looked delectable. He knew what waited underneath that material. He knew what waited for his touch — and his alone. "They're all I have. For now, they'll have to do."

A thought arose. Torin had things delivered to a P.O. box all the time for Paris to pick up. Perhaps Maddox would have him order dresses like those he had seen on the television while watching one of those silly movies with Paris. Low cut. Maybe high heels, too, and some jewelry. And maybe the sexy — what did Paris call it? — lingerie Ashlyn had wished for.

"We'll talk later," she said, stomping to his side. Not a question, he noticed, but a demand.

"Yes." He tried not to smile. "We will talk."

"You're going to answer all my questions. No evasions." She stared up at him, eyes narrowed.

Perhaps. "You had best behave while I'm gone. Remember how I told you it was dangerous to make me mad?"

"What, you'll spank me if I'm a bad girl?"

The provocative comment surprised him. Gods, where had this little firecracker come from? He'd seen her scared, shocked, sick, aroused, but not feisty like this. Amazingly, the spirit did not erupt at her defiance. Did not compel him to lash out. He thought perhaps it . . . No. Impossible.

The spirit of Violence did *not* smile.

"You don't want to know what I'll do," he said when he found his voice, "so do not tempt me."

She rose on her tiptoes, her warm breath fanning his ear. The hard peaks of her nipples abraded his chest. He waited, unable to breathe as he anticipated what she would do next. He might not know where the firecracker had come from, but he knew she excited him.

"Maybe I like tempting you," she whispered. She bit his earlobe. "Think about that while I'm locked away."

He would. Oh, yes. He would.

CHAPTER THIRTEEN

Ashlyn stared at the splintered door that had just been slammed in her face by Maddox, trapping her inside another bedroom. Another prison. Oh! That man was infuriating. He'd tenderly, wildly pleasured her in a way that should have embarrassed her — *had* embarrassed her until that first wondrous lave of his hot tongue — and then he'd become a warrior again, hard and harsh and determined.

Yet still she'd desired him.

He'd threatened to lock her away with another innocent woman — a woman he had *already* locked away. Shameful behavior, to be sure.

Still she'd desired him. Had even bitten his earlobe and tried to tempt him to finish what they'd started in that shower. But he'd resisted, escorting her down the hallway and into this room, where he'd dumped her without a kiss or even a word.

And still she foolishly desired him.

She wanted him to hold her, to cuddle her as she'd always dreamed someone would. She wanted him to talk to her and get to know her. And then she wanted him to freaking make love to her! All the way, this time. Nothing held back.

This desire she had for him was too strong and she didn't understand it. He was ruthless and cryptic and temperamental. He was spawned from hell itself. But he was also kind, caring and the best thing to ever happen to her body. Oh yeah. And he was silence. As if she could forget about that. Damn it!

"Who are you?" a female voice suddenly asked.

Pulled from her musings, Ashlyn whipped around. Danika and three other women, ranging in age from late seventies to twenty-something, peered over at her with equal measures of concern and fear. Dear God. Maddox had *four* women locked away? Was this to be an immortal's harem?

Well, you do have the costume.

Danika stepped forward. "She's the sick one. The one I —" she coughed "— healed."

"Thank you for that," Ashlyn said softly, not sure what else to say to this stranger who wasn't a stranger.

Danika nodded in acknowledgment. "You look better." Her gaze raked over Ashlyn before slitting with suspicion. "Miraculously better, to be honest."

"I wish I could explain it, but I can't. Once the nausea passed, my strength returned. Seems those 'small pebbles' did the trick, after all." Ashlyn studied her, as well. "You look better, too. You've lost that lovely green tint."

"Well, that was the first time I ever rode a man to fetch painkillers." Danika anchored her hands on her hips. "So what brings you to Castle Spook? Were you kidnapped, too?"

Ashlyn wasn't given time to answer.

"Who are these people?" a slightly older version of Danika asked. "*What* are they? Danika said one of them has wings."

If they didn't already know, she wasn't going to be the one to break it to them.

With barely a pause, the oldest of the group asked, "Do you know a way out?"

All of the women closed in on her as they spoke, encircling her. They peered at her hopefully, as if she held all the answers and could save them from the vilest of fates.

She held up her hands, palms out. "Everyone slow down." *Kidnapped,* Danika had said. Why would Maddox have done such a thing? "Are any of you hunters or bait?"

Every time Maddox said those two words, there was disgust in his voice.

"As in, do we hunt treasure? Bait a hook?" Danika's face scrunched in confusion, but there was a hard glint in her green eyes. "No."

"As in, I have no idea. I was hoping someone here would know." Voices of the past began to edge their way into her mind. One conversation after another. "No. No, not again." She felt herself pale, heat evaporating from her skin, leaving only a cold, trembling shell. *Breathe. Just breathe.*

"I think she's getting sick again," Danika said, concerned. "Can you make it to the bed?" she asked Ashlyn.

"N-no. I just want to sit."

Suddenly a pair of hands settled on top of her shoulders, easing her to the floor. Ashlyn went willingly, her legs becoming too weak to hold her up. Shuddering, she drew air into her lungs.

They're going to kill us.

We have to escape.

How? Hysterical laughter.

If we have to jump out the window, then we jump. They want to infect us with some sort of disease.

We jump, we die.

We stay, we die.

The voices belonged to these women, Ashlyn realized. Every word they'd spoken in the room was going to play through her head. Damn it, she'd gotten used to the silence. Had assumed she'd have peace as long as she stayed out of the dungeon. Hopefully, they hadn't been here long enough to have too many conversations.

I miss Grandpa. He'd know what to do.

Well, he's not here, is he? We have to figure it out on our own.

A buttered roll and a glass of apple juice were shoved under her nose. "Here," Danika said gently. "These might help."

Who's talking? Who said that?

Who are you talking to, Dani?

Uh, no one.

Ashlyn accepted both with shaky hands. On and on and on their exchange tumbled. Sometimes, as it had been in the dungeon, the conversations seemed one-sided. She couldn't hear who the women were talking to; she only knew they *were* talking to someone other than themselves.

She heard Danika say, *If — if I* am *a healer, will you swear to spare my mother, sister and grandmother? They haven't done anything wrong. We came to Budapest to get away, to say goodbye to my grandpa. We —*

But she didn't hear the comment before

it. Or after. Why?

The men were immortal, but she'd heard immortal creatures speak before. Vampires, goblins, shape-shifters, even. Why not the demons here? They had to be the ones Danika had been speaking to.

Ashlyn nibbled at the bread and sipped the juice, trying to tune out each new discussion. She hummed. She meditated. The women attempted to engage her, but she simply couldn't respond. There were too many voices vying for her attention.

One by one, the women gave up. How many minutes or hours passed after that, she didn't know. So many times she almost called for Maddox, but she held the pleas back, biting her tongue until she tasted blood. He had chores to do, he'd said. Besides, she didn't want to be a burden. A nuisance.

That's what you came here for, she reminded herself. *To demand that these men teach you how to control your powers, even if it meant becoming a nuisance to them.*

But that had been before Maddox actually entered her life. Now she wanted him to be her lover (if he would, the jerk), not her nursemaid. Again.

You hear a . . . a . . . voice? In your mind?
Yes.

And it's not your own?
Maybe, probably. I don't know.

Blessedly, the murmurings did stop, ending at the moment of Ashlyn's entrance. Relieved as she was, she had to admit she had learned several new tidbits of information. The first and most significant: Danika *had* heard of hunters — she'd told her family about them.

"Hunters," Ashlyn said, lifting her gaze. Danika was looking out the room's only window, a window none of the women had been able to pry open. Ashlyn had heard them try and fail. "What are they? Don't lie to me this time. Please."

Startled, Danika jumped and turned, hand over heart. "Better again, eh? Why should we trust you? You could be working for those men. They might've sent you here to learn something from us, and when you learn it, they'll storm inside and kill us."

"True." After all, these women only knew she'd been sick and snuggled up to their enemy. "But you saved me. Why would I want you hurt?"

Danika peered over at her but said nothing.

"You'll just have to trust that I'm not here to trap you or hurt you. We're in the same situation, you and I."

"But what about the angry one? Maddox. You're dating him."

Dating wasn't exactly the word she'd use. Ashlyn tried to picture Maddox sitting across from her in some candlelit restaurant, drinking wine and listening to soft music. Her lips lifted in a smile. "Maybe. So?"

"So, that makes you one of them."

"I'm not," she insisted. "I just got here. Yesterday, in fact."

Danika's eyes widened, her golden lashes hitting her equally golden eyebrows. "Now I know you're lying. He cares for you, that much was obvious. A man doesn't show that much compassion to a woman he's just met."

Yes, he'd been compassionate. Yes, he'd been kind. Tender. Unerringly sweet. The fiercest man she'd ever met had mopped her brow and cleaned her face. "Again, I can't explain it. I'm not lying."

A minute ticked by in silence.

"Fine." Danika's shoulders lifted in a deceptively casual shrug. "You want to know about hunters, I'll tell you. Not like it's crucial info, anyway." Inhale, exhale. "When the winged man, Aeron, took me into the city, he spotted a group of men. They were armed like soldiers and they were sneaking around back alleys as if they didn't want to be seen."

So far, that told her nothing.

"Aeron muttered *Hunters* under his breath and whipped out a dagger." Anger began to color Danika's soft timbre. The memory obviously wasn't her favorite. "He would have fought them if he hadn't been carting me around. He said so. He also said those men had come to kill him and his friends." She spoke the last in a deep, dark tone, mimicking Aeron. Ashlyn nearly smiled at the gloom-and-doom inflection. "I wanted them to fight, distract him so I could run. But they didn't. They didn't see us."

Ashlyn frowned. Hunters of the immortal. Wasn't that basically what she did for the Institute? She listened to conversations to find — hunt — those who were not exactly human. *Stop right there. The Institute studies, observes, renders aid when needed and takes extreme action only when threatened.*

She took comfort in that. The employees were utterly scientific when dealing with the creatures they found, not predatory.

They were not always so fair-minded with her.

The first time an attempt had been made against her, it was because she'd stumbled across a recent conversation a coworker had had with a child. He'd lured that sweet, innocent little girl . . . he'd threatened . . . he'd done terrible things. Sickened, Ashlyn had turned him in. He'd retaliated by trying to shoot her. McIntosh, always close by her side, had thrown her down, saving her life.

The second time, she was nearly stabbed in the back — literally — by a woman intent on keeping her affair a secret. McIntosh had once again acted as her bodyguard, shielding her and taking the slice instead.

The third and final time, about eleven months ago, she was poisoned. Luck had been on her side. She'd managed to throw up most of it. Ah, sweet memories. To this day she still didn't know why, didn't know which secret she'd divined that someone had been willing to kill to keep.

McIntosh did everything in his power to protect her. But sometimes that wasn't enough, so she'd learned to rely only on herself and trust no one — which made her sudden eagerness to depend on Maddox all the more confusing.

"Aeron, uh, was bad-mouthing you, too," Danika said, breaking into her thoughts.

Ashlyn blinked in surprise. "Me? Why?"

"Said you were bait, whatever that means."

Her shoulders slumped as she said, "Maddox calls me bait, too. I still don't know what that is." How could she refute something she didn't comprehend? Unless . . . wait. If she was right about hunters stalking immortals, that had to mean bait was the lure. Dangle it in front of an immortal and a hunter could ensnare him in a trap.

Why that . . . that . . . asshole! She'd come here for help, not to draw him out of his lair so that he could be slain. "Idiot!" she fumed.

"Don't call me names," Danika snapped.

"I wasn't talking about you. I was talking about *me*." She'd let Maddox kiss her, had let him put his fingers and tongue inside of her, had even been desperate for more. And all the while he'd thought her capable of such a vile, duplicitous act. He probably thought she was easy, too — hence his surprise when he'd discovered she was still a virgin.

Tears of shame stung her eyes.

"They tricked you, huh?" Danika asked gently.

She nodded. Had Maddox wanted her, even a little, or had he simply wanted to seduce her for information about her obviously nefarious plan? She suspected the latter, and it hurt. Cut deep. How many times had he accused her or questioned her with suspicion in his eyes?

No wonder he'd so easily resisted her bumbling attempt to talk him into finishing what they'd started. No wonder he'd dumped her here. *Idiot!* she thought again. Yes, that's what she was. Her only excuse was that she didn't have a lot of hands-on experience with men. *And this is why!* They were bastards. Users and seducers.

"Tell me about the voice you're hearing," she said to Danika. Anything to get her mind off Maddox — before she burst into sobs of disappointment and resentment.

Danika's expression iced over. "I haven't mentioned any voice to you. They've been watching us, haven't they? Is there a camera hidden in here or something?"

"I don't know." Ashlyn raised her knees and propped her chin in the dent between them. "Maybe there's a camera, maybe there isn't. Given how confused they were by Tylenol, I'm not sure any of them would know how to operate one. In any case, that's not how I learned about the voice."

Did Danika have an ability similar to Ashlyn's? Ashlyn had never met another like herself, but she was learning to expect the unexpected here. "Tell me the rest. Please. We're in this together. We can help each other."

"There's nothing to tell." Danika stalked

through the room, feeling the walls. "I'm going crazy. There, is that what you wanted me to admit? Some guy started talking in my head this morning. We've had some real stimulating conversations."

One voice. A man's. Not many voices, male and female. Not Ashlyn's ability, after all. "Tell me," she urged again. Her stomach chose that moment to rumble, a booming concerto in the uncomfortable silence that followed. "What has he said to you?"

With a scowl, Danika plucked a piece of cheese from the platter perched on the vanity. She tossed it at Ashlyn before commanding her family to help search for cameras. Just in case. "He asked for the 411 on our captors."

"Like?"

"Like their daily routine, what weapons they have and what security system the fortress has." She laughed, but there was no humor to the sound. "I think it's my mind's crazy way of coping with what's happened."

Ashlyn didn't think so. Those questions were too invasive, too specific, the kind of information a soldier would want to gather on his enemy.

So . . . if it wasn't Danika who wanted data on the men, who was it? And who had the power to ask without benefit of a body?

■ ■ ■ ■

"I'm sick of this shit," Paris grumbled. "Just once today, I'd like to stay in town and relax after screwing, rather than rushing back here. Hello, I can't flash like Lucien." He plopped in front of the TV screen and turned on his favorite Xbox game. Naked mud wrestling. His color was high and the strain had vanished from his features. "What's the meeting about this time? And FYI, I didn't see any Hunters."

"That's because all you see are potential bedmates," Aeron replied.

"And there's a downside to that?" Paris asked, unperturbed.

"Stop arguing," Lucien said. "We've got some business to take care of, and I don't think anyone's going to like what they hear."

Maddox leaned back on the couch and scrubbed a hand down his face. Violence pounded through him, hot and dark. Hotter than usual. Darker than usual. Barely caged. It didn't like being away from Ashlyn. The woman who had tried to lure him to bed. The woman he'd turned away. What kind of idiot turned away a woman such as her?

She'd wanted him, for gods' sake.

He'd wanted her just as badly. Still

wanted. Wanted her supple body wrapped around his, wanted her mouth on his. Or on his cock. He wasn't picky. He wanted her cries of abandon in his ears, her sweet taste in his mouth.

He should have taken her when he'd had the chance. Instead, he'd deposited her in Lucien's room after removing the barricade — overkill, if you asked him, when there was a perfectly good lock on the knob — and cleaned his own. Then he'd found himself summoned to the entertainment room where there was, apparently, nothing but more bad news to pass around.

"Tell them, Aeron," Lucien said on a sigh.

Pause. Then, "I've felt the first stirrings of Wrath. Nothing drastic. Yet." He propped himself against the far wall. He pounded a fist into the stone behind him as if to punctuate his admission. "It's manageable, but I'm not sure how long that will last."

"He can smell the humans now, and their scents won't leave his nose," Reyes said.

Maddox wondered at the fury in the man's tone.

Paris paled. "Fuck. That was fast."

"No one knows that better than me," Aeron replied.

Maddox suppressed a growl. How much more would he and the others be forced to

318

endure? He'd learned a bit ago that there *were* other Hunters out there, hiding in town. According to Aeron, they appeared even stronger and more capable than their predecessors.

Because of what Ashlyn had revealed about her ability, Maddox had to wonder if they were here for *her,* too. A woman whose job it was to listen for nonhuman creatures would be a valuable tool indeed. The very notion infuriated his demon, made them both want to torture, maim, *kill.*

"I'm not sure how much longer I can go without hurting them." Aeron rubbed the back of his neck. "Already I see their bloody bodies in my mind and I like it." There at the end, his voice cracked. A slight change, but there all the same.

"Does no one have an idea?" Reyes tossed his knife in the air, caught it and tossed it again. "Anything that might save them?"

Silence.

"Talking about it is pointless," Torin finally said. "We're only tormenting our-selves, trying to come up with a solution that isn't there. We can't approach the Titans; they'll give us all another curse. We can't set the women free and tell them to hide. Aeron will only be forced to follow them. So, I say let him do it."

Reyes glared at him. "That's a little callous even for you, Disease."

What would he do if Aeron were ever ordered to kill Ashlyn? Maddox wondered. Cruel as he was learning these new gods were, he suspected they'd issue the command without hesitation. He leapt to his feet with a roar, smashing his fist into the wall.

All conversation stopped.

The act felt good, so he did it again. And again. His hands had yet to fully heal from his battle with Aeron, and this didn't help. The spirit must truly feel bonded to Ashlyn, too, because even it wanted to kill something at the thought of losing her. *Go get her. She's ours. She belongs to us.*

Almost always before, he and the spirit had disagreed. Man and beast, each against the other. To share a common desire was shocking. He punched the wall again and stone crumbled to the ground.

"The little woman isn't calming us, I see," Torin said with a short laugh.

Maddox turned away from him in time to catch Aeron exchange a loaded glance with Lucien. "What?" he snapped at them.

Lucien held up his hands, all innocence.

"Nothing," Aeron said. "Just . . . nothing."

"How many times do you have to be told? She's Bait, man." Reyes gave his dagger a final toss, end over end, and the tip embedded just above Maddox's shoulder. "Surely you know that by now."

"If you don't, you're a fool," Aeron said, maintaining that conversational tone. "Maybe I'll kill your precious Ashlyn when I kill the others, and break her spell over you once and for all."

Just like that, the spirit erupted fully, washing over him, consuming him. *No one threatens our woman.* No one. Black spots winked over his vision, followed quickly by red.

"Ah, hell," Lucien said. "Look at his face. You knew better, Aeron."

Knocking over tables and kicking chairs, Maddox fought his way toward Aeron. He left a trail of destruction in his wake, even picked up the plasma screen and tossed it to the ground, shattering it.

"Hey," Paris protested, as his game went silent. "I was winning."

Only one word drifted through his mind: *kill. Kill, kill, kill. Kill.* Woe to anyone who was foolish enough to get in his way. When he reached Aeron, the man had already unsheathed two blades. Maddox didn't bother with a weapon; he would flay the bastard with his bare hands. He wanted blood soaking his fingers, wanted bones scattered on the — Ashlyn's face suddenly flashed through his mind.

Her head was thrown back, her golden hair wet and cascading down her back. Water droplets slid over her stomach and caught in her navel. Pleasure shuddered through her.

Reyes and Lucien leapt on him, dragging him to the ground and shoving Ashlyn from his head. He bellowed, a howl so loud he expected glass to shatter. Fists flew — his, theirs, he didn't know. Someone kneed him in the stomach, knocking the breath from his lungs, but he didn't stop.

Kill. Kill.

If he'd had fangs he would have bitten, so badly did he crave the taste of blood. He would have drained someone dry. As it was, he brought up a booted foot and kicked somebody in the cheek. Grunted in satisfaction when he heard a howl.

"Pin his fucking legs."

"Can't. Got his arms."

"Knock him out, Paris."

"Sure. Want me to spew diamonds from my ass while I'm at it?"

A fist collided with his jaw. His teeth rattled and he tasted the blood he'd craved.

"That's for ruining my game." Paris. "Bunny was about to spread oil on Electra."

"I'll kill you. I'll —" Ashlyn's pleasure-drenched image flashed once again. Her eyes alight with passion. Her head thrown back as she enjoyed his mouth on her, licking every drop of her femininity.

He stilled, realization slamming into him. What was he doing? What the hell was he doing? He didn't want blood and death on his hands. He didn't. He wasn't a monster. He wasn't Violence.

Suddenly he was ashamed of his actions. He should have had more restraint. He knew better.

Panting, he tried to sit up. The men tightened their grips. He relaxed, not forcing the issue. *No more,* he vowed. *No more attacking my friends.*

We have to protect Ashlyn, Violence growled.

A desire to protect? From the demon?

We will, just not this way. Not like this. The more he gave in to the spirit, the more he became Violence. When had he stopped fighting against it so fervently?

Sometimes, when he was alone, he liked to think that if he'd been born a human, destruction would have been the furthest thing from his mind. He would have married, had a loving wife and laughing children who played at his side while he carved. Carving furniture — chests, dressers, beds — had once been a pleasure for him.

Since he had destroyed everything he'd ever created, he'd given up the hobby.

"He's stopped moving," Reyes said with surprise.

"I can't see the spirit anymore." Aeron. Confused.

"Hey. We didn't even have to chain him." Paris.

"This is a first." Torin. Still laughing.

They released him and stepped away in unison. Maddox shook his head, trying to clear his thoughts and piece together what had just happened. He had been consumed by Violence, yet he hadn't murdered everyone in his path. Nor had his friends been forced to bind him to impede him.

Gingerly, he sat up and glanced around the room. Total destruction greeted him. Wood splinters, ripped foam cushions, black TV shards. Yes, he'd been consumed.

His brows puckered in confusion. Usually he had to be knocked out and chained. Or beaten so badly he could only wait in bed until Pain and Death came for him. Yet thoughts of Ashlyn had soothed him completely.

How?

"Good now?" Reyes asked him.

"Yes." The word was raw, hoarse. Someone must have choked him.

He pushed to his feet and stumbled to the couch. No cushions, not anymore, but he didn't care. He fell onto the hard springs. They squeaked under his weight.

"Good thing Torin knows how to invest," Paris said, glancing around as he sat beside Maddox. "Looks like it's time to splurge on new furniture."

"Where were we?" Lucien asked, getting them back to the business at hand. There was a cut on his forehead, one that hadn't been there a few minutes ago.

A wave of guilt swept through Maddox. "I'm sorry," he said.

Lucien blinked at him in surprise, but nodded.

"The women," Reyes grumbled, settling at Maddox's other side. "I say we give it more time. Unlike some of us —" he sent a pointed look in Maddox's direction "— Aeron has his spirit under control right now, whether it's stirring or not."

"I agree." Lucien walked to the overturned pool table, the scent of roses drifting from him.

A nice smell, but not as good as Ashlyn's,

all honey-warm and spiced with secrets and moonlight. Ashlyn . . . Thinking about her again caused his body to harden, to ready. Should have taken her when he'd had the chance, he thought again. Should have penetrated that tight, wet sheath.

"Uh, I'm happy to sit close to you and everything, but I had no idea *you* would like it so much," Paris muttered.

For the first time in hundreds of years, Maddox felt a blush creep into his cheeks. "It's not for you."

"Thank the gods," was his friend's reply.

"Speaking of gods, Maddox, now might be a good time to tell the others about the voice you heard," Lucien prompted him.

Maddox didn't want to burden them but knew there was no other choice. "Very well. Someone came to me, in my head, commanding me to send every one of you to a cemetery tonight at midnight, unarmed."

Lucien motioned to Aeron. "You know these new gods better than any of us. What do you make of this? Does it sound like something the Titans would do?"

"I'm not an expert on them, but I do not think so, no. There would be no reason to concern themselves with our weapons. Useful as they are in battling Hunters, they'd be futile in a war with the gods."

Paris *woohoo*-ed, and everyone shot him a surprised glance. He shrugged sheepishly. "Got my game back on with the mini-TV I'd stashed in case something like this happened."

Maddox rolled his eyes.

"Let's assume for the moment that the voice belongs to a Hunter," Lucien said, bringing them back to the main topic. Again. "That means we're now dealing with a Hunter who has a formidable ability. And since it's doubtful he's working alone, we have to wonder if his friends have similar powers."

Aeron said, "We're stronger than mere mortals, special powers or not. We can take them."

"Yes, if we can outwit them. Remember Greece? The Hunters were not as strong as we were but they managed to hurt us time and time again. Now a trap has most likely been set in the cemetery." Maddox eyed each of them in turn. "I can't go — I'll be dead — but everyone else can. You can turn their trap against them and kill *them*."

Lucien shook his head. "At midnight, Reyes and I will be here, with you. That leaves Paris and Aeron, since Torin can't leave, either. We can't send the two of them to fight a battle when we don't know the odds."

"Let's leave now, then," Maddox said. He hated leaving the fortress, but he would do it. To protect Ashlyn, he would do anything. If this new breed of Hunter meant her harm . . . "There are seven hours until midnight. That's plenty of time for me to fight and return."

Everyone blinked at him in silent surprise. He'd never offered to go into the city before.

"Someone has to stay here and protect the women," Reyes finally said.

"I agree." He couldn't, wouldn't, leave Ashlyn alone, defenseless. What if she became sick again? What if Hunters were able to breach the fortress and hurt her?

"Well, I *don't* agree." Lucien gave them both an apologetic smile. "Killing the Hunters is more important than guarding the women."

Since they'll be dead soon, anyway. He didn't have to say it when they were all thinking it.

Reyes's hands fisted. Maddox ground his teeth together.

"Someone stays behind to guard," he said, "or you fight without me." Aeron might be Wrath and Lucien might be Death, but no one fought like Violence. Taking him into battle all but guaranteed their victory.

"We'll go without you," Lucien said, finality in his tone.

So be it. He wasn't leaving Ashlyn unprotected. The fortress was well-fortified, yes, but it couldn't stab an opponent, rendering him ineffective. It couldn't sweep her away from danger and into safety's arms. "Tell me what you intend to do, then, to ensure victory."

A pause. Lucien and Aeron exchanged a tense look. Before he could comment, Lucien bent down and picked up a long, rolled-up paper that had fallen to the floor during Maddox's tirade. He strode to the couch and unrolled it, anchoring it on the edge. "Would've been nice to do this on the coffee table," he muttered. "Even the pool table. As thorough as you are, though, you overturned and cracked both."

"I have already apologized," Maddox said, guilt increasing. "And tomorrow I will repair them."

"Good." Lucien pointed to the paper. "As you can see, this is a printed map of the city. Earlier, when we were planning and you were otherwise occupied, we decided to set a trap in this abandoned area." His finger circled a bumpy-looking stretch of land to the south. "There are hills and no houses, which makes it the perfect place to strike. We'll wait there and let the Hunters come to us."

"That's it? That is your plan?"

"Well, that and kill them." The fragrance of roses became stronger as Lucien's eyes glittered menacingly. "It's a good plan."

"They may not come. They may be at the cemetery."

"They'll come," Lucien insisted.

"How do you know?"

He paused, glanced at Aeron once more. "I have a gut feeling."

Maddox snorted. "Your gut could be wrong. We should at least secure the hill before you go so that no one sneaks up while you're gone and I'm dead."

"Fine," Lucien said with a sigh. "Let's get to work."

CHAPTER FOURTEEN

Hotel Taverna, Budapest

Sabin, keeper of Doubt, lay on his bed, staring up the suite's virginal white ceiling. He'd traveled from New York to Budapest with one goal: finding Pandora's box and destroying it. All right, two goals. So far, no luck. But he *had* found the warriors who had walked away from him thousands of years ago. Men he'd once fought beside. Men he'd once loved.

Men who now hated him.

He sighed. Since his arrival three days ago, he'd caught a glimpse of Paris here and there, but hadn't made his presence known, unsure of the reception he'd receive. Would he be attacked on sight or embraced as the prodigal son?

Damn, but he almost feared finding out. He'd nearly decapitated Aeron when the warrior tried to stop him from burning Athens to the ground in an effort to draw out the Hunters responsible for their friend Baden's death.

A few times since coming here, Sabin had tried to stealthily infiltrate their midst, to learn everything he could about these warriors he'd once considered brothers yet who were now strangers to him. They had revealed nothing. So he had turned his attentions to the humans surrounding them. Only one had heard him. A woman. She hadn't given him any new information, either.

All he knew was that six warriors were alive and kicking in that massive fortress on the hill, and they were armed out the ass.

That, he'd already learned from a Hunter he'd interrogated a month ago. The very Hunter who had told him, with great reluctance, about the search for Pandora's box. How finding the box would mean the end of the Lords of the Underworld, for the demons would be sucked back inside its walls and the warriors unable to survive without them.

Apparently, Hunters had been planning for weeks to storm the fortress and capture the warriors inside, but hadn't found a way in yet. The fact that they wanted to capture rather than destroy plagued Sabin with questions. Did the warriors here know where the box was? Did they care? How did they feel about Hunters these days? They'd walked away from the fight once. Would they do so again?

He uttered another sigh. There'd be time for thinking on that later. Right now, he had another mystery to solve. The changing of the guard, so to speak. From the hands-off Greeks to the control-freak Titans — a worry he hadn't expected.

He didn't know these new gods, but he didn't think he liked them. There'd been murmurs of war and domination all through the heavens when they'd summoned him, forcing him to stand in a circle of unfamiliar faces and answer their questions.

What is your ultimate goal?

What are you willing to do to reach it?

Are you afraid of dying?

Why they'd summoned him and not the others, he didn't know. He didn't know anything, really. Not anymore. He wasn't even sure Maddox would tell the others to visit the cemetery.

He hoped they came. The time had come to make his presence known; he simply wanted to have the advantage when he did so.

If only I could lie . . . It would have made things a whole lot easier.

But Sabin *couldn't* lie — if he tried, the demon went crazy and Sabin passed out cold. Strange reaction to wickedness, but he could not stop it. What he *could* do was project his thoughts into another's mind, filling them with mistrust and worry as he wove a web of doubt through questions and observations.

Neither questions nor observations were lies, now were they?

Plugged in as his demon was to doubt, Sabin had heard Maddox praying for the human girl and had swooped in, creating even more doubt about whether she could survive without the aid of a god. That she *had* survived worked in Sabin's favor, allowing him to demand payment.

On the off chance the warriors arrived — they'd be armed despite his command, he was sure — Sabin and his men were going to be there, waiting. Hoping. How would they react to this unexpected reunion?

With hatred, most likely.

"Shut the hell up," he told the spirit. He didn't mind using it against others, but he hated when the stupid thing tried to weaken *him*.

The door to his suite swung open.

He gripped the blade strapped to the back of his neck, preparing to strike. When he spotted his guests, he relaxed.

"What kind of welcome is that?" Kane asked.

Cameo, Amun and Gideon flanked him. They'd been together since Baden's death, when they'd given themselves over to their demons. Anything to help punish those who had taken one of their own.

The destruction they had caused, the people who had been hurt . . . Sabin shuddered, remembering. It had taken a long time to find themselves again, but by then it had been too late. They could never fully immerse themselves into society, could never be anything other than warriors.

Hunters wouldn't let them.

More than destroying Baden, they had slaughtered any human the warriors favored and destroyed any home they'd ever made. For that, Sabin would fight them for the rest of his days. Aka eternity. Until the last one fell, defeated, he would fight.

Sabin sat up and anchored his weight on his elbows, leaning back against the headboard. "Anything?"

"Plenty," Gideon said.

"Nothing," Kane countered with a roll of his eyes.

Gideon was possessed by the spirit of Lies. Unlike Sabin, the man couldn't utter a single truth. Everyone in the room knew to believe the opposite of whatever he said.

Sabin pinned Gideon with a next-time-just-keep-your-mouth-shut look and the man shrugged, as if to say he'd do what he wanted, when he wanted. No "as if" about it, actually. Gideon did do whatever he wanted. Always had. Rebellion swam in his blood.

He was tall, a warrior like Sabin, but that was where the similarities ended. While Sabin had brown hair, brown eyes and a roughly hewn face, Gideon was pure punk, embracing the modern Goth look, throwing in a little grunge and mixing it all together with movie-star flair.

He'd colored his pale hair bright, metallic blue. Said he'd done it because it really made his eyes pop. Of course, that was a lie. He'd probably crafted the look as a warning to humans. *Approach at your own peril.*

He was pierced and tattooed all over his body. He only wore black, and he never left home without a full arsenal strapped to his body.

Well, none of them did, really.

"Where's Strider?" Sabin asked.

Gideon opened his mouth to answer — with a lie — but Kane, possessor of Disaster, interrupted, "He couldn't accept defeat. He's still looking."

Of course. Sabin should have known. Because Strider held Defeat inside of him, he had to win, no matter what he was doing — war, cards, Ping-Pong — or he suffered physically, unable to move from bed for days.

Sabin had told his team to talk to the locals with the goal of learning something new about the Lords or the box, so Strider would not return until he did so.

Cameo, the only woman in their cursed group, plopped into the plush lounge across from him. Once, she, too, had been an immortal warrior to the gods. Like the other warriors, she'd been offended when Pandora was chosen to guard *dimOuniak.* But unlike them, she hadn't resented the fact that a female guard had been chosen — only that the female selected hadn't been herself. He still remembered her enormous smile the day they'd decided to topple Pandora. It was the last smile Sabin had ever seen on her face.

"The locals are unwilling to give us any information," she said. "For some reason they consider the warriors — get this — *angels* and don't want to betray them."

Sabin had a hard time listening to her.

She was the saddest excuse for flesh he'd ever seen.

Oh, she wasn't ugly. Far from it. She was small and delicate, with black hair and amazingly bright silver eyes. But she now held the spirit of Misery inside her, so laughter, giddiness and joy were not a part of her life.

Sabin had tried for hundreds of years to cheer her up. No matter what he did, what he said, she always looked on the verge of suicide. Truly, all the sadness in the world was swimming in those silver eyes and layered in her voice. He'd always wondered how she persevered without going mad.

He rubbed his jaw as his gaze sought Amun. "Did *you* learn anything?"

Amun leaned against the far wall, a dark slash in contrast to the stark white of the room. Dark skin, dark eyes, dark everything, Amun could divine secrets — deep, deep secrets — when in close proximity with someone.

Had to be a burden, knowing the ugliest secrets of those around him.

Maybe that was why Amun rarely spoke. Afraid he'd spill unthinkable truths. Afraid he'd cause widespread panic.

"Nothing to help our cause," Cameo answered for him in that death-warmed-over tone of hers. "Except for the women who've slept with Paris and Maddox and only know the size of their cocks, the townspeople have always remained at a distance from the warriors, so they don't know enough for Amun to divine a secret."

Okay, seriously. She made him want to plunge a knife in her heart, right here, right now, rather than wait for her to do it. Anything to stop the sadness.

Before he could respond, the door burst open a second time and Strider entered, claiming everyone's attention.

His light hair was in tangles around his face, his blue eyes bright. Dirt streaked his sharp cheekbones and blood was sprinkled on his chin. But his strides were smooth, unburdened, so Sabin knew the man had found something.

Sabin straightened abruptly. "Tell us."

Strider paused in the center of the room and grinned. "As we suspected, Hunters are already here."

Cameo shifted in a movement of total grace and elegance completely at odds with her suicidal expression. "Let's capture and question them and find out if they know more than we do."

"No need," Strider said. "I already detained one."

"And?" Sabin asked excitedly.

"Like that Hunter told you last month, they're here to capture the Lords on the hill. They've got someone on the inside."

"I'm delighted to hear this," Gideon said.

Strider ignored him. They all did.

"No mention of the box?" Kane asked. As he spoke, a lightbulb shorted out in the lamp beside him, spraying sparks in every direction.

"None."

The lamp tipped over, nailing Kane in the head.

Sabin shook his head. The man was a walking disaster. Literally. Whenever Kane stepped into a room, things went to hell pretty quickly. Sabin expected the ceiling to cave at any moment. And yeah, it had happened before.

Kane brushed the tiny flames from his hair and rubbed his temple, hazel eyes showing no emotion. Without a word, he moved away from the hazardous lamp and eased onto the floor as far away from everyone as he could get.

Sabin cast a glance out the French double doors that opened onto a comfortable balcony with a romantic view of the city. Not that he had room for romance in his life. Women tended to run screaming from

340

him — if he didn't run screaming first.

He didn't mean to, but he made them doubt themselves in every way imaginable. Their life choices, their appearance, their everything. They cried. Always. Sometimes they tried to kill themselves. And he just couldn't take it anymore. Couldn't take the guilt that came with his unstoppable actions. So now he stayed away. Far, far away.

Sabin tamped down a wave of regret. Night had fallen and he could see the twinkling city lights. The moon was full, bright and clear. A golden beacon in the black velvet sky. Cold air wisped inside, dancing the sheer white curtains against the wall.

A night for lovers.

Or death.

"Where are the Hunters now?" he asked.

"Meeting at a club, according to my source. I already checked it out, and it's about five minutes from here," Strider said.

Sabin had wanted to be at the cemetery, but now he wanted to be at the club. Unfortunately, he couldn't be in both places at once. In an echo of the choice that had faced him centuries ago, he again found himself torn between Hunters and his old friends.

He gave the room another inspection, as if

341

the answer was hiding somewhere in the shadows. "I need one of you to go to the cemetery tonight. Fully armed. I did my best to draw the warriors there. You can decide what to do if you see them. The rest of us will visit the club."

"I'll take the cemetery," Kane said. He didn't sound excited. Rather, he sounded resigned. "The club might collapse if I go."

True.

A chunk of plaster chose that moment to dislodge from the wall and slam into Kane's skull. Good thing the man had a mane of thick tabby-cat hair to soften the blow. As it was, he winced.

Sabin sighed. "If all goes well, we might get the answers we've been waiting for and finally, once and for all, be able to destroy Pandora's box." *Before the Hunters find it and suck our demons back inside, killing us.* "Now let's move out."

CHAPTER FIFTEEN

Damn, damn, damn.

Time had gotten away from him. Maddox had become completely absorbed as he'd placed traps along the hill: pits to fall into, trip wires, nets. Should have done it long before today, but they hadn't wanted to hurt any of the deliverymen bearing supplies or the women who came looking for Paris.

Every time Maddox had thought he was done, Lucien had given him another task.

Now it was eleven-thirty, and there was no time to see Ashlyn. No time to kiss or hold her. *If* he decided to see her again, he thought darkly. After his outburst today, he'd be a fool to ever approach such an innocent again. Still, he wanted to be near her. Craved it. Surely there was a way. So far, he'd kept himself under control around her.

But what happened when she pushed him past the edge of reason? When, not if. What would he do when the spirit erupted, as it inevitably would?

"May the gods smile on us this night," Lucien muttered.

Maddox, Reyes and Lucien raced through the intricate hallways of the fortress toward Maddox's bedroom. Always better to chain him early. Less chance for destruction that way. His stomach already ached.

Reyes had already grabbed the sword — the very one Maddox had used to slay Pandora all those years ago. It hung at the warrior's side, glinting in the moonlight that seeped through the windows, taunting Maddox even now.

He passed Lucien's bedroom and brushed his fingertips over the door. Ashlyn was inside. What was she doing? Was she thinking of him?

They rounded a corner, closer . . . closer . . . *I'm not ready,* the spirit whined. A first, since the bloodlust always sated it. Maddox wasn't ready to die, either. Not this time.

Footsteps echoed, an ominous war beat.

He passed the last window in the hallway, the largest. It looked over the hill, down onto the snowcapped trees. What he would have given to run through those trees, to feel the snow drift over his skin. What he would have given to take Ashlyn out there, right now, and make love to her on the cold, hard ground, where she'd be bathed in moonlight like a wood nymph. No violence. Just passion.

"Perhaps we can convince these Titans to release you from this curse," Lucien said, dragging him from his musings.

For the first time in hundreds of years, he felt a stirring of hope. Maybe, despite everything, the Titans *would* release him if he asked. They had once craved peace and harmony for the world. Surely they — *You know better.* Look at what they were making Aeron do.

Maddox's hope fell away from him in little pieces, like leaves from a winter tree. Already the Titans had proven themselves crueler than the Greeks had ever been. "I do not think I want to risk it."

"Maybe there is an alternative to the gods," Reyes said.

If so, they would have found it by now, but he didn't say that aloud. A few seconds later, the trio entered his bedroom, shoving the thick wooden door out of the way. Dread heated Maddox's blood as he climbed onto the bed. He lay down. The fresh cotton sheets were cold, scentless, and bore no trace of Ashlyn. Still, he had the memory.

Last time he'd lain here, he'd held her in his arms, comforted her. Breathed her in. Contemplated making love to her. Savored her taste in his mouth.

His dread increased as Reyes chained his wrists and Lucien his ankles. "When this is over," he said, "check on Ashlyn. If she is well, leave her in the room with the other women. If not, lock her in another room and I will care for her in the morning. But no more dungeons. No more cruelty. Feed her, but do not give her wine. Understand?"

The two men shared another of those tense looks they'd exchanged earlier and stepped away from the bed, out of spitting range.

"Reyes," Maddox said, a warning. "Lucien," he added, a curse. "What's going on?"

"About the woman," Lucien began, refusing to face him. There was a poisoned pause.

"I'm trying to remain calm," he said, even as a black haze shuttered over his vision. "Tell me you have not done anything to her."

"We haven't."

He released a breath, his eyesight returning to normal.

"We haven't done anything to her," Lucien continued, "but we're going to."

The promise hit Maddox's ears then registered in his mind a moment later. He bucked against the chains. "Let me loose. Now!"

"She's Bait, Maddox," Reyes said quietly.

"No. She isn't." Feeling panicked, as if he were stuck in a nightmare he couldn't awaken from, he told them of her ability and his suspicion that she'd been followed unknowingly. "She's cursed, like we are. Cursed to hear ancient conversations."

Lucien shook his head. "You're too enthralled with her to admit the truth. That she may have a strange ability only solidifies my belief that she is Bait, exactly like the voice you heard in your head today. How better to learn about us? How better to discover the best way to defeat us?"

Maddox strained his neck forward, nearly ripping the tendons. "Hurt her, and I will kill you. That is not a threat, it's a vow. I'll spend the rest of my days seeing to your torture and ultimate death."

Reyes tangled a hand in his hair and the inky locks stood up in spikes. "You're not thinking clearly now, but someday you will thank us for this. We're taking her into the city. We're using her to draw out the Hunters. That is the piece of the plan we didn't tell you."

Bastards. Betrayers. He'd never suspected his friends, the very warriors who shared in his misery, would be capable of this. "Why are you telling me now? Why are you doing this?"

Reyes looked away from him, but didn't answer. "We'll do our best to bring her back in the same condition she leaves in."

Once again Maddox jerked on the thick chains, using all of his might. He didn't shatter the impossibly strong links — the gods themselves had made these chains — but he did bend the metal headboard. Rage exploded through him, so fervent and sinister he couldn't see, couldn't breathe. Had to get to Ashlyn. Had to protect her. She was innocent, fragile, would never survive if a fight broke out.

And if the enemy captured her . . .

He bucked and roared and bucked some more. "Ashlyn!" he screamed. "Ashlyn!"

"I don't understand how he can be this fierce over one woman," he faintly heard Lucien say.

"Such devotion is dangerous," Reyes replied.

He blocked the sound of their chatter. "Ashlyn!" If she heard him, she could run to him, unlock him, and he could protect her. He could — no. She was trapped inside

Lucien's room, and he had put her there. He had made sure she couldn't escape. And even if she did make it here, would the two men he'd once considered friends attack her?

He pressed his lips together and bit down on his tongue. For hours — minutes? seconds? — he fought silently but failed to free himself. Lucien and Reyes watched without a word, never relenting. He cursed them with his eyes, promising retribution.

Help Ashlyn hide, he prayed. *Let her remain hidden until I come for her.*

A sharp pain stabbed his side.

Midnight had finally arrived.

He groaned. The spirit churned inside of him, a poisoned hailstorm, a bundle of lightning, a tempest of destruction. Man and demon melded with a common goal. Surviving this, so that they could defend their woman.

But Reyes rose over him, sword in hand. His face was devoid of emotion. "I'm sorry," he whispered.

When the blade cut into Maddox's stomach, slicing through skin, organ, bone, he couldn't hold back his screams any longer.

The door to the bedroom creaked open slowly, and all but Ashlyn and Danika shrank as far away as possible. They grabbed each other's hands. All evening, Ashlyn had been seething with the need to confront Maddox. Danika had wanted to confront Reyes. Instead they had ended up sharing their life stories.

Rather than freaking Danika out, Ashlyn's past seemed to ease the girl's suspicions. In turn, Ashlyn had been outraged at Danika's kidnapping. How strange to think that in this place of death and fear, Ashlyn had found not only her first would-be lover but also her first real friend.

An angel stepped inside the room.

Silver hair produced a halo around his head; his green eyes sparkled like emeralds. A demon should not be so beautiful. But he was covered in black, as Ashlyn would have expected, with a black shirt, black pants and black gloves. Worse, he held a gun in one of his outstretched hands.

She'd seen him before, in Maddox's room. Last night — was it only last night? — when Maddox had been stabbed. This man hadn't participated, but he had watched. And he hadn't tried to help.

"Ashlyn," he said, eyes searching for her.

Fear tightened her throat. He knew her name? Why hadn't Maddox come? Had he washed his hands of her already? Did he now want her dead?

Trying not to whimper, she pushed Danika behind her. "I'm here," she managed to squeeze out. Part of her expected to be shot that very second.

She wasn't.

The man remained in place, though his gaze moved across the room, past the bed and dresser until it collided with hers. "Come with me."

She felt rooted to the floor, frozen. "Why?"

He cast a harried glance over his shoulder. "I'll explain on the way. Now hurry. If they see you, I won't be able to save you."

Danika was suddenly in front of her, a bundle of fury. "She's not going with you. None of us are, no matter how many guns you point at us. You and your buddies can go fuck yourselves."

"Maybe later," he replied dryly, keeping his sights on Ashlyn. "Please. We don't have much time. Do you want to see Maddox again or not?"

Maddox. Just hearing his name caused her heart rate to spike. *I must be the stupidest girl in the world.* She gave Danika a hug and whispered, "I'll be okay." She hoped.

"But —"

"Trust me." She pulled from the girl's hold and trudged forward. The white-haired angel backed away from her as if she were a stick of dynamite.

"No one else move," he said, practically cartwheeling in his haste to keep distance between them. "I'll shoot first and ask questions later." Still watching her, he stopped in the hall.

When Ashlyn stood in front of him, he added, "Don't touch me. Bad things happen when people touch me. Don't even get close enough to fall into me if you trip." His tone was deadly serious, his eyes now flat.

"Okay," she said, confused. Still, she tucked her hands behind her back, just in case she forgot, and waited for him to lead the way.

He moved a wide circle around her, keeping the gun trained straight ahead, and shut and locked the door. Ashlyn didn't try to rush him. Fear once again held her bolted in place.

"What bad things?" she couldn't help but ask when he turned back to her.

He leapt into motion, throwing over his shoulder, "Disease. Agony. Death." He sheathed the gun at his waist. "My skin cannot touch another living thing without causing a plague."

Dear Lord. Whether it was true or not, the idea alone was enough to keep her away from him. She suspected he spoke true, however. Each time she'd seen him, he'd done his best to remain out of the way, removed from everyone around him. Not the actions of an evil man, but a man who cared more about others than he did himself. Her heart softened toward him. *Stupid idiot.*

"What's your name?"

"Torin," he said, seeming surprised that she cared.

"You don't plan to kill me, do you, Torin?"

He snorted. "Hardly. If I did, Maddox would cut out my heart and fry it for breakfast."

"Okay, that was a little more information than I needed," she said, yet she couldn't help but experience a silly, schoolgirl rush of happiness. Did Maddox care about her, then? Even a little? If so, where was he? Why hadn't *he* come for her?

Torin led her through the hallways, quiet, even his footfalls muffled. A few times he stopped and listened, then motioned for her to hide in the shadows. "Keep it down," he told her when she opened her mouth to ask a question.

"Anytime you're ready to talk, *I'm* ready to hear about what's going on," she whispered.

He ignored her. "We're almost there."

"Where?" The more she walked, the more she thought she heard . . . what *was* that?

A second later, she knew.

Her stomach cramped, the noise becoming all too clear. Screaming. Agonized, pain-filled screaming. She'd heard that torturous suffering only once before and it had been once too often.

"Maddox," she gasped out. Not again!

She was so close now, she could make out the deep timbre of his voice, his and the second voice that sometimes peeked through it, both broken and cracked. She wanted to vomit. Urgency pulsed through her. She almost raced in front of her guide, but held her ground, afraid he'd reach out to stop her. "Hurry, Torin. Please hurry. I have to help him. We have to stop them."

"In here," he said, opening a door and stepping out of the way. She raced into the room, already searching for Maddox. She saw an antique chest, a bearskin rug, a canopied bed, but no Maddox. Confused, concern intensifying, she spun around.

"Where is he?" She had to get to him. Didn't matter what he'd done to her or how he felt about her.

He shouldn't have to suffer like that.

"Don't worry about Maddox. You know

he'll be fine. Worry about yourself. They were going to take you into the city, and I couldn't let them. Maddox would have murdered us all in our beds. So, for the sake of my life if not yours, be quiet. They don't have a lot of time to search for you. Behave and you might survive." He shut the door in her face with a soft snick.

A *click* echoed as the lock engaged.

Dread, fear and uncertainty fought for dominance inside of her. She didn't know if Torin had been telling the truth and she didn't care. She had to get to Maddox. Another of his shouts pierced the air and seemed to cut through plaster and rock, wrapping around her.

Tears stung her eyes. She rushed to the door, trying to turn the knob with a shaky hand. It didn't budge. Damn it! She'd be quiet, but she was *not* staying in this room.

Ashlyn wheeled around and again surveyed the area, trying to see it through a thief's eyes. Dust covered everything, as if the room had been forgotten for years. No knickknacks, either. Nothing she could use to smash the lock.

She moved to the window and swept the drapes aside, instantly gaining a view of the mountain, white and majestic. A balcony led — she looked, gasped. Down, down,

down. *Only if you fall.* Thankfully the double glass windows opened easily. Ignoring the sudden blast of frigid air, she peeked right, then left. A few feet over was another balcony.

Maddox bellowed, loud and long.

Palms sweating, she raced to the bed, an idea forming in her mind. A dangerous idea. A stupid idea. "The only idea," she muttered, sweeping up the covers and sheets with a flick of her wrist.

Dust filled her nose and mouth and she coughed but didn't slow. She tied one end of the sheet to one end of the comforter. "It's been done in movies. You'll be okay." Maybe. Actors had nets — and stunt doubles. She had neither.

Another bellow.

Her stomach churned as she returned to the windows. The oversized T-shirt and sweatpants she wore did little to protect her against the elements, but she stepped onto the balcony without any hesitation and hissed in a breath. The stone was ice-cold against her bare feet and the wind was bitter.

Fingers shaking, breath misting, she tied an end of the makeshift rope to the balcony railing. Double knotted. Triple knotted. Gave a jerk.

It held.

But would it hold her weight? After puking her guts out earlier, she was probably a few pounds lighter, so that was one point in her favor.

Shaking more violently now, she climbed over the metal bars. Rust left a dirty trail on her clothing. She kept her gaze level. "You have nothing to worry about. There's not a ten-million-foot drop."

She descended the blanket. A creak. A rattle. Her heart almost stopped. "Maddox needs you. He might even care about you. Or he might think you're a liar and an evil killer, might not even like you and might have tried to seduce answers from you — but either way he doesn't deserve this. You're the only one in this place who thinks so, so you're it. His only hope."

God. I sound like the princess from Star Wars.

But she was desperate to fill the silence she'd so prized. Otherwise, she'd think about falling and death — or worse, failure. "You're doing good. Keep it up."

She lost her voice when she found herself hanging freely. A lump formed in her throat. *Please, Lord. Don't let me fall. Don't let my hands sweat any more than they already are.*

She leaned forward, rocking the sheet . . .

an inch. Damn. She leaned backward. An inch. Forward, back. Forward, back. Soon she had a nice swing. But the sheet slipped a little — or maybe she did — and she screamed.

Just a bit more. I can do it. Picking up speed, she continued to rock back and forth. Finally, she was close enough to the second balcony to reach out and grab — damn! She'd missed.

On the next forward swing, she reached out again. Her fingers hit the rail but failed to catch. Back she flew, slipping another notch.

Concentrate, Darrow. She reached out again and this time she was able to hook her fingers tightly, not letting go, even when the rope tried to jerk her backward. With a grunt, she threw all of her weight forward, grabbing on to the bar with her other hand and releasing the sheet. Then she made the mistake of looking down.

The lower half of her body dangled over fifty feet of jagged mountain.

She couldn't help it; she yelped.

For several heart-pounding moments, she kicked her legs up, trying to curl them around the bar as she'd done with her fingers. Slipping . . . slipping . . . Finally her knee latched.

Muscles burned and strained as she hoisted herself up. It was cold outside, yeah, but she was sweating. Her legs rattled as she tried to pry open the window that led into the new room. It resisted. Several minutes of beating and kicking passed before she succeeded. She climbed inside, nearly collapsing with relief.

The room was dark and dusty, just like the other had been, but she could hear Maddox moaning and fighting once again. *Please don't let me be too late.* Closer now . . . so close . . .

She tiptoed to the door and inched it open. No one was in the hallway. Suddenly Maddox's voice went quiet. Too quiet. She covered her mouth with her hand to prevent a cry. There was muttering —

". . . shouldn't have told him."

"He needed time to calm down. Now he has it."

"He might never calm down."

"Doesn't matter. It was the right thing to do." A pause. A sigh. "I'm eager to finish this and remove at least one burden from our lives. Let's grab the girl and go."

Trembling, she pressed herself against the wall and surrounded herself with shadows. Footsteps echoed. A door creaked open, then closed. More footsteps, these moving away from her.

Ashlyn sprang into motion. She raced into the hall, caught a glimpse of two men rounding a corner and opened the door to Maddox's room.

She almost vomited.

He lay on the bed, the bed where he'd held her so tenderly only hours ago, blood pooling around him. His chest was bare and she could see six gaping wounds where a sword had pierced. She could see inside his body. Oh God. She covered her mouth with her hands.

In a shocked trance, she found herself walking toward him. *Not again,* she thought. *Not again!* The brutality was astonishing.

Why did those bastards keep doing this to him? He was a demon, they were demons, but that wasn't reason enough. "There's no reason good enough," she sobbed. Cruel and heartless, that's what they were.

Slowly she reached out and smoothed her hand over Maddox's brow. His eyes were closed; blood streaked his face, splattered in a random pattern. No, not random. Ashlyn thought perhaps she saw the shape of a butterfly, all angles and sharp curves.

Blood even ran down his wrists and ankles where he'd pulled at his bonds.

Another sob bubbled in her throat and

overflowed. Her knees collapsed, and she was suddenly kneeling beside him. "Maddox," she whispered brokenly. "I'm here. I won't leave you." She gazed about for a key to unchain him, but found nothing.

Reaching out, she clasped his lifeless hand. He was immortal. He'd awakened from this once. He could do it again. Right?

Flames licked at him. Burning like acid. So hot. Melting him, destroying him bit by bit. The air was heavy, black and thick as his body disintegrated. So much pain.

"Maddox."

He heard the voice, familiar, sweet, and he stopped writhing, heat suddenly forgotten. "Ashlyn?" He scanned the depths of the hell he'd returned to but saw only cave after cave of flame. Heard only whimpers and shouts. Had Ashlyn died? Had she been sent here to suffer, too?

That could only mean Lucien and Reyes had killed her. "Bastards!" Maddox howled. They had killed her, and now he would have to kill them. *With pleasure,* the spirit growled.

"I'm here," she said. "I won't leave you." A sob this time.

"Ashlyn," he called. He'd bargain with the cruel new gods. He would get her out of here. Whatever was needed. He would agree to stay here forever, even. Anything to set her free.

"I won't let you go. I'll be here when you awaken. *If* you awaken. Oh God."

His brow furrowed in confusion before melting away once again. Her voice wasn't an echo inside of hell. It was an echo inside his mind. But that made no sense. That was not possible.

"How could they have done this to you? How?"

Was she . . . with his body? Yes, he realized a moment later. Yes, she was. He could almost feel her hand clutching his, her warm tears dripping onto his open chest. He could almost smell her sweet honey scent.

As his charred flesh burned and reformed, burned and reformed, she whispered to him, comforting him. "Wake up again, Maddox. Wake up for me. You have a lot of explaining to do, and I won't let you go until you tell me the truth."

He wanted to obey and fought to escape the deep, deep pit in which he found himself, doing all he could to project his spirit back into his body. He wanted to see her, to hold her, to protect her. But the fire enveloped him in a smoldering embrace, trapping him. He gritted his teeth, wrestling,

362

struggling, battling again and again. He would battle all night, if he had to. He would battle until Lucien came for him.

He would be with Ashlyn again.

His connection to her was too strong, too deep, too ingrained, to be ignored or denied. In such a short amount of time, she'd somehow become the center of his universe. His only reason for living. It was as if she belonged to him. As if she'd been born just for him.

Now that he'd found her, nothing would come between them.

"I'll stay here all night," she said. "I'm not going to let you go."

He was smiling as the flames consumed him again.

CHAPTER SIXTEEN

The time for war had arrived.

Aeron was glad. He seethed with the need to battle, to slay. Maybe, if he maimed a few Hunters, he would stop imagining his blade slicing through Danika's neck, followed quickly by her sister's . . . her mother's . . . and lastly, her grandmother's.

He hadn't told the others, but the need to kill was more than an ignorable flicker inside him now. It was beginning to color his every thought and make him crazed. The gods had not exaggerated. The beast inside him was eager to follow the order he'd been given.

Worse, the stirrings seemed to increase with every hour that passed.

And they would only grow stronger, he knew. They would grow and grow and grow until at last he destroyed those four innocent women.

He worked his jaw. Hopefully he could

suppress the thirst for blood, if only for a little while. *I'm a monster, as bad as the spirit inside me.* If the warriors failed to think of a way to save those women, well, Aeron knew he would have to kiss the last remaining vestiges of himself goodbye. He would be a demon.

Aren't you already?

"Think Maddox's woman is out here?" Paris asked, interrupting his brooding thoughts.

"Could be." They hadn't been able to find her and had soon given up their search, coming into the city anyway. He was furious that Bait might even now be on the loose.

Had the Hunters already been warned of the Lords' arrival?

Lucien had flashed into the cemetery first, but hadn't seen anything suspicious. Still, Torin had been sent in afterward to wait, watch and take surveillance pictures with a few of his toys. Sending him had been a last resort. He'd protested, but in the end had agreed to go. At least the cemetery's inhabitants were already dead, rendering Disease harmless.

Now Aeron and the others moved swiftly through the cobbled streets of Buda. Without Ashlyn, they had to draw the Hunters out another way. They had chosen to be the Bait themselves.

Midnight might have come and gone, but the city was far from ready to sleep. People sat at lighted tables, the innocent playing chess, the more jaded selling a few hours of fun. Buildings towered on each side, a symphony of curves and points. A few cars meandered past.

Humans jumped out of the warriors' way, snatches of gossip and speculation drifting through the moonlight. *The angels have come down from their mountain . . . think they're after those men who were asking about them, the ones at Club Destiny . . .*

"Men were asking about us," Aeron said, teeth clenched. Even as he spoke, a woman crossed the street to greet them, her expression glazed as she stared at Paris.

"A kiss," she beseeched him.

"Always." Paris smiled and lowered his head to grant her request.

Aeron barked, "Later. Take us to this Club Destiny." If Promiscuity started kissing, Promiscuity would not stop kissing until clothes were shed and passion-cries were ringing.

"Next time," Paris told the woman, regret in his tone, and moved on, leading the way to the club.

"Promise?" she called. But she snapped out of her lust-haze when Lucien passed her, blanching at his scarred face.

A few minutes later, the warriors stood just inside the club's entrance, surveying the scene. A crowd of humans danced in a fast, gyrating rhythm, multicolored lights pulsing around them. Those who spotted them gasped. Most backed away — angels, indeed. A brave and foolish few stepped closer.

Standing there, Aeron could sense . . . something. A slight hum of power, perhaps. He frowned.

"See them?" Reyes asked, gaze scanning. His posture was tense. Pain seemed more on edge than ever tonight. His hands were swollen, as if he'd followed Maddox's lead and ruined an entire room.

"Not yet, but I know they're here." Aeron fingered the blade hidden at his side. *Where are you?* Who *are you?*

"Hello, heaven. Look at those sweet little morsels," Paris said, his voice husky with arousal.

"Mind out of their pants," Reyes snapped.

Aeron wished that were *his* only worry. Needing sex. Human females regarded him with fear, like the blonde who'd nearly popped a vessel today at the thought of being touched by him. And he was happy about that. They *should* fear him. He wouldn't mean to, but he'd chew them up and spit them out in a single bite.

"Five minutes," Paris said, the words thick with pleasure. "That's all I need."

"Later."

"Now."

"What are you, a child? Your cock is not a toy, so stop playing with it for one damn night."

"Gods. It can't be," Lucien suddenly said, his stunned tone ending the squabble. He motioned to the back of the club with a grim tilt of his chin. "Look."

Every gaze followed his to a group who stood near the back of the club, watching them.

Aeron hissed in a breath and palmed one of his blades. Seemed the day's surprises weren't over. "Sabin." He had never thought to see Doubt again. The man he'd once considered a friend had held a knife at his throat, had cut and cut deep. "What's he doing here? Why now —" His words jammed to a halt as the answer hit him. "He's still warring with the Hunters. *He* probably brought them to our doorstep."

"Only one way to find out," Lucien said, but none of them moved forward.

Aeron knew why his own feet had turned to lead. That dark, fateful night was playing through his mind.

"We have to kill them," Sabin had screeched. "Look what they did to Baden."

"We have done enough of that," Lucien had replied in that calm voice of his. "We have caused them and their loved ones far more pain than they have brought us."

Cold rage had washed over Sabin's face. "Does Baden mean nothing to you, then?"

"I loved him just as much as you did, but more destruction will not bring him back," Aeron had spat, turning his back, unable to stand the pain in Sabin's eyes. Pain that was mirrored inside him. "I cannot take much more, for my heart grows blacker every day. I need peace. Sanctuary."

"I would rather die than allow a single Hunter to live."

"We killed the man who removed his head. Let that be enough."

"Enough? I held Baden's lifeless body in my arms, his blood seeping all the way to my soul, and you want me to walk away? You are worse than the Hunters." Sabin had attacked then, the blade embedded before Aeron ever sensed it coming.

A fair fight, he could have forgiven. An attack from behind? Hell, no.

After Aeron had fought him off, he'd just wanted to leave. Leave Greece, the war, the hated memories. But Sabin and a few others still had wanted more blood.

That was when the Lords had divided. Irrevocably.

He studied them now, these warriors he knew but didn't. They appeared the same, though their attire had changed with the times. Gideon had blue hair, an unholy gleam in his electric-blue eyes — a gleam that was more than feral, more than predatory. Reminded Aeron of Lucien the one and only time he'd exploded in a temper, nothing and no one able to restrain him.

Cameo was still the prettiest woman he'd ever seen, but damn if he didn't want to stab himself in the heart just from looking at her. Strider was still handsome, though the years had etched ruthlessness on the planes of his face. Amun had discarded his robes for a black shirt and jeans.

Where was Kane? Had the Hunters gotten him, too?

Sabin and the others began a slow, steady approach. He kept his eyes on them as he and the others finally moved forward, as well. The two groups met in the middle of the dance floor, humans quickly scrambling out of their way.

"What are you doing here?" Lucien demanded. Aeron noted that he spoke in English, probably so that the dancers would not understand him.

"I could ask you that, as well," Sabin replied in the same language.

"Here to stab someone else in the back, Doubt?" Aeron asked him.

Sabin popped his jaw. "It's been a couple thousand years, Wrath. Ever heard of a thing called forgiveness?"

"That's funny coming from you."

A muscle ticked below the warrior's right eye. "We didn't come here to fight you. We came to fight Hunters. They're in town, in case you hadn't heard."

Aeron snorted. "We heard. Did you lead them here?"

"Hardly." Sabin ran his tongue over his teeth. "They learned about you *before* we did."

"How?"

Sabin shrugged. "Don't know."

"I highly doubt you'd travel all the way to Budapest to fight. You could have stayed in Greece for that," Lucien said with the slightest hint of bite in his tone.

"Fine. You want the truth?" Strider splayed his arms, showing he was weaponless. "We need your help."

371

"Hell, no." Paris shook his head. "We don't even need to hear how or why, 'cause the answer won't change."

You don't really think you can beat these men, do you? The uncharacteristic doubt whispered through Aeron's mind, quickly solidifying and raking sharp claws in his thoughts.

"We are not the same warriors we used to be," Cameo said, drawing attention to her sad eyes. "Hear us out, at least."

Everyone cringed. She spoke as if every sorrow in the world rested on her delicate shoulders. Probably did. Listening to her, Aeron wanted to sob like a human baby.

"We *do* need your help. We're looking for *dimOuniak*. Pandora's box. Do you know where it is?" Sabin asked tightly.

"After all these years, you want the box?" Lucien seemed bathed in confusion. "Why?"

If you engage them, you might be killed. Or maimed. Why not give them what they want and return to life as normal? Aeron's fists tightened. Damn it. He was strong and capable. There was no reason to doubt himself like this. *Doubt . . .*

A growl rumbled in the back of his throat as he recalled his former friend's ability. "Get out of my head, Sabin."

"Sorry," the warrior said with a weak

smile. "Habit."

He should have launched his dagger then and there. "So you're the one who tried to lure us to the cemetery unarmed." Not a question. "I thought you didn't want to fight us," he added dryly.

Sabin's smile became sheepish. "Wasn't sure of my welcome and didn't want to tempt Fate. And since I failed to draw you there, Kane's going to have a boring night with the corpses. What are you doing here, by the way? Did you hear the Hunters would be here, too?"

"We sent Torin to the cemetery, so Kane's night will be anything but boring," Lucien told him, gaze scanning the club. "And yes, we tracked the Hunters here, though I don't see them."

"Disease is with Kane?" Frowning, Sabin whipped a black box from his pocket. Even as he did so, Reyes had a knife pointed at his neck, obviously thinking the man was going for a weapon. When Reyes realized it was a walkie-talkie, he lowered his blade.

Frown deepening, Sabin raised the radio to his mouth and said, "Kane. Stand down. Friendly fire."

"Roger that. I know," was the staticky reply.

Sabin returned the radio to his pocket.

"We good now?"

"Not even close," Aeron snapped.

Strider stood there shaking angrily, his blistering gaze circling the area. Several people had begun dancing again, high on alcohol and lust as they writhed against each other. "Do you know about the Titans?"

Lucien looked at Aeron before nodding. "Yes."

Cameo bit her lip. "Any idea what they want from us?"

Gods, Aeron wished the woman would keep her mouth closed. "No," he answered before someone could speak for him. He didn't want anyone else knowing what he had been commanded to do.

"Listen, old friends, I know you hate us," Sabin said. "I know we want different things. But one thing we all have in common is a will to live. About a month ago we learned that Hunters are searching for Pandora's box. If they find it, our demons are in danger of being sucked inside. That means we're in danger of dying."

"How do you know it hasn't been destroyed already?" Reyes asked with a frown.

A moment passed, the erratic pulse of muscle the only sound.

"I don't, but I'm not willing to take a

chance that *maybe* it's gone forever."

All these years, Aeron had given the box very little thought. His demon had been inside of it, now it wasn't, and he'd accepted the consequences of his actions, end of story.

Now he thought back to the fateful night of his demon's release, trying to remember what had happened. He had helped fight off Pandora's guards while Lucien had opened the box. The demons had sprung out, seemingly unstoppable as they flew at the guards, devouring their flesh.

The scent of blood and death had infused the air, blending with the screams. Something had wrapped around Aeron's neck — a demon, he knew now — and he'd lost his breath. He'd fallen to his knees, no longer able to hold his own weight, and crawled through the entire chamber, searching for the box, desperate to find it. But he never had. It had vanished as if it had never been.

Lucien ran a hand through his midnight hair. "We don't know where it is. All right?"

A woman suddenly smashed herself into Paris, licking at his neck. Paris closed his eyes and Reyes shook his head. "We should take this conversation elsewhere."

"Let's go to your fortress," Sabin suggested. "Perhaps, together, we will remember *something* about the way it was taken."

"No," Aeron and Reyes said simultaneously.

"Well, I could happily stay here all night," Gideon said, obviously irritated.

Aeron had forgotten how quickly Gideon's lies could rub his nerves the wrong way.

"Your fortress?" Sabin prompted. "I'm ready to leave when you are."

"No," Aeron said again.

"Fine. We'll stay here. Just give me a moment to send everyone home." Sabin closed his eyes, expression growing intense.

Aeron watched him carefully, gripping his dagger, not knowing what to expect. The music stopped abruptly; the dancers ceased moving. Uncertainty fell over each of their features as they began muttering and walking toward the doors. In a matter of minutes, the entire building had emptied out.

Sabin's shoulders slumped and he expelled a long, exhausted breath. His eyelids cracked open. "There. We're alone."

Amun, who hadn't spoken a single word during the entire exchange, tilted his head to the side and stared at Aeron intently, his eyes like a laser beam into his forehead. Amun's face was unreadable, and that made Aeron uneasy. Possessed as the warrior was by Secrets, could he guess what Aeron guarded deep in his soul?

Amun's gaze suddenly met his, and there was regret and knowledge in his dark eyes. Aeron stiffened. Oh, yes. He could guess.

Sabin's chest expanded as he clearly fought for patience. "Why don't we strike a deal? We'll take care of the Hunters who have invaded your city if you'll help us find the box. It's a fair exchange. We've battled them for years and know just how to strike."

"I found one earlier and interrogated him," Strider said. "That's how we knew to come to the club, but so far we've seen no trace of the rest."

Aeron caught a flash of movement in the far shadows and frowned. "Someone stayed behind," he muttered. Everyone stiffened.

That's when Aeron saw the outline of four more humans, all male and all well-muscled, even in silhouette. His frown deepened as he drew in a whiff of gunpowder. "Hunters," he growled. "How's that for a trace?"

Even though they had killed Baden, Aeron had been prepared to leave them alone. He'd caused them just as much pain centuries ago, after all. But they had come here. They would start a new war if given the chance.

Realizing they'd been spotted, one of the humans stepped forward.

The strobe light was still spinning, spitting those fractured beams of light in every direction. They danced over the mortal's young, determined face. He was smiling. He rubbed his right wrist with his left thumb, and in the wild light Aeron could just make out the symbol of infinity he traced.

"Who would've thought we'd get all the world's evil together in the same room at the same time?" The man held up a small black box, two wires hanging from its sides. "Seriously, is it Christmas?"

Several of the warriors growled. Some withdrew guns, some preferred their sharpest daggers. All were ready to battle. Aeron didn't wait — he found that he couldn't, didn't want to, was *eager* to act. Wrath had already judged this man and found him guilty of the crime of killing innocents in his quest to kill Lords.

Aeron tossed his blades, end over end, and both embedded to the hilt in the man's chest.

His eyes bugged and that white-toothed grin froze on his face. He didn't die immediately, as he would have if this had been one of Paris's movies. He fell to his knees, panting, in pain. He'd live for a while yet, but there was nothing anyone could do to save him. "You'll pray for death when we're done with you," he gasped.

"Burn in hell, demon!" one of the other mortals shouted, tossing a dagger of his own.

One of the warriors fired his gun as the blade pierced Aeron's chest. Aeron frowned. Gazed down at the pearl handle winking in the light. His heart continued to pump, slicing open with every beat. Ouch. They had quick reflexes. He would have to remember that.

Lucien and the others sprang forward.

The Hunter didn't back down. "I hope you enjoy the fire," he said, swiping up the black box his fallen friend had dropped.

Boom!

An explosion rocked the entire structure, blasting through stone and metal. Aeron was lifted off his feet and thrown into the air like a sack of feathers.

Defeated by humans. Unbelievable.

It was the last thought to drift through his mind before his world went black.

CHAPTER SEVENTEEN

Maddox became aware of his surroundings with a jolt. Dead one moment, fully conscious the next. Ashlyn slept in the crook of his arm, her pliant body curled around him.

He glanced down at himself. She must have cleaned him and even managed to change the sheets despite his chains because the blood was gone. His scabs were back and stretched across his stomach and his ribs.

Ashlyn's soft honey-colored hair ticked his chin; her warm exhalations fanned his skin. Alive and here. With him. He hadn't imagined it. *Straight from hell into heaven.*

Come morning, he usually felt the need to destroy something. To fight. To forget the flames and the pain by giving in to the numbness and darkness of the spirit. Not so right now.

He felt — dare he believe it? — at peace.

Ashlyn looked so relaxed, he was loath to

awaken her. No, not relaxed, he realized on closer inspection. Tearstains were evident on her cheeks and teethmarks marred the lushness of her lips, as if she'd bitten down hard and repeatedly.

He longed to caress a fingertip over the curve of her cheek, but couldn't. Damned chains. "Ashlyn. Beauty. Wake up for me."

A soft moan parted those lips.

Sunlight caressed her as he craved to do himself, bathing her luminous skin and paying her absolute tribute. Her lashes were feathered, still damp from her tears, like strands of ribbon covered with dew.

She'd cried at his suffering. When was the last time someone had cried over him?

"Ashlyn."

She moaned.

He lowered his head and kissed the tip of her nose. As always, spears of electricity slammed into him. She must have experienced it, too, gasping out his name and jolting upright. The cover fell to her waist, revealing the baggy T-shirt she wore. *His* T-shirt. He liked her in his clothing, liked that she was covered by material that had once covered him. Lock after lock of hair fell down her shoulders and back.

When her gaze landed on him, she released a trembling sob and threw herself into his wide-open arms. "You're alive. You came back from the dead again."

"Unlock me, beauty."

"I don't have the key."

"It's under the mattress." Lucien had stopped carrying the key years ago when Maddox managed to snap it from its chain around his neck. "Why didn't they take you?"

"Torin hid me. Oh." She hurriedly dug under the springs, found it and released him. She fell back into his side, the scent of her skin distracting him from wondering why Torin would have done such a thing. "I'm so glad you came back to me."

He wound his arms around her waist, rubbing his hands up and down her back, soothing, calming. His joints protested, but he didn't stop. "I came back. I'll always come back."

"I don't understand," she said on a shaky breath. Her body trembled. "Why do they keep doing this to you?"

"Another curse." His voice cracked with emotion. "I killed a woman, and now I must die as she died." He had not wanted Ashlyn to know what he'd done, but it wasn't fair to keep her in the dark when she'd revealed all her secrets.

Ashlyn gripped him tightly. "Who was

she? Why did you kill her?"

"The woman I told you about. The warrior, the one given the task I desired for myself. Pandora."

Her eyes stretched wide. "*The* Pandora?"

"Yes."

"*That's* the box you opened? Dear Lord, I don't know why I didn't piece this together before. Why didn't the gods just put the demons back inside the box?"

"Punishment. But more than that, the box was gone, with no way to be re-created."

"How did you kill . . ."

"My demon had overtaken me, and —" Again he could hear the torment in his own voice, and wondered what Ashlyn thought. "I lost control, became Violence completely, and my sword did irreparable damage to her. I have regretted the action ever since, doubt me not."

"But immortals can't be killed eternally. Right? I mean, you're proof of that."

"Most *can* be killed. Not easily, but it is possible."

"Well, everyone makes mistakes, and you've paid for yours," she said, her understanding surprising him. Warming him. Felling him. "I sort of wish you'd killed those gods who cursed you, too, because they're vile, disgusting —"

Wincing, he plastered a hand over her mouth, cutting off her words. "She did not mean it," he said, eyes traveling ceilingward. "I will willingly take any punishment meant for her as my own."

Lightning did not strike them. The earth didn't rumble. Locusts didn't swarm, eating at their flesh. Maddox slowly relaxed. "Never curse the gods. They hear all." Unfortunately.

She reluctantly nodded and he removed his hand.

"I'm not bait," she said.

"I know you're not."

"Really?" she asked hopefully. She angled her head, peering up at him.

"Really."

Her features softened; she even smiled. "What convinced you?"

"You." He looked at her in wonder because it was still a surprise to him. "Your sweetness, your ability. Your virginity."

"So you . . . wanted me?" she asked, unsure now. "Not because you desired answers from me but because . . ."

"But because," he assured her. "You make me burn."

Happiness sparkled in her eyes, like rays of sunshine stamping out the night. She snuggled still deeper into his side, breasts meshing into his chest. "I'm glad the Institute brought me to Budapest."

His body had begun to stir, to ready, to desire more. Until the Institute was mentioned. Violence growled. "You are not going back to them."

"You and your demands." Not realizing his sudden turmoil, she continued blithely, "You know, I've heard a few tidbits about Pandora's box here and there. Did I tell you that the Institute is always interested in tracking down supernatural relics mentioned throughout history in myth and legend?"

He stiffened. "Will you tell me what you heard about the box?"

"Let's see . . ." She tapped her chin. "I heard that the box is hidden. Where, I don't know. But supposedly it's guarded by Argus and even the gods themselves can't get to it."

Maddox absorbed this news with shock. Argus was a huge beast with over one hundred eyes, enabling it to see everything that happened at all times. Legend claimed it had been killed by Hermes, but legend was often a lie told by the gods to fool mortals.

"I also heard a conflicting story," Ashlyn continued, "that the box is actually guarded by Hydra, not Argus. The common denominator in both stories, though, was that the —" She gave another gasp.

"What?"

"If the box ever resurfaced, the demons would be sucked back inside. That's good, right?"

He shook his head. "For the world, perhaps, but not for me. Without the demon, I will die."

"How can you know that? I mean —"

"I know it," he interrupted, thinking on what she had said. Hydra. A poisonous serpent with multiple heads. If that was true, the box was buried deep in the ocean. But which story was he to believe? One or both or neither? If the rest of what she had heard could be believed, that the demons could be sucked back inside if the box were found . . .

"I could, I don't know, do a more thorough search for the box. Make it my top priority."

"No!" That would entail having her leave the fortress, placing her in danger. "I know I told you to tell me everything, but now we must choose a less volatile topic." Violence was prowling his mind, more agitated with every word. While Maddox now believed the demon did not want to hurt Ashlyn, he wasn't willing to take a chance. He would talk about flowers and moonbeams — he cringed — if it meant maintaining this delectable inner peace.

"Is there a way to break your death-curse?" Ashlyn asked. So much for flowers and moonbeams.

"No." He shook his head. "There is no way."

"But —"

"No." He would not allow her to try and bargain with the gods, hoping to find a way to save him. He was not saveable. More than that, he was not worth the effort. He was more monster than man, even if he sometimes tried to convince himself otherwise. "That is a subject best dropped, as well."

She trailed a fingertip down his sternum, deliciously warm breath fanning him. "What subject *can* we talk about, then?"

He splayed his fingers over her bottom and squeezed. "Have you heard any more voices during your time here?"

"Unfortunately." She arched slightly, the action nearly imperceptible, in an effort to be closer to him. "I heard every word spoken by those four women. Who, by the way, should be released immediately."

"They stay."

"Why?"

"That, I cannot tell you."

She drummed her fingertips. "At least tell me what you plan to do with them. They're nice. They're innocent. They're scared."

"I know, beauty. I know."

"So you're not going to hurt them?" she insisted.

"No. *I'm* not."

Her palms flattened, just above his heart. "Does that mean someone else is?"

His blood heated erotically, singeing his veins. "I'll do everything in my power to make sure they aren't. All right?"

Her lips pressed into his neck and her tongue flicked over his pulse. "All right, but I'm going to do everything in *my* power to make sure they aren't, either."

He hated denying her anything, so he clasped her chin, forcing her to face him, and gave her what he could. "I'm sorry you had to listen to their conversations. Never again will I put you in a room where humans have been."

"It wasn't so bad this time." Her fingers curled around his wrists, soft, gentle. "And I don't hear anything when you're around, no matter who's spoken."

"I wonder why. I am not complaining — I am glad, just curious."

"Maybe the voices are afraid of you."

He almost grinned.

"Actually, *I* wonder why I can't hear any of your friends' past conversations. I mean, I've always been able to hear other supernatural beings."

"Maybe we operate on a higher tier of existence."

She did grin.

"Still, we will make sure I am always around you," he said, and it would be his pleasure. "That way, the voices will never bother you again." *What about when you're dead?* The thought caused him to stiffen. There was no one to watch her then. No one to protect her.

Sensing his anger, she frowned. "What's wrong?"

"Nothing." He would not think of the coming death now. He had Ashlyn in his arms and he was going to enjoy her, savoring this small amount of time they had together. "No more talk of the women or curses."

"Well, now you've taken away most of our common ground." Her gaze lowered, fastening on his lips. She shivered. "I've traveled all over the world for the Institute, but I never dreamed I'd meet someone like you."

"Strong?"

A chuckle escaped her. "Yes."

"Handsome?"

"Of course."

"Sharp of wit and skilled with a sword?"

"Absolutely." Another chuckle. "But I mean a man . . . friend . . . guy. Oh, I don't know what to call you!"

He savored her amusement — and her earnest words. "Just call me yours. That is all I want to be."

Everything about her softened. "Tell me something about yourself." She tugged her face from his clasp and once again snuggled into his body. She didn't remove her hands from his wrists but slid them down his arms and around his neck, as if she feared letting him go, even for a second. He feared it, too. He wanted her desperately. And would have her, he swore, after they showered, all traces of blood and death removed. "Something you've never told anyone else."

He could tell her that he liked classical music rather than the hard rock his friends preferred, but that information lacked the deeply personal touch she obviously craved. And Maddox found that he wanted her to know him better than anyone else in the world.

His sense of peace — true peace — deepened. All because she was here with him.

Because she had cried for him and cared for him. Because she didn't judge his past sins or revile him. Because she wanted to learn about him, too. Because only he eased her torment.

Because, when she looked at him, she didn't see Violence. He suspected she saw man. *Her* man. A heady thought. Drugging. Shocking. Enough to earn his eternal devotion.

"There have been a few times over the years that I wished to be human. And have a wife and —" he gulped, confessing "— children." He'd never told his friends, who would have laughed. *He* should laugh at the ridiculousness of it.

Violence? Near children?

Ashlyn didn't laugh, didn't scold him. "That's a beautiful dream," she said, and there was a wistful catch in her voice. "You'll make a wonderful father. Fierce and protective."

Humbled by her proclamation, though he knew he would never be given the chance to prove her words, he traced circles over each of her vertebra. "Tell me one of your secrets now."

Shivering, she drew her finger over the ridged peak of his nipple. His cock jumped in response; his blood blistered. No longer simply heating, but already an inferno. Still, he didn't kiss her, didn't roll on top of her. However much it pained his body, now was a time for talking.

"I didn't learn to read until last year," she admitted shamefully. "Until then, I had to give all of my reports verbally, rather than typing them, and everyone knew why. I just couldn't concentrate long enough to decipher the words. The voices were always there, disturbing me. When I was a kid, my boss would read stories to me, fairy tales so magical I could almost block out the whispers. That was when I became determined to learn on my own. But it took a long time to actually do so."

He didn't care if she could read or not. But she cared, and he sought to comfort her. "That you learned at all is worthy of praise."

She gifted him with a brilliant smile. "Thank you."

"I didn't learn to read until hundreds of years after my possession, and then I only did so because I didn't like others knowing something I did not. See? You are ahead of me already."

She chuckled, relaxing further. "Once I learned, I went online and ordered every romance novel I could find. They're fairy tales for grown-ups. They were delivered straight to my door and I devoured them as fast as I was able."

"I will have Paris buy you some in town. An entire boxload."

"That would be lovely. Thank you," she said again, giving him another of those smiles.

His chest ached as he kissed the top of her head. "I've seen a few romance novels." Paris had left a few lying about the fortress, and Maddox had — maybe, perhaps, might have, would never admit it aloud — picked them up. "Had I read them —" cough, cough "— I would probably think they were —" sexy, fun, enlightening "— interesting."

Her gratitude morphed into pure wickedness. "Maybe . . . maybe we can read one together or something."

"I would like that."

As hungry as he was for her, Maddox found it amazingly pleasant to pass the time just talking. She told him how she'd spent part of her childhood inside a lab, being tested — sometimes painfully, which meant he now had a list of scientists to kill — and how she still spent most of her time alone, just to escape the noise. She'd never really been part of a family. Only one man had ever treated her as anything more than an animal, and Maddox found himself indebted to that human.

But Maddox seethed with the need to chase away those memories and replace them with better ones, happier ones. More than that, he seethed with the need to avenge her. "You deserved better," he said, Violence finally stretching its arms and yawning.

"I didn't mind my upbringing," she said. "For the most part, that is. I was always hearing things, so solitude was actually welcome."

But she'd missed playing and being touched, loved. He heard it in her voice, a need she couldn't quite hide. *You know her so well, do you?* Yes, he thought. He did. A part of him, a part buried so deep he hadn't realized it was there until she had materialized in his life, had known her from the beginning.

She was his. His woman. His . . . everything.

He caressed her arm and felt a small, hard, unnatural lump. He frowned and glanced down. "What's that?"

"Birth control," she said, cheeks heating to a dark pink. "Standard agency procedure. A while back, a woman was raped on the job by a rabid goblin. She became pregnant and the child was . . . not normal. Now the Institute teaches us self-defense and gives all female employees the option of having the implant."

Violence arched its back and fluttered open its eyes, awakening further. The thought of this delicate beauty being forced was abhorrent to both man and spirit. She was a virgin, but that didn't mean she had been left completely alone. "Were you ever hurt?"

"No," she assured him. "But I knew if the voices ever overtook me I wouldn't be able to protect myself."

Violence did not relax.

"Tell me about *your* childhood," she said. Her fingertip again grazed his nipple. She rubbed against him, caught herself and stopped.

His skin tightened with awareness. So did hers; he knew it. From the beginning, he'd always seemed to know when she was aroused. And right now, the woman was definitely aroused. "I did not have a childhood. I was created already a man, already a soldier."

"I'm sorry," she said softly. "I forgot."

I want her so badly. Last time he had stopped himself from taking her fully because she was a virgin. He was the same man he had been yesterday — he'd still never had a virgin and still wasn't exactly sure of the best way to go about it — but none of that mattered now. He'd almost lost her. She had almost been taken from him.

He would not wait another moment.

He would be as gentle with her as he was able. And if the spirit sought to intrude, well, he'd allow Ashlyn to chain him. "I want to make love with you, Ashlyn."

Breath caught in her throat as she inched her fingers over the ropes of his stomach. Stopped at his scabs, then his navel, circled. Moved down another inch. Stopped again. "You do?"

Want her, need her, want, need. Soon . . . now . . . Maddox thought perhaps she wanted to touch lower, to hold his cock, but hadn't quite worked up the nerve. *Yes, yes.* He would have smiled but he and the demon were too primed.

The more she touched him, the more he — they — wanted her. Her sweet scent was in his nose, firing his blood all the hotter. That sweetness trickled all the way to his bones, igniting all sorts of needs. "Oh, yes."

"I want you, too," she whispered on a tremulous breath. "But . . ."

No more waiting. Must have, must have, must have. A sense of ferocity pounded through him. *Ours,* the spirit said. *Mine,* Maddox corrected. "I want to be inside you. No more waiting."

She stilled, air wheezing from her.

"I need you to understand that I'm keeping you. You will stay here with me, and I will protect you. Together we will learn how to stop the voices for good."

"M-Maddox." Whatever else she meant to say was lost as she pressed her lips together.

Yes. Must keep. "I won't hurt you," he said, more for himself and the spirit than for her.

"I know you won't hurt me. But I do have a life and a job."

Keep!

"I'm going to stay for as long as I feel like staying, but I need your promise that you won't lock me up again. When your friends come for you to —" she gulped "— kill you, I want to be with you. I swear I won't attack them, even though I'll want to, but I need to hold your hand. I can't stand the thought of you dying alone."

In that moment, Maddox fell completely, absolutely, irrevocably in love with her.

Mine, mine, mine. She was more important than breathing, more necessary than food or water or shelter. In a thousand lifetimes of war and violence and rage, she gave him kindness. Serenity. Compassion. Trust. Woe to anyone — even the Lords of the Underworld, even the gods — who tried to hurt her. He'd thought it before, but it became a blood oath now. Whoever attempted to harm her from this moment on would die at Maddox's feet.

Lucien and Reyes hadn't taken her last night as they'd claimed, and that saved their miserable hides. Barely. They would pay, though. Oh, they would pay. Violence needed some sort of retribution before it could forget.

"I don't want you to have to watch. I won't be alone, sweet. Pain and Death will be with me."

"Yeah, but they won't snuggle you."

He contained his grin. "You are mine, woman, and I am yours. Until you, my life was desolate. I existed, but I didn't truly live. Now I live, even in my death." The words were as close to marriage vows as he would ever come, he was sure. She would always be his, and he would always be hers.

Tears welled in her amber eyes. "That's the most beautiful thing I've ever heard."

"All I want you to do is think about what you are asking." If he had to watch *her* die over and over again . . . Sickness churned inside of his stomach. "The blood, the horror of it . . ."

"I know what I'm asking," she said, determined. "I still want to stay with you."

Once again, need replaced all else. "You're going to take a shower. Paris says human women love them, that they help relax and soothe." He sat up, dragging her with him. *Finally, finally.*

No, not yet. Soon. He would make Ashlyn's first time special, even if it killed him.

She twirled the ends of her hair around her finger. "Are you going to join me again?"

Maddox forced himself to shake his head and the spirit roared in fury. *Why not now?* "If I shower with you, I'll take you. Totally and completely."

Her gaze slanted over to him, hot, so hot, and he felt the force of it vibrate through him. "Like I told you, I know what I'm asking," she whispered.

Gods, he wanted to kiss her. But if he kissed her, he wouldn't stop kissing her until he was inside her, pumping, pounding, sliding. "There's something I have to do first."

"Afterward . . ." She didn't finish her sentence, but then, she didn't have to.

"Afterward," he promised. Oh, yes. Afterward.

Slowly, the spirit smiled. For the second

time in two days, man and demon were in perfect agreement.

CHAPTER EIGHTEEN

Ashlyn hurried through the shower, wondering what it was that Maddox had to do. The water was hot, soothing, and washed away the trials of the night. Not the hated memory of holding her lover's bloody body in her arms, but the physical effects. The fatigue, the nearly debilitating sense of despair, the rage at what had been done to the man she was coming to love.

The man who might be coming to love her in return.

The feelings might have come upon them quickly, but it just felt right. She wanted so badly to be with Maddox. Wanted so badly to hold and touch him, to give and receive pleasure. To bask in these new feelings of rightness. He no longer considered her Bait, and he wanted her to stay with him. Now and always. Her lips lifted in a slow, happy grin.

How am I going to break his death-curse?

The thought drifted through her mind, overshadowing everything in its path. Her smile faded. Surely there was something she could do to save him from an eternity of dying, only to be resurrected knowing he'd have to die again. No one deserved to be tortured like that.

Ashlyn rested her forehead against the dewy white tile. Surely somewhere in the world, in some time period, a human had talked about the gods and how to break their stupid, unfair curses. She'd probably heard something over the years, but if so, it had blended into all the other voices.

Now, at least, she knew what to listen for.

Maddox wouldn't want her to leave the fortress for that, she was sure, so she'd have to go without telling him. Besides, she couldn't hear the voices when he was around.

Until you, my life was desolate, he'd said. *I existed, but I didn't truly live. Now I live, even in my death.* Fierce protector that he was, he'd consider his own suffering a small price to pay for keeping her safe. Already she knew that much about him.

She'd leave at night, while he could do nothing to stop her, then sneak back in the morning.

Don't think about that now. There's time

enough for spy games later. In just a little while, she was going to make love with a man. With Maddox. His big, strong hands were going to caress her entire body. His mouth was going to taste her. His penis was going to slide deep inside of her.

She shivered. *First desperate to leave, now desperate to stay.* Somehow, some way, she was going to contact McIntosh and let him know she was okay. Not now, though. After. After she experienced the most intimate of acts and knew how it felt to be joined with someone.

Selfish of her, yes. But she couldn't have stopped herself for any reason.

Without a doubt, Maddox was going to finish what they started this time. The tight coiling of his muscles as he'd held her on the bed had promised as much. And the white-hot look he'd given her before leaving the room had only solidified the knowledge.

No longer would she worry that he'd abandon her afterward, as so many men had done to so many women throughout the centuries. Maddox was intense and passionate and different. He didn't need to lie or issue false promises to get what he wanted. He had only to take.

Yet he chose not to. He wanted her to give.

Warm water soon became cold. Ashlyn

turned the knobs, shutting off the steady stream. *Drip, drip.* Almost time, she thought, and moisture instantly pooled between her legs. Her nipples were as hard as rocks.

Droplets slid down her skin, chilling her. She imagined Maddox licking them off, shivered again and nearly moaned. She grabbed a towel and patted herself dry as best she could before anchoring the fluffy white material under her arms so that it draped from breasts to knees. Eager, she exited the bathroom on a cloud of steam.

Maddox wasn't in the bedroom.

She frowned . . . until her toes brushed something soft and she glanced down. Violet silk scarves formed a winding trail, leading from the bedroom to the room next door. When she stood in the entryway, she gaped in delighted surprise.

She'd been in this room before, when she'd crawled over the balcony and through the window, but it hadn't looked like this. Dust had covered everything then. The sheets, even. Now it was a room made for pleasure. Sconces glowed from the walls, golden light flickering over a bed of black silk. Maddox had cleaned it. For her. Her heart swelled in her chest, beating wildly.

Where was he?

The balcony doors were open, inviting

fresh, cold air inside. She approached, her heated blood making her indifferent to the frigid temperature. Maddox gripped the balcony rail, his back to her, dark hair — damp, she noticed — in disarray. His shoulders were wide, tanned and bare.

She'd never seen his bare back before.

There was a huge butterfly tattoo that stretched from the top of his shoulders to just below the waist of his pants. It was red, almost neon, and it looked angry. Mean. As if it could leap off his back and slice her in two. Odd, she mused. Butterflies were such delicate creatures, she never would have imagined one could appear so menacing. Or that a man as, well, manly as Maddox would have such a design tattooed on his body.

"Maddox," she whispered, her voice breathless.

He whipped around as if she'd shouted. A frown tugged at his sensual lips. In that moment, he wasn't the lover who'd left her to shower and prepare for hours of pleasure. He was the warrior who'd tried to leave her in the forest alone.

"Everything okay?"

"There is a blanket tied to that balcony." He pointed to the right, but didn't remove his narrowed gaze from her face. "Do you know anything about that?"

Besides their night in the forest, he'd rarely looked at her in anger. That was usually directed at someone else. So having those violet eyes — now framed with red the exact neon shade of his tattoo — aimed at her like an accusing finger was a bit disconcerting.

Good news? Angry he might be, but that freaky skeletal mask hadn't descended over his features. Empowered by that, Ashlyn raised her chin and stepped toward him. "Yes. I know something about the blanket."

"If you were anyone else," he said tightly, "I would think you tied the cover to the rail so that Hunters could climb inside the fortress."

"But you don't think that of me?" If the question had had teeth, it would have bitten him. Hard.

"No," he said, and she relaxed. Slightly. "So tell me," he continued, "what *did* you use it for?"

Confession time. "I told you that Torin hid me, right? Well, he locked me up so that your other friends couldn't find me, which I don't fully understand yet, so don't ask. I heard you shouting and did what was necessary to reach you."

He took a menacing step toward her, then

stopped himself, as if he feared getting too close to her just then. "You could have fallen to your death," he said quietly.

"But I didn't."

"You dangled in the air, Ashlyn."

Don't back down. Not during this critical moment. They'd just established that they liked each other and that they were both willing to take their relationship to the next level. Whatever happened here would set the stage for future fights. And there would be fights. He was too stubborn, and she too determined.

"Yes," she agreed. "I did."

"Do not ever — ever! — do that again." He closed the rest of the distance between them and leaned down, obliterating her personal space. "Understand?"

Her heart kicked into supersonic hyperdrive. "Tell your friends not to lock me up, and *then* I'll swear it."

His eyes widened with disbelief. Did he expect her to sob out an apology? "I'm going to kill them," he snarled, surprising her. "You could have died out there."

As he maneuvered around her, she saw death in his eyes. Oh, no, no, no. There would be no leaving her. There would be no beating his friends. Not now. Ashlyn reached out without hesitation, without fear, curling her hand around his wide, solid bicep. Growling, he spun and faced her.

"This day isn't going to be ruined by more pain," she told him.

"Ashlyn."

"Maddox."

He could have shoved her away. Could have rejected her, cursed her. Hit her. Instead, he redirected the focus of his emotions. "You could have died out there." With a low, animalistic growl, he meshed his lips against hers. His tongue shoved inside her mouth, past her teeth, thrusting hard.

Finally. Thank you, Lord, finally. She tasted a blend of fury and passion and heat, and it was the most decadent flavor she'd ever encountered. Intoxicating. Her blood instantly sparked.

"Don't want . . . to hurt . . . you," he snarled, speaking between kisses.

"Can't."

"Hurt . . ."

"Won't."

His head tilted to the side as he deepened the kiss, took more of her mouth, feeding a hunger that lived deep inside her. She loved it, embraced it. Maddox was passion, total, breath-stealing passion, and he was ferocious in the giving and taking of it. As she'd wanted; as she'd needed.

"I'm going to give you what you crave, and I swear to the gods I will not hurt you," he said.

"I want you and everything you have to give. Everything."

He gripped her ass and jerked her against him, pushing the air from her lungs. Breathless, she wound her legs around his waist. He backed her into a wall. Cool stone dug into her bare back, but she didn't care.

Wildness had never been a part of her life. Home, work, home, work. That's all her life had consisted of, really. She'd told Maddox that she'd been glad for her solitude, but the truth was, there were times she'd been starved for touch. Any touch.

This was more than she'd ever dreamed.

His erection pressed between her open thighs, not entering, not yet, but hard and hot through his pants, through the towel, hitting her exactly where she needed it most. A moan burst from her. She gripped him, nails digging into his chest. His nipples were so hard, they abraded her skin.

"Feels good," he said, palming one of her breasts. His touch wasn't gentle, but it wasn't rough, either, offering the perfect balance of pleasure and pain. He shook, as if he were holding himself together by a single strand of control.

"Yes." *Yes.* Her stomach quivered, shooting jolts of blissful, melting heat through the rest of her body. Over and over she arched forward, back, forward, rubbing against his shaft. She'd never been so wet. She'd never felt so needy, achy. Never wanted to drown, to die, to live, to fly all at the same time — but she did now.

"Want it . . . like in the books you read?" He bit at her chin, down her neck.

"Told you. Want you. Only you." The nips stung, but he licked at each twinge until it became sensitized, further kindling her desires. He shoved at the towel and pinched her nipples then, fingers a little rougher than his teeth had been. There was a rumbling in his chest, a sound of primal urges that mirrored her own.

"Towel. Off." He didn't wait for her response, but jerked the material from her and tossed it over his shoulder.

Icy air kissed her skin. Rather than wrap her in his arms, warming her, he pulled back and looked at her. Just looked, up and down, slowly, lingering, savoring. Somehow his gaze was hotter than a touch, obstructing the cold.

When he peered at her like that, she felt like a goddess. A siren. A queen.

"Beautiful," he said. "So beautiful." His

hands followed the same path his eyes had taken. He touched her entire body, leaving no place unexplored.

"Yours."

"Mine." He licked and sucked her collarbone, leaving a sizzling trail. "You are the most perfect thing I have ever beheld." He cupped each of her breasts again. "Perfect pink nipples made for my mouth."

"Taste them."

He laved one nipple, that wicked tongue flicking back and forth, then turned his attention to the other. Then he backed her to the center of the room and dropped to his knees.

Her eyes closed in absolute surrender. Amazing things happened when this man got on his knees. Decadent things. One of his hands snaked around her middle, hugging her close. And as he continued to lave her, he caressed her thighs with his free hand.

Touch there . . . right there . . . Oh! Every time his fingers brushed her clitoris, they darted away before exploring fully. Frustrated, she almost fell. He held her up, his teeth grazing her flesh. "Need more," she told him.

"Soon."

"Maddox," she said, desperate. If he'd just

sink a finger inside her, she'd come. More than she wanted to come, however, she wanted to explore him. "Touch you, too." She was panting, barely able to get the words out.

He was on his feet before she could blink, staring down at her with his eyes on fire, a collage of red, black and purple. Without a word, he swooped her up and tossed her onto the bed. Cool silk slid over her heated skin. And then he was on top of her, pinning her down. His weight was surprisingly luscious and more sensual than she could ever have anticipated.

Golden light bathed him, created a halo. He really was an angel just then. *Her* angel. Her savior and her lover. "Take off your pants," she commanded. His bare chest burned her deliciously, and she could hardly wait to feel his bare legs . . . his hard, swollen penis, nothing in the way.

He didn't comply. Shivering, she reached for his waistband to push at his pants.

He shook his head, stilling her. "When they come off, I'll be inside you." His voice was low, gravelly.

"Good. I want you inside me."

"Not done tasting." He eased off her a little and trailed a finger down the planes of her stomach.

Oh God. "Yes, taste more. I want . . . I need . . ." More of everything. If he wouldn't let her remove the pants, she'd work around them. She worked her hand underneath, gripped him.

He hissed in a breath. His eyes closed briefly. "Ashlyn."

He was so big, she couldn't close her fingers. Thick, full, amazing. As she skimmed her hand up and down, up and down like she'd seen him do in the shower — oh, so good, never stop — he finally, *finally* worked a finger inside of her. She gasped at the heady sensation.

He stilled. "Good?"

"Good," she said on a moan.

Propelling back into motion, he pumped his finger in and out. Slowly at first . . . faster . . . faster . . . she arched into the inward glide, loving the stretch, trying to tighten her muscles and hold him deep.

"More?"

"More," she breathed.

A second finger thrust inside, stretching her farther. Her knees squeezed his thighs, surrendering to his every whim. Her gaze met his. Sweat beaded on his face and tension bracketed his mouth.

"Hot," he said. "Wet."

"Big," she said, squeezing him. "Hard."

"All yours."

"Mine," she agreed. *I want him forever. Now and always.* "More."

He slammed a third finger inside her and there was a slight burn. She loved it, loved the miracle of being filled by him. "Mine," he said. His cock surged in her hand. "Ready, beauty?"

"Yes. Oh, yes. So ready." More than ready. Never had she wanted anything so intensely. It was something she gladly would have given her life to experience. "Yes. Please."

She kneaded his back, scratched at his skin as he shoved his pants to his ankles and kicked them off. No underwear. He was finally, totally, blessedly nude.

"Look at me."

She did, their gazes as tangled as their bodies.

The hard tip of his penis pressed between her legs, but didn't fully enter. She arched her hips, urging him on. He didn't move any deeper. Despite his claim that he'd be inside her the moment his clothes were shed, he resisted.

"Need a moment . . . to get spirit . . . under control," he bit out. "Don't want to leave. Don't want to walk away. But the urges . . ."

"Mmm, urges. Yes."

"No. Dark. Violent. Hard."

"I'm not scared." No, she was excited, willing to take him *and* the spirit. It was a part of him, so she'd love it, too.

"Should be scared." The sweat that had beaded on his temples dripped onto her cheek, the frosty air doing nothing to cool him down. "Haven't done it this way in thousands of years. Haven't looked at a woman while . . ."

He didn't finish, but she could guess what he'd been unable to say. He hadn't looked at a woman while making love to her. Ashlyn met his gaze again, all the love she felt for him shining brightly. She didn't try to hide it, couldn't. "I don't want to wait anymore."

"Must."

She drew up her knees, trying to urge him forward, but he braced a palm on the headboard, refusing to budge. Grrr! She didn't want him to fear hurting her. "Pound. Bite."

"No. Not with you."

"Pound me. Bite me. I won't break."

"I won't hurt you." He shook his head, refusing to look at her. "Won't hurt you. Promised."

Make him lose control. Prove to him that he can't hurt you, no matter what he does. Yes, she thought, cupping his jaw and forcing him to peer down at her. If he held back this time, if he continued to fear the things he wanted to do to her, he'd eventually stop touching her altogether. He'd leave her.

"Give me all you've got. Just do it now," she told him on a moan, once more trying to slide herself down on his thick length. "I'm so wet, I'm already in pain."

His shallow pants filled her ears. "Just a few more minutes. I'm just going to hold you, then I have to leave."

No, not okay.

She traced her fingertips down his back, loving the feel of velvet poured over electrified steel. His tattoo had looked so real, she'd expected it to be raised, but it wasn't. It was smooth and as warm as the rest of him.

"If you won't take me . . ." She tried to appear innocent as she massaged his butt. The muscles contracted on contact. "I'll take you."

Without another warning, she tightened her grip and jerked at the same moment as she arched forward. Maddox's arm bent and he slammed inside her. A cry spilled from her lips, pained and blissful all at once.

Maddox's control shattered.

He roared, loud and long, pulling back

and slamming forward over and over again. She gasped, feeling him so deeply she'd never again be able to think of herself as simply Ashlyn. She was now Maddox's woman.

He bit the cord of her neck and she trembled. Back he continued to slide, forward he continued to slam. The entire bed shook, metal legs screeching against the floor. He gripped one of her knees, anchoring it on the curve of his arm, spreading her legs farther apart and giving him deeper penetration.

"I'm sorry," he chanted. "I'm sorry."

"Don't be. Yes, yes!" she cried.

His tempo increased and his thrusts became harder. "Ashlyn," he panted. "Ashlyn."

She was on fire, burning from the inside out. Her pulse points hammered in tune with his strokes. Back and forth her head thrashed as she became mindless to anything except the pleasure.

He pinched her nipples and that made her hotter.

He scraped his teeth over her throat and that made her wetter.

He squeezed her thighs tightly and that made her needier. "Sorry," he said again. "So sorry. Wanted to be gentle."

"Love it hard. Want harder." Gentle could come later, after her need had been sated. After he realized she could — and quite happily — take anything he had to give. "Close. So close." Almost there. Just needed . . .

He tangled his hand in her hair and jerked her face to his, thrusting his tongue inside her mouth. His decadent taste flooded her, a drug, a shot of heroin. In that instant, she erupted. Burst. Flames of ecstasy consumed her.

Her entire body shuddered and wept. A scream was ripped from her as white light and shadows flashed through her mind. She was dying slowly, dying quickly. Just . . . dying. Flying to heaven.

"Ashlyn," Maddox shouted as he, too, erupted. Hot seed spurted inside her, pulsing deep . . . so deep . . . His muscles tensed. "Mine." He bit down on her neck again, as if he couldn't help himself.

This time, he drew blood.

It should have hurt, did hurt — so good, so good — but it made her come again. She trembled and arched against him, crying out with the heady bliss of it. Never would she have thought pleasure and pain could mix so potently. Never would she have thought one could trigger the other. But they did. And she was glad.

He collapsed on top of her, again panting, "Sorry. So sorry. Didn't mean —"

"No sorries. I'm glad." Satisfaction hummed through her as she accepted his weight. Satisfaction and true happiness. "Always want it this way."

He rolled to his back, taking her with him. Boneless, she lay on his chest. He wrapped his arms around her, holding her, smoothing his hands down her back. "You would have liked gentle better. Especially for your first time."

Slowly she smiled. "I doubt it, but I'm willing to let you try and convince me."

Amazement flickered in his eyes a split second before he had her straddling his waist. "That will be my pleasure."

CHAPTER NINETEEN

Never, in all his life, had Maddox been so sated. Not in all his thousands of years.

Thrice he'd made love to Ashlyn and now she was sleeping next to him, tucked into his side, breath traipsing over his ribs. After hard and fast, then slow and tender, she'd claimed she needed a reminder of what hard and fast was like before deciding which she liked better.

He'd been shocked, awed and humbled by her words, for he'd shown her the worst, the beast, the part of himself that he despised, but she had not run screaming. Hadn't cried. No, she had asked for more.

He grinned at the memory. A true, unrestrained grin, he thought, amazed. When the spirit had demanded Maddox mark her, he'd been helpless to do anything but obey. So he had bitten her and drawn blood. Everything virtuous inside of him had screamed in protest, ashamed. But she had liked it; she truly had not minded, had even bitten him in response. And now he felt free. He did not have to fear his reactions with her. *He did not have to fear.*

She was everything he had never known he needed, everything he could never live without. She had . . . tamed him. She had charmed the spirit. He'd told her his plan to keep her, and he'd meant it. She belonged with him, now and always.

Slowly he traced a fingertip over her spine. She murmured in her sleep and burrowed deeper against him. Her breast pressed against his underarm, spearing him with heat. What a treasure she was. He'd gone into the forest looking for a monster, but found salvation instead.

With Ashlyn, Violence was not truly violent. Instead, the spirit was made into something beautiful. Dark, yes. Always dark. But sensually so. Not evil, but needy. Not destructive, but possessive. Two days ago, he would not have thought such a thing was possible.

Ashlyn. Demon tamer. He chuckled softly, careful not to wake her. After their excess, she needed to conserve her energy. He had plans to ravish her lat—

Below them, a door slammed. A man cursed. Maddox recognized the raspy baritone instantly. Reyes had returned.

Maddox's mood instantly thundered from contentment to anger. They had unfinished business, he and Reyes. A warning was in need of delivery. Something to show the warrior that any attempt to hurt Ashlyn would come with consequences.

Maddox rolled from the bed, pausing to make sure he had not disturbed his woman. Her eyes remained closed, lashes casting shadows over her rosy cheeks.

Quietly he dressed. T-shirt, pants, boots. Daggers. *She's ours. No one hurts her.* The spirit wanted vengeance, as well, and was seething under his skin, in his blood, spreading flames, blistering . . . melting . . . but Maddox did not lose control.

I am angry, yet I am dictating my own actions, he thought, baffled. *I decide.* It was strange. Wondrous and exhilarating. And he owed this newfound control to Ashlyn.

With a backward glance at her sleeping form, he stalked from the room. The spirit's mood blackened with every step away from her, but still it never managed to regain command.

Maddox found Reyes in the foyer, but the warrior was not alone. The rest of the Lords were also there, every one of them cut and bleeding and covered in black soot. There were also men Maddox did not recognize —

No, surely not, he thought, blinking. "Sabin?"

No one paid him any heed. Sabin — dear gods — was too busy peeling off his shirt and studying a deep gash in his side. Lucien had his arm wrapped around . . . Strider. Cameo sat on the floor with her knees drawn up to her chest. Her dark hair was singed at the ends and the left side of her face was burned. Gideon and Amun were propped against the wall, as if they couldn't stand on their own.

Seeing the warriors after so many years was like a blow to the stomach. What were they doing here? Why had they come?

Paris groaned, drawing his attention. The warrior's forearm was broken so badly the bone peeked through the skin. Aeron was . . . Maddox frowned. Aeron was cuffed to the banister and cursing loudly. Blood dripped from his forehead, a crimson river. "Kill. I must kill," he said, voice thick and layered with malevolence. "I need their blood. Hmm, blood."

Just as the Titans had vowed, Wrath must have taken over. That meant the need to slay those four women now consumed him. Would he have to be chained from now until the Lords found a way to save them — or until they were dead?

With the thought, hatred spilled through Maddox. Hatred for the Titans, for bringing his friend to this point. Hatred for the Greeks for their initial curse, the Hunters for their relentless pursuit and, most of all, his younger self for opening the box on that disastrous night.

"What's going on?" Maddox demanded. That he did not simply attack proved just how much Ashlyn had changed him. "Did you set off one of our traps on the hill?"

A few of the warriors glanced up at him, though most ignored him. "No," Sabin muttered. "Those we avoided."

"Bomb," Reyes said, not bothering to look up. He was in the process of removing his boots — boots that were practically melted to his feet. He was smiling.

"One of ours?" Maddox insisted, not trusting a word out of Sabin's mouth.

"Hardly. I know better than to blow myself up." Reyes sighed, finally deigning to look at him. There was confusion in his eyes. "Why aren't you railing on me?"

Quick as a snap, Maddox unsheathed a dagger and hurled it end over end toward the warrior. In a blink, he'd unsheathed the other one and hurled it at Lucien. The blades sailed over each man's left shoulder and lodged in the wall behind them. "Have no doubt, if you ever plan something like that again, I *will* kill you."

Lucien's gaze was flat. He appeared calm, and yet Maddox sensed something bubbling under that serene surface. His features were strained, as if he were a block of ice that had been hammered at one too many times. Was he ready to crack? "You should be glad we failed to find her. I am. The Hunters played us like violins, drawing us to a specific location and greeting us with bombs."

Bombs. A new war truly had begun, then. Maddox descended the rest of the steps, teeth grinding together. He stepped around a bucking Aeron and was punched in the thigh for his efforts. That was better than being stabbed, he supposed.

"So why is Sabin here?" He did not face the man in question. "Did *he* bring the Hunters?"

"Apparently, the Hunters were already here. Sabin followed them and now wants us to help him find *dimOuniak*." Reyes tossed his ruined boots aside. Raw, oozing blisters covered his bare feet.

"Sorry to spring our old friends on you." Gripping his broken arm, Paris slammed it against the wall, popping the bone back into place. He winced, paled. "But it's amazing what decisions you'll make when your brains are splattered over a nightclub dance floor."

Lucien flattened his palm on the wall and leaned over, grimacing. "By the time we gained our bearings, the Hunters were gone. They had not left a trail and we didn't know if they would be lying in wait at Sabin's hotel. Here, at least, we knew we'd all be safe, since Torin has us under surveillance."

"They knew what they were doing, and had obviously been preparing for a long, long time," Reyes said. "What I want to know is why they didn't stick around to chop off our heads while we were incapacitated."

"They're planning something else." Paris rolled his shoulder. "Have to be."

Everyone turned to Sabin.

He shrugged. "They're out for blood. Expect anything."

Reyes nodded. "We should gear up and find them before they try anything else."

Sabin cleaned his face with his T-shirt, saying, "I remember a time when you would rather have split with your friends than attack Hunters."

"No," Lucien told him. "We split with

friends who wanted to destroy the entire city and everyone in it. We split with friends who attacked one of our own."

Eyes stark, Sabin spun away.

Maddox gazed around the foyer, studying the weary group one by one. "Where is Torin?"

A deadly stillness came over Lucien. "He hasn't returned from the cemetery?"

Cemetery? Torin had ventured outside the fortress? What else had Maddox missed while he was dead? "I don't think so. I did not hear him come in, but I was . . . occupied."

Frowning, Sabin withdrew a walkie-talkie. "Kane. Do you read?"

Nothing.

"Kane."

Again, nothing. A little panicked now, Sabin repeated, "Kane. Answer me."

Nothing.

Everyone looked at everyone else.

Lucien ran a hand over his jaw, his features more frazzled than before. "We have to find Torin before someone else does. Gather bandages, Maddox, and meet us upstairs. I want to be out the door in ten minutes."

A feminine gasp suddenly rang in his ears. Maddox whipped around, only to see Ashlyn standing at the top of the staircase.

Those long locks he so loved spilled down her sides, and her eyes were wide, concerned. She wore one of his shirts and had those black sweatpants bagging over her legs.

In seconds, he was beside her and dragging her behind him, blocking her from view. He didn't know if he could trust the newest additions to the "family." Not really. Not anymore. Too much time had passed for him to feel any kind of kinship.

"I guess I don't have to ask who the human belongs to," Sabin said dryly.

"What happened to them?" Ashlyn asked, horrified. She peeked around his shoulder. "They're so bloody. And who are the new guys?"

"A bombing. The men are . . . like us."

"Five minutes and a knife," Aeron shouted, jerking at his bonds. "That's all I need."

Blanching, Ashlyn grabbed hold of Maddox's arm.

Reyes stepped up to the now-cursing prisoner and punched him in the face. Once, twice, three times. He punched until Aeron slumped to the ground. Maddox thought he heard Aeron utter, "Thank you," but he could not be certain.

As the warriors limped upstairs, Maddox

kept Ashlyn behind him. When they were alone, he turned to her and trailed a fingertip over her jaw. "Go back to my room. Please," he added. "I'll be there as soon as possible."

Determined, she peered up at him through the thick fan of her lashes. "I can help them, and so can the other women. Danika helped me when I was sick, remember? She's good in times of crisis. So am I."

He gave a quick shake of his head. "I don't want you near them."

"If I'm going to stay here, I have the right to get to know your friends."

"Not all of those men are my friends. Those who are, you can get to know another day. Right now, you need rest."

"No, I don't." She anchored tight fists on her hips. "I refuse to lounge in bed all day when I can be productive."

"Rest is productive."

"No, it's not."

"I do not know some of those men, Ashlyn. Not anymore. If one of them were to try to hurt you . . ." Even saying the words sparked a deep rage inside of him.

"I want to help. I've never been part of a family before." Suddenly appearing more vulnerable than he had ever seen her, she flicked her gaze to her hands, which were twisting the fabric of her shirt. "All I've ever done is stand off to the side and listen, and all I've ever wanted to do is be a part of something. Let me help your family, Maddox."

Something knotted in his chest. He could deny this woman nothing. Not even this. He would watch the men closely, hover over her shoulder if necessary, but he would not stop her from giving aid.

"Go to my room and gather all the towels you can carry." He always had an overflowing supply. "Do you know how to find the entertainment room?"

She shook her head and he gave her directions. When he finished, a delighted smile lit her face. "Thank you." She rose on her tiptoes and brushed a soft kiss on his mouth.

He shouldn't have, but he immediately deepened it, backing her against the wall. She made him forget everything but desire. Her flavor flooded him, that unique drug he'd never get enough of. One of her legs lifted and wound around his waist.

That quickly, passion trembled through him. His cock throbbed and his hand shook with the need to rip away her clothing and discover her naked curves once again. To plunge inside her body as surely as her tongue plunged inside his mouth, hot and wet, meeting him thrust for thrust. She moaned. He swallowed the sound. Delicious.

"Maddox!" Reyes rumbled from down the hall. "Sometime today."

With regret, he tore away from Ashlyn, severing all contact. Safer that way. One touch would lead to one more kiss. One more kiss and he would carry her back to his room, friends — and enemies — forgotten.

"That was . . . nice," she said, fanning herself.

His eyelids were heavy as he studied her. Her lips were red, swollen and moist, and she traced her tongue over them as if savoring the lingering taste of him. He had to look away, but his gaze was drawn back in the next instant. Her eyes were bright and golden, fevered. For him.

A pulse hammered at the base of her neck. He found himself reaching out to stroke it, but stopped himself in time. None of that. Not now.

"Maddox," Lucien called.

"I said, are you coming?" Reyes shouted.

"Towels," he said to Ashlyn, then turned on his heel before he talked himself into staying.

That man fires me up, Ashlyn thought, watching Maddox stride down the hallway. He flew around the corner, disappearing from view. Her heartbeat still drummed erratically.

Smiling dreamily, she traced her fingertips over her tingling mouth. Good thing Maddox had walked away. A few more seconds of that devastating kiss and she would have allowed him — ha, *begged* him! — to take her right here, where anyone could watch them.

She heard a man grunt, another shout profanities, and snapped to attention. No time to moon over Maddox now. She jumped into motion. The air was chilly, a little damp, but invigorating. She loved the stained-glass windows here, the glistening stone that spoke of endurance and the passage of time.

She'd like to visit the site of the bombing and listen to the conversations that had taken place there. *Like to? Darrow, you* will. More often than not, she hated her gift. There was no real purpose for it and no job meaningful enough to warrant her constant suffering. For Maddox, though, she'd happily, eagerly, tune in to the voices, over and over again. She didn't like the knowledge that there were men out there, hiding, waiting to kill him.

When she snuck out to listen for ways to break his death-curse, which she planned to do tonight, she'd find out where the bombing had taken place and go there. If she was lucky, she'd learn where the hunters were hiding *and* how to save Maddox from dying.

Probably wishful thinking on both counts, but hope was a silly thing.

Her gaze snagged on a trail of blood, and her mouth fell open in horror. Only when she realized the injured warriors must have been up here did she relax.

. . . somewhere. Right?

The tiny bit of conversation suddenly whispered through her mind, surprising her. The new guys? Ashlyn stopped, one foot in midair. Her ears twitched as she listened, but nothing else assaulted her. Odd. That had been a man's voice, and hadn't been there a little while ago.

She walked another step. Nothing. Changed directions, another step.

Yes. I'm betting on it.

There. Another snatch. Gulping, she continued in that direction . . .

Come on, this way . . . where are they . . . hopefully still out . . . lost too many with those fucking booby traps . . . took too long to clean the mess . . . do they know . . . fight . . .

. . . and soon found herself in front of the door that blocked Danika and her family from freedom.

Ah, hell. Someone — several someones, actually — had sneaked inside. Not the new guys, then. Were they still there? Had they hurt the women? Ashlyn's hand shook as she reached for the knob. Wait. Maybe she should run and tell Maddox.

The intruders might be hunters.

She swallowed past the lump in her throat. If they were the very men who'd planted that bomb, they could be planting another right now. She backed away, meaning to alert Maddox. *You can't leave Danika and the others here, Darrow.*

"They'll be fine," she whispered. According to Maddox, hunters only wanted to hurt immortals. Right? Right. She backed up another step. Telling Maddox was the smart thing to do. He could stop them, she couldn't.

But another step and conversation slammed into her mind.

Where is she?

I wish to God I knew.

434

Do you think they . . . killed her?

It's possible. Hell, worse *is possible. They're* demons. Pause, sigh. *Damn it, I should have put more guards on her.*

Her boss, she realized. Dr. McIntosh was here. She should have been relieved to hear him, glad that he'd cared enough to track her down. But . . . he'd had men guard her? How had he infiltrated the fortress?

Ashlyn, honey. If you can hear this, meet us at Gerbeaud at —

What if she's locked up? She won't be able to leave on her own.

Hush. I hear someone coming.

Then, quiet.

She scrubbed her fingers back and forth across her brow, trying to start a fire of intelligent thought. Were they still here? What would Maddox do if he found them? What would they do to Maddox? Panic raced through her. *Okay, okay. Think, Darrow. Think.*

In the end, she didn't have to make a decision after all.

The door in front of her opened and McIntosh peeked into the hall. His eyes widened when he saw her. His familiar, plain face comforted her — but for the first time, it also made her uneasy.

"Ashlyn! You're alive!"

"McIntosh, I — I —"

"Shh, not here." He snaked out an arm and jerked her inside the room, softly shutting the door behind her. The first thing she noticed was Danika and her family, passed out on the floor.

"Oh my God." She moved toward them but her boss's grip tightened, keeping her in place. Several other men were casing the room, looking for . . . what, she didn't know. Nor did she recognize them. She'd never seen them at the Institute.

One of the men coughed, a gut-wrenching gag following, drawing her eye to him. There was blood on his hands. Sweet Jesus. He coughed again, doubling over. He was alarmingly pale and there were bruises under his eyes. Another cough.

"Be quiet," McIntosh whispered fiercely.

"Sorry. Throat hurts."

"It didn't five minutes ago."

"Does —" cough "— now."

Ashlyn broke free of her boss's hold and rushed to Danika, crouching beside her. "Is she . . ." She felt for a pulse. *Thump, thump.* Thank God.

"Just sleeping," McIntosh assured her.

Relief sagged her shoulders. "Why would you do something like this? Why did you knock them out?" Even as she spoke, bits of their conversation played through her mind.

Who are you? Danika demanded. *What are you doing here?*

I'll ask the questions. Who are you? her boss asked.

Prisoners.

Were you looking for the box, too?

Ashlyn's heart sank at the query.

Box? Danika's confusion was clear by her tone.

Did they tell you where it is? McIntosh's excitement rang loud.

He must have grabbed her, because she grated out, *Let go of me.*

Did they?

Reyes! Reyes, help!

Shut up, or I'll be forced to silence you myself.

Reyes!

There must have been a struggle because Ashlyn could hear huffing breath, grunts of effort, Danika's family gasping and then crying, and then suddenly silent. More conversation about drugging the women and using them as bait later if necessary.

Hunters, she realized, closing her eyes in horror. She'd suspected yesterday when speaking with Danika, but had promptly dismissed the thought, reminding herself how good and noble the Institute was. To be honest, a part of her had assumed no one would be able to keep such a secret from *her*. But these men *were* hunters. No denying it now. Opening her eyes, she fixed them on her boss.

Nausea churned in her stomach. He'd known about the box all along. He'd been searching for it, but hadn't told her. Oh God.

He'd lied to her. She'd devoted her entire life to a cause that didn't exist. McIntosh had read her fairy tales all those years ago, told her she was special, that she had a higher calling. She'd thought she was making the world a better place. Instead, she'd helped him destroy people, maybe innocents. A sense of betrayal washed through her, so strong it nearly dropped her to her knees.

"You don't study the creatures I find for you, do you?" she asked softly. "Hunter."

"Of course I do," he said, offended. "I'm a scientist, after all. Not every Institute employee is a Hunter, Ashlyn. You're proof of that. Ninety percent of our work *is* merely observation. But when we uncover evil, we stamp it out. No mercy."

"What gives you the right?"

"Morality. The greater good. Unlike the demons here, I am not a monster. Everything I do, I do for the safety of mankind."

"How did I not know?" she gasped out. "How did I not hear?"

He raised his chin, his eyes asking her to understand. "Only a few do the actual dirty work. And we never spoke of it on the premises. Nor did we let you into the places we'd been."

"All these years." She shook her head, dazed. "No wonder you barely let me out of your sight. You didn't want me to stumble on information I wasn't supposed to have."

"You want information? I can show you pictures of the things these demons have done. Things that will make you vomit. Things that will make you want to scratch out your own eyes, just so you never have to see such an image again."

She clutched her stomach. "You should have told me the truth."

"I wanted you to stay as removed as possible. I do care about you, Ashlyn. We knew there were two groups of demons. We've been fighting one for years and were always searching for the other. Then one of our female operatives discovered Promiscuity. We brought you to Budapest to listen and learn everything you could about these new enemies. You were never supposed to get close to them."

Her life's work had turned out to be something malicious and sick. *I was such a fool.* "You came to kill these men, but they treat the people of Budapest only with kindness. They donate money as if it's water and keep criminal activity at a minimum. They keep to themselves and hardly venture out. *You* bombed a nightclub."

McIntosh approached her, his expression determined. "We didn't come to kill them. We can't. Not yet. Years ago, it was discovered that to kill a Lord was to release its demon upon the world — a demon who's nothing more than a twisted vessel of destruction, warped from its captivity. No, we're here to capture the warriors. When we find Pandora's box, we can lock away the demons and dispose of the men who house them. *You* found that out for us, remember?" He reached her and grabbed her shoulders. "Do you know where it is? Did they tell you?"

"No."

"You had to have heard something. Think, Ashlyn."

"I told you. I don't know where it is."

"Don't you want to live in a world free from evil? Free from lies and misery and violence? You hear more of each in a day than most people do in a lifetime." He studied her for a long while, frowning. "I've nurtured your talent for years. I gave you a place to stay, food to eat and a life as peaceful as possible. All I asked in return was that you used your gift to find the creatures living among us."

"And I've always done so. But I haven't heard anything new about the box," she insisted, sickened.

His frown deepened. "You must have. You weren't a prisoner like these women. You were freely roaming the halls." As he spoke, his eyes widened, as if his own words had offered a startling revelation. He released her and reached into his pocket, withdrawing a syringe filled with clear liquid. "Are you working for the monsters now, Ashlyn? Is that what's going on? Were you working with them all along?" The betrayal in his voice would have been laughable if she hadn't been so frightened.

She backed up a step, then another. Her back hit a brick wall and she tried to jump away. Strong arms banded around her, holding her in place. Not a brick wall, after all. A man. A hunter. She struggled to free herself.

"Where's the box, Ashlyn?" the doctor demanded. "That's all I want. Tell me where it is and I'll let you go."

Calm down. Stall him. Distract him. When she didn't appear with the towels, Maddox would come looking for her. "You're a hunter, but you don't have a tattoo on your wrist." Hadn't Maddox said something about tattoos? "Why is that?"

He held up his arm and pushed the sleeve of his shirt down. An intricate black, sideways figure-eight stared at her. "I simply made sure you never noticed it. My father took me to get it on my eighteenth birthday when I made my vow to continue the family legacy."

How had she never known? She felt so stupid. The woman who had thought herself impossible to deceive had been fooled for years. Shame and guilt joined ranks with her betrayal and fear.

Just keep him talking. "Why the symbol of infinity?" she asked, barely managing to find her voice.

"Our purpose is an eternity without evil. What better symbol?"

"But the men here, they aren't evil. They really aren't. They've taken care of me. They've helped me. If you'd just get to know them, you'd —"

Hate fell over his face like a curtain. "Get to know a demon?" He cracked his jaw. Stepped closer. "Those creatures of the underworld need to be destroyed, Ashlyn. *They* toppled Athens. The people they killed, the pain they caused . . ."

"But hurting them makes you as evil as you claim they are. Have you not already killed people to get to them?"

Without warning his arm whipped out, slamming the syringe into her neck. A sharp pain, a warm rush. She tried to jerk away. Too late. She was suddenly so light-headed she could hardly move. A strange lethargy worked its way through her body, weaving weakness and shadows in her blood, her dizzy mind.

"Sleep," McIntosh said.

And she did.

CHAPTER TWENTY

Maddox could not believe what he was seeing. A hallucination? A nightmare? He had left the injured warriors to check Torin's room for any sign of the man's return. To his alarm, he had found blood smeared throughout the hallways. Now he stood in Torin's doorway, and he saw that Torin had indeed returned. He lay on the floor in a puddle of thick, dark blood. So dark it appeared black. Even his silver hair was tinted with that lethal red-black liquid.

A deep gash slashed his neck.

Someone had either tried to sever the head from his body and failed or had cut him to slow him down — and succeeded. Torin's eyes were closed but his chest rose every few seconds. He was still alive. But for how long?

Bile rose in Maddox's throat — bile and rage and determination. Had Torin crawled home from the cemetery after this happened? Or had someone sneaked inside the fortress, attacking him from behind in the hall? Had Kane done it? Or a Hunter? Maddox scanned the room, dread building. No sign of Hunters, nor of Kane.

He shouted for his friends as he considered his options. Torin was like a brother to him; he couldn't leave him like this to suffer. But he couldn't touch him, either. Though Maddox himself would not become sick, he would undoubtedly spread the disease to Ashlyn.

Ashlyn. Had the culprit gotten to her, too? No. No! *Help Torin and find her!*

Again, he called for the warriors.

Skin to skin he could not risk with Torin. He would have to wear gloves. Urgency spilling through him, Maddox sprinted to the closet and withdrew one of the many pairs of black gloves Torin had stored there. He hastily pulled them from their sealed package and slid them onto his hands before draping a black shirt around his neck, protecting the skin there.

He bent down and scooped the injured man into his arms. He carried him to the bed and wrapped a T-shirt around his bleeding neck, applying pressure to stop the flow. It was strange to be this close to him after centuries of distance.

Slowly Torin's lashes cracked open, and Maddox found himself staring into pain-drenched green eyes. Already Violence was preparing for battle, sharpening its claws, demanding action.

"Hunters," Torin gurgled. The word was barely audible. "On hill. Coming here. Fight. Want box. Touched me. Took Kane." He passed out after that, arm falling limply to the floor.

Damn. Having done all he could, Maddox sprinted from the room, intent on finding Ashlyn and the others. *Stay calm. She's all right.* But the thought of her hurt or worse . . . "Ashlyn!" If the Hunters had gotten hold of her after they'd touched Torin, she could very well die of disease.

A familiar black haze descended over his vision.

She wasn't in his room, and it did not look as if she'd been there at all. The towels were undisturbed. She was not in the women's room, either. In fact, none of them were. No. *No!*

From the corner of his eye, he caught the glint of silver. He strode onto the balcony, nearly breaking through the glass doors to get there. A rappel wire was hooked to the rail and hung all the way to the ground.

Man and spirit bellowed in unison. There

was no sign of the Hunters on the hill, which meant they were already a good distance away. Sweet gods, the Hunters had her. The Hunters had touched Torin and had then touched Ashlyn.

Sick to his stomach, he barreled toward the entertainment room. He removed the gloves and extra T-shirt along the way, dropping them on the floor wherever he happened to be.

"Towels?" Lucien asked when he spotted him. Obviously, he hadn't heard Maddox's cries for help. But he saw his friend's expression and frowned.

Maddox told the group what he'd discovered, the broken, panicked admission rushing from him. Each of them snapped to attention and clamored around him. Each of them paled.

"Did they breach our walls?" Paris demanded.

"Yes." Maddox turned to Sabin with a snarl. "Did you help them?"

The man held up his hands, the picture of aggravated innocence. "I was being blown to bits, too, remember? And my goal has always been their destruction."

"What of Danika?" Reyes asked roughly.

"Gone."

Reyes's eyelids squeezed closed.

"Torin needs medical attention," Paris said. "How are we going to manage that?"

"He'll have to heal on his own. Gods, there's going to be a plague," Lucien said grimly. "We can't stop it now."

Maddox's hands tightened into fists. "I don't care if there's a plague or not. My woman is out there. I'll do whatever is necessary to save her."

Strider stepped forward. "Kane was in that cemetery with Torin. He might have followed him back. Did you see him?"

"Torin said there was a battle on the hill. Kane was taken."

"Fuck," Sabin snarled, slamming his fist into the wall.

How had a day so bright with promise combusted so quickly?

"I'll go into town with you," Reyes said to him. He'd cleaned some of the soot from his face, but his feet were still charred and bare.

"I'll search the rest of the fortress." There was a blazing fire in Lucien's mismatched eyes. Aeron had once claimed that Lucien possessed a temper darker than the most violent of storms. Maddox hadn't believed him then. He believed now. "I'll make sure they aren't still here, hiding."

After seeing that rappel wire, Maddox

doubted it. "Five minutes," he said to Reyes before racing to his room and loading his body with weapons. Knives, guns, throwing stars.

Hunters were going to bleed tonight.

Reyes watched Maddox with shock.

They had stalked the streets of Budapest until finally stumbling upon a group of four Hunters. They were now in the forest, surrounded by trees and safe from the prying eyes of humans. Night had fallen and flaxen rays of moonlight slithered over nature, beast and human alike.

Maddox had attacked without warning.

He wore the veil of Violence, and it was no longer a mere shadow. It had taken over his face completely, a skeletal visage straight out of nightmares. Quickly he — it — killed two of the Hunters with a simple slash of his blade, their necks slit, just as had been done to Torin. They fell to the ground, instantly dead.

Reyes remained in place. He wasn't sure Maddox was aware of his surroundings, much less of who he fought. And if Reyes were to intervene, he suspected he would be slashed, as well.

His own rage was as fierce as Maddox's. For some reason, he felt responsible for

Danika and was infuriated that she had been taken out from under him. So what that she was already marked for death?

"Where is your leader?" Maddox quietly asked as he stalked around the two Hunters still breathing.

"D-don't know," one of them said with a whimper.

"Where are the women?"

"Don't know," the other cried. "Please. Please don't hurt us."

Maddox showed no mercy. He fingered the bloody tip of his blade, running his tongue over his teeth. The blood splattered over that skeleton-face added all kinds of eerie. "Where were they taken?"

"D—"

"Say it, and I'll cut out your tongue. You'll watch as I eat it," Maddox warned.

Reyes didn't recognize that voice. It was lower, harsher, than Maddox had ever sounded before. He was all beast, no trace of man.

"I want to know where they are."

"I do—"

The man didn't have a chance to finish his sentence. Maddox spun toward him, arm rising. He sliced down. One moment the man was alive. The next he was dead, blood pouring from his neck.

That's when the sole survivor whimpered. Coughed.

"I'm only going to ask once more," Maddox said, and the Hunter coughed again. "Where were they taken?"

"McIntosh didn't tell us," was the trembling response. "Just said we were to watch the city and radio if we saw one of the Lords. Except for Miss Darrow, there wasn't supposed to be a woman inside the fortress. Please. They just want the girl and the box. They planned to sneak inside, grab her and look for it. That's all."

Reyes stomped over and grabbed the radio that was strapped to one of the corpses. He hooked it to the back of his belt, planning to listen and see what he could learn. Right now there was only silence.

Maddox peered at him and Reyes nodded. Without a word of warning, Maddox reached over and snapped the man's neck, letting him fall in a heap with his friends. They couldn't have allowed him to live. He was a Hunter. He was infected. And he'd played a part in Ashlyn's disappearance.

"What should we do next?" Reyes stared up at the heavens, part of him hoping the answer would fall from the stars.

"I do not know." Maddox felt nearly mad with worry as he echoed the unfortunate

Hunters' words. Violence had taken over and ruled him totally, but in the back of his mind, he was aware. If he didn't find Ashlyn soon, he would have to wait until morning, when he returned from the dead. And if he had to wait . . . if Ashlyn had to spend the night with Hunters . . .

He wanted to kill them all.

"Let's search the town one more time. There has to be a trace," Reyes said. "We have to have missed something."

Side by side, they strode back into the city. Not many people were out, but those that were stayed clear of them. The bombing had probably ruined the illusion that they were angels. That and the fact that there was blood on Maddox's hands and splashed on his face.

When he and Reyes stood in an alley, a dirty, urine-scented place that closed in on him like a life-sized coffin, he stopped and looked toward the velvety heavens as Reyes had done. Helplessness bombarded him, a poor companion to the rage and dark urges he already felt.

Ashlyn was his reason for living.

He loved her. He had known it before, but he was sure of it now. She was gentleness and she was light. She was passion and she was calm. Hope and life. Innocence and . . . everything. She was his everything.

Now that he'd found her, he could not imagine his life without her. It was as if she were the missing link, the final element of his creation, the only thing that completed him.

He had promised her that he would always protect her.

He had failed.

Roaring, he punched the wall beside him. He felt shredded inside.

A newspaper danced at Reyes's ankles and the warrior bent down, grabbed it and crumbled it into a ball before tossing it aside. "We're running out of time."

"I know." *Think!* "The Hunters would not have taken the women out of the city. They'll be focusing all their energies on searching for the box, and they must think we have it to have entered the fortress as they did."

"Yes."

"Most likely, they're still here in town. Hiding."

"I would not doubt if they hoped to use the women as a trade for the box," Reyes said. "We should arrange one."

From his tone, Maddox knew he did not mean a fair one. They would take the women and leave only bloodshed behind.

"How?"

Reyes held up the walkie-talkie. They listened to it for several long, agonizing moments, but it offered nothing except static — even when they requested an audience.

"Damn this! I don't want to return to the fortress empty-handed, but I don't know what else to do." Reyes sounded tortured by the thought. "Midnight approaches."

All Maddox knew was that he needed Ashlyn safe and whole and in his arms. Gaze still on the heavens, he splayed his arms wide. "Help us," he and the spirit shouted as one. "Help us. Please."

Nothing. The heavens did not open up and pour out a tide of rain. Lightning did not strike. All remained as it was. The stars twinkled from their inky perches. His eyes narrowed. When this was over, he and those uncaring, selfish gods were going to have a reckoning. Whatever had been done to Ashlyn, he would mete out to them. A thousandfold. "Let us circle the area one last time."

Reyes nodded.

Fifteen minutes later, Reyes and Maddox were exiting a chapel they had quietly searched when they spotted an old man across the street. He was dirty, unkempt, wearing only a thin, hole-infested coat. And

454

he was coughing. A bone-deep, spit-up-a-lung cough.

Maddox recalled the night Torin had come into this very city — a city much different than it was today. Huts rather than buildings. Mud streets rather than cobblestone. The people had been the same, though. Fragile, weak, unsuspecting.

Torin had removed his glove and caressed the cheek of a woman begging for his touch. A woman he had longed for from afar for years. His resistance had crumbled and he'd hoped, just once, that someone would survive. That love would conquer all.

An hour later, the woman had started coughing. Just like the old man was now.

An hour after that, the rest of the village had followed suit. In the days that followed, most of the townspeople had died terrible deaths, their skin pockmarked and every orifice of their bodies bleeding.

Maddox cursed under his breath. Ashlyn was out there somewhere, with the very Hunters who had caused this new epidemic — for that's what it would be. An epidemic.

Violence sank fully into the shadows of his mind, as if it respected that Maddox needed to take charge. He and Reyes crossed the street with heavy footfalls, closing the distance between themselves and the old man.

Most of the area was still deserted, people tucked safely in their homes. Tomorrow, they would not be safe even there. "I need to speak with you," Maddox called to the old man.

Coughing, he stopped. His eyes were fevered as he gazed up at Maddox. When he saw the warrior, he gave a start. "You're one of them." He doubled over from another cough. "The *angyals.* My parents told me bedtime stories about you. I've wanted to meet you my entire life."

Maddox barely heard him. "You might have been in contact with a group of men. Strangers to the city. They might have been in a hurry and would have had tattoos on their wrists. They might have had five women with them." He tried to temper his voice, to keep his fury and concern and desperation to a minimum. It would not do to scare the old man into a heart attack.

Although, that might be merciful. The death that would soon claim him would not be a kind one. Yes, Lucien was going to be a busy man.

Reyes described the Hunters he had seen at the club, then described the women.

"Saw the little blonde you're talking about," the man said. Cough. "There were three women with her, but I don't recall what they looked like."

Danika, then. But who had been with her? Her family, most likely. That meant Ashlyn was . . . no. No! She was alive. She was fine. "Where did they go?" he gritted out, unable to temper his reaction this time. Urgency rushed through him. "Tell me. Please."

Confusion flitted over the man's weathered face and he wobbled, nearly falling. Coughed. "Were running down that street, chased by someone tall. A man." He pointed, coughed. "Nearly toppled me over."

"Which direction did they travel?" Reyes demanded.

"North."

"Thank you," Reyes said. "Thank you."

The old man coughed and collapsed to the ground. Though loath to lose any more time, Maddox crouched beside him. "Sleep. We . . . bless you."

The human died with a smile, as Maddox never had. *Ashlyn,* he silently called. *I am coming for you.*

CHAPTER
TWENTY-ONE

Ashlyn awoke with a gasp, ice-cold water dripping from her face. A moment passed, her ragged breaths the only sound, before she oriented herself. Her shirt was plastered to her skin, nearly ice. Her watery gaze was hazy at first, but the room soon came into view. Stone walls, dark, scuffed. Bars on one side that looked into a narrow stone hallway. Chains hung in the far corner.

Don't panic, don't panic. Next she saw a familiar thinly lined face. At one time, McIntosh would have been a welcome sight. Now, she felt hate pour through her.

Tossing the now-empty bucket aside, he sat on a wooden stool in front of her. She was cuffed to a chair, arms stretched behind her, she realized, and tried to pull free. The cold metal dug into her skin, but the cuffs didn't open.

"Where am I?" she demanded.

"Halal Foghaz." His voice was rougher

than usual. Scratchy.

Prison of the Dead.

"Some of the worst criminals in Budapest's history were kept here until they revolted and slaughtered their guards. The place was closed down. Until a few weeks ago."

Her eyes narrowed to tiny slits.

"Relax," he told her. He was pale, his eyes rimmed with red. He coughed. "I'm not the dragon you always feared when I read you those fairy tales."

The reminder of the years they'd spent together didn't soften her. "Let me go. Please." Droplets of water trickled into her mouth, droplets that were fused with dirt and she didn't want to think about what else. Grains scratched at her gums. "What did you do to the men, the warriors? Where are the other women?"

"I'll answer your questions in good time, Ashlyn. Right now, I want you to answer mine. Okay?" He coughed again. At least he sounded reasonable. Not like the crazy fanatic she'd encountered in the fortress.

She shivered in cold. "Okay." But then she could say no more, voices crashing into her mind. She stiffened.

She thought she heard McIntosh sigh, thought she heard him utter, "I see you're in no shape to answer questions now. I'll be back when the voices quiet." She thought she heard footsteps, the bars slam shut. And then she heard only the voices.

There were so many, so many. Prisoners, killers, murderers, thieves. Rapists. Oh God. A man was raping another man, and the victim was screaming in pain and humiliation.

"Maddox," she whimpered. Her hands were locked together by those cold metal links, so she couldn't even cover her ears. So loud, so loud, so loud. "Maddox." His image formed in her mind, strong, determined. His violet eyes were tender, his lips soft from kissing her. Dark hair hung over his forehead.

I'm here, he mouthed. *I'm here. I will protect you always.*

Instantly the voices slowed, quieted. They didn't vanish completely, but they were no longer debilitating. She blinked in surprise. How? That had never happened before. Was Maddox close by?

His face shimmered, faded as hope swelled inside her chest. As his image vanished, however, the voices grew louder. Louder. Eyes widening, she pictured him again. Again, the voices slowed. Again, they became manageable.

If the situation hadn't been so dire, she would have grinned. *I can control it on my own. I can control it!* The knowledge was astounding. Amazing. Wondrous. No more hiding away. No more avoiding heavily populated areas. No more!

Uh, Darrow. Hate to be the downer at this party, but you're trapped. With a hunter. Remember?

As if hearing her internal dialogue, a voice chuckled gleefully. *I know how to escape. You want in on the action or do you want to stay in this shithole? All we gotta do is a little digging.*

The man from the past wasn't talking to her, but to another prisoner. Their conversation caught her attention, causing her ears to twitch. Never releasing Maddox's image, she listened to instructions about exactly where to go. Soon she *was* grinning.

"Thank you," she whispered when the voices stopped their chatter.

"Yeah, yeah. You're welcome," a new voice said. Present, not past.

Smile collapsing, she narrowed her gaze and searched the cell. She was alone, yet something . . . thickened the air. Hummed with power and energy. "Who's there?"

"You want to know how to break a curse or what?" A woman's voice. A declaration, not truly an inquiry. "I thought I heard you asking about that before."

Ashlyn felt a tingle of heat trail from one shoulder to the other, as if someone ran a fingertip over her skin. Then a warm breeze danced in front of her. Still she didn't see anything. Whatever she was dealing with, she knew it wasn't human. An immortal? One of Maddox's gods?

"Yes," she answered on a trembling breath. "I did."

"Cool. I can totally help with that."

Cool? Totally? From a potential goddess? Where were the *thous* and *thys?* "Will you help me escape, too?"

"One thing at a time, kitten." Something shimmered in the corner, then long white hair came into view. Next she saw a tall woman with the body of a supermodel — a body clad in a red crop-top and a black skirt so short it barely covered the line of her panties. Tall, inky boots. Then, finally, a face materialized and Ashlyn found herself beholding the incarnation of loveliness. Features so perfect, so sublime and majestic they could only belong to a god. "Your friend, captor, *whatever,* mentioned fairy tales, yes?"

Had delusion set in or was this woman for real? "Yes."

"So you already have the answer. Think about the stories." Frown. A lick of a bright pink lollipop. "What did they teach you?"

Real enough for me, Ashlyn thought. "To search for a prince?"

"Ick. Wrong. Think, girlie. I want to get back."

Back to where? What was this being's name? And why was she here, helping?

"I said think, and babe, you don't look like you're thinking. You're sizing me up. You want a piece or something?"

Of her? "No. Of course not."

A shrug. "Then I suggest you get to it."

Okay, okay. Thinking . . . It was hard to recall story details when the need to escape weighed so heavily, but somehow she managed it. The prince in *Sleeping Beauty* fought through thorns and fire to slay the dragon and save his woman. In *Maid Maleen,* the princess dug through the walls of the tower she had been locked in for seven years, her determination to live and find her prince giving her strength. In *The Six Swans,* the princess gave up her voice for six years to set her brothers free from a terrible curse.

Ashlyn had always sighed over those stories, had tucked them deep in her heart to remember when she was alone. She had always secretly wanted a prince to gallop into the Institute and sweep her onto his white steed, riding off into the sunset to a land untainted by old voices. He never had. And that had been for the best, because she'd learned to rely on herself.

"Well?"

"Fairy tales teach determination, perseverance and sacrifice. Well, I'm determined, I'll persevere, but what do I sacrifice?" A shudder racked her. Would she be asked to sacrifice her relationship with Maddox? He was everything to her. To save him, though . . . anything. Even — her stomach clenched, churned — that. "I'm not a princess, and my life is hardly a fairy tale."

A chuckle. "Well, don'tcha want it to be?" A pause. "Ah, shit. Your enemy approaches. Think about what I said and we'll powwow later."

"But you didn't really say anything!"

A second passed and the air seemed to deaden, all sense of life vanishing.

"Better now?" McIntosh suddenly asked.

Ashlyn's eyelids popped open. When had she closed them? McIntosh stood behind the bars. He coughed, this one so strong it doubled him over. He only managed to stay upright by gripping the metal. He looked sicker, paler than when she'd last seen him.

"Better," she said softly. Had she just

imagined that entire encounter with the kind-of-invisible goddess?

He unlocked the bars and stumbled inside. Coughing, he pocketed the key. He didn't make it to the stool but collapsed on the dirt behind it. One minute passed, two. He didn't move, didn't make a sound.

"McIntosh? Are you okay?"

Finally, movement. He shook his head, as though he needed to dislodge a thick fog. "Picked up a little cold," he said. "Most of the men did." He rolled to his back and eased to a sitting position, wincing all the while.

She frowned. "How long have we been away from the fortress?"

"The better part of the day."

A day? So sick, so quickly? "None of you appeared sick before."

"Weren't." He coughed yet again and this time blood trickled from the side of his mouth. "Some are sicker than others. Damn winter germs. Pennington actually died, poor bastard. Well, maybe lucky." He scooted back until he rested against the bars.

Died? From a common cold?

"You need a doctor."

Anger flashed in his dark eyes and he made a visible effort to pull himself together. "What I need is that box. Those men are evil, Ashlyn. With their presence alone they spread lies and pain, doubt and misery. They're the reason for war and famine and death." Coughing again, he reached into his pants pocket and weakly tossed several photos in her lap. "We've fought these bastards for as long as I can remember. Their evil does not stop."

She looked automatically. And gagged. Decapitated bodies, a hand attached to nothing, blood flowing like rivers.

"The men you keep defending did this."

Not Maddox, she thought, tearing her gaze away. He wouldn't have done that. He couldn't. "The men I met aren't the source of the world's evil." She gentled her tone. "They could have hurt me, but didn't. They could have raped or killed the other women, but didn't. They could have stormed Budapest and slaughtered its people, but they didn't do that, either."

His head lolled to the side and for a moment she thought he'd fallen asleep — or died. This was no cold. Couldn't be. Before her eyes, red pockmarks were appearing on his face. "McIntosh?"

He jerked awake. "Sorry. Dizzy."

"Unlock me. Let me help you." *Let me escape.*

466

"No. Questions first," he said weakly. "Don't trust you anymore."

"Unlock me, and I'll tell you anything you want to know."

"Told you. Don't trust you. You've been with those monsters. They've corrupted you."

"No, they didn't. They *helped* me."

"*I* helped you. I made sure you were protected from harm. I gave you a life even your parents would have denied you."

"Yes, you did help me." Just not the way she'd needed. He'd helped her because it benefited him. "Now unlock the cuffs and let me help *you.*"

A soft sigh escaped him, but ended on a cough. When the fit subsided, he gasped out, "You should have gone home like I told you. But you defied me and your guards failed to report in. By the time I checked your location, it was too late. Wish I had gotten to you sooner, but couldn't just knock on the door. Had to plan."

"Checked my location? What plan?"

"The explosion. Distract the creatures to get you back. GPS. In your arm."

Oh God. They had detonated that bomb because of *her.* Guilty tears stung her eyes. *My fault.* They all could have died because of her. "I don't understand about the GPS."

She could barely get the words past the hard lump in her throat.

"Not birth control like we told you. Chip. We've always been able to track you."

Her mouth fell open as another hot flood of betrayal washed through her. Betrayal and hurt and fury, all blending with her guilt. How dare they! Never had she felt more violated. She wanted to cry; she wanted to scream. For once in her life, she wanted to kill.

Guess I was bait after all, she thought almost hysterically. However unintentionally, she'd led the hunters straight to Maddox's doorstep.

"We let one of our guys be captured yesterday," he said, his eyes glazed and far away. "He led the demons to a club. We left them there when we could have taken them. For you." He gave a weak smile before hunching over from another round of coughing. When he quieted, she saw that red branched from his eyes like molten rivers of poison.

"Unlock me, Dr. McIntosh. Please. I've aided you all these years. Don't leave me here to die."

He didn't respond for several seconds. Then, surprising her, he lumbered to his feet. He hobbled to her and knelt behind her. Grip weak, he undid the cuffs. The metal fell to the ground with a thump, and she was free.

She moved from the chair and crouched beside him. He was breathing heavily, struggling for every shallow intake of air. He didn't look like he'd survive the hour. Despite her anger, despite all he'd done, she felt pity rise up inside her. "Where are the other women?" she asked gently, choosing information over escape.

A pause. A wheezing exhalation. "Should be on a plane to New York."

"Where in New York?"

He closed his eyes, seeming to drift.

"McIntosh! Stay awake and talk to me."

His eyelids flickered open and closed, his body growing more and more pliant. "They'll be . . . traded for box. You'll see one day," he whispered. "Better place without them." He opened his eyes again and focused on her. "Pretty thing. Father would be proud." His sentences were no longer coherent, just disjointed pieces of thought flowing from his mind in no particular order. His eyes closed again, and this time they stayed closed. "What's wrong with me?"

"I don't know." Her voice trembled. "You need a hospital."

"Yes." But he died a heartbeat later, head falling to the side, body going completely limp.

Ashlyn covered her mouth with her hand. McIntosh was dead. He had betrayed her, yes, and a part of her hated him for that. But the little girl inside her still craved his approval.

Trembling, tears again burning her eyes, she pushed to her feet. She didn't take the key from his now-open hand because she didn't need it. She planned to use the same escape route the prisoner had used.

But first . . . *Go on. It'll hurt, but you have to do it.* Hand shaky, she picked up the stool McIntosh had been sitting on earlier and slammed it into the metal bars until one of the legs snapped off. She used the jagged edge to scratch desperately at her arm. She winced, nearly cried out. Blood flowed, and she whimpered at the pain. Finally she reached the GPS chip. She dug it out and tossed it on the floor, hiding it in the dirt.

Hurry, Darrow. Hurry. She couldn't risk running into any more of the Institute's employees up top. Most were probably sick, like McIntosh had said, but that didn't mean the ones who were well would let her waltz out. Bringing the prisoner's voice to her mind, she stumbled to the cell's only

470

toilet and twisted the bolts that fastened it to the wall. Some didn't want to budge and she had to force them, nearly breaking her fingers as she did so. When the last fell onto the dirt, she kicked the toilet aside.

A man-made hole stared up at her, a hole someone had dug straight to the outside world. She didn't want to crawl through the tight, black space, but with only one backward glance at McIntosh's prone body, she entered the opening. Total darkness surrounded her.

"Don't panic," she said, the prisoner's voice echoing hers in her mind. Her exhalations ricocheted from the muddy walls. A rat scampered past her fingers.

She hissed in a breath.

Forever she crawled, her legs burning from exertion. Wouldn't have been so bad, but it was an uphill climb. Chunks of dirt fell on her, even filled her mouth, coated her tongue. *Keep going. Just keep going.*

She felt like the princess in *Maid Maleen* just then, fighting her way free. The thought brought her mind back to that strange conversation she'd had with the goddess. Or hallucination. Ashlyn would never again wish to be inside a fairy tale.

A light appeared at the end of the tunnel, small but visible. Relief flooded her, and she quickened her movements. A second later, she found a small opening. Even a child couldn't fit through. "No. No!" She clawed and clawed and clawed.

After an eternity, she caught a glimpse of moonlit sky. Arms nearly sagging in relief and fatigue, she pulled herself up onto the cold, hard ground. She stood, her knees knocking. Snowcapped trees towered all around her. She shivered, Maddox's baggy clothes doing little to keep her warm.

A man screamed, a tortured sound.

She stiffened. Maddox. Maddox! Midnight must have arrived. She looked around, spotting the fortress on the horizon, but the scream hadn't come from that direction. When she heard him again, she kicked into gear despite her exhaustion, following the sound. Another scream. A roar.

"I'm coming. I'm coming."

As she ran, Ashlyn began to cough.

CHAPTER
TWENTY-TWO

When Maddox awakened, terror was already gripping him. Ashlyn needed him.

He was . . . not in the forest, he realized. No, he was in his own bed, his own bedroom, staring up at the vaulted ceiling as he did every morning. But he was not chained.

How? Why?

Sunlight streamed through the window, warming him. He'd failed to find Ashlyn and the time for his death had arrived, preventing him from searching further. Reyes, he thought then. Reyes must have dragged him home.

Maddox bounced out of bed, determined to renew his search. He would find her today, no matter what. *We'll destroy the world piece by piece until she's recovered.*

There would be no resting until —

A woman's cough stopped him midstep. He had been about to hit the hallway running, but now spun around. Ashlyn lay on his bed. Shock slammed into him with the force of a sword through the gut.

He scrubbed a hand over his face, afraid to believe. Still the vision remained. Relief swamped him, overshadowing the shock, and he ran back to the bed. A wide grin stretched his face as he fell to his knees, thanking the gods, reaching out to gather his woman in his arms.

She coughed again.

He froze, realization setting in. His grin disappeared. *No!* Not Ashlyn. But he studied her more closely. She was pale, too pale, and there were dark circles under her eyes. Little pink splotches marred her pretty skin.

He could have torn out his own heart.

He had suspected . . . he had feared . . . and now his worst fear had come true. The Hunters had exposed her to disease. They had probably died, one by one, allowing her to escape and find him.

Allowing her to come home to die.

"No!" he roared. He wouldn't let her; she was his life. An eternity roasting in hell was preferable to a single minute on this earth without her.

Reyes stomped into the room, as if he had been waiting for some sign of life. He was grim and angry as a storm cloud, ready to erupt. "Has she woken yet?" He had so many cuts on his arms it was hard to tell where one began and another ended.

"No," Maddox replied brokenly.

The warrior looked her over. "I stayed nearby. She coughed all night. I'm sorry." Then, in a comforting tone, he added, "Most die within hours of becoming infected, but she's managed to stay alive. Perhaps she'll survive."

Perhaps wasn't good enough. Maddox laid a hand over her too-hot brow. Commands began to spill from him. "Get me cool rags. And more of those pills, if we still have Danika's purse. Water, too."

Reyes rushed to obey, returning shortly with everything Maddox had wanted. Ashlyn refused to awaken, so he crushed the pills and dumped the powder into her mouth. Next he poured the water down her throat.

She coughed and gagged, but did eventually swallow. Finally her eyelids flickered open and she squinted against the light. "Home," she said when she spied him, her voice hoarse. "Hurt. Worse than before."

"I know, beauty." Softly he kissed her temple. While he could be infected by Torin, he could not be infected by a human. Not that it mattered. He would have touched and held her anyway. "You're going to get better this time, too."

"Boss . . . Hunter. Dead."

He nodded in acknowledgment, not wanting to speak what he was feeling about the man's death. Satisfaction.

"What of Danika?" Reyes asked, stepping forward. "I followed the hole you came through and found the prison and the dead Hunters, but Danika was not inside."

"Might be . . . on her way to . . . New York," Ashlyn said haltingly.

Reyes paled, the color draining from his face as though it were being sucked out by the vacuum Aeron always grumbled about using. "They told you nothing else?"

"I'm sorry." She coughed.

Madox winced at the terrible, rattling sound. He laid one of the cool, wet rags on her brow. She sighed, closed her eyes. Reyes tangled a hand in his hair, clearly frustrated, needing to pace, needing pain.

"Go," Maddox told him. "Find her."

The warrior glanced at Ashlyn, then Maddox, then nodded. He left without another word.

Maddox remained with Ashlyn for hours, mopping her brow, forcing her to sip the water. He recalled seeing Torin do this all those years ago, after he'd touched the human woman and the plague had taken root.

476

For a time, Maddox thought Ashlyn's will to live was stronger than the disease, for she had not died like the others. That, or perhaps something — someone — was helping her. But then her cough had become bloody, her body too weak to sit up. Her throat became so swollen she was no longer able to swallow. How much longer could she last?

Not knowing what else to do, Maddox bundled her up and cradled her in his arms. He did not speak to his friends as he carried her out of the fortress. They did not ask his intentions, probably too afraid he would become violent. He would have. The spirit churned inside of him, worried for her, too, wanting to destroy, to maim, to kill. This time in helplessness and frustration, not fury.

Down the hill and into the city he raced, the moonlight a mocking reminder of his failure to help her yesterday, too. *Save her, have to save her.* She never made a sound, too weak now even to cough. The streets were barren, no one outside. *Whatever it takes, save her.*

He carried her straight to the hospital, a place he had found yesterday in his fruitless search for her. The building was filled, nearly bursting from its seams, hundreds of humans inside, coughing. Dying. He did not want to leave her, was afraid to trust them with her life. But he did not know what else to do.

In a crowded, white hallway, he found a gloved and masked man issuing orders. "Help me," he said, cutting into the man's speech. "Help her. Please."

Distracted, the white-coated man glanced at Ashlyn and gave a weary sigh. "Everyone needs help, sir. You'll just have to wait your turn."

Maddox pinned him with a fierce stare and knew Violence flashed over his face. Knew his eyes burned bright red.

"You're — you're — one of them. From the hill." The man gulped. "Lay her there." He pointed to a bed with wheels at the end of the hall. "I'll care for her myself."

Maddox did as instructed, then kissed Ashlyn's soft lips. Still no response. "Save her," he commanded.

"I'll — I'll do my best."

Please let her survive. He wanted to stay with her, guard her, watch over her. Take care of her. More than anything, he wanted her with him. But he walked away from her then, and into the night. Midnight approached.

In the morning, he would return. Woe to

the world — woe to the *gods* — if she was not here, alive and well.

Reyes cursed as he searched the airport, nearby hotels. Medical clinics. He'd seen more of the city in two days than in all his centuries living here. He felt like a caged animal, seething with a need to act but ultimately powerless. Danika was still out there. Maybe sick, like Ashlyn. Maybe dying. And he could not find a single sign of her.

Night had fallen once again, and he was surprised to realize he'd raced to the same alleyway he and Maddox had discovered last night. He could see where Maddox had punched the wall in rage. The stone was cracked and dented.

Reyes was close to hopping on a plane to New York, but knew he could not stray very far from Maddox's side. When the gods had cursed Maddox to die every night, they had cursed him, as well, tethering him to the warrior as surely as if they'd used iron chains. Why him, rather than Aeron, he did not know. All he knew was that, at midnight, he would be forced to return to the fortress. Always he would return.

He'd taken off several times before, testing his boundaries, testing the gods' reaction, but always he was pulled to Maddox at midnight.

"Damn this!" He unsheathed one of his daggers and slashed the tip across his thigh. Fabric tore and blood leaked from the wound. What was he going to do? There was a need inside him, a deep need he'd never experienced before, to save, to rescue. To protect. But only Danika. Only to look into those angel eyes again and feel another flicker of pleasure.

A pleasure he was never supposed to experience.

But he had experienced it, and now he wanted more.

The gods would not have ordered Aeron to hunt her down and kill her if she could die from Torin's disease or if Hunters were destined to render the final blow. The thought brought both comfort and anger.

Perhaps Reyes should release Aeron — whom he had locked in the dungeon before leaving the fortress — and follow him to Danika, for surely Wrath would be able to scent her out so Reyes could free her from the Hunters.

No, he realized. Reyes would not be able to follow him if Danika were not close by. And if Aeron reached her first she would die, no doubt about it.

Forget her. She's a human. There are thousands. Millions. You can find another woman who looks like an angel.

"I don't want to find another," he shouted. But he could not keep Aeron chained forever, and he knew it. "Damn this."

Stop acting like a baby, a female voice said inside his mind, surprising him. *Look on the hill and shut the hell up already. You're giving me a major headache.*

His shoulders stiffened. He scanned the area, knife at the ready. He saw no one.

What are you waiting for? the voice said again. *Hurry.*

A god? One of his own kind? Couldn't be Doubt, for the speaker was clearly female. Reyes didn't waste any more time trying to reason it out. He sprinted into motion, and ten minutes later, he stood at the edge of the hill.

Danika was there. She and a man — Kane, he realized — were lying on the ground, both of them moaning.

Anger filled him at the notion that she was injured, even as relief poured through him. Shockingly, she looked as if she'd been climbing back up, trying to reach the fortress. Rocks were scattered around the pair as if they'd fallen from the sky, the couple the target.

Reyes scooped her up, never wanting to let her go, and nudged Kane with the toe of his boot to wake him. He kept the hilt of his dagger at hand, just in case. He wasn't entirely comfortable having the other Lords back in his life.

Kane grunted. Opened his eyes. Grabbed for the gun sheathed in his waistband. Reyes kicked it out of his hand.

"Go ahead and kill each other," Danika said weakly. Her blond hair was matted with blood. In that instant, Reyes thought he knew the dark, consuming violence Maddox must experience whenever he thought of Ashlyn being hurt.

"How are you hurt?" If Disaster had —

"Rocks fell," she said, cutting off his furious thoughts. "From a mountain, I guess. He pushed me out of the way to avoid the worst of it and I tripped, hit my head."

Reyes relaxed, but only slightly. "Thank you," he said to Kane.

The man nodded, rubbed his temple as if in regret, and stood.

"Where's your family?" Reyes asked Danika. He could have remained just as he was for all eternity.

"Flying somewhere you'll never think to find them." She wouldn't meet his eyes and struggled against his hold. "Now put me down."

Never, he wanted to say. "No. You're too weak to walk." Turning to Kane, he switched to Hungarian so that Danika would not understand. He hoped. "How did you save her? And do not answer in English." He only prayed *Kane* understood him.

"Hunters were on their way to the fortress when Torin and I ran into them," was the reply, also in Hungarian. Of course the man would speak it, Reyes thought. He would not have traveled to Buda unprepared. "We fought, but there were so many. . . . He was cut and I was taken. They made the mistake of putting her in the same van they'd stashed me in. The tires blew and the vehicle flew off the road."

"And the Hunters are now . . . ?"

"Dead."

Good. Though a part of him yearned to kill them all over again. Something painful. Something slow and lingering. His gaze locked on Danika, searching for any sign of Disease's infection. Her skin glowed health-ily and there was no telltale cough. So, she *had* remained unaffected. For the reason he feared?

"Why did you come back?" he asked her, reverting to English.

"*He* made me," she said, pointing to Disaster. "Is Ashlyn okay? I heard them talking about —" she choked on a sudden sob "— hurting her to draw you guys out so they could find some stupid box."

"She has been found," he said, tightening his hold. Her pain was like a hot poker stabbing straight into his chest — and for once he didn't enjoy the sensation. "She's very sick."

Danika swallowed. "Will she . . ."

"Only time will tell." Reyes motioned for Kane to go ahead of them. The warrior nodded and leapt into motion. "Death waits in town, Danika. You will stay at the fortress until the Hunters are destroyed and the sickness passes."

"No. I won't." She struggled against him, trying to push away from his torso and jerk her legs to the ground. "I want to go home *now*."

"Moving like that simply presses your body against mine."

She stilled, and he was both glad and disappointed. He hadn't lied. Her body was warm, fragrant with pine, and every time she had moved, his nerve endings had come alive.

He started walking up the hill, taking a different path than Disaster. Just in case.

Reyes's relief at Danika's safe return was still so vast he shook with it.

"Am I to be your prisoner again?"

"Guest, as long as you stay put." When it was safe, he would set her free, allowing her to live out the rest of her life as she pleased. However long it was. "We've had to lock Aeron in the dungeon. You are not to go down there. Ever. Understand?" He let all of his rage, all of his torment, drip from his voice. "He will kill you without blinking."

"Yet another reason I want to go home," she said, shuddering. "Things like this don't happen there."

"And where is home?"

"Like I'm going to tell you. *Kidnapper.*"

If he had his way, she'd soon tell him everything there was to know about her. They would spend their short time together in his room, in his bed. His cock jumped to attention as he imagined all that angel hair splayed on his pillow . . . those lush breasts pink and ripe . . . those sweet legs parted . . .

Perhaps she would never want to leave.

Ha! Women like her never wanted men like him. He cut himself for pleasure, for relief. He had to. Sometimes, he felt he would die if he didn't. If she knew, she would scoff at him. And that would be for the best. She was better off away from him, away from Wrath.

When the sickness passed, he *would* let Danika go. He couldn't go with her to protect her — not that she would want him to — and he couldn't stop Aeron from doing his duty.

For Reyes, there could be no happy ending.

Chapter
Twenty-Three

Ashlyn hovered in a realm of unconsciousness. Shadows were all she knew. Shadows and a single voice, all the voices of the past and present receding in awe of this one. It was one she'd heard before. Ethereal, like a phantom. A very modern phantom who was slightly bored and still sucking on a lollipop.

"I'm baaack." Chuckle. "No need to express your joy. I feel the love. So, hey. Did you think about the fairy tales or what?" that female voice from the cell said. The goddess. "I've got, like, a week, tops, before I'm found out so I need to blow this joint el pronto."

"I thought about it," Ashlyn tried to reply, but the words wouldn't form.

"Good."

Okay, so the goddess heard her anyway. *Sacrifice,* she projected in her mind. *I have to sacrifice something to break Maddox's curse.*

"Ding, ding, ding. And what do you need to sacrifice, girlie?"

I still don't know. Or rather, still didn't want to consider. *What's your name?* That was a much simpler topic.

"My name is . . . Anya."

Anya. Pretty. But there'd been a brief hesitation, as if she'd had to think about what to say. Was there a goddess named Anya, or some variation of the name? Ashlyn's mind came up blank. *Are you —*

"Uh, discussing sacrifice here. Concentrate. I'm not disobeying direct orders just so you can piss on this sweet little revolt I've got going. I asked you a question and I'd like a straight answer."

Sacrifice. Right. Concentrating was difficult when one's mind was like mush. One thing she knew with clarity, though, was that life without Maddox would be intolerable. Still, she *would* give him up to save him.

"That's better," Anya said, reading her thoughts again. "But you're not thinking big enough. C'mon, did you miss the most important lesson of those fairy tales of yours? Now's your chance to prove that worthless boss taught you something of value after all."

Value. The single word slammed into her and suddenly Ashlyn knew. Her blood chilled just thinking about it. *The best kind of sacrifice is a life for a life.*

"There you go. I knew you had the answer. That means yours for his, honey bear. Are you strong enough?"

For him? Anything. Even pain, even death. Saving him was more important than keeping him.

"Alrighty, then." Anya clapped. "Let's get this party started. Wake up. He needs you."

Maddox's image rose in her mind and she thought perhaps she felt his hand gripping hers, willing strength into her body. Then . . . something, a presence, a warmth, invaded her body, sweeping through her and mending the rawness of her lungs, the bruised muscles in her ribs and sides.

She pried her eyelids open — and found Maddox peering down at her. He looked tired, but he saw her and grinned, and it was the most beautiful sight she'd ever seen.

Could she really give him up?

Three days later, Ashlyn was strong enough to leave the hospital. Maddox carried her back to the fortress without a word — no car for this he-man — and straight to his room. She spied a few of the warriors in the hallways. Some looked grim, others angry, but they all nodded at her, as though they accepted her presence now, even if they didn't like it.

Once the bedroom door was shut and locked, Maddox set her on her feet, letting her body slide down his. He dropped his arms to his sides, severing contact.

"Have you learned anything new about the women?" she asked, not moving away from him. His heat enveloped her and his nearness tantalized her.

"They've been freed. All except for Danika, who is driving Reyes crazy, insulting him at every turn." He studied her face intently. "How are you feeling?"

"Good," she said, and she meant it. She still had a mild cough and a slightly raw sensation in her chest, but she was nearly healed. Which meant it was time. Time to save him.

He needs you, the goddess Anya had said.

Ashlyn wasn't going to tell Maddox about Anya. He'd ask questions; questions she didn't want to answer. She knew what she had to do to release him from his curse — knew it, hated it, but was going to do it — and couldn't let him stop her. Couldn't let *her* stop her. The thought of being without him filled her with despair.

I don't want to say goodbye.

Tears threatened to spring to her eyes, so

she forced herself to smile. This was *her* fairy tale, and she was going to save her prince. *Just . . . Don't say goodbye. Not yet.* She'd enjoy the rest of the day with him, talking to him, touching him as she hadn't been able to do while in the hospital.

"I want you," she told him. "I want you so badly."

"I want you, too." There was a sudden glint of wickedness in his purple eyes. "I feel like an eternity has passed since I last touched you."

But they just stared at each other, neither one reaching for the other yet.

"I want you to know . . ." she bit her lip and peered down at her booted feet. Confession time. "I love you."

Shock blanketed Maddox's face and his mouth flailed open and closed.

"It's too soon," she said for him, "our lives are too different and I'm responsible for a lot of the crap you've had to deal with this past week, but I can't help it. I still love you."

Finally, he reached out. His fingers cupped her cheeks and gently forced her to face him. Tenderness overshadowed the shock. "I love you, too. So much. I'm a violent man with violent emotions, but I do not want you ever to fear that I'll become violent with you. I *can't* hurt you. It would be worse than cutting out my own heart."

Joy fluttered inside her, more than she'd ever thought possible. Tears filled her eyes. She leaned into his chest, needing him more than ever before. He lowered his head, slowly . . . pure temptation . . . his gaze never leaving hers. Their lips brushed, a gentle kiss of beauty and of love.

His tongue slid inside her mouth. Over and over, forever and ever, he kissed her, savoring her, enjoying her. She felt his elation, his wonder, both emotions mirrored inside her.

"So beautiful," he whispered.

"I love you," she said again.

"Love you. Need you."

Piece by piece, he removed her clothing and piece by piece she removed his, glorying in every new inch of skin revealed. He was so big and hard. So . . . hers. She gloried in touching him, savoring him and memorizing him. He was banked ferocity and he loved her.

Hearing him say those words had given her a sublime sense of peace. Once, after she was sick the first time, he'd called this her home. It was, she realized. It was the only home she'd ever really known. How unlikely that a man of violence would be the one to give it to her. That he would be the one to drive out the memory of padded rooms, crazed noise, solitude and ultimate betrayal. How . . . extraordinary.

"I'm going to worship you," he said. "With my mouth, my hands." He dropped to his knees.

"No." Ashlyn gripped his shoulders and tugged him up.

He frowned, confused.

"My turn." This time, *she* knelt. *She* worshipped him. Her mouth enclosed his thick length, so hard and hot, taking him all the way to the back of her throat. She'd never done this before, but she knew the way of it, having heard it described in excoriating detail by numerous women.

His hands gripped her hair, and he moaned. "Ashlyn."

Performing the act wasn't something she'd thought she'd like, but Ashlyn found that she loved it. Loved his pleasure in it. Up and down she sucked him, enjoying the way he trembled, circling her tongue over the round head before diving down to the base. She cupped his testicles. Giving Maddox pleasure brought her more satisfaction than anything else she'd ever done, made her wet and aching, a slave to desire.

He thrust, hard, caught himself and tried

to slow. She increased her speed, taking all he had to give. Wanting him to thrust, wanting it hard.

"Ashlyn, Ashlyn." With a roar, he spilled his hot seed into her mouth.

She swallowed every bit of it. When his last shudder subsided, she pushed to shaky feet. His eyelids were at half-mast, his bottom lip swollen as if he'd chewed on it to keep from shouting in pleasure, in agony. His face was cloaked by that skeletal mask, letting her see both man and beast. Both were staring at her with love and tenderness, a need so deep it was infinite.

He would willingly die for her. She knew it; soul-deep, she knew it. *I can do no less for him.*

"I'm not going to lay you down on the bed," he said huskily.

"Wh-what?"

"I'm going to take you against the wall, each stroke measured. Deep. No longer two bodies but one."

She would have melted into a puddle if he hadn't caught her. He did that to her, felled her with his beautiful words. Her arms wound around his neck, locking them together. Eternity in his arms wouldn't have been enough.

His lips descended to hers and he fed her

a kiss that was slow and sweet, hot and needy. Step by step, he backed her into the wall as he'd promised. Cool stone pressed into her naked back and she gasped.

On and on he continued to kiss her, kneading her breasts, paying tribute to her nipples. Soon she was writhing, panting, moaning. Begging.

"More," he promised. "I'll give you more."

Let this last forever. "I love you. I love you so much."

Lifting her up, he braced her against the stone with his hips, not entering — oh, please enter, no, savor — and anchored her legs around his waist. She squeezed him tightly, but he forced her to release her hold and spread her knees, opening herself up to him. Cool air kissed the most private part of her.

Two of his fingers traced a fiery path down her stomach and played at the fine tuft of hair. Eyes closed, she tried to arch her hips and lead those fingers into her core. She was dripping with need.

She'd wanted him the first (thousand) times they were together, but this . . . this was true need, being with the man she'd given her heart to. This was more than sex, more than pleasure. This was destiny, a melding of souls.

"Touch me, Maddox."

"I am, love. I am."

"Deeper."

"Like this?" His fingers inched down . . . down . . . then stopped at the moist slit.

"More."

"Like this?" Another inch.

"More. *Please*."

He shook his head and with his free hand clasped her chin and angled her to meet his loving gaze. "You don't have to beg me, Ashlyn. Ever. Your every desire is my pleasure to give." Those two fingers at last slid home.

Her back arched. He worked in and out, his thumb rubbing her clitoris. Oh God. "Yes!" That was exactly what she'd needed, what she'd die without. "Yes, yes. More."

A third finger instantly joined the play, increasing the pleasure, intensifying the sensation.

"Yes. Just like that," she said on a wispy catch of breath.

"So tight and wet."

"For you."

"Only me."

Too much . . . not enough . . . Fast, lingering. Fast. She arched, riding his fingers, slipping and sliding against them. Her clitoris was swollen, desperate. "Need . . . need to come."

"Need to feel you." He surged inside her, his fingers there one second, his cock there the next. He filled and stretched her; he completed her.

She gasped and moaned, on fire, burning deliciously. *My life was worth living for this alone — for this man, for his touch.*

"Love you," he grunted against her throat.

"Love you, love you, love you," she sang in harmony with his thrusts.

He nuzzled her throat, as though he could lick her words into his body. He kept his thrusts slow and measured, just like he'd promised. "Never felt anything like this. Never want it to end."

She felt it, too. A sizzling burn in her blood, electric, awakening every cell. "So good."

"Forever," he said.

"Forever." *You'll have my heart forever.*

He surged inside her one last time, hitting so deep she felt him in every part of her body. Hitting her exactly where she needed him, branding her. Her orgasm ripped through her. She screamed his name, clutching him close.

He roared hers, holding her protectively. Heat enveloped them, so much heat. A heat that would never die.

"Mine," he said, brushing a soft kiss on her lips.

"Yours." *Always.*

Maddox carried her to the bed and gently laid her down. He settled beside her, cocooning her. They didn't speak for a long while, just enjoyed each other. *A little longer,* she prayed. *Give me a little longer.*

"I missed you," he finally said.

"I missed you, too. More than I can say." She draped her leg over his. "What happened while I was gone?"

He traced a lazy circle on her back, saying, "Aeron has been placed in the dungeon. As I mentioned, Reyes is trying to woo and repel Danika at the same time, and Danika had to be locked in his room to keep her from escaping. Torin was injured, but is on the mend. Sabin and the others, the men you saw here after the bombing, have moved in. At the moment, we've reached a truce. Not a comfortable one, but a truce nonetheless."

Wow. Never a dull moment, it seemed. "I don't like Danika being locked up."

"Trust me, beauty, it is for her own good."

She sighed. "I trust you."

"What . . ." He paused. Stiffened. "What did the Hunters do to you, Ashlyn? I have to know."

"Nothing, I swear," she assured him. "I have to tell you something." *Please don't stop loving me.* "I brought them here, Maddox. Me. I'm so sorry. I didn't mean to. Really. I didn't. They tricked me and —"

"I know, beauty. I know."

Relieved, she relaxed. He truly loved her, to forgive her so easily for something he'd almost killed her over before. She hugged him tight. "Before he died, my boss told me that they plan to find Pandora's box and suck your demons inside."

"We were told the same thing." He suddenly yawned. A peaceful smile lifted the corners of his lips. "I owe the gods a thank-you for bringing you back to me, but I find I'm too tired to approach them right now. I need little rest, but I have gotten none these past few days."

"Go to sleep. I need you to keep up your strength," she said huskily.

He chuckled, a sound of absolute joy. "Your wish is my pleasure."

CHAPTER
TWENTY-FOUR

"He sooo does not owe the gods. He owes me. But I swear this is totally my last favor to you. I put him to sleep. Don't waste any time."

Ashlyn froze as Anya's voice penetrated her mind. *No, not yet,* her body whined. *I need more time with him.*

"Choice is yours, chica. I'm signing off."

And she did. Anya's hum of energy died, leaving the room deflated.

Shaking, Ashlyn pushed from the bed and sneaked from the room — but not before giving Maddox one last wistful glance. She hated to leave the decadence of his arms, but wouldn't risk losing this chance.

"This is for the best," she told herself. "He's not going to die again. Not when I can save him."

For fifteen minutes, she roamed the halls of the fortress, knocking on bedroom doors. No one answered. Not even Danika. All the while the halls echoed with the sound of someone shouting profanities. She heard chains rattling. Aeron, she realized and shuddered. He scared her.

Finally, she found one of the immortals. The silver-haired angel who'd taken her from Danika's room and hidden her in another. Torin. Disease. He was lying on a bed, a red towel wrapped around his neck. His skin was pale, he'd lost a little weight and the lines around his eyes and mouth were taut with pain. But he was breathing.

She didn't wake him. She did approach the side of the bed to whisper, "I wish I could touch you, hold your hand and thank you for hiding me that day. I was able to reach Maddox and hold him that night."

His eyelids fluttered open.

Startled, she jumped backward. Their gazes met and she relaxed. There was gentleness in his green eyes, and she liked to think he would have said, "Welcome home," if he'd been able. "I hope you get better soon, Torin."

He might have nodded, but it was hard to tell.

Her nerves on edge, she continued her search.

Finally, she located a group of them. Her heart hammered in her chest as she studied them, unnoticed. They were working out, bench-pressing and squatting more weight than five humans combined could have done. The one named Reyes was pounding away at a punching bag. Sweat poured down his bare chest, ribboned with flecks of blood.

He was the one who always wielded the sword. She tried not to hate him for it.

"Ahem," she said, drawing everyone's attention.

All of them paused, peered at her. A few narrowed their eyes. She lifted her chin. "I need to talk to you," she said, aiming the words at Reyes and Lucien.

Reyes went back to his punching bag. "If you're going to try to talk us out of killing Maddox tonight, save your breath."

"I'll listen to you, sweet," the tallest of the group said. Paris was his name. Blue eyes, pale skin, brown and black hair. Pure sex, Maddox had said, and she believed him. The words had been delivered as a warning to stay away.

"Quiet," Lucien said. "If Maddox heard you, he'd go for your head."

A blue-haired man faced her. "Want me to kiss them for you?"

Kiss them? She'd only seen him once before. In the foyer, right after the bombing, but he hadn't struck her as a kisser. He

502

looked as if he wanted to kill them.

Reyes growled, "You shut up, too, Gideon. And don't cozy up to her. She's taken. I'll have to hurt you."

"I'd hate to see you try," the now-grinning man said.

She blinked. How odd. His words said one thing, his tone quite another. Well, whatever.

"You're right," she told Reyes. "I don't want you to kill Maddox tonight. I want you to —" *oh God, are you really going to say this?* "— kill me instead."

That got everyone's attention. They stopped what they were doing, weights dropping, the treadmill grinding to a halt, and stared at her, gaping.

"What did you just say?" Reyes gasped out, wiping sweat from his brow.

"Curses are broken through sacrifice. Preferably *self*-sacrifice. If I sacrifice myself, dying in place of Maddox, his curse will be broken."

Silence.

Thick, heavy silence. She only wished it were comfortable.

"How can you be sure?" Lucien asked, those odd eyes somber. "What if it doesn't work? What if Maddox's death-curse isn't broken and you've died for nothing?"

She gathered her courage, wrapping it

503

around her like a blanket in the winter. "At least I will have tried. But, uh. I kind of have it on the highest authority that this will work."

"The gods?"

She nodded. Well, Anya had never verified that little tidbit. Ashlyn had just assumed.

Again, silence.

"You would do that?" Disbelief filled Paris's electric eyes. "For Violence?"

"Yes." Thinking of the pain she would endure terrified her, but she didn't hesitate with her answer.

"I stab him," Reyes reminded her. "That means I would have to stab you. Six times. In the stomach."

"I know," she said softly. She gazed down at her bare feet. "I see it in my mind every day, and I relive it every night."

"Let's say you do break his curse," Lucien said. "You will have condemned him to a life without you."

"I'd rather he live without me than die repeatedly with me at his side. He suffers so much and I just can't allow it."

"Self-sacrifice." Reyes snorted. "Sounds ridiculous to me."

Ashlyn raised her chin another notch and tried the same logic the goddess had used on her. "Look at the world's most beloved fairy tales," she said. All that magic, all those happily-ever-afters. "Selfish queens always die and the good princesses always win."

Reyes snorted again. "Like you said, fairy tales."

"Aren't all fairy tales based in fact? You yourself are supposed to be nothing more than a myth. Pandora's box is a story parents read to their children at night," she countered. "That means life itself is a fairy tale. Like the characters, we all live and love and search for a happily-ever-after."

They continued to stare at her, something unreadable in their eyes. Maybe . . . admiration? Minutes dragged by, torturously slow. She'd made her decision and if she had to stab herself to carry it out, she would.

"All right," Lucien said, shocking her. "We'll do it."

"Lucien!" Reyes scoffed.

Lucien peered over at Reyes, and Ashlyn could see hope lighting his severely scarred face. "This will free us, too, Reyes. We'll be able to leave the fortress for more than a single day. We could travel if we wished. We could leave — and stay gone — when we craved solitude."

Reyes opened his mouth, closed it.

"In the movies Paris has forced us to watch," Lucien continued, "good always overcomes evil with an extreme act of self-sacrifice."

"Human movies mean nothing. If we do this, we could be cursed even more. Punished for defying the gods' will."

"For Maddox, for freedom, why not risk it?"

"Maddox will not like it," Reyes said, but there was hope in his voice now, too. "I think . . . I think he would rather have the human."

That observation warmed her, but she didn't back down. She couldn't — wouldn't — let Maddox suffer like that night after night, knowing there was something she could do. He'd paid for his crimes, plus interest.

An eye for an eye, she thought. He'd given her peace. She would do the same for him.

"Sometimes what we want isn't what we need," Lucien said. His voice had dropped and an edge of wistfulness seeped from it. What did he want that he didn't need?

"All right," Reyes finally said.

"Tonight," Ashlyn insisted. "It has to be tonight." She didn't want him to suffer yet again, nor did she want to risk changing her mind. "Just . . . give me as much time as possible with him, okay?"

Both men nodded grimly.

506

■ ■ ■ ■

Maddox saw to Ashlyn's every need for the rest of the day. He fed her by hand and loved her body so many times he lost count. He talked about his plans for their future together. How her new job could be helping the warriors search for Pandora's box — if she so desired. How they would wed and spend every waking minute together — if she so desired. How they would seek a way to save her from aging so that they could have an eternity together — if she so desired. He would carve her anything she wanted, and she could read him passages from romance novels. If she so desired.

She laughed with him, teased him, loved him, but there was a quiet desperation about her that he did not understand. A sadness. He didn't press her. They had time. For once, he viewed time as his friend. She couldn't know that she had tamed him. Tamed the spirit. And that now, both existed to please her.

"What's wrong, love?" he asked. "Tell me and I will make it better."

"It's almost midnight," she said, trembling.

Ah. He understood now. He gazed down

at her. They sat on the edge of his bed and he clasped her hand in his. Moonlight bathed her lovely features, illuminating the concern in her eyes. "I will be fine."

"I know."

"Hardly hurts, I swear."

That earned him a soft chuckle. "Liar."

Her laughter warmed him, inside out. "I want you to stay in another bedroom tonight."

She shook her head, tickling his arm with strands of her hair. "I'm going to stay with you."

He sighed. There was such determination in her voice. "All right." He wouldn't permit himself any reaction to the stabbing. He would not make a noise, would not move a muscle. He would die with a smile on his face. "We will —"

Reyes and Lucien entered the bedroom, more grim than he'd ever seen them. He wondered at their mood, but decided not to question them in front of Ashlyn. No reason to heap anything else on her right now; she was about to watch him be murdered.

Maddox placed a swift kiss on Ashlyn's lips. She gripped his head, urging him to linger. She was fierce, almost desperate. He allowed himself a moment more. Gods, how he loved this woman.

"We will finish this tomorrow," he said. Tomorrow . . . He could hardly wait.

He lay down on the cotton sheets and scooted to the headboard. Reyes shackled his wrists, Lucien his ankles. "At least turn away when they begin," he said to Ashlyn.

She smiled a sad smile and crouched beside him. She stroked his cheek, softly, a butterfly caress. "You know I love you."

"Yes." And he had never been so glad of anything in his life. This woman was his miracle. "And you know I will love you forever and afterward."

"Listen, Maddox . . . Don't blame anyone but me for this, okay. You've suffered enough, too much, and as the woman who loves you, it's up to me to save you. Know that I do it willingly, because you mean more to me than my own life." She kissed him again, briefly this time, and stood. She turned to Lucien and Reyes. "I'm ready."

His brows drew together in confusion, dread on its heels. "Ready for what? What would I blame you for?"

Reyes unsheathed his sword, the blade whistling against the air. Maddox's dread increased. "What's going on? Tell me. Now."

No one said a word as Reyes approached Ashlyn.

Maddox strained against his chains. "Ashlyn. Leave the room. Leave the room and do not return."

"I'm ready," she whispered again. "Should we go to another room?"

"Ashlyn!" Maddox snarled.

"No," Lucien said. "You said you wanted the ultimate sacrifice, remember? He has to watch and understand what you're doing for him."

Her eyes met Maddox's, pooled with unshed tears. "I love you."

In that moment, he realized exactly what they planned. He bucked and fought for freedom. He shouted profanities even Paris would not utter. All the while, hot tears streamed down his cheeks. "No. Do not do this. Please, do not do this. I need you, Ashlyn. Reyes, Lucien. Please. *Please!*"

Reyes hesitated. Swallowed.

And then he stabbed Ashlyn in the stomach.

Maddox screamed, straining so forcefully the metal links cut all the way to the bone. If he kept it up, he would lose his hands and ankles. He did not care. Only one thing mattered, and she was dying in front of him. "No! No! Ashlyn!"

Blood poured from her stomach, wetting her shirt. She pressed her lips together, somehow remaining silent and upright. "I love you," she repeated.

Reyes stabbed her again. With each new cut, Maddox felt his ties to midnight slacken, as if invisible chains that had bound him for thousands of years were slowly lifting away. And he wanted them back! He wanted Ashlyn.

"Ashlyn! Reyes! Stop. Stop." He openly sobbed, helpless, furious. Dying himself, though he felt stronger than ever. "Lucien, make him stop."

Death lowered his gaze, saying nothing.

At the third thrust of the blade, Ashlyn did fall. She did scream. No, that was him. She only whimpered. "Doesn't . . . hurt," she gasped out. "Like you said."

"Ashlyn." Her name trembled from his lips, the plea desperate. Raging. Violent. "Oh, gods. No. Ashlyn. Why are you doing this? Reyes, stop. You must stop!" He could not say it enough.

Her eyes met his again, and there was so much love in them he was humbled. "I love you."

"Ashlyn, Ashlyn." He jerked and the chain sank deeper, cut harder. "Hold on, beauty. Just hold on. We'll patch you up. We'll give you Tylenol. Do not worry, do not worry. Reyes, stop. Do not do this thing. She is innocent."

Reyes did not heed him, but stabbed her again and again. Her eyes closed. And then he paused. Gulped. Looked up at the heavens and then over at the still-silent Lucien.

"Don't take her! Please don't take her."

Finally the sixth blow was delivered.

"Ashlyn!"

Blood flowed around her now-lifeless body, a crimson pool. Tears continued to rain from Maddox's eyes. Still he struggled. Still the ties to midnight waned. "Why? Why?"

Blessedly, Lucien unlocked him. His hands and feet were barely attached as he collapsed onto the floor and crawled, leaving a trail of blood behind. He gathered his woman in his arms.

Her head lolled to the side. Dead. She was dead, while he felt the weight of the death-curse turn to mist inside his body, evaporating as if it had never been. "No!" He sobbed, great wrenching sobs. Though breaking the curse had once been all he'd cared about, he would rather endure a thousand more than lose this woman. "Please."

"It is done," Reyes said grimly. "Let us hope her sacrifice was not in vain."

Maddox buried his face in Ashlyn's hair and rocked her in his arms.

CHAPTER
TWENTY-FIVE

Maddox cradled his lover for what seemed an eternity, willing her to awaken. He could not stand the thought of life without her. Would rather die himself.

Lucien and Reyes hovered behind him, silent.

"Take my spirit to hell for eternity," he cried to the heavens. "Anything but this. Bring her back. Let me take her place at death's door."

All eternity? a voice purred. It was not Sabin speaking in his head this time, but a female. *Now that's commitment.*

He did not hesitate. "Yes. Yes! Forever. All eternity. I cannot live without her. She is everything to me."

I like you, cowboy, I really do.

"Do you hear a woman in your head, too?" Lucien asked, his shock clear.

"Yes," Reyes said with equal bafflement. "Who are you?"

Your new best friend, sugar.

"Help me, then," Maddox pleaded.

Silly immortal. For days I've been breaking the rules — which is kinda a hobby of mine — to help you. Not sure I want to keep it up, though. You and your woman are serious time-consumers.

"Please. Help her, and I'll never need another moment of your time. I swear it. Just give her back to me. Please. *Please.*"

You insulted the big dogs last week, Violence, and I really liked that. Made me sit up and take notice, to be honest. Not many people break from the mold anymore, you know? And for a Lord to do it . . . rockin'! Know why?

"No." And he did not care.

Awesome. Lesson time.

"Ashlyn is —"

Not going anywhere. Now hush it. I need to lay some background so you understand exactly what I'm risking for you.

As he rocked Ashlyn in his arms, he pressed his lips together, fighting his desperation, his urgency.

So anyway, the Titans are in control, the bastards, and they totally plan to take the world back to what it was in their heyday. A place of peace, a place of worship, blah, blah, blah, where humans bow and sacrifice to them, and all that shit. In a few days, two temples will suddenly rise from the sea. You just wait. It will be the beginning of the end, for sure. She paused dramatically. *I don't know whether the Tities want you guys dead or not in the big scheme of things, but I do know they plan to use you to get what they want.*

"The women. Danika," Reyes said.

Bingo. Something about her bloodline, maybe a prophecy. I'll have to study up 'cause I'm mostly drawing a blank. But you can see my dilemma, right? By helping you, I'm really going to piss off the new management.

"Do you wish me to kill them for you?" Maddox rushed out. "I will do it. I will." However much time it took, whatever he had to do. He would find a way.

"Maddox," Lucien warned. "Stop. Before you bring a far worse curse upon our house. She's going to help you. She's just pretending she's got to bargain. Right, goddess?"

Oh, a Smartie McSmartpants, she purred. *You're a sexy one, I'll give you that.* She uttered another sigh, dreamy this time, before collecting herself. *No time for that. Unfortunately. Like I was saying before, the little woman really impressed me. I didn't think she'd do it, truth be told. What a show, though, right?* Chuckle. *If I had bodily functions, I think I would have peed my pants.*

"Goddess. Focus. Please."

"Maddox," Lucien warned again.

Anya. My name is Anya. And I'm not, technically, a goddess myself, just the daughter of one, so stop lumping me in the same category as those jackoffs. Angry sigh now.

"What can I do? Tell me! I will do anything." Maddox thought Anya might have been sucking on a piece of candy, for there was a slurp and a pop and a strawberry and cream breeze.

Your woman gave up her life for yours. Are you willing to do the same? Because you should know, my powers are contingent on others' actions and I can't do anything unless you do. Oh, and there's the little matter of payment.

"Yes. I will sacrifice anything for her." Again, no hesitation. "I will give whatever payment you ask."

There was another sucker-slurping pause. *All right, here's the scoop. I've got Titans chasing me down. Don't ask me why. It's a long story. Anyway, they're hunting me like a freaking animal and have been for, like, days. If I ever come to you for help, you're going to give it. Understand?*

"Yes. Anything."

Not just you, sweetness. All of you.

For a moment, neither Lucien nor Reyes responded. Maddox was close to leaping at them and cutting both their throats. Then, "Yes," they said in unison.

Okay, then. A deal is struck. Your woman will wake up, and she'll be bound to you. She'll live as long as you do. Not a bad deal for a mortal, really. But if one of you dies, you both die. Got it?

"Yes, yes."

If you try and renege, know that I'll kill you, which will kill her. Her voice dripped to a sugary hum. *I'll cut off your heads and feed them to the gods on a silver platter.*

"I understand. I accept," he said immediately.

One heartbeat passed. Another. Then there was a purr of satisfaction and Maddox was suddenly caught up in a whirlwind. Ashlyn was ripped from his bloody arms and he bellowed, reaching for her. She still lay motionless, but her blood seemed to be flowing back into her body.

Maddox was thrown back on the bed and the chains once more banded around him, his wrists and ankles healing in seconds. Reyes and Lucien walked to the center of the room — but they were walking backward.

Time was reversing at an accelerated

speed, Maddox realized, shocked. He'd seen many things in his long life, but never this.

Reyes stood in front of Ashlyn, pulling the sword out of her rather than thrusting it in. Rather than falling, she rose.

As suddenly as the whirlwind began, it stopped. Everyone looked around in confusion.

"What happened?" Ashlyn asked, incredulous. "I was dead." She held up her arms, looking them over, then felt her stomach, searching for wounds. "I know I was. I can still feel that blade cutting through my — Oh my God, Maddox, what did you do? Did the curse reverse, too?"

"That was . . . I do not have words," Reyes said, frowning. "I stabbed her."

They had all retained their memories of the event, yet as of now the event had not actually happened. "Free me," Maddox shouted. "The chains."

Expression confused, Lucien obeyed.

Maddox leapt to his feet and pulled Ashlyn into his arms, kissing her face and squeezing as tight as he could without crushing her. She laughed, then drew back to study him. "But the death-curse —"

"*Is* broken. I swear it. I feel its ties no more."

Enjoy yourselves, boyz, 'cause now you're

free from Maddox's curse, as well, Anya's voice suddenly sang. *Don't worry, though. I'm sure your demons will keep you plenty miserable. Just don't forget our deal. Ta-ta for now.*

Reyes's body jolted and Lucien's head was thrown back. They shook, their knees gave out and they fell to the ground. Both remained there, panting, for a long while. They looked up at the same time, their eyes meeting.

"I do not have to kill Maddox anymore," Reyes said, awed. "The pull of his death is gone. Gone!"

"The death-curse truly is broken," Lucien said, his tone as close to joyful as Maddox had ever heard it. "Thank you, Ashlyn. Thank you. You are a remarkable human."

"I'd like to say it was my pleasure," she teased with a grin.

"You died for me," Maddox said, claiming her attention and blocking his friends from his focus. Only one person mattered right now. And he was shocked and overcome and furious at her. "You died for me," he growled.

"I'd do it again," she said. "I love you."

He swung her around and she squealed happily. "Never again, woman. You will never leave me again."

"Never."

"Reyes, Lucien. *You* will leave," he said without taking his eyes from Ashlyn.

They quietly exited the room, gifting him and Ashlyn with privacy. Maddox stripped her and kissed her stomach, where she'd been stabbed.

"I need you," she breathed.

And he needed her. Now and always. He penetrated her, unable to stop, and moaned at the pleasure.

"I love you," he told her, slowly pumping inside her.

"I love you, too." She sighed, her head thrashing from side to side.

"Thank you. For what you did, thank you." No one had ever sacrificed so much for him. "Just . . . do not ever let yourself be killed again. Understand?"

She laughed, but he stroked her deeply, exactly where she liked and her laugh became a moan. "Then don't get yourself cursed again, my sweet prince."

"Cursed? Love, I have been blessed with a prize beyond measure."

"So have I, Maddox," she said, and they both climaxed. "So have I."

The next afternoon, Lucien called a meeting.

Ashlyn perched on Maddox's lap, happier

than she'd ever been. All of her dreams had come true. She could control her ability with thoughts of Maddox and he could stop the voices altogether. True love really did conquer all.

She even had a family. A real family, with a feud and everything. The two groups of men were stiff and distant with each other, though as polite as demons could be. She was determined to heal that rift, like the sister she felt she was.

Since the (reversed) stabbing, most of the warriors had treated her with affection, ruffling her hair when they saw her, joking with her about being stuck with Maddox for eternity. Except for Disease, who was still recovering from his wounds. Torin *did* wink at her, though. Ashlyn knew the man had to feel terrible about accidentally unleashing illness on the townspeople. The effects had been — were — devastating, yes, but thankfully modern medicine had helped contain the outbreak. Maybe he would take comfort in that. And when he healed, he could help the warriors rebuild Club Destiny, giving something back to the town.

Life was good. So much better than she could have ever imagined. She grinned.

Lucien stood at the front of the room and said, "I have talked with Sabin and, as you know, I have decided to help him search for the box. It is time the damned thing was found. As long as it's out there, the demons are in danger of being sucked inside. Which means we're in danger of dying."

"Damn Hunters," Ashlyn said, and Maddox squeezed her waist.

"They're dead, killed by Disease," Reyes pointed out.

Ashlyn shook her head, hating to correct him. "You killed some of them. Not all. McIntosh was merely vice president of the Institute. I never actually met the president, not in all the years I worked there. I was told he never goes out in public. I hadn't thought about it before, but now it sounds suspicious to me. Besides that, there are a lot more employees, spread out all over the world. And maybe other Hunters who aren't even affiliated with the Institute."

There was a murmuring among the group.

"We hoped the box was here in Budapest," Sabin said, stepping to Lucien's side and frowning when the warrior tensed, as if expecting an attack. "The interrogation of a Hunter, at least, led us here. But . . ."

"They have found no sign of it," Lucien finished for him. "And they would like our help."

"You want me to help search for that box,

you're going to have to give me some direction," Reyes said. He was on edge, Ashlyn knew, because Danika had sneaked out of the fortress that morning without a good-bye. No one had gone after her. Ashlyn was sad, having lost her first female friend, but knew it was better that way.

They had to free Aeron sometime.

Maddox had told Ashlyn about Aeron, how the man needed to kill Danika and her family. That was the only dark spot in Ashlyn's life. But Maddox also mentioned that Reyes was determined to protect the woman, even though he was fighting the need.

Ashlyn liked to think Anya would ultimately help Danika the way she'd helped her. If Anya *could* help, that is. Maddox had also told her that Anya had confessed to being chased by the Titans. She was some sort of supernatural being who could pop in and out of buildings, remain cloaked in invisibility and reverse time, yet she feared being overtaken — which meant she *could* be overtaken.

"Watch your tone, Pain," Cameo said, standing on Lucien's other side. "You're bringing down morale."

Okay, two dark spots, Ashlyn mused. Cameo made Ashlyn's heart weep every time she looked at her. The woman needed love. So far, though, none of the men seemed taken with her, as beautiful as she was. Everyone kept their distance, as if they feared they'd kill the woman — or themselves — if they got too close. Well, they weren't the only males in the world. Surely someone out there could fall in love with Misery.

"Ashlyn has heard conflicting stories," Maddox said. "Will you tell them?"

She nodded. "One says the box is being guarded by Argus. The other says the box is hidden deep in the sea, guarded by Hydra, but I don't know where."

Everyone groaned.

"Any ideas where we should start?" Lucien asked her.

She shook her head.

"Anya mentioned the surfacing of two temples," Maddox said. "These temples were probably used by the gods and will not have been contaminated or picked over by humans. The moment they surface, some of us should search them. Perhaps we will find something to lead us to the correct path."

"Excellent." Lucien nodded. "Someone will have to stay here with Aeron and Torin and guard the fortress."

"Ashlyn and I will stay. We'll read tomes and texts."

"And I'll listen for clues in town," she added.

Maddox squeezed her closer to his side and whispered, "I need you so badly."

"Good. Because I plan to see to *all* your needs," she told him seductively.

His mouth softened and his violet eyes dipped to her lips. "Right now I'm picturing you in a black leather suit with a sword at your side. I had Paris buy such an outfit in town earlier, as I know how you like your sexy garments."

She melted against him, so filled with love it bubbled out of her in a continuous stream. "When I wear it, will I be fighting to protect my virtue or fighting to take yours?"

"Mine, of course."

Arousal thrummed to instant life and she shivered. "Wanna blow this meeting and go to our room? We can get a recap later."

"More than I can say."

They stood. And the man with the blackest violent streak in the whole wide world chased her laughingly from the room, leaving everyone staring after them in wonder and envy.

Perhaps their time would come. . . .

ABOUT THE AUTHOR

New York Times and *USA TODAY* bestselling author **Gena Showalter** has been praised for her "sizzling page-turners" and "utterly spellbinding stories." The author of more than seventeen novels and anthologies, Showalter is celebrated in a wide variety of genres for her breathtaking romances featuring dark, seductive heroes and strong, appealing heroines. Readers can't get enough of her trademark wit and singular imagination, whether she's writing paranormal stories about vampires, nymphs and superheroes, white-hot contemporary romance or young adult alien huntress books. Her newest series, Lords of the Underworld, promises to be her sexiest and most addictive yet. Don't miss this intoxicating blend of dangerous passion, demons and other supernatural forces, and immortal men who are hotter than hell!

To learn more about Gena and her books,

please visit www.genashowalter.com and www.genashowalter.blogspot.com.

MAR 31 2009	DATE DUE	
12-22-09		
6/21 IR		
SF MAR 2011		
SC NOV 2012		
BC JUN 2013		

	DATE DUE	